Oriental Odyssey - II

The Devil Worshippers

Unabridged Translation of the
Original Karl May Manuscript Published under the Title

Giölgeda padishahnün
[In the Shadow of the Padishah]

A Travel Narrative
by
Karl May

Translated by
Michael M. Michalak

Original German text by Karl May [1842 – 1912]
First published 1881-1888
in 'Deutscher Hausschatz' in serial format

English translation by Michael M. Michalak

ISBN: 0-9718164-1-7

This book is printed on acid free paper.

Nemsi Books - rev. 1.0 – 06/24/2002

Acknowledgments

We would like to thank the following people for their encouragement and advice during the arduous and sometimes frustrating task of translating the original Karl May work from German into English.

Walther Ilmar	For his encouragement and suggestions as well as his investigation of the legality in using the original work published on the Karl May Gesellschaft web site.
Karlheinz Everts	For giving us the permission to use the texts published at the Karl May Gesellschaft web site.
Theodor Wolfgang Michalak	For his research and assistance in identifying the meaning of obscure German words and dialects.
Angelia Baldwin **Britta Werner**	For reading the manuscript and providing some valuable feedback before the book was published.

Our appreciation and thanks is extended to all of you and your contribution was much appreciated.

Michael M. Michalak – Translator and Editor
Elaine Adair-Michalak – Editor

I also wish to give a very special thank-you to my wife, Elaine, who despite her battle with cancer persevered in editing the greater part of this book prior to her untimely death on the 31st May 2001. Despite her illness, she insisted on completing the editing of the manuscript that was translated up to that point in time. Thank you, Elaine, for your labor of love. Your energy and drive will be a constant reminder of your inner strength to me. I will continue our project just as we had planned.

Michael

In Memory of

Elaine Teresa Adair-Michalak

24th September 1963 - 31st May 2001

You were all things to me. And I am less than whole without you.
You walked by my side in life, wherever our journey took us.
Each step we took together confirmed our shared bond.
We are as one and shall remain entwined throughout Eternity.

This book, and all those that follow
Are dedicated to you,
My sweet Elaine.

Foreword

Those of you dear readers who have enjoyed the first part of '*Giölgeda padishahnün*' or 'In the Shadow of the Padishah' can now finally read the remainder of this narrative.

This second book is the continuation of a series known as 'Der Orientzyklus', or 'Oriental Odyssey', as I finally decided to call this series. Karl May was quite adamant that his writings were 'travel narratives' and to honor the author's intent, I have chosen to call this series an 'odyssey', which according to the Oxford dictionary is 'a long adventurous journey'.

I started this second volume of the 'Oriental Odyssey' in January 2001, shortly before publishing the first book in this series. My wife Elaine was diagnosed with cancer whilst we were working on the first book. Between doctor appointments and hospital visits, Elaine still edited what I translated and found comfort in this fictional world. She was proud when she was finally able hold the first book of our work in her hands in March of that year and desired to see the completion of the second and subsequent books of this series. But death claimed her before she could read the entire story as it unfolded. Her loss has of course delayed the completion of the work we had started together, but after many months of inactivity and grief, I again resumed this epic work. On the 23rd February 2002, I finally completed the translation we started together. I was driven by my memory of her courage and perseverance and my promise to her that our project of translating Karl May's original manuscripts into English would continue.

With the assistance of a friend, I have now established a new publishing company, named 'Nemsi Books', which will publish the continuing unabridged translations of Karl May's original works in both hard cover and soft cover formats. So, dear readers; if you have grown fond of these adventure narratives, more will be published in due course and in formats that can either grace the bookshelves of your library or accompany you on your own travels.

It was our, and still is my intention to publish all the writings of the original series as numbered editions. Thus; 'Oriental Odyssey I' – 'In the Shadow of the Padishah – Through the Desert' is followed by 'Oriental Odyssey II' – 'In the Shadow of the Padishah – The Devil Worshippers' and will be followed by 'Oriental Odyssey III' – 'Travel Adventures in Kurdistan' and so on.

We would like to remind our readers that the original series, which was later edited and published as a set of six books that embodied the collection of Karl

May's Travel Adventures in the Orient, is not the basis for this translation. Rather we had chosen to use the serialized version as it appeared in the 'Deutscher Hausschatz' [German Home Treasure] from 1880 to 1884.

This 'Oriental Odyssey' series is thus the first and only unabridged English translation of Karl May's original work and for the first time, after more than a century, it is finally available to English language readers in all its glory.

During the years since Karl May wrote these narratives, the German language has undergone changes in spelling and use of idioms. Our task then was not just translating the original work from one language into another. Rather it was a matter of extensive research. Terms such as 'Barbier' [barber] and other professions are no longer in common usage and could not be found in even the most comprehensive translation dictionaries. Old spellings such as 'Muth' [courage] and 'Thier' [animal] still use 'th' which has been discontinued and replaced with 't'. Also, we grappled with the terseness of the dialogue that was employed in the original German version. How could we best represent this without ambiguity, and still keep the translated version true to the original author's style. We opted to retain the terseness and only added ' . . .<the character> said/muttered/grumbled . . .' whenever it became unclear as to who was speaking. Similarly, we divided long and convoluted sentences and added a reference to the name or title of the specific character when this became unclear.

During the translation of this second book, I came across a single sentence paragraph that stated '*Dieser lag rauchend am Boden.*' - literally translated this would state; '**That one lay smoking on the floor.**' Taken out of context, this sentence conjures up a number of images, and is a perfect example why German can not be translated into meaningful English prose without some additions or explanations. Contextually the sentence states; 'The Arab was lying on the floor, smoking his pipe.' - Therefore 'That one' should be identified for the reader; that is one should say 'The Arab' or more accurately, 'The Haddedihn'. And whilst the reader may be aware that in the Orient, every man is smoking a pipe of one kind or another, the reference to 'smoking' is quite vague. Today, 'smoking' would be assumed to mean 'smoking a cigarette' which is clearly not what the Arab was smoking as he lay on the floor. But '...lay smoking on the floor' is not good English prose either '...lay on the floor, smoking.' would be better. Yet this is overly terse. Hence the clarification, 'The Arab was lying on the floor, smoking his pipe.' presents the reader with a fuller picture of the scene so briefly described by Karl May. I would like to stress that whilst we decided to add such descriptive references to the English translation, we did not take away anything from Karl May's original writing. Nothing has been added to what Karl May had intended -

yet some purists may claim that the text has been edited because of these clarifications. I can not stress this enough to readers of this translation. The text presented here is as Karl May wrote it - except for the few additions and clarifications that needed to be made to transition his narrative into readable English prose. I do not claim it to be perfect, nor do I claim it to be definitive. I simply claim that it is the original Karl May – 'warts and all' - fashioned into English prose for the English language reader.

In those instances where the German idioms could not be rationally translated, we have translated the idiom virtually verbatim and added a note at the end of this book.

We hope that you, the reader, will enjoy this second tale in these gripping adventure stories of the 'Oriental Odyssey', involving the characters Kara Ben Nemsi and Hajji Halef Omar.

Yes, there will be more. And in the true Karl May style we invite you, dear readers, to follow us further on our epic journey through the Turkish Empire and to patiently await the completion of the third book of our series; 'Oriental Odyssey III' – 'Travel Adventures in Kurdistan'.

Michael M. Michalak – Translator and Editor
Elaine Adair Michalak – Editor

DISCLAIMER

The translator and editor wish to advise that they do not endorse or confirm any of the views, interpretations, representations, or conjectures of the original author. Where we have recognized an inaccuracy of fact we have added a footnote to that effect; but it was not our intention to correct or edit the original text, nor censor or enhance the work of Karl May.

On the whole we have made no attempt to anglicize the foreign words (i.e. Turkish, Arabic etc.) that appear in the text. They appear in the original Germanic form, with a few exceptions – e.g. 'sh' being substituted for '*sch*' in non-German foreign words, and 'j' replacing the Germanic form of '*dsch*' and '*tsch*'. We do not attest to the accuracy or authenticity of these foreign words, or to their spelling or definition, except where specified.

The Devil Worshippers
[Continuation of 'A Desert Battle']

Chapter 21

And so it came to pass that I was in Mosul awaiting an audience with the Turkish Pasha.

I planned to travel with Mohammed Emin into the mountains of Kurdistan to free his son, Amad el Ghandur, from Fort Amadijah by either cunning or by force; a task that would not be easy to accomplished. The brave Sheik of the Haddedihn would have dearly loved to bring all his warriors and battle his way through the Turkish territories and attack Amadijah openly; but there were a hundred pressing reasons that made the execution of such a fantastic plan impossible. A lone man would have more hope of success than an entire horde of Bedouin, and Mohammed Emin had finally agreed with my proposal to carry out this venture with just three men. These three were Mohammed Emin, Halef and myself.

Of course it had taken considerable persuasion to convince Sir David Lindsay, who would gladly have joined us, that his complete incapacity for the language as well as his inability to fit in would bring us more harm than good. He had finally decided to remain with the Haddedihn and to wait with them for our return. There, he could make use of the wounded Greek, Alexander Kolettis, as an interpreter and dig for 'fowling-bulls'. The Haddedihn had promised to show him as many ancient ruins as he desired. He did not accompany me to Mosul because I advised against it. He would be of no use to me there and the only reason that would prompt him to go, namely to seek the protection of the English Consul, did not need to be pursued as the protection of the Haddedihn was, for now, sufficient guarantee of his safety.

The dispute that had existed between the Haddedihn and their enemies was settled. The three defeated tribes had agreed to leave hostages with the victors. So it came about that Mohammed Emin's people would not miss him. Of course, he did not ride to Mosul either, since his presence there would pose a great danger to his person; rather we agreed to meet at the ruins of Khorsabad in the old Assyrian *Saraghum*. We had ridden together through Wadi Murr, Aïn el Khalkhan and on to El Kasr. There we had separated; I had traveled to Mosul with Halef; and with the aid of a raft the Sheik had crossed over the Tigris in order to make his way to our rendezvous point via the river that flowed alongside Jebel Maklub.

And what was my purpose in Mosul? To perhaps seek out the representative of England and ask for his protection? That never entered my mind, for I was as secure without his protection as I would have been with it. But I did have to visit the Pasha, an unavoidable necessity, for I wished to equip myself with everything that our task might require.

The heat in Mosul was terrible. A glance at the thermometer showed me that at ground level, it was 116 degrees Fahrenheit in the shade. I, however, had arranged lodgings for myself in a *sardaubs* [cellar]. Most of the inhabitants of this city preferred to linger in these places during the summer season. Halef sat with me and polished his pistols. A long silence had existed between us, but I recognized that something was weighing heavily on this little man's heart. Finally he turned to me abruptly and said:

"I had not thought of it, *Sihdi*!"

"Thought of what?"

"That we may never see the Haddedihn again."

"Ahh! And why not?"

"You intend to go to Amadijah, *Sihdi*?"

"Yes. You have known this for a long time."

"I have known it, but I did not know the way that leads there. *Allah il Allah*! It is the way to death and into *Jehennah*!"

He made such a worried face, as I had never seen before.

"That dangerous, Hajji Halef Omar?"

"You do not believe it, *Sihdi*? But have I not heard that on this trek you desire to visit the three men that call themselves Pali, Selek and Melaf, the three men whom you rescued from the island of the Abu Hammed, and who, after they had recovered in the Haddedihn camp, returned to their homeland?"

"I will visit them."

"Then we are lost. You and I, we are both 'True Believers'; but every believer that goes to them will loose life and heaven."

"That is news to me Hajji Halef! Who has told you this?"

"Every Moslem knows it. Have you not yet discovered that the land in which they live is called *Shaïtanistan*?"

Ah, now I knew what he meant. He was afraid of the *Jesidi* - the 'Devil Worshippers'. I acted as though I knew no such thing and asked:

"*Shaïtanistan*, the country of the Devil? Why?"

"The *Radjahl el Shaïtan* live there, the men of the Devil, who pray to *Shaïtan*."

"Hajji Halef Omar, where do such people who pray to the Devil exist around here!"

"You do not believe it? Have you never heard of such people?"

"Oh yes; I have even seen such people."

"And yet you appear not to believe me?"

"I truly do not believe you."

"Even if you have seen them yourself?"

"Yes, though not here. I was in a country, far, far away on the other side of the great sea; the *Francs* call it Australia. There I discovered wild men who believe in a *Shaïtan* they call *Yahu* [See Trans. Notes Ch 21. 1], whom they pray to. But there are no people here who pray to the Devil."

"*Sihdi*, you are smarter than I and much smarter than most people; but sometimes your cleverness and wisdom desert you. Ask any man that you meet and he will tell you that in *Shaïtanistan* they pray to the Devil."

"Were you there, when they prayed to him?"

"No. But I have heard about it."

"Were those people, from whom you have heard this, there?"

"They were told by others."

"Then I will tell you that no man has ever seen this, for the *Jesidi* permit no one who holds a different belief than theirs to be present at their religious services."

"Is that true?"

"Yes. At least it would be a very rare exception if they permitted a stranger to attend."

"Yet it is known what they do."

"Well then?"

"Have you not heard that they are called *Jeragh Sonderan*?"

"Yes."

"That must be an evil name; I do not know what it means."

"It means something like 'Extinguisher of Light'."

"You see, *Sihdi*! In their religious services, where even women and girls are present, the light is extinguished."

"Then someone has told you a great lie. They have confused the *Jesidi* with another sect [the Assyrian in Syria], where such a thing is said to occur. What else have you heard about them?"

"In their holy house stands a rooster or a peacock to whom they pray - that is the Devil."

"Is he truly the Devil?"

"Yes."

"Oh you poor Hajji Halef Omar! Do they have many holy houses?"

"Yes."

"And in each is a rooster?"

"Yes."

"How many Devils must then exists! I thought there was only one?"

"Oh *Sihdi*, there is only one, but he is everywhere. They also have fallen angels."

"In what respect?"

"You know, the Koran teaches that there are only four archangels, namely *Jebraïl* [Gabriel], who is the *Ruh el Kuds* [The Holy Ghost] and is united with Allah and Mohammed, just like the Christians have the Father, Son and Holy Spirit. Then there is *Azraïl*, the angel of death, who is at times, also called *Abu Jahah*; then there is *Mikaïl* [Michael] and finally *Israfil*. The devil worshippers have seven archangels and they are called *Gabrïel*, *Michaïl*, *Rafaïl*, *Azraïl*, *Dedraïl*, *Azrafil* and *Shemkil*. Isn't this right?"

"It is not wrong, for I also believe that there are seven archangels."

"You? Why?" He asked in astonishment.

"The holy book of the Christians says so [Tobais 12 V 15, Revelation 1 V 4 and 4 V 5], and I believe that more than the Koran."

"Oh *Sihdi*, what do I hear! You were in Mecca, you are a Hajji and believe more in the *Kitab* of the infidels than the words of the Prophet! Now I am not surprised that you desire to go to the *Jesidi*!"

"You can return. I shall go alone!"

"Return? No! It is perhaps possible that Mohammed only spoke of four angels, because the other three were not in heaven when he was there. They had things to do on earth and so he did not meet them."

"I tell you, Hajji Halef Omar that you do not need to fear the 'Devil Worshippers'. They do not pray to *Shaïtan*, they don't even call him by name. They are clean, faithful, grateful, brave and honest; these traits you rarely find among the 'True Believers'. Besides, you will not lose your soul, for they will not force their belief upon you."

"They will not force me to pray to the Devil?"

"No. I assure you!"

"But they will kill us!"

"Neither you nor I."

"But they have killed many others; they did not kill Christians though, only Moslems."

"They defended themselves during an attempt to annihilate them. That is why they kill only Moslems, for they were attacked by them and not by Christians."

"But I am a Moslem!"

"They are your friends because they are mine. Did you not nurse three of their men until they were well again?"

"It is true, *Sihdi.* I will not leave you, I will go with you!"

I heard steps descending the stairway. Two men entered. They were two Albanian Aghas of the irregular troops of the Pasha. They remained by the entrance and one of them asked:

"Are you the infidel whom we should guide?"

From the moment I was announced to the Pasha, I had deliberately discarded the Koran that was hanging around my neck. I wished to avoid being seen with this symbol of pilgrimage.

The one asking the question expected an answer of course, but I did not give him one; I behaved as though I had neither heard nor seen him.

"Are you deaf and blind that you do not answer?" he demanded rudely.

These Arnauts [Albanian irregular troops of the Pasha] are rough, unrestrained and dangerous people, who at the slightest provocation not only reach for their weapons but also use them; it was not my intention, however, to accept their behavior without consequence. Therefore I spontaneously drew my revolver from my *hawk* [belt] and turned to my servant:

"Hajji Halef Omar Agha, tell me if someone is here!"

"Yes, there is someone here."

"Who is it?"

"Two *sabits* [officers], who wish to speak with you."

"Who sends them?"

"The Pasha, may Allah grant him a long life!"

"That is not true! I am Emir Kara Ben Nemsi; the Pasha - may Allah protect him! - Would send me polite guides. Tell these men, who use insults for greetings, that they should leave. They should repeat the words that they spoke to me to whomever sent them!"

Their hands clasped the grips of their pistols and they looked at each other. I casually pointed the barrel of my weapon at them and frowned as menacingly as possible.

"Hajji Halef Omar Agha, what have I commanded you?"

I saw in the little man's face that my demeanor was entirely to his liking. He too had his pistols in his hands and now he turned to the men at the entrance with a proud countenance:

"Hear what I have to say to you! This brave and famous *Effendi* is the Emir Hajji Kara Ben Nemsi, and I am Hajji Halef Omar Agha Ben Hajji Abul Abbas Ibn Hajji Dawuhd al Gossarah. You have heard what my *Effendi* has said. Go and do as he has commanded!"

"We will not go! The Pasha has sent us!"

"Then return to the Pasha and tell him that he should send respectful messengers! He who comes to my *Effendi* must remove his shoes and recite the greeting."

"To an infidel . . . "

Now I stood before them.

"Be gone!" I ordered them.

"We have . . . "

"Out!"

Suddenly Halef and I were alone again. The officers must have recognized that I would not permit them to give me orders. One has to understand how to deal with Orientals. Any Westerner who believes himself mistreated has no one to blame but himself. A little personal courage and if possible a great dose brazenness supported by that lovely virtue, which one would call coarseness back home, but which, under certain circumstances produces the best results.

Certainly there are circumstances where one is forced to endure one or more instances of unpleasantness. In such cases, it is advisable to conduct oneself accordingly. Of course it does require complete knowledge of the circumstances and due consideration of each particular case. A good deal of experience is also necessary in order to decide what would be better and wiser: roughness or patience and will power, the hand on the weapon or - the hand in the purse.

"*Sihdi*, what have you done?" cried Halef.

He feared, despite his fearlessness, the consequences of my act.

"What have I done? I have shown these two louts the door!"

"Do you know of the Arnauts?"

"They are bloodthirsty and vindictive."

"That they are. Did you not see one of them shove that old woman to the ground in Kahira, just because she did not scamper out of his way? She was blind."

"I did see this. But these two will not intimidate us."

"And do you know the Pasha?"

"He is a very good man!"

"Oh, very good, *Sihdi*! Half of Mosul is empty because they all fear him. Not a day passes without ten or twenty people receiving the *bastinado*. He who is rich shall not be alive tomorrow, and his fortune will belong to the Pasha. He agitates the Arab tribes against one another and then makes war upon the victor so he can take the spoils. He speaks to his Arnauts thus: 'Go, destroy, murder, but bring me the spoils!' They do it and he becomes richer than the Padishah. Whoever is his confidant today will become the Pasha's prisoner tomorrow and the day after tomorrow he will lose his head. *Sihdi*, what will he do to us?"

"We must wait and see."

"I want to tell you something, *Sihdi*. As soon as I see that he plans to do something evil to us I will shoot him down. I will not die without taking him with me."

"You will not get into such a situation, for I will go alone."

"Alone? I will not permit that. I am going with you!"

"May I take you along when he commands to see me alone?"

"*Allah il Allah*! Then I will wait here. But I swear to you by the Prophet and all the Caliphs: if you are not back here by this evening, then I will send the Pasha word that I have an important message: he will admit me, and then I will send both pistol balls through his head!"

He was serious and I am certain that he would have done this, that brave little man. Such an oath he would not have broken.

"But what of Hanneh?" I asked.

"She shall cry, but be proud of me. She would not love a man who allows his *Effendi* to be murdered!"

"I thank you, my good Halef! But I am convinced that it will not come to that."

After a while we again heard footsteps. An ordinary soldier entered. He had removed his shoes outside.

"*Salaama*!" he greeted.

"*Salaam*! What do you want?"

"Are you the *Effendi* who wishes to speak with the Pasha?"

"Yes."

"The Pasha - may Allah grant him a thousand years! - Has sent you a sedan chair. You shall be taken to him!"

"Go back up. I will follow shortly!"

When he had gone Halef said:

"*Sihdi*, do you see now that it becomes dangerous?"

"Why?"

"He does not send an Agha, but rather an ordinary soldier."

"That may be; but do not worry!"

I ascended the few steps. Ah! Before the house stood a troop of about twenty Arnauts. They were armed to the teeth, and one of the two Aghas who had previously visited was in command. Two *Hammals* carried the sedan chair.

"Climb in!" the Agha commanded me with a dark expression.

I did so without inhibition. This escort made me think that I was a prisoner of sorts. I was carried away at a trot until we reached a gate.

"Climb out and follow me!" the Agha commanded in the same brusque tone he had used earlier.

He led me up a stairway to a room in which many different officers stood, they examined me with sullen looks. By the doorway sat several civilians - inhabitants of the city - one could see that they did not feel comfortable in this lion's den. I was announced immediately; I took off my sandals, which I had worn for precisely this purpose, and entered:

"*Salaam aaleïkum*!" I greeted, whilst folding my arms across my chest and bowing.

"*Sal* . . . " the Pasha interrupted himself, but continued immediately: "Your messenger said that a *Nemje* wished to speak with me?"

"It is so."

"Are the *Nemsi* Moslems?"

"No. They are Christians."

"Yet you dare to speak the greeting of a Moslem!"

"You are a Moslem, a favorite of Allah and a favorite of the Padishah - may God protect him! - Should I salute you with the greeting of the heathens that have no God and no holy book?"

"You are bold, stranger!"

He cast a strange and sly look upon me. The Pasha was not a big man and lean of build, his face would have been ordinary if it did not display the lines of cleverness and cruelty so obviously. His right cheek was greatly swollen and next to him was a silver dish filled with water, which served him as a spittoon. His clothing was entirely made of silk. The hilt of his dagger and the *agraffe* about his turban sparkled with diamonds; his fingers glittered with rings, and the water pipe from which he smoked was the most precious I had ever seen.

After he had examined me from head to foot for a while, he asked further:

"Why have you not introduced yourself through a Consul?"

"The *Nemsi* do not have a Consul in Mosul, and the other Consuls are as strange to me as they are to you. A Consul cannot make me better or worse than I am, and you have sharp eyes; you do not need to learn of me through the eyes of a Consuls."

"*Mash Allah*! You do indeed speak very boldly! You speak as though you were a great man!"

"Would another kind of man dare to visit you?"

This was of course spoken quite insolently, but I saw at once that it made the expected impression.

"What is your name?" He inquired.

"*Hasredin* [Highness], I have different names." I replied.

"Different? I think that a man has only one name!"

"Usually. With me, however, it is different, for in every country and with each people that I visit, I am named differently."

"Then you have seen many lands and many people?"

"Yes."

"Name these people!"

"The *Osmanli* [Ottoman Turks], French, English, Spanish . . ."

I could name a pretty row of names and of course I placed the *Osmanli* at the beginning. His eyes grew larger with each name and finally he blurted:

"*Hei-hei*! [Exclamation of surprise] Are there that many peoples on the Earth?"

"Many, many more!"

"*Allah akbar*, God is great! He created so many nations, like the number of ants in an anthill. You are yet young. How can you have visited so many countries? How old were you when you left the land of the *Nemsi*?"

"I numbered eighteen years when I went across the sea to *Jeni-dünja* [America]."

"And what do you do?"

"I write books and articles for newspapers, which are then printed."

"What do you write about?"

"Mostly I write about what I see, what I hear and what I experience."

"Do the men that you meet also appear in these *chaberler* [newspapers]?"

"Only the best."

"Even I?"

"Even you."

"What would you write about me?"

"How should I know this at this time, oh Pasha? I can only describe people in the manner that they have behaved towards me."

"And who reads this?"

"Many thousands of people of high and low standing."

"That includes Pashas and sovereigns?"

"Even them."

At that moment the sound of a thrashing echoed from the courtyard, accompanied by the moans of the one being punished. I listened involuntarily.

"Don't listen to that," warned the Pasha. "It is my *hekim*."

"Your physician?" I asked in surprise.

"Yes. Have ever had *dish aghrisi* [toothache]?"

"As a child."

"Then you know how it goes. I have a sick tooth. That dog was supposed to take it out; but he was so awkward that he hurt me. He is now being flogged for that; and now I cannot close my mouth."

Not close his mouth? Could the tooth already be partially extracted? I decided to make use of this.

"May I look upon the sick tooth, oh Pasha?"

"Are you a *hekim*?"

"On occasion."

"Then come here! It is at the lower right!"

He opened his mouth, and I looked in.

"Would you permit me to feel the tooth?"

"If it will not hurt!"

I nearly laughed into the Pasha's severe face. It was the eyetooth, and it hung so loosely between the swollen gums that I needed to use only my fingers to complete the interrupted extraction.

"How many strokes will the *hekim* receive?"

"Sixty."

"Will you forgo the remaining strokes if I take out the tooth without hurting you?"

"You cannot do it!"

"I can do it!"

"Good! But if you hurt me, then you get the remaining stokes."

He clapped his hands and an officer entered.

"Releases the *hekim*! This stranger has bought mercy for him."

The man left with a very astonished face.

Now I stuck two fingers into the Pasha's mouth, pressed first on the neighboring teeth - for the magical effect - then took hold of the sick eyetooth and removed it. The patient twitched his eyelids but appeared not to know that I already had the tooth. He grabbed my hand quickly and pushed it away.

"If you are a *hekim*, then why do you probe so long! There lies the tool!" he pointed to the floor. I held the tooth unseen between my fingers and stooped down. The object that I saw lying there was a very old and desiccated goat's foot, next to it lay a pair of dental forceps - but what a contraption! One could have lifted all kinds of flat steel from the smith's fire with this one. A little sham could do no harm. I inserted the goat's foot into the Pasha's, not altogether small, mouth.

"Pay attention, see if it hurts! *Bir - iki - ij* - one, two, three! Here is the wayward one that has caused you so much pain!"

He looked at me amazed.

"*Mash Allah*! I felt nothing!"

"So practice the physicians of the *Nemsi*, oh Pasha!"

He felt inside his mouth; he examined the tooth, and only then was he convinced that he was free of it.

"You are a great *hekim*! What shall I call you?"

"The *Beni Arab* call me Kara Ben Nemsi."

"Do you remove every tooth as well as this?"

"Hmm! Under the right circumstances!"

He again clapped his hands and the same officer appeared once more.

"Ask around the house if there is anyone with a toothache!"

The adjutant disappeared and I felt as though I had developed a toothache myself, despite the very gracious countenance of the Pasha.

"Why did you not follow my messengers immediately?" he asked.

"Because they insulted me."

"Tell me!" He demanded.

I reported the affair. He listened attentively and then raised his hand threateningly.

"You were wrong. I had commanded your presence and you should have come immediately. Thank Allah that he gave you the gift to extract teeth without pain!"

"What would you have done to me?"

"You would have been punished. How, I do not know right now."

"Punished? That you would not have done!"

"*Mash Allah*! Why not? Who would have prevented this?"

"The Sultan himself."

"The Sultan?" he asked, amazed.

"None other. I committed no crime and may certainly demand that your Aghas show me some respect. Or do you believe that it is not necessary for you to consider this *tirsheh* [parchment]? Here take it and read!"

He opened the parchment and touched it to his forehead, mouth, and heart after he had glanced at it.

"A *Bu-djeruldi* from the Sultan - May Allah bless him!"

He read it, folded it and returned it to me.

"You stand in '*Giölgeda padishahnün*'! How did you come by it?"

"You are Governor of Mosul! How did you come by it, oh Pasha?"

"Really, you are very bold! I am Governor of this local district because the sun of the Padishah illuminates me."

"And I stand in '*Giölgeda padishahnün*', because the grace of the Sultan shines upon me. The Padishah gave me permission to visit all his lands and I will write great books and newspaper articles about them, telling how I was received by his people."

That appeared to make an impression. He pointed to the precious *Smyrna* carpet next to him.

"Seat yourself!" he commanded.

He then ordered the Negro lad who cowered before him to attend to his pipe, to serve coffee and to bring me a pipe.

Even my sandals were brought to me, and I had to slip them on immediately. Then we sat together, smoking and drinking, as though we were old acquaintances. He appeared to find more and more pleasure in my company and to prove this in deed he called upon the two Aghas of the Arnauts. He looked upon them with an expression that suggested nothing less than some great fortune smiled upon them and asked:

"You were to bring this *Bei* to me?"

"You commanded it, oh Lord!" answered one.

"You did not greet him! You kept your shoes on! You even called him an infidel!"

"We did so because even you called him that."

"Silence, you dog; and I say, did I really called him that!"

"Lord, you have . . ."

"Silence! Did I call him an infidel?"

"No, oh Pasha."

"And yet you claimed that I did so! Go down into the courtyard! Each of you is to receive fifty strokes on the soles of your feet. Go outside and announce this!"

This was surely endearing proof of our friendship. Fifty blows? That excessive. I would have granted them ten or fifteen. I therefore had to intercede on their behalf.

"You judged justly, oh Pasha," I said. "Your wisdom is sublime, but your righteousness is greater still. Grace is the right of all emperors, all kings and rulers. You are the sovereign of Mosul, and you will allow your grace to shine upon these two men!"

"Upon these scoundrels who have insulted you? Isn't that the same as insulting me?"

"Lord, you stand so sublime over them like the star over the earth. The jackal howls at the stars but they listen not and shine on. They will praise your goodness in the West when I tell of how you answered my plea."

"These dogs are not worth it; but so that you see that I love you, I will commute their sentence." He turned to the two men and growled; "Get out of here and let your faces remain unseen today!"

When they had left the room, he inquired: "In which country were you last?"

"In Egypt. And then I came to you through the desert."

I said this because I did not want to lie to him and neither could I tell him that I had been with the Haddedihn.

"Through which desert? Through the desert of the Sinai and of Syria! That is an evil way, but thank God that you have chosen it!"

"Why?"

"Because otherwise you would have come amongst the Shammar-Arabs and would have been murdered by them."

If he had known that which I neglected to mention!

"Are these Shammar so bad, Highness?"

"They are an impudent, predatory rabble that I will cast asunder. They pay neither tax nor tribute, and therefore I have already begun to destroy them."

"You sent troops against them?"

"No. The Arnauts are to be employed for greater things."

These 'greater things' were easy to guess: The pillaging of his subjects and the enrichment of the Pasha himself.

"Ah, I have guessed!" I declared.

"What have you guessed?" He demanded.

"A smart ruler spares his subjects and attacks his enemies by causing two friends to fall out!"

"*Allah il Allah*! The *Nemsi* are not stupid people. I have truly done this."

"Has it worked out?"

"Badly! And do you know who is to blame?"

"Who?"

"The English and a foreign Emir. The Haddedihn are the bravest among the Shammar. They were to have been destroyed without the blood of my men being spilled, so we sent three other Arab tribes against them. Then this Englishman came with this Emir and enlisted yet other tribes, who helped the Haddedihn. My allies were all killed or captured. They lost the greater part of their herds and must now pay tribute."

"To which tribe does this Emir belong?"

"No one knows; but it is said that he is not a man. He kills the lion at night, alone. His bullets find their mark across many miles and his eyes burn in the darkness like the fires of hell."

"Can you not capture him?"

"I will try, but there is little hope. The Abu Mohammed captured him once; but he escaped them by riding through the air."

The good Pasha appeared to be a little superstitious. He had no idea that this 'Devil's spawn' sat at his side and drank coffee with him.

"From whom did you hear this, Highness?"

"From an *Obeyed* who was sent to me as a messenger when it was already too late. The Haddedihn had already taken the herds away."

"You will punish them?"

"Yes."

"At once?"

"I wish to, but I must unfortunately grant them more time, although my troops are already gathered. Have you been to the ruins of *Kufjunjik*?"

"No."

"There all the troops that will move against the Shammar are gathered; but now I will send these men to another place."

"May I ask to where?"

"That is my secret, and no one may learn of it. You probably also know, that diplomatic secrecy must be well preserved."

Just then the man who had been dispatched with the order to search out anyone with a toothache entered. I sought to read the result of his search in his face. It would in no way be pleasant for me to have to root about the palisade of teeth within some Arnauts maw with the aid of an old goat's foot or some monstrous forceps - and then to do so as painlessly as it was expected of me.

"Well?" asked the Governor.

"Forgive me, oh Pasha; I have found no one that suffers from *Dish aghrisi*!"

"And you do not suffer from this either?"

"No."

My heart became lighter. The amiable Pasha turned to me regretfully:

"It is a shame! I wished to give you the opportunity to have your art admired. But perhaps we will find someone tomorrow or the next day."

"Tomorrow and the next day I will no longer be here."

"No? You must stay. You shall live in my palace and be served as I am. - Go!"

This last word was directed at the officer, who removed himself.

I answered: "And yet I must depart for now, but I will come again."

"Where do you wish to go?"

"I want to go up into the Kurdish Mountains."

"How far?"

"That is still undecided; perhaps up to *Tura Shina* or even to *Julamerik*."

"What do you want there?"

"I want to see what kind of people live there and which plants and herbs grow in that region."

"And why must this occur immediately, that you cannot remain here with me for some time yet?"

"Because the plants that I seek may otherwise wilt."

"You do not need to learn about the people up there. They are Kurdish robbers and some *Jesidi*, whom Allah will condemn! But why the herbs? Ah, you are a *hekim* and need herbs! But have you not considered that the Kurds will perhaps kill you?"

"I have been with worse people than them."

"Without accompaniment? Without Arnauts or *Bashi-Bozuks*?"

"Yes. I have a sharp dagger and a good gun and . . . I also have you, oh Pasha!"

"Me?"

"Yes. Your power does extend as far as Amadijah?"

"Exactly that far. Amadijah is the boundary fort of my district. I have cannons there and a garrison of three hundred Albanians."

"Amadijah must be a very strong fort!"

"Not only strong, but totally invulnerable. It is the key fort against the land of the free Kurds. But even the subjugated tribes are stubborn and wicked."

"You have seen my *Bu-djeruldi* and will, I am sure, grant me your protection. That is my request and the reason I came to you."

"That shall be granted to you, but under one condition."

"Which is?"

"That you return and be my guest."

"I accept this condition."

"I will send two *khawassen* [policemen] with you, they shall serve you and protect you. Do you know that you will pass through the lands of the *Jesidi*?"

"I know it."

"They are an evil, disobedient people, one needs to show one's teeth to them. They pray to the Devil, 'extinguish the lights' and drink wine."

"Is the latter that bad?"

He looked at me searchingly.

"Do you drink wine?"

"Very gladly."

"Have you wine with you?"

"No."

"I thought, if you had ... then ... I would visit you before your departure."

To be allowed to hear this indicated that I must have already won his confidence. I could make use of this and therefore said:

"Visit me! I can probably get some wine."

"Even such that spits?"

He obviously meant champagne.

"Have you drunk such wine before, oh Pasha?"

"Oh no! Don't you know that the Prophet forbids the drinking of wine? I am a faithful follower of the Koran!"

"I know this. But one can make such spitting wine artificially and then it is not real wine!"

"You can make spitting wine?" He asked hopefully.

"Yes."

"But it takes a long time - perhaps some weeks or even some months?"

"It only takes a few hours."

"Will you make me such a drink?"

"Gladly, but I need a few things that are essential for the process."

"What do you need?"

"Bottles."

"I have those."

"Sugar and raisins."

"You shall have these from me also."

"Vinegar and water."

"My *mudbachji* [cook] has these."

"And then a few things that one can only get from a pharmacy."

"Are they *ilajlar* [medicines]?"

"Yes."

"My *hekim* has a pharmacy. What else do you need?"

"Nothing. But you must permit me to prepare the wine in your kitchen."

"May I watch so that I can learn how to prepare it?"

"That is almost impossible, oh Pasha. To prepare wine that a Moslem is permitted to drink, the kind that spits and cheers the soul, this is a great secret!"

"I will give you whatever you demand!"

"Such an important secret one does not sell. Only a friend may be taught it."

"Am I not your friend, Kara Ben Nemsi? I love you and would gladly grant all that you request of me."

"I know it, oh Pasha, and therefore you shall discover my secret. How many bottles shall I fill for you?"

"Twenty. Or is this too much?"

"No. Let us go to the kitchen!"

The Pasha of Mosul was a secret subject of 'King Bacchus'. Our pipes were lit anew and we proceeded into the kitchen.

The gentlemen in the waiting room were astounded when they saw me with the 'peace pipe', walking at the Pasha's side in a comradely fashion; but he paid them no heed. The kitchen was at ground level and was a high, dark room with a monstrous hearth, over which hung a giant kettle full of seething water that was reserved for the preparation of coffee. Our entrance did not cause surprise so much as horror. Five or six fellows sat in a circle on the floor smoking, steaming cups of mocha were before them. The Pasha had probably never been in his own kitchen before, and upon his appearance, the people there froze in terror. They remained seated and stared at him with wide-open eyes.

He stepped into their midst and let loose an tirade of kicks whilst shouting:

"Up, you *jürückji* [idlers], you slaves! Do you not know who I am, that you remain seated, as though I were but one of you?"

They leapt up and prostrated themselves on the ground before his feet.

"Do you have hot water?"

"It boils there, Lord," answered one who appeared to be the cook; for he was the fattest and dirtiest of them all.

"Get me raisins, you lout!"

"How many, Lord?" The fat one wheedled.

"How many will you need?" he asked me.

I checked the quantity of the water and then pointed to an empty container.

"This *bardak* [pitcher], three times full."

"And sugar?"

"As much again."

"And vinegar?"

"Perhaps a tenth part."

"Did you hear this, you *kerkmaklar* [monsters]? Get going!"

They hurried out and soon returned with the ingredients. I directed that the raisins be washed and then all the ingredients be put into the boiling water. A western champagne producer would have laughed at my brewery, but I had little time and needed to do this as quickly as possible and yet not burden the memory of this noble Pasha with too many chemical procedures.

"Now into the pharmacy!" I urged him.

"Come!"

He walked ahead and led me into a chamber that was on the same level. There the poor *hekim* was lying on the floor, his feet wrapped in bandages. The Pasha gave him a kick as well.

"Get up, *zeddikler* [repugnant one], and show me and this great *Effendi* the honor that is due to us. Thank him, for he has asked that I cease your punishment. Know this, you *kabaji* [no-good], he has taken out my tooth without my even feeling it. I command you to thank him!"

Oh what joy to be the personal physician of a Pasha! This poor blighter threw himself before me and kissed the hem of my old *haïk*. The Pasha then asked:

"Where is the pharmacy?"

The physician pointed to a large, worm-eaten box.

"Here, oh Pasha!"

"Open it!"

I was treated to the sight of a confused disorder of paper bags, leaves, canisters, amulets, tar-sticks and other assorted items, the character and use of which was completely unknown to me. I inquired after bicarbonate of soda and cream of tartar. Of the first there was enough, of the latter only a little was at hand; but it would do.

"Do you have all you need?" the Pasha asked me.

"Yes."

He gave the physician a parting kick and commanded:

"Buy a greater quantity of these things and remember their names. I need them urgently, in case a horse gets sick. If you forget the names you will receive fifty, carefully counted, blows!"

We returned to the kitchen. Bottles, varnish, wire and cold water were brought and then the Governor chased all that were present from the room. No person except himself should, even if only slightly, share in the great secret of how to prepare this wine that was - no wine at all – and therefore permissible to be drunk by a good Moslem without any pangs of conscience. We cooked, brewed, cooled, filled, corked and sealed, the sweat dripped from the Pasha's face, and when we were finally finished, the servants were permitted to enter so that they could move the bottles to the coolest place in the cellar. One bottle, however, the Pasha took with him to 'proof', and he carried it in his hot little hands through the waiting room and into his chamber, where we sat down once more.

"Shall we drink?" he asked.

"It is not cool enough yet."

"We shall drink it warm."

"Then it will not taste so good."

"It must!"

Of course it had to, for the Pasha commanded it! He called for two *kadehs* [glasses] to be brought, forbade anyone, even the herald, to enter and then loosened the wire around the neck of the bottle.

Pop! - The cork flew to the ceiling.

"*Allah il Allah*!" he cried in fright.

The artificial wine gushed from the bottle. I tried to catch it in my glass.

"*Mash Allah*! It truly spits!"

The Pasha opened his mouth and shoved the neck of the bottle between his lips. It was almost empty when he pulled it away and stopped it with his finger.

"*Saltanatly* - Grand! Listen my friend, I love you! This wine is even finer than the waters of Zem-Zem!"

"You think so?"

"Yes. It is even better than the waters of *Hawus Kewser*, from which one will drink in Paradise. I will not just send two, but four *khawassen* with you."

"I thank you! You have noted well how one prepares this wine?"

"Very well. I will not forget it!"

Without consideration for my needs or the fact that two glasses were available, he set the bottle to his lips again and only put it down when it was completely empty.

"*Bom bosh*! It has run out. Why was there not more!"

"Now you know how precious my secret was?"

"By the Prophet, I see this! Oh, you *Nemsi* are very clever people! But permit me to leave you for a moment!"

He got up and left the room. When he returned, after some time, he was carrying something under his kaftan. When he had sat down, he pulled it forth. It was . . . two more bottles of wine. I laughed.

"You have brought them yourself?" I asked.

"*Kendi* - Myself! No one may touch this wine that is 'not wine' except me. I have commanded it below, and whoever dares to touch a bottle from this point on will be whipped to death!"

"You still want to drink?"

"Should I not? Isn't this drink delicious?"

"But I tell you that this drink has a better taste when it has cooled."

"How must it taste then when it is so delicious now! Allah be praised, He Who creates the waters, the raisins, sugar and medicines for the joy of the 'True Believers!"

And he drank without concern for me. His face expressed the greatest bliss and when he had finished his second bottle, he said:

"Friend, no one can equal you, neither a believer nor an infidel. Four *khawassen* are too few for you; you shall have six!"

"Your kindness is great, oh Pasha; I know how to praise it!"

"Will you also write of what I drank?"

"No, about that I will be silent; for I will not write of that which I also shared."

"*Mash Allah*, you are right! I drink without thinking of you. Pass me your glass, I will open this other bottle."

Now I finally got to taste my artificial product. It tasted exactly like warm soda water mixed with raisin broth and sugar; to the unpretentious palate of the Pasha, it must have been a joy.

"You know," he said and took another long pull at the bottle, "that six *khawassen* are still too few? You shall have ten!"

"I thank you, oh Pasha!" if this drinking continued, I would be forced to continue my travels with an entire army of *khawassen*, and under the circumstances that would have been quite troublesome.

"So you go through the land of the 'Devil Worshippers'," he touched on the old subject. "Do you know their language?"

"Is it Kurdish?"

"A Kurdish dialect. Few of them speak Arabic."

"I do not know it."

"Then I will provide you with an interpreter."

"Perhaps this will not be necessary. Kurdish is related to Persian, and that I do understand."

"I do not understand either, but you know best whether you need a *dragoman*. Don't stay in their land too long, though. Do not rest amongst them, rather ride through their land quickly."

"Why?"

"Something terrible could happen to you."

"What?"

"That is my secret. I can only tell you that it could become dangerous and that is why I am sending a guard along with you for your protection. Drink!"

This was now the second secret to which he had alluded.

"Can your people only accompany me to Amadijah?" I asked him.

"Yes, for my power reaches no further."

"What is the territory beyond there?"

"The territory of the Kurds of Berwari."

"What is their capital city called?"

"The capital is the castle Gumri, where their *Bei* lives. I will give you a letter, but I cannot promise you that this document will be of benefit to you. How many companions do you have?"

"One servant."

"Only one? Do you have good horses?"

"Yes."

"That is good for you, for a good horse is often the key to the life and freedom of its rider. And it would be a great misfortune if something were to happen to you, for you are the owner of a splendid secret, which you have revealed to me. But I also wish to express my gratitude to you. Do you know what I will do for you?"

"What?" I asked.

He emptied the bottle and answered with a most benevolent expression:

"Do you know what the *Dish-parassi* is?"

"I know it."

"Well?"

"It is a tax, which you alone can demand."

I described this very vaguely, for the *Dish-parassi*, the 'tooth compensation', is a monetary tax that is raised wherever the Pasha rests whilst on his travels. It is for his teeth, being that they are worn down by the chewing of the local food; for this the local inhabitants must render compensation.

"You have guessed it," he said. "I will give you a letter commanding that you will be paid the *Dish-parassi*, wherever you go, just as though you were me. When do you wish to depart?"

"Early tomorrow morning."

"Wait, I will get my seal and have the letter written at once!"

He stood and left the room. Because the Negro had to carry his pipe after him, I remained alone. Next to where the Pasha had sat were some papers, with which he might well have been occupied when I first arrived. I quickly opened one document. It was a map of the valley of Sheik Adi. Ah! Could this map be connected with his secrets? I could not pursue this thought further, for the Governor returned. At his command, his cipher clerk appeared to whom he then dictated three letters. The first was to the Kurdish *Bei*, the second to the commander of Fort Amadijah and the third to all village chiefs and other authorities. Therein it was written that I had the right to raise the *Dish-parassi*, and that the inhabitants should fulfill my requests as though they had been demanded by the Pasha himself.

What more could I ask for? The purpose of my presence in Mosul was more than fulfilled, and this miracle had been achieved, apart from my boldness, through bicarbonate of soda.

"Are you satisfied with me?" he asked.

"Endlessly, oh Pasha. Your kindness shall crush me with good deeds!"

"Don't thank me now, but later."

"I hope that I will be able to!"

"You will!"

"By what means?"

"That I can tell you. You are not only a *hekim*, but also an officer."

"Why do you think this?"

"A *hekim* or a man who writes books would not dare to visit me without being accompanied by a Consul. You have a *Bu-djeruldi* from the Sultan, and I know that the Padishah sometimes permits foreign officers to travel through his lands in order to give him military reports. Admit it, you are one of these!"

This erroneous supposition could only be to my advantage, and it would have been very unwise of me to refute it. But I did not want to lie and I therefore carefully composed the following diplomatic phrases:

"I cannot confess it, oh Pasha. If you know that the Padishah sends such foreign officers then you have probably also heard that this occurs mostly in secret. Would you be permitted to expose such a secret?"

"No. I don't even intend to entice you to talk about it, but you will thank me for it. That is what I meant earlier."

"How can I prove my appreciation to you?"

"When you return from of the mountains of Kurdistan, I will send you to the Shammar Arabs, especially to the Haddedihn. You shall travel through their territories and then report to me on how I can defeat them."

"Ah!" I said in apperception.

"Yes. This will be easier for you than for one of my people. I know that the officers of the *Francs* are smarter than our own, although I myself was a colonel and performed great services for the Padishah. I would have asked you to look at the lands of the *Jesidi*; but it is too late for that, as I already have the information I need."

These words confirmed my earlier suspicion. The troops at Kufjunjik were ready to attack the 'Devil Worshippers'. He continued:

"You will travel very quickly through their territory and not wait until the day when they celebrate their great festival."

"Which festival is that?"

"The festival of their saint; it will be celebrated at the grave of their Sheik Adi. Here you have your letters. Allah be with you! At what time will you leave the city tomorrow?"

"At the time of the first prayer."

"The ten *khawassen* shall then be at your dwelling."

"Lord, two will be enough."

"You don't understand. Ten are better than two; remember that. You shall have five Arnauts and five *Bashi-Bozuks*. Return soon and do not forget that I have given my affection to you!"

He gave me the sign of dismissal, and I left the house, which I had entered some hours before almost as a prisoner, with my head held high. When I had reached my dwelling, I found Halef bristling with weapons.

"Allah be praised that you return, *Sihdi*!" He welcomed me. "If you had not been here at the setting of the sun, I would have kept my word and shot the Pasha!"

"I would not tolerate that; the Pasha is my friend!"

"Your friend? How can a tiger be the friend of man!"

"I have tamed him."

"*Mash Allah*! Then you have worked a miracle. How did this happen?"

"It was easier than I suspected. We stand under his protection and will be given ten *khawassen,* who will accompany us."

"That is good!"

"Perhaps not! He has also given me letters of recommendation and the right to raise the *Dish-parassi*."

"*Allah akbar*, then you have also become a Pasha! But tell me, *Sihdi*, who must obey whom: I the *khawassen* or they me?"

"They you, for you are not a servant, but rather Hajji Halef Omar Agha, my companion and protector."

"That is good, and I say to you that they will know me, if it occurs to them to deny me the respect that is my due!"

The Governor had kept his word. When Halef arose at dawn the next morning and stuck his head out of the door, ten men greeted him, who were mounted on horses before it. He awakened me at once and I of course hurried to inspect my 'protectors'. There were, as the Pasha had promised, five Arnauts and five *Bashi-Bozuks*. The latter wore the usual clothing of the Turkish military. The Arnauts wore crimson velvet outer-vests, green, decorated velvet under-vests, wide sashes, red trousers with metal shin-armor and red turbans, they carried so many weapons with them that one could have armed a troop three times their number with their knives and pistols alone. The *Bashi-Bozuks* were commanded by an old *Buluk-Emini* [fourier or clerk of a company] and the Arnauts by a wild looking *onbashi* [commander of ten men].

The *Buluk-Emini* appeared to be a unique character. He rode no horse, but rather a donkey, and wore the sign of his rank - an enormous inkwell - upon a strap around the neck. In his turban several dozen quills were wedged tightly. He was a fat little man who had no nose; yet the larger was his moustache that hung from his upper lip. His cheeks looked almost blue and were so fleshy that the skin could scarcely cover them, and for the eyes there remained enough room for them to open just far enough to admit a little light into the brain when it was necessary.

I gave a bottle full of *Racki* to Halef and commanded him to welcome these brave heroes with it. He stepped out to them, and I stood so that I was able to observe the process.

"*Sabahiniz chajir* - Good morning, you valiant fighters! Be welcome to us!" He began.

"*Sabahiniz chajir* - Good morning!" echoed the troop in unison.

"You have come to accompany the famous Kara Ben Nemsi on his journey?"

"The Pasha sends us for this purpose."

"Then I will tell you that my name is Hajji Agha Halef Omar Ben Hajji Abul Abbas Ibn Hajji Dawuhd al Gossarah; I am the marshal on this journey and Agha of him whom you should accompany, and you must, therefore, follow my directions and obey them. What was the order that the Pasha gave you?"

The *Buluk-Emini* answered in such a thin high-pitched voice that it sounded like someone blowing on a rusty F-trumpet:

"I am *Buluk-Emini* of the Padishah, whom Allah may bless, and my name is Ifra. Remember this name! The Pasha, whose most faithful servant I am, gave me this inkwell and these quills in addition to much paper in order to write down everything that happens to you and us. I am the brave leader of these men and will prove to you that . . ."

"Silence, *eshekun-atli* [donkey rider]!" the *onbashi* interrupted him while he stroked his huge beard. "What are you? Our leader? You dwarf! You master of the inkwell and of the geese that are the origin of your quills! That is what you are and nothing more!"

"What? I am *Buluk-Emini* and my name is Ifra. Courage ..."

"Silence, I tell you! Your courage grows in the feet of your donkey, may Allah burn it; for this creature has the miserable custom of meandering through the day and braying at the sky at night. We know you and your donkey, but it is certain which one of you two is the *Buluk-Emini* and which is the donkey!"

"Beware your tongue, *onbashi*! Don't you know that I am so brave I even ventured to that place in the battle where noses are hacked off? Look at my nose, which unfortunately is no longer present, and you will marvel over the audacity with which I fought! Or perhaps you don't know about that story, the story of the loss of my nose? Then hear it! It was at the time when we fought before Sebastopol against the *Moskows*; there I stood in the thickest part of the battle and had just raised my arm to ... "

"Silence! Your story has been heard a thousand time already!" - and turning to Halef he continued: "I am the *onbashi* Ular Ali. We have heard that the Emir Kara Ben Nemsi is a brave man and we like that; we have further heard that he spoke for our Aghas, and that we like even more. We will protect him and serve him, and he shall be satisfied with us!"

"Then I ask once more, what orders did the Pasha give you." Halef continued.

"He has ordered us to ensure that the Emir is treated as a best friend, like the brother of the Pasha."

"Then we will receive free shelter and nourishment everywhere?"

"Everything that you, and we, will need."

"Has he also told you about the *Dish-parassi*?"

"Yes."

"That will be paid in coin?"

"Yes."

"How high will it be?"

"As high as the Emir wishes it."

"Allah bless the Pasha! His intellect is as bright as the sun, and his wisdom illuminates the world. You shall be content with us. Are your ready to commence the journey?"

"Yes."

"Have you got food?"

"For a day."

"But no tents!"

"We do not need any, for each evening we will find a good dwelling."

"Do you know that we will go through the land of the *Jesidi*?"

"We know it."

"Do you fear the 'Devil Worshippers'?"

"Fear? Agha Halef Omar, have you ever heard that an Arnaut was afraid? Or is perhaps a *Merd-it-Shaïtan* - a man of the Devil, Shaïtan himself? Tell the Emir that we are ready to receive him!"

After a while I let my horse be led out and followed behind him. The ten men stood at attention before me, each at the head of his horse. I merely nodded, then mounted my beast and indicated that they should follow me. The little troop set itself in motion.

Chapter 22

We rode across the pontoon bridge and found ourselves on the left shore of the Tigris, outside of the city of Mosul. There I first called the *onbashi* to my side and asked him:

"Whom do you serve now, me or the Pasha?"

"You, oh Emir."

"I am satisfied with you. Send the *Buluk-Emini* to me."

He returned to his position. Then the little fat one approached.

"Your name is Ifra? I have heard that you are a brave warrior."

"Very brave!" he assured me with his trumpet-like voice.

"You can write?"

"Very well, very beautifully, oh Emir!"

"Where have you served and fought?"

"In all the lands of the earth."

"Ah! Name these lands for me."

"What for, Emir? There would be more than a thousand names!"

"Then you must be a very famous *Buluk-Emini*."

"Very famous! Have you never heard of me?"

"No."

"Then you surely have not traveled much in your life, otherwise you would have heard of my fame. For example, I must tell you how I lost my nose. That was the time we were before Sebastopol and fighting against the *Moskows*; there I stood in the thickest part of the battle, I had just raised my arm ..."

At that moment he was interrupted. My raven-black stallion definitely could not stand the odor of his donkey; it snorted angrily, hackles raised, it snapped at the *Buluk-Emini's* little gray beast. The donkey reared up on his hind legs to avoid the bite, turned aside and ran - yet it was no mere evasion but a true escape. It ran over hill and dale ahead of us; the little *Buluk-Emini* could hardly keep his place astride the donkey and soon both were gone from view.

"That happens to him often!" I heard the *onbashi* say to Halef.

"We must go after him," answered Halef; "otherwise we lose him."

"Him?" laughed the Arnaut. "It would not be a pity to lose him. But do not worry! It has happened to him a thousand times already and he has never been lost."

"But why does he ride such a beast?"

"He must."

"Must? Why?"

"The *jüsbashi* [captain of one hundred men] desires it. He makes sport with Ifra and the donkey."

As we had passed between Kufjunjik and the cloister of Saint George, we saw the *Buluk-Emini* halt before us. He awaited our approach but called from afar:

"Lord, you perhaps believed that the donkey ran away with me?"

"I was certain of it." I called back.

"You err, Emir! I only rode ahead to scout out our way. Do we follow the Khausser or do we ride along the usual path?"

"We stay on the path."

"Then permit me to tell you my story later. I will now serve you as a guide."

He rode ahead. The Khausser is a brook or stream that springs from the northern reaches of the Jebel Maklub and waters many village lands along its journey to Mosul. We rode across a small bridge and from then on kept the stream to our left. The ruins and the village of Khorsabad are roughly seven hours ride to the north of Mosul. The area consists of marshy ground, from which rise poisonous gases. We moved swiftly in order to reach our goal, but we probably had another hour's ride before us when we met a troop of some fifty Arnauts. At the head of the convoy rode the officers and in their midst I spied the white garments of an Arab. As we came closer I recognized . . . Sheik Mohammed Emin!

Oh dear! He had fallen into the hands of these people; he, an enemy of the Pasha who had already taken his son prisoner and dispatched him to Amadijah. The question now was, had he tried to defend himself; but I could not detect a single wounded man. Had they caught him while he slept? I had to attempt to rescue him from these dangerous people. Therefore I stopped in the middle of the path and let the convoy approach.

My troop dismounted to rest by the side of the road. Halef and I remained on our horses. Their leader detached himself from the others and rode towards us at a trot. Directly before me he reigned in his horse and asked; whilst ignoring my resting men:

"*Salaam*! Who are you?"

"*Aaleïkum*! I am an Emir from the west."

"Of which tribe?"

"Of the tribe of the *Nemsi*."

"Where do you intend going?"

"Towards the east."

"To whom?"

"To everyone!"

"You answer very briefly, fellow! Do you know who I am?" He replied indignantly.

"I can see who you are."

"Then reply more appropriately! With what right do you travel here?"

"With the same right with which you ride!"

"*Tallahi* - by God, you are very bold! I ride by the order of the *Mutessarif* of Mosul; you can believe that!"

"And I travel here by the order of the *Mutessarif* of Mosul and the Padishah of Constantinople; you can believe that!"

He opened his eyes a little more and then demanded:

"Prove it!"

"Here!"

I handed him my authorization. He opened it with the prescribed formalities and then examined it. He folded it again carefully and returned it to me and said in a very courteous tone:

"You yourself bear the blame for my speaking harshly to you. You saw who I was and should have answered more courteously!"

"You yourself bear the blame for that not having happened," I answered him. "You saw my troop, which attests to my being a man that enjoys the friendship of the *Mutessarif*, and you should have questioned me more courteously! *Aghaja benden jok selam ejle*; *sabahnitz chajir ola* - greet your master many times from me; good morning!"

"*Bash üstüne sultanum* - as you order, my Lord!" he answered.

I turned away. It had been my intention to free Mohammed Emin, but I had noticed, immediately upon speaking with the officer, that this was not necessary. The officer's troop had halted some distance behind him and was watching me more than their prisoner. Mohammed Emin made good use of that circumstance at once. He was bound only lightly and sat on an inferior Turkish horse. At the rear of the troop was his magnificent mount, its saddle still laden with all his weapons. I noticed his success in freeing his hands and just at this moment, when my conversation was at an end, he raised himself up to a standing position on the back of his Turkish horse.

"Halef, watch out!" I murmured to my servant, who had been watching as intently as I had.

"You and I, between them and him, *Sihdi*!" he answered me.

He had understood me immediately. The Haddedihn chief dared a series of bold leaps from croup to croup of the horses halted behind him. The riders of these beasts had not expected such audacity, and before they could grab him, he had reached his own horse – dropped into the saddle, torn the reigns from the hands that held them and galloped away diagonally, neither up nor down the path but straight towards the stream.

A chorus of surprised and angry voices sounded behind him.

"The prisoner escapes," I shouted at their leader; "let us chase after him!"

At the same time I turned my horse and raced after the escapee. Halef held himself at my side.

"Not so close to me, Halef! Further away! Ride so that they cannot shoot without hitting us!"

It was a fast, wild hunt that followed. To our good fortune, the pursuers only sought to catch up to Mohammed Emin at first, and when they saw that his horse was superior to theirs, they then decided to use their weapons. By this time though, the lead that he had won was too great. Then too, their guns were of little use as Halef and I were not riding in a straight line before them but rather in an erratic manner; I also did everything possible to make it seem as though my horse were being stubborn. He appeared to halt, buck and then brake into a run, he turned and reared, turned on his own axis and then shot ahead to either the right or the left before turning sharply in the proper direction. Halef did likewise and so the Turks could not shoot for fear of hitting us.

The Haddedihn chief had driven his horse fearlessly into the waters of the Khausser. He managed to cross successfully, as did Halef and myself; but before the others could do likewise we had gained a considerable lead. We raced ahead, always towards the northwest until we had ridden for some two hours. We then came upon the road which led from Mosul to Raban Hormuzd via Telkeïf and which runs parallel to the one we had intended to take in order to reach Khorsabad, Jeraijah and Baadri. Only here did Mohammed Emin halt his horse. He saw only the two of us for the others had disappeared beyond the horizon quite some time ago.

"Allah be praised!" he cried. "*Effendi*, I thank you, you have taken their hands from their guns! What do we do now so that they do not follow us?"

"How did you fall into their hands, Sheik?" asked little Halef.

"He will tell us that later; he has no time for it now," I answered. "Mohammed Emin, do you know the marshy land that lies between the Tigris and Jebel Maklub?"

"I once rode through the same."

"In which direction?"

"From Baa Sheika and Baazani across Ras al Aïn towards Dohuk."

"Is the marsh dangerous?"

"No."

"Do you see that peak, there in the northeast, which might be reached in three hours?" I asked them both.

"We see it." They responded simultaneously.

"There we will meet again, for here we must part. We must not follow the road as we would be seen and our destination surmised. We must ride into the marsh, and do so individually, so that our pursuers, when they reach here, will not know which tracks to follow."

"But what of our Arnauts and *Bashi-Bozuks*, *Sihdi*?" asked Halef.

"They don't concern us now. They are more of a hindrance to us than an advantage; they provide no more protection than my passports and papers. Halef, you part here and head towards the south; I will ride the central route and the Sheik rides north: - Each of us must ride at least a half-hour's distance from the other."

The two separated from me and I headed away from the road into the marsh, which did not truly possess the properties of a swamp. My companions disappeared from my sight and I headed alone towards the goal that we had set before us.

For many days now I had found myself in a state of excitement such as I had not felt in a long time. There is no land on earth that hides as many riddles as the ground that was now stirred by the hooves of my horse. Quite apart from the ruins of the Assyrian and Babylonian empires, which are apparent at every step, now the mountains appeared before me, the slopes and valleys of which are populated by peoples whose nationality and religion can only be determined with great difficulty. Members of these nations, tribes and sects might also be encountered at every step - the 'Light Extinguishers', 'Fire Worshippers', 'Devil Worshippers', Nestorians, Chaldeans, Nahumites, Sunnites, Shiites, Nadjijetes, Ghollates, Rewafidhites, Muatazilctites, Wachabites, Arabs, Jews, Turks, Armenians, Syrians, Druse, Maronites, Kurds, Persians and Turkmenites. Who can say what mistakes or violations a stranger might commit under such circumstances! These mountains reek to this day with the blood of those who fell victim to racial hatred, wild fanaticism and the desire for rape or bloody vengeance.

Here human abodes depend on the mountainous terrain they are in the form of caves and crevasses, like the nests of vultures that are always ready to fall upon the ignorant victim. Here, the system of oppression, the careless exploitation of that wrathful bitterness produces a state in which one cannot determine a friend from a foe, and the Word of reconciling love, that was taught by the messengers of Christ was taken away by the wind. The American missionaries may speak of success: - the field is ready to receive the mustard seed. Other men of God may do and dare all. In the Kurdish Mountains animosity flows like a river into a wild whirlpool, which will only rest when a mighty fist successfully grinds the rocks to dust and then conquers the hatred and manages to crush the head of the horrible, softly creeping blood feud. Then their paths will be free for the feet of those that 'preach peace and announce salvation'. Then no inhabitant of these mountains will say: 'I became a Christian because otherwise I would have received the bastinado from the Agha.' And that Agha was - a strict Mohammedan. [See Translation Note Ch 22. 1]

The mountain grew larger and larger before me, or rather I came closer to it. The ground was soft and damp, but there were only a few places where the hooves of my horse had sunk to any depth, and finally there was dry land. The fever zone of the Tigris was behind me. I now saw a rider approaching on my right and before long I recognized Halef, with whom I was soon united.

"Did you meet anyone?" I asked him.

"No, *Sihdi*."

"No one saw you?"

"No one. Far to the south, on the path that we left, I saw a little man walking, he towed an animal behind him. But I could not recognize him."

"Can you recognize that one over there?"

"Oh *Sihdi*, that is none other than the Sheik!"

"Yes, that is Mohammed Emin. He will be with us in ten minutes."

And so he was. He recognized us and quickly joined us.

"What now, *Effendi*?" he asked me.

"That will depend entirely upon what you have experienced. Were you perhaps observed?"

"No. Only a shepherd drove his herd past me in the distance."

"How were you captured?"

"You should not have sent me to the ruins of Khorsabad [This name is most probably an abbreviation of Khosrauabad, the seat of the Khosroes]. Until this morning I remained hidden in the southern section, then I took a position closer to the road in order to watch for your arrival. There I was spied by the soldiers and surrounded. I could not defend myself for they were too many. As to why they took me prisoner, I do not know."

"Did they ask you of your tribe and your name?"

"Yes; but I advised them falsely."

"These people are inexperienced. An Arab would have recognized you from your tattoo. They took you prisoner because the troops of the Pasha camp in the ruins of Kufjunjik – those that are designated to move against the Shammar."

He was startled and drew up his horse.

"Against the Shammar? Allah help us; then I must return immediately!"

"That is not necessary. I know the Governor's plan."

"What is this plan?"

"The move against the Shammar is, for now, only a ruse. The *Mutessarif* will first attack the *Jesidi*. The *Jesidi* must not be allowed to suspect this, and that is why the Pasha lets it be known that he intends to move against the Shammar."

"Do you know that for certain?"

"Definitely, for I have spoken with him myself. I am to return and scout out the pastures of the Shammar."

"But if the Pasha finishes with the *Jesidi* quickly, then he will use the opportunity to send his army against the Shammar."

"He will not be done with the *Jesidi* that quickly; you can depend on that. By then the brief springtime will be over."

"*Mash Allah*, what does spring have to do with this war, *Effendi*?"

"A great deal. As soon as the hotter days come, the plants will wither and the plain will dry out. The *Bedawi* migrate with their herds to the mountains of the Shammar or the Sindshar, and the army of the Governor would die miserably."

"You are right, *Effendi*. Then we shall continue confidently on our way; but I am unfamiliar with this way."

"To the right we have the road to Ain Sifni, to the left the road to Jerraijah and Baadri. But until we reach Baadri we must not be seen and thus it will be necessary to keep to the shore of the Khausser. When we have Jerraijah behind us we no longer need to hide."

"How far is it to Baadri?"

"Three hours ride."

"Lord, you are a great Emir. You come from a land far from here and yet you know this area better than I!"

"We were to go to Amadijah, so I had inquired about the area through which we were to travel. That is all! Now forward!"

Although the two paths that we wished to avoid were barely half an hour's ride from us, we were lucky to remain undiscovered. When we saw people coming from the right, we rode to the left, and when we noticed people to the left, we rode to the right. Of course my telescope assisted me greatly in this and to it alone we owed our thanks when we finally looked upon Baadri and knew we were safe.

We had now been in the saddle for nearly ten hours and were rather tired when we reached the row of hills at the foot of which lay a village. This was the residence of the spiritual leader of the 'Devil Worshippers' as well as the worldly home of the tribe. I asked the first man that we met for the name of the *Bei*. He looked at me with some embarrassment. I had not considered that most of the *Jesidi* do not speak Arabic.

"*Bei nije demar* - what is the name of the *Bei*?" I asked again, in Turkish.

"Ali *Bei*," he answered me.

"*Ol nerde oturar* - where does he live?"

"*Gel, seni götirim* - come, I will lead you!"

He led us to a great, stone building.

"*Ijerde otur* - He lives within," said the man; then he departed.

The village was extraordinarily lively. I noted that besides the houses and huts there were also many tents, before which horses and donkeys were tethered and between which numerous people moved to and fro. Their number was so great that our arrival appeared not to have been noticed.

"*Sihdi*, look here!" said Halef. "Do you know that one?"

He pointed to a donkey that was tethered before the entrance of a house. Truly, it was the donkey of our fat little *Buluk-Emini*! I dismounted and entered. I heard the thin high-pitched voice of the brave Ifra:

"And you really will not give me another room?"

"I have no other," replied another voice in a very dry tone.

"You are the *Kiajah* [Head of the village]; you must arrange another!"

"I have already told you that I don't have another. The village is full of pilgrims; there is no empty place. Why does your *Effendi* not carry a tent?"

"My *Effendi*? He is an Emir, a great *Bei*, who is more famous than all the *Jesidi* princes in these mountains!"

"Where is he?"

"He will arrive later. First he has to catch a prisoner."

"Catch a prisoner? Are you crazy?"

"An escaped prisoner."

"Ah, I see!"

"He has a *Firman* from the Sultan, a *Firman el Onsul* [Passport from the Consul], a *Firman* and many letters from the *Mutessarif*, and here are my papers as well."

"He should come himself!"

"What? He has the *Dish-parassi*, and you say that he should come himself! I will speak with the Sheik!"

"He is not here."

"Then I will speak with the *Bei*!"

"Go to him!"

"Yes, I will go. I am a *Buluk-Emini* of the Sultan, I receive thirty-five piaster a month [7 German Marks] and do not need to fear any *Kiajah*. Do you hear?"

"Yes, thirty-five piaster a month!" the response sounded almost jovial. "What else do you get?"

"What else? Listen! Two pounds of bread, seventeen lot [1 lot - a measure varying between 15.5 grams and 16.6 grams] of meat, three lot of butter, five lot of rice, one lot of salt and one and a half lot of condiments daily, as well as soap, oil and boot polish. You understand me? And if you laugh at my nose, which I no longer have, then I will tell you how I lost it! That was a long time ago, when we stood before Sebastopol; I found myself in the thickest rain of bullets, and . . ."

"I don't have the time to listen to you. Shall I tell the *Bei* that you wish to speak with him?"

"Tell him. And don't forget to mention that I will not be turned away!"

My person had been the subject of this rather loud discussion. I entered and Mohammed Emin and Halef followed behind. The *Kiajah* was about to open a door but turned at our sudden appearance.

"Here comes the Emir himself," said Ifra. "He will show you to whom you must listen!"

I first turned my attention to the *Buluk-Emini*:

"You there! How is it that you are in Baadri by yourself?"

His face showed embarrassment, but he answered nonetheless:

"Have I not told you that I would ride ahead, Excellency?"

"Where are the others?"

"*Iflemish* - disappeared, vanished, blown away!"

"Where to?"

"I do not know, Highness."

"You must have seen!"

"Only a little. When the prisoner escaped, they all rode after him, even my people and the Arnauts."

"And why not you?"

"*Benim eshek* - my donkey did not want to, Master. And besides, I had to ride to Baadri, to ready your quarters."

"Did you note the escaped prisoners features?"

"How could I? I was lying face down on the earth and when I arose, to join the hunt, he was already too far away."

This was very pleasing to me since it assured the safety of Mohammed Emin.

"Will the others follow soon?"

"Who knows! Allah cannot be divined; he leads the believers here and there, to the right and to the left, as it pleases him, for the way of man is written in the *Kitab takdirün* - in the 'Book of Providence'."

"Is Ali *Bei* here?" I asked the village elder.

"Yes."

"Where?"

"*Bu kapu esheri* - behind this door."

"Is he alone?"

"Yes."

"Tell him that I wish to speak with him!"

While he entered the other room, Ifra poked the little Halef in the side and said softly, while looking at Mohammed Emin:

"Who is this Arab?"

"A Sheik."

"Where does he come from?"

"We met him along the way. He is a friend of my *Sihdi* and he will remain with us."

"*Wer jok Bakhshishler* - does he give many gratuities?"

"*Bu kadar*- a great many!" said Halef, whilst extending all ten fingers.

That was enough for the good *Buluk-Emini*, as I could read from his satisfied demeanor. The doors now opened and the village elder returned. Behind him appeared a younger man of admirable stature. He was tall and slim, had regular facial features and eyes that held an uncommon gleam. He wore trousers that were covered with fine needlepoint patterns, a rich jacket and a turban, from beneath which a substantial quantity of splendid curls cascaded. In his belt was simply a knife, the hilt of which was engraved with an artistic design.

"Chosh geldin demek - Be welcome!" he said, whilst he offered his hand, first to me, then the Sheik and finally Halef. The *Bashi-Bozuk* he did not appear to notice at all.

"*Mazal bujurum sultanum* - forgive me, Lord, that I enter your house," I answered. "The evening is near and I wanted to ask you if a place exists within your domain where we might rest our heads."

He studied me intently from my head to my feet and then answered:

"One should not ask the wanderer from whence he comes and to where he goes. But my *Kiajah* tells me that you are an Emir."

"I am not an Arab, nor a Turk, I am a *Nemsi*, from the Far West."

"A *Nemsi*? I do not know these people and I have never seen one of them before. But I have heard of one *Nemsi* whom I would like to meet."

"May I ask why?"

"Because three of my men owe their lives to him."

"How so?"

"He freed them from their captivity and brought them to the Haddedihn."

"Are they here in Baadri?"

"Yes."

"And are their names Pali, Selek and Melaf?"

He took a step back in surprise and said.

"You know them?"

"What was the name of the *Nemsi* to whom you refer?"

"He was called Kara Ben Nemsi."

"That is my name. This man here is Mohammed Emin, the Sheik of the Haddedihn, and the other is Halef, my companion."

"Is it possible? What a surprise! *Seni gerek olarim* - I must embrace you!"

He pulled me towards him and kissed both my cheeks; he did similarly with Mohammed and Halef, but he omitted the kissing. Then he took my hand and said:

"*Jelebim mahalinde geldin* - Lord, you come at the right time. We are to have a great feast, at which we do not customarily permit strangers; but you shall partake in our joy. Remain here for these happy days and even longer!"

"I shall, provided that the Sheik agrees."

"He will agree."

"You must know that his heart drives him on as we will explain to you."

"I know it. But enter. My house is your house and my bread is your bread. You shall be our brothers for as long as we live!"

As we stepped through the doorway I heard Ifra say to the village elder:

"Have you heard, old one, what a famous Emir my *Effendi* is? Learn to value me in the same manner. Remember this!"

The room that we entered was decorated in a simple manner. The Sheik and I were seated alongside Ali *Bei* who still held my hand and once more studied me intently.

"So you are the man who vanquished the enemies of the Haddedihn!"

"Do you desire to color my cheeks with modesty?"

"Who also killed the lion in the night without aid! I wish I were like you! Are you a Christian?"

"Yes."

"The Christians are mightier than other peoples; but I too am a Christian."

"Are the *Jesidi* Christians?"

"They are all things. The *Jesidi* have taken for themselves only the good from all religions . . ."

"Do you know that for certain?"

He frowned.

"I tell you, Emir, that in these mountains no single religion can survive; for our people are divided, our tribes are split and our hearts torn asunder. A good religion must teach love; but a free love - a love that grows from deep within cannot take root with us for the ground is full of hate, vengeance, betrayal and cruelty. If I had the power, then I would preach love, but not with my lips, rather with my sword in hand, for where a noble flower shall flourish, the weeds must be eradicated first.

Do you think perhaps that a sermon can make a *karanfil* [carnation] from a *zehr-lahana* [poisonous weed]? The gardener can enhance the bloom of the poisonous weed, but the poison will continue to lurk within. And I tell you that the sermon of my sword shall make lambs from wolves. Whoever hears this sermon will be happy; but whoever resists it - they I shall crush. Only then can I restore the sword to its scabbard and return home to my tent, to rejoice in my work. For once love has entered, it is truly as the Holy Book of the Christians says; *Muhabbet bitmez* - Love never ends!"

His eyes shone, his cheeks had flushed and the tone of his voice came from deep within his heart. He was not only a handsome man but a noble one as well; he knew the sad state of his land and perhaps had the stuff to be a hero.

"You therefore believe that Christian preachers who come from far away cannot be effective?" I asked him.

"We *Jesidi* know your Holy Book. It says: '*Chüdanün söz jekij dir, bi jatlar tashlar* - the Word of God is a hammer that shatters rocks.' But can you crush water with a hammer? Can you crush the mist, which rises from the swamps and kills life, with it? Ask the men that came from *Jeni dünja* [America]! They have taught and spoken much; they have given many beautiful gifts and sold many beautiful things, they have even worked as *basmaji* [printers]. And the people have listened to them, have taken their gifts, have permitted themselves to be baptized and then went on to rob, steal and kill as before. The Holy Book was printed in our language, but no one understood the dialect and no one here can read or write. Do you believe that these holy men will teach us to read and write? My quill is now made only of sharp steel."

The *Bei* continued his speech.

"Go to the famous Rabban Hormuzd cloister, which once belonged to the Nestorians. Now it belongs to the *Katuliklar* [Catholics], who converted Alkosh and Telkef. Some poor *Abdelar* [monks] starved on the dry heights, where two bare olive trees now mark their passing. Why is it so and not otherwise? We do not have *Jeboshu* [Joshua], who ordered: *'Günesh ile kamer, sus hem Gibbea jakinda hem dere Ajala* - Sun, stand still at Gibeon and, moon, in the valley of Ajalon!' We do not have the hand of *Shimsa* [Samson] that forced the wicked to behave well at the point of his sword. We do not have *Johan Dawuhd* [Shepherd David], who vanquished the murderer *Joliah* [Goliath] with his slingshot. We do not have the flood that drowned the godless, so that *Nauah* [Noah] could kneel down with his kindred before Allah beneath the seven-colored bow. Does it not say in your book: '*Insanlar jeza estemez-ler dan ruhuma* - the people do not want to be punished by my spirit'? If I were a *Musa* [Moses], I would send my Jeboshu and my Kaleb through all the valleys of Kurdistan and would level the ways with my sword. Your Kitab says of this: '*Wazar-lar sallami, der-ler ughurü* - they preach peace and announce salvation'!

You look at me with astonishment; do you think that peace is better than war and the shovel is better than the club? I believe that too. But can you think of a peace that is not won with the saber? Must we not carry the club here so that we can work with the shovel? Look at yourself, only yourself! You carry many weapons and they are better than those which we posses. Why do you carry them? Do you also carry them in the land of the *Nemsi* when you travel?" He asked.

"No," I had to admit.

"There, you see! You can go to *kilise* [church] and pray to Allah without worry. You can seat yourself before a teacher and listen to his voice without anxiety. You can honor your parents and advise your children without fear. You live in the Garden of Eden undaunted, for your snake's head has been crushed. But we still wait for a hero who will still and calm the '*shamata arasynda daghlere'* – 'clamor in the mountains', of which your book speaks. And I tell you that he will yet come. It will not be the Russian nor the English, not the Turk, who sucks us dry, and not the Persian, who lies to us and cheats us so honorably. We once believed that it was Bonaparte, the great Shah of the French; but now we know that the lion cannot expect help from the eagle, for their domain is so different. Have you heard how the *Jesidi* have suffered?"

"Yes."

"We lived in peace and harmony in the land of Sindshar; but we were oppressed and expelled. It was early in the year; the river broke its banks and the bridge was washed away. There lay our elders, our women and children, down at the water's edge by Mosul. They were driven into the rushing waters or slaughtered like wild animals. On the terraces of the city stood the people of Mosul; they cheered at the bloodbath. Those that survived did not know where to rest their heads. They went into the mountains of Maklub, Bohtan, or Sheikhan, to Missuri, and Syrian and even across the Russian border. There they acquired a home, there they worked, and when you see their homes, their clothes, their gardens and their fields, then you rejoice; for there rules purpose, order and cleanliness, whilst all around them you see only dirt and apathy. This tempts those neighbors around them, and when they need money and people, they fall upon us and murder our happiness and us. We celebrate a feast in three days, a feast in honor of our great saint. We have not been able to celebrate this feast for many years, because the pilgrims would have been risking their lives to make the pilgrimage to Sheik Adi. This year however, it appears as though our enemies intend to remain peaceable and thus we will honor our saint after such a long time. *Jelebim mahalinde geldin* - You came at the right time. Whilst we reject strangers at our feast; you, the benefactor of my people shall be welcome to us."

Nothing was more pleasing to me than this invitation, for it was an opportunity to observe and study the traditions and customs of these enigmatic 'Devil Worshippers'. The *Radjahl el Shaïtan* or *Chalk-shaïtanün* ['Devil's People'] have been described to me as terrible people and yet to me they appeared in a much better light, so much so that I was eager to educate myself about them.

"Accept my thanks for your benevolent offer," I answered. "I would like to remain with you very much, but we have a duty to fulfill, which requires that we leave Baadri soon."

"I know of this duty," he replied. "You can partake of our feast nonetheless."

"You know of our task?"

"Yes, you wish to go to Amad al Ghandur, the son of Sheik Mohammed Emin. He is in Amadijah."

"How do you know this?"

"From the three men whom you rescued. You will not be able to free him just now."

"Why not?"

"The *Mutessarif* of Mosul appears to fear an attack by the Kurds of the east and thus has sent many troops to Amadijah, of these a considerable number have already arrived in Amadijah."

"How many?"

"Two *jüsbashi* [captain, commander of one hundred men] with two hundred troops of the sixth infantry regiment. Anatoli Ordüssi, of Diarbekir; and three *jüsbashi* with three hundred troops of the third infantry regiment. Irak Ordüssi, of Kerkjuk; all together five hundred men, commanded by a *bimbashi* [major, commander of one thousand men]."

"And Amadijah is twelve hours from here?"

"Yes; but the path is so difficult that you cannot reach it in a day. One usually camps in Cheloki or Spandareh overnight and rides the following morning over the steep and arduous Gharah mountains, behind which lies the plain and the rocky peak of Amadijah."

"What troops are in Mosul?"

"Parts of the second dragoons and of the fourth infantry regiment of the division Irak Ordüssi. And they are on the move. One unit will move against the Bedouins, and another will move across our mountains and march to Amadijah."

"What is the number of the latter?"

"A thousand men under the command of a *Miralai* [colonel], and they also have a *Alai-Emini* [regimental quartermaster] with them. I know this *Miralai*; he slew the wife and two sons of Pir Kamek [Jesidic Saint] and his name is Omar Amed."

"Do you know where they will assemble?"

"Those who are destined for the Bedouin camps are hidden at the ruins of Kufjunjik; I have discovered from my scouts that they will break camp the day after tomorrow. The others will be ready to march much later."

"I believe that you have been informed incorrectly by your scouts."

"How so?"

"Do you really believe that the *Mutessarif* of Mosul is sending troops from as far as Diarbekir to move against the Kurds of the east? Was not the second infantry regiment, Irak Ordüssi, which is in Suleimania, much closer? And does the third regiment in Kerkjuk not consist, for the most part, of Kurds? Do you believe that he would make the mistake of sending three hundred of these men against their own tribe?"

He frowned in contemplation and then said:

"Your summation is clever but I do not follow."

"Do the troops that are in Kufjunjik have cannons?"

"No."

"If one intended to engage on a plain then one would certainly take *topdshi* [cannons]. A troop that does not carry artillery, is certainly destined for the mountains."

"Then my scouts have misinterpreted the situation. The people at the ruins are destined for Amadijah and not for the Bedouins."

"They will break camp the day after tomorrow? Then they arrive here on the day of your great feast!"

"Emir!"

He spoke this single word as an expression of extreme terror. I continued:

"Notice that neither the southern nor the northern side provide passage into Sheik Adi, only the western and eastern boundaries permit access by troops. Ten hours from here, in the west, a thousand men are gathering at Mosul, and twelve hours from here, in the east, five hundred men are joining up in Amadijah. Sheik Adi will be encircled and no escape will be possible."

"Lord, is this so intended?" He moaned.

"Do you honestly believe that five hundred men are enough to invade the territory of the Kurds of Berwari, of Bohtan, Tijari and Chal, Hakkiari, Karitha and Tura-Ghara, Baz and Shirwan? These Kurds would be able to assemble an opposing force of six thousand men by the third day."

"You are right, Emir; it is aimed at us!"

"Now that you have been convinced by reason, accept this then: I have it directly from the lips of the *Mutessarif*, that he intends to attack you in Sheik Adi."

"Really?"

"Listen!"

I told him of my discussions with the Governor, which corroborated my previous conclusion. When I finished, he arose and paced up and down several times. Then he offered me his hand (when he had resumed his seat).

"I thank you, oh Lord; you have saved us all! If five hundred *jenkdshi* [soldiers] had attacked us without warning we would have been routed; but now it would please me if they really came. The *Mutessarif* has intentionally lulled us into a false sense of security so that we would be induced to make a pilgrimage to Sheik Adi. He has planned it all very cleverly; but one thing he has not considered - the mice that he hopes to catch will become so numerous that they will tear apart the cat. Be so good as not to mention what we have discussed to anyone, and permit me to leave you for a short while."

He arose and left the room.

"How do you like him, Emir?" asked Mohammed Emin.

"As much as you!"

"And this is supposed to be a *merd-es-Shaïtan*, a 'Devil Worshipper'?" asked Halef. "I imagined a *Jesidi* to have the maw of a *kurdsh* [wolf], the eyes of a *kaplan* [tiger] and claws like a *vampyr*!"

"Do you still believe that the *Jesidi* will steal Paradise from you?" I asked with a smile.

"Just wait, *Sihdi*! I have heard that the Devil often takes on a pleasing shape to cheat the 'True Believer'."

The door opened and a man entered, his appearance was quite unusual. His clothes were of the purest white and his hair, which he wore in long tresses down his back, was white as snow. He might have been eighty years old; his cheeks were hollow and his eyes rested in deep sockets, but his gaze was fearless and hard, and the way he entered and closed the door showed the surprising flexibility of his body. The full raven-black beard that hung to his belt was in marked contrast to the snowy hair on his head. He bowed before us and greeted us in a resonant voice:

"*Günesh-iniz söjündürme-sun* - May your sun never darken!" And then he added: "*Hun be kurmangji zanin* - Do you speak Kurdish?"

The last question was spoken in the Kurmangji dialect, and as I, quite unintentionally, hesitated in answering he said:

"*Shima zazaja zani*?"

This question was spoken in the Zaza dialect. Both these dialects are the most commonly spoken of the Kurdish languages, neither of which was familiar to me at that time. I therefore did not understand the words, but guessed their substance and answered in Turkish:

"*Seni an-lamez-iz* - we do not understand. *Jalwar-iz söjlem türkje* - please speak in Turkish!"

As I spoke, I arose to offer him my place, as was proper considering his age. He took my hand and asked:

"*Nemsi sen* - are you the German?"

"Yes."

"*Izim seni kujaklam-am* - Permit me to embrace you!"

He embraced me joyfully but did not take the offered place; instead he seated himself in the seat that the *Bei* had previously occupied.

"My name is Kamek," he commenced. "Ali *Bei* sent me to you."

"Kamek? The *Bei* has already spoken of you."

"In what circumstance did he mention me?"

"It would cause you pain to hear it."

"Pain? Kamek knows no more pain. All pain that a human heart is capable of feeling I have suffered in a single hour. How can it harm me anymore?"

"Ali *Bei* said that you knew the *Miralai* Omar Amed."

He did not flinch and his voice sounded calm when he answered:

"I know him but he does not yet know me. He killed my wife and my sons. What of him?"

"Forgive me; Ali *Bei* will tell you himself!"

"I know that you were asked not to speak of this; but Ali *Bei* has no secrets from me. He has informed me that you told him of the intentions of the Turks. Do you really believe that they will come to disturb our feast?"

"I believe it."

"They shall find us better prepared than at the time when I lost my soul. Do you have a wife, and children?"

"No."

"Then you cannot comprehend that I live and yet died long ago. You may yet experience it. Do you know Tel Afer?"

"Yes."

"You were there?"

"No, but I have read about it."

"Where?"

"In the descriptions of this land and even in the . . . you are a Pir, a famous holy man of the *Jesidi*, you know of the Holy Book of the Christians?"

"I posses a part of it, it is called *Eski-Saryk* [Old Testament], in the Turkish language."

"Well, then you must have read the book of the Prophet Isaiah?"

"I know it. Jesaja is *biringji pejghamber on altinün* - the first of the sixteen prophets."

"Then look up the thirty-seventh chapter of that book. There, the twelfth verse reads: 'Have the gods of the nations delivered them, which my fathers have destroyed, as Gozam, and Haram, and Rzeph, and the children of Eden, which were in Telassar?' That Telessar is Tel Afer."

He looked at me in amazement.

"Then you know the cities of our land from this holy book that has already existed for thousands of years?"

"So it is."

"Your *Kitab* is greater than the Koran. But listen! I lived in Mirkan, at the foot of Jebel Sindshar, when the Turks attacked us. I escaped with my wife and my two sons to Tel Afer, for it was a fortified city. I had a friend there who offered me refuge. Yet even there the madmen entered to kill all the *Jesidi* who had sought refuge. My hiding place was discovered and my friend was shot for his charity. I was bound and led outside of the city with my wife and children. There the fire burned in which we were to find death, and there flowed the blood of the tortured. A *Mülasim* [lieutenant] stabbed me with his knife through my cheeks to cause me pain. Here, you can still see the scars. My sons were courageous youths, they saw my torment and seized him. For that they were also bound and so too was their mother. Their right hand was cut off and they were carried to the fire. Even my wife was burned to ashes and I was made to witness it. Then the *Mülasim* pulled the knife out of my face and slowly, ever so slowly, pressed it into my chest.

When I awoke it was night and I was lying beneath many corpses. The blade had missed my heart, but I was lying in my own blood. A Chaldean found me in the morning and hid me in the ruins of Kara-tapeh. Many weeks passed before I could get up and my hair had turned white in the hour in which my loved ones died. My body lived again, but my soul was dead. My heart had vanished; in its place beats and ticks a name, the name of Omar Amed, for that was the name of that *Mülasim*. Now he is a *Miralai*."

He had told the story in a flat and indifferent tone of voice, which had more of an effect on me than would the fiery expression of relentless need for vengeance. The story sounded so monotonous, so mechanical, as though it were being told by one who was under an anesthetic or even one who was sleep walking. It was terrible to hear.

Chapter 23

After a pause I asked:

"You intend to seek vengeance?"

"Vengeance? What is vengeance?" he answered in the same tone. "Vengeance is an evil, malicious deed. I will punish this man and then my body will go to that place where my soul has preceded it. - You will remain with us during our feast?" he digressed.

"We are yet undecided."

"Stay here! If you go now your quest will fail; if you stay, then you still have hope that it will succeed; for there will be no Turk in the way and the *Jesidi* could easily offer you support you."

He spoke now in a different tone, and his eyes had taken on the same lively expression that they had held earlier.

"Our presence can only disturb your feast," I said with the intention of perhaps discovering something of his sect.

He shook his head slowly.

"Do you believe the tall tales or rather the lies that are told about us? Compare us with others, and you will discover cleanliness and purity. Purity is what we strive for; purity of life and of spirit, purity of speech and purity of wisdom. Pure is the water, and pure is the flame. That is why we love the water and baptize with the same. That is why we honor the light, as a symbol of a pure God, of which your *Kitab* declares that - he lives in the *atesh* - in the light, which no one can reach. You bless yourselves with *su ikbalün* - blessed water, and we bless ourselves with *atesh ikbalün* - the blessed fire. We dip our hand into the flame and bless our brow with it, as you do with the water.

You say, *Azerat Esau* [the Lord Jesus] has been on earth and will come again; we know this too, that he was once among men, and we also believe that he will come again, to open the gates of heaven. You honor the savior who lived on earth; we honor the savior who will come again. We know that he was a man, but we do not know when he will return. That is why we do as he ordered his disciples to do, when he found them sleeping in the *Baghje Gethseman* [Garden of Gethsemane]: '*Gözetyn namaz kalyn ansizdan üzerine warilmemish olursaniz* - Wake and pray that you are not attacked!' That is why we make use of the *choros* [rooster], a symbol of vigilance. Do you not do the same? I have been told that the Christians adorn the roofs of their temples and houses with a rooster - a rooster made of *teneke* [tin] and covered with *altun* [gold]. You use a tin rooster and we use a living one. Are we therefore idolaters or bad people? Your priests are wiser and your teachings are better; we would have better teachers if we had wiser priests. I am, among all the *Jesidi*, the only one that can read your *Kitab* and write, and that is why I speak to you as no one else can."

"Why don't you ask for priests that can teach you?"

"Because we do not wish to participate in your disunity. The teachings of the Christians are divided. If you can assure us that you are united, then they will be welcome among us. If the Christians of the west send us teachers and each teach a different lesson, then they do a great harm to themselves. *Azerat Esau* says in your *Kitab*: '*Im jol de gerjeklik de ömir de* - I am the way and the truth and the life.' Why do the westerners have so many ways, so many truths, if there is only one living truth? That is why we do not argue about the savior who has already been here, but we keep ourselves pure and await the one who shall come."

Ali *Bei* entered again, and it was - admittedly - very pleasing to me. My desire for knowledge with regard to the 'Devil Worshippers' had very nearly caused me embarrassment at the hands of this simple Kurd. I am a mere layman not a theologian, yet I was forced to remain silent as he reproached the church of my homeland because of its split in doctrine - alas, alas!

The Pir arose and offered me his hand.

"Allah be with you and also with me! I go on the path I must follow, but we shall meet again."

He offered his hand also to the others and departed. Ali *Bei* waved after him and said:

"He is the wisest among the *Jesidi*; no one is equal to him. He was in Persia and India; he was in Jerusalem and Stambul; he has seen everything and studied everywhere, he has even written a book."

"A book?" I asked in amazement.

"He is the only one that can really write. His desire for our people is that we become as clever and as civilized as the western nations. And that we can only achieve by learning from the books of the Franks. So that these books may be transcribed into our language, he has written down many hundreds of words in our dialects. That is his book."

"That would be priceless! Where is this book?"

"In his home."

"And where is that?"

"In my house. Pir Kamek is a holy man. He wanders throughout the land and is welcome everywhere. The whole of Kurdistan is his home, but his preferred residence is with me."

"Do you think that he would show me his book sometime?"

"He would be glad to."

"I will ask him at once! Where did he go to?"

"Stay! You will not find him for he has gone to watch over his people. But you shall see the book; I will fetch it for you. Before I go, promise me that you will remain with us!"

"You mean we should re-schedule our ride to Amadijah?"

"Yes. Three men came from Kaloni. They belong to the branch of the Badinan from the tribe of Missuri and are agile, brave, clever, and true to me. I have sent them to Amadijah, to scout out the Turks there. They will also attempt to find Amad el Ghandur; this I have especially advised them, and until they bring news, may you be happy here!"

We were most happy to agree and accepted his offer, and Ali *Bei* embraced us with joy once again when we told him.

"Now come with me so that my wife can meet you as well!"

I was surprised at the invitation, but later discovered that the *Jesidi* do not segregate their wives as the Mohammedans do. They lead a patriarchal life and in the Orient I have never been so reminded of my native German family life as here. Of course the ordinary people did not posses the clarity of religious insight as Pir Kamek did, but compared to the sly Greek, haggling and immoral Armenian, the vengeful Arab, the lethargic Turk, hypocritical Persian and the thieving Kurd, I had to admire the wrongly accused, often besmirched 'Devil Worshipper'. His culture swayed between Chaldeism, Islam and Christianity, but nowhere should the last find such a fertile ground as here with the *Jesidi*, if the devout messengers would but understand that the traditions and customs of these people must be taken into account.

Outside of the house sat the *Buluk-Emini* next to his donkey. Both were eating; the donkey ate grain and the *Bashi-Bozuk*, dried figs from Sindshar, of which he had several strings, which were laid out before him. And whilst he chewed, he told those standing around him of his many heroic deeds. Halef settled next to him and we three walked to another part of the building that served as the home of the mistress.

She was young and carried a small boy in her arms. Her beautiful long, black hair had been plaited into many braids and her brow was covered with many pieces of gold.

"Be welcome, you men!" she said in an unpretentious, simple manner and offered us her right hand.

Ali *Bei* introduced us. Her name unfortunately escapes me. I took the child from her arms and kissed him. She appeared to take that as a compliment and an honor. The little *Bei* was of course a likable little fellow, kept very clean and quite different from the overfed Oriental children of the same age so often seen among the Turks. Ali *Bei* asked me where we wished to eat: either in our rooms or here in the home of his wife, and I chose the latter immediately. The little 'Devil Worshipper' appeared to enjoy my company; he looked at me mischievously with his flashing, dark eyes, ruffled my beard, squirmed with delight and stammered a word occasionally, a word which neither he nor I understood. As far as Kurdish goes, we were on the same rung of comprehension and that is why I kept hold of him even throughout the meal, for which his mother rewarded me by serving me the choicest morsels and afterwards showed me about her garden.

The tastiest dish of the meal was the *kursh*, it is made from cream, which is baked in an oven then sprinkled with sugar and drenched in honey. What impressed me most in the garden was a tree with flame-colored blossoms that produces bloom upon bloom and is called '*Bint el Onsul'* – 'Daughter of the Consul', by the Arabs.

Ali *Bei* showed me my room. It was situated on a platform on the roof, where I could enjoy the view. When I entered I noticed a small notebook on the low table.

"That is the Pir's book," explained Ali in answer to my questioning glance.

I took the book immediately and seated myself on the divan. The smiling *Bei* left me, so as not to disturb my study of this priceless find. The notebook was written in an Arabian-Persian script and contained a considerable collection of words and idioms in many Kurdish dialects. I soon noted that it would not be difficult to make myself understood in Kurdish, once I had managed to master the phonetic sound of the letters. Here were the practical examples of meanings and I decided to use our visit to practice the language as much as possible.

In the meantime dusk had approached and at the brook below, where girls fetched water with a number of boys assisting them, the following song was sung:

"Ghawra min ave the Bina michak, darjin ber pishte Dave min chala surat ta kate Najalnik ak bjerdza ma, bishanda ma Rusete."

[Freely translated: 'A Christian girl comes to fetch water, fetch water, I stand in the background and breath in anticipation that I will touch her cheek once with my lips, even if I am sent to Russia in chains.']

It was a rhythmic and melodious tune, such as one does not often hear in the Orient. I continued to listen, but sadly no additional verse followed and I arose to go outside where the people busied themselves, for more and more strangers arrived; tent was erected next to tent. One could not help but notice that an important feast was at hand. As I stood before the door I noticed a considerable gathering around the little *Buluk-Emini,* who spoke loudly.

"I have fought at Sayda," he announced importantly, "and then on the island of Candia, where we defeated the Emperor. After that I fought in Beirut under the famous Mustapha Nuri Pasha, whose brave soul now lives in Paradise. I still had my nose then but I lost it in Serbia, where I went with Shekib *Effendi* when Kiamil Pasha chased away Michael Obrenowitsch."

The good *Bashi-Bozuk* appeared to have forgotten exactly where he had lost his nose. He continued:

"I was attacked behind Bucharest. Although I defended myself valiantly; already twenty of the enemy lay dead on the ground; one of them swung at me with his saber; the blow should have cleaved my head, but since I pulled back, so it hit only my no . . ."

At that moment a scream came from nearby, a scream as I had never before heard in entire my life. It sounded like a high pitched steam whistle followed by the gobble of a turkey and that was joined by a groaning whimper not unlike that many-voiced lament an organ makes when it loses its wind in the middle of play. Those present stared at the being that was the source of this enigmatic primitive sound. But Ifra said unperturbed:

"What are you marveling at? It was my donkey! He does not like the dark; that is why he brays all though the night until the light returns."

Hmm! If this was the case then the donkey was quite a charming creature! With a voice like that it could raise the dead! Who could think of sleep during the night when one had to listen to the impromptu musical sounds of this four-legged Jenny Lind [See Translation Note Ch 23. 1]. It appeared to have a descant trombone for lungs, a bagpipe for a windpipe and a throat composed of the stops and valves of a hundred clarinets.

By the way, this was now the third time that I had heard the tale of the lost nose of the *Buluk-Emini*. It would appear that it was 'written in the book of fate' that he should never finish this saga.

"This animal cries like that the whole night?" someone asked.

"The whole night," he confirmed with the resignation of a martyr. "Every two minutes."

"You should discourage this habit!"

"How?"

"I don't know!"

"Then keep your advice to yourself! I have tried everything without success: - beatings, hunger, thirst."

"Tell him in earnest words so that he knows his transgression!"

"I have told him with earnest and loving words. He looks at me, listens to me quietly, shakes his head and . . . continues to cry."

"That is strange. He understands you; he certainly understands you, but does not care to do you that favor."

"Yes, I have often heard that animals understand man, for sometimes they are possessed by the soul of one of the departed, who must atone for his sin in this manner. The fellow that possesses this donkey must have been deaf, but certainly not mute."

"You must discover which tribe he belonged to. In what language do you speak to the donkey?"

"In Turkish."

"What if the soul belongs to a Persian, an Arab or even a *giaur*, who does not understand Turkish?"

"*Allah akbar*, that is true! I had not thought of that!"

"Why does the donkey always shake its head when you talk to him? His spirit does not understand Turkish. Speak to him in another language!"

"But what if I can't find the right one? I will ask my Emir. Hajji Halef Omar tells me that he can speak the languages of all people. Perhaps he can discover where the spirit of my donkey lived. *Soliman* [Solomon] could understand all animals."

"There have been others that have understood. Do you know the story of the rich man, whose sons could even talk with stones?"

"No."

"Then I will tell you! *De vachtha beni Israil meru ki dauletlü, mir; du lau wi man, male wi pür, haneki wi ma. Va her du lavi wi va hania khoe parve dikerin, pew jun, jek debee ...*"

"Stop!" interrupted Ifra. "In what language do you speak?"

"In ours. It is Kurmangdshi."

"I don't understand it. Tell the tale in Turkish!"

"Then you have the same problem as the spirit of your donkey who only understands his own language. But how can I tell you a Kurdish story in Turkish? It will sound entirely different!"

"Try it!"

"I will see! So, at the time of the children of Israel there was a rich man who died. He left to his two sons many riches and a house. When the two sons wanted to divide the house, they argued about it. One said: 'It is my house!' The other said: 'It is my house!' Through the Will of God a baked brick came to life in a wall and said: 'What, are you not ashamed? This house is neither yours nor his. I, a man, who was a king, was great in this world for three hundred years; I died. Three hundred years I lay in my grave, wasted and become dust. A man came and baked me into a brick. For forty years I was a house; it decayed. For three hundred and seventy years I lay in the field; another man came and again made me into a brick and used me in this house. In this house I have remained for three hundred and thirty years and I do not know what I will be from this day forth. In the meantime my soul does not pain me ..."

He was interrupted. The donkey, because clearly it could not understand Turkish, was bored; it opened its mouth and let forth a double shriek, the sound of which could only be compared to a hornpipe combined with a broken tuba. A man struggled through the gathered crowd and entered the hallway. Here he noticed me.

"Emir, it is true that you have arrived! I only just heard because I was in the mountains. How happy I am! Permit me to greet you."

It was Selek. He took my hand and kissed it. This symbolic act of respect is common among the *Jesidi*.

"Where is Pali and Melaf?" I asked him.

"They met Pir Kamek and have gone down to Mosul with him. I have to deliver a message to Ali *Bei*. Will I see you again later?"

"I intended to go to Ali *Bei* myself. Is this message perhaps a secret?"

"Possibly; but you may hear it. Come, Emir!"

We walked to the home of the mistress, where the *Bei* was. It appeared that entry here was permitted to anyone. Even Halef was there. The good Hajji was once again busy eating.

"Lord," said Selek, "I was in the mountains above Bozan and have to report something."

"Speak!" The *Bei* offered.

"May all hear it?"

"All."

"We believed that the *Mutessarif* of Mosul sent five hundred Turks to Amadijah, to protect it against the Kurds. But that is not true. The two hundred men who came from Diarbekir marched via Urmeli, and are now hidden in the forests of Tura Gharah."

"Who told you this?"

"An *odundshi* [lumberjack] I met from Mungeyshi. He was going down to Kana Kujjunli, where his rafts are. And the three hundred men from Kerkjuk are likewise not on the way to Amadijah. They went via Altun Kiupri to Arbil and Girdashir and are currently above Mar Mattei on the Ghazir river."

"Who told you this?" The *Bei* asked again.

"A Kurd from Zibar, who traveled on the canal to Bozan by way of Dohuk."

"The Zibar are reliable people: they never lie and hate the Turks. I believe what these two men have said. Do you know the Idiz Valley ['The Valley of Scoundrels'] at Ghomel, branching off above Kaloni?"

"Only a few know of it, but I have been there often." Selek assured him.

"Could one convey horses and cattle from here to there in order to hide them?"

"If one knows the forest well they will be successful."

"How much time would be required to send our women, children and animals there?"

"Half a day. If we go via Sheik Adi, then climb up the steep ravine behind the shrine, no Turk will know what we are doing."

"You have the best knowledge of that area. I will talk more with you, until then you will be silent and tell no one. I wanted to ask you to serve the Emir, but you will be needed elsewhere." The *Bei* concluded.

"May I send him my son?"

"Do it!"

"Does he speak good Kurdish?" I asked.

"He understands Kurmangdshi and Zaza."

"Then send him to me; he will be most welcome!"

Selek departed as a meal was being prepared. Since the hospitality of the *Jesidi* is boundless, as many as twenty people were present, and in honor of Mohammed Emin and myself music was provided. The band consisted of three men who played the *thembure*, *kamanje* and the *bülure*, three instruments that were comparable to the flute, guitar and violin. The music was soft and melodious; all in all, I noted later, that the *Jesidi* had much better musical taste than the followers of Islam.

While we ate, the son of Selek arrived; I retired with him to my quarters so that I could study Pir Kamek's manuscript with his help. The horizon of learning that this young man possessed was quite small, yet I found it sufficient to still my desire for knowledge. Pir Kamek was the most learned among the 'Devil Worshippers' and only with him could I find the experience and vision with which I had initially been surprised. The others were simple disciples, and I did not wonder that they accepted the symbol for a thing without question and that their customs were more habit and blind belief than inner conviction. The mystery of their worship was what held them bound, as in all the Orient a tendency to the dark and arcane was preferred to the unveiled light of day.

Our discussion did not pass undisturbed, for, at fairly regular intervals of a few minutes, the disgusting, marrow-penetrating cry of the donkey sounded; this could not be tolerated for much longer. Yet it was tolerated and even laughed at for as long as there was activity in the village, and still more pilgrims arrived. However, as the clamor quieted and everyone sought rest, the loud interjections of the gray-coated beast became intolerable; various voices arose, first muttering sullenly, then growing to a loud squabble.

Instead of dissuading the donkey, the angry calls seemed to entice him to greater and stronger feats of voice; he forgot about his bawling; the pauses between his cries became less and less until finally they united into a single symphony that could only be described as infernal.

I arose to go and offer assistance when a muddled din sounded from below. A crowd advanced upon the little *Buluk-Emini*. What was being negotiated between them I could not determine; in any case, he was so cornered that he was at a loss as to how to help himself, for a moment later I heard steps approaching my door. He entered.

"Do you sleep already, Emir?"

The question was quite superfluous for he saw that the both of us were still dressed and reading from the book; but in his fear he could not find a better introduction.

"You ask that? How can one sleep with the terrible serenade that your donkey sings!"

"O Lord, that is it! I cannot sleep myself. Now they all come to me and demand that I move that animal into the forest and tie it up there, otherwise they will shoot it dead. It must not come to that; for I must return it to Mosul, otherwise I will receive the bastinado and lose my rank."

"Then move it into the forest."

"O Emir, I cannot!"

"Why not?"

"Shall I let it be eaten by wolves? There are wolves in the forest!" He moaned.

"Then remain there with it and watch over it!"

"*Effendi*, two wolves might come!" The *Buluk-Emini* cried in shock.

"So?"

"Then one would eat the donkey and the other would eat me!"

"That would be very good, for then you would not receive the bastinado."

"You jest! Some say that I should come to you."

"To me? Why?"

"Lord, do you believe that the donkey has a soul?"

"Of course he has one."

"Perhaps he has a different one than his own!"

"Where would his own be? Perhaps you have swapped: His soul is inside you, and yours is inside him. Now you are the donkey and are as fearful as a *tawshun* [rabbit], and he is the *Buluk-Emini* and roars like an *arslan* [lion]. What can I do about it?"

"Emir, It is quite certain that he harbors another soul; but not a Turkish one, for he does not understand the language of the *Osmanli*. But you speak all the languages of the earth, and that is why I beg you to come down. If you speak with the donkey, you will soon discover who dwells within him, be it a Persian or a Turkmene or an Armenian. Perhaps it is even a Russian that possesses him, for he leaves us so little peace."

"Do you really believe that ..."

At that moment the animal raised its voice once again, and with such gusto that the entire mutinous assembly joined in.

"*Allah kerihm*, they will murder my donkey. Lord, come down quickly, otherwise his life is forfeit and his soul too!" He pleaded, then ran ahead as we followed him.

Should I have some fun? Perhaps it would be unjust, but his ardent belief that some foreign soul possessed this gray beast had put me in a mood that I found hard to suppress. When I arrived below, the crowd shifted its attention to me.

"Who knows of a means to silence this animal?" I asked.

No one answered. Finally Halef said:

"Lord, only you alone can make that happen!"

My Hajji belonged to these 'True Believers'. I stepped up to the donkey and grasped its halter. After I had laid a few foreign language questions upon it, I held my ear to its nose and listened. Then I acted as though surprised and turned to Ifra.

"*Buluk-Emini*, what was your father's name?"

"Nachir Mirja."

"That is not it. What was your father's father's name?"

"Muthallam Sobuf."

"It is he! Where did he live?"

"In Hirmenlü at Adrianopel."

"That is right. He once rode from Hirmenlü to Thassköi and to annoy his donkey, he tied a heavy rock to its tail. But the Prophet has said: '*Esheklerin sew* - love your donkey!' That is why the spirit of your grandfather has to atone for that deed. He was made to turn around at the Ssirath Bridge, which leads to Paradise and to Hell, and he took possession of this donkey. In life he tied a rock to his donkey's tail and now his soul can only be released if a rock is bound to his own tail now. Do you wish to release him, Ifra?"

"O, Emir, I will do it!" he cried. He was closer to tears than to laughter, for the image of his grandfather languishing in this donkey must have been terrible for a true Moslem such as he. "Tell me everything that I must do to save the father of my father."

"Fetch a stone and a rope!"

The donkey noted that we were captivated with it; it opened its mouth and brayed.

"Quick, Ifra! This will be the last time that he yammers."

I held the animal's tail, and the little *Bashi-Bozuk* tied the stone to the end of it. When this operation was over, the donkey turned its head to face its rear in order to remove the rock with its teeth; of course this did not work. Then it tried to throw off the rock with a flick of its tail; but the stone was too heavy and the tail only swayed like a small pendulum, it came to rest immediately, with the stone knocking against its hind legs. The donkey was visibly in a quandary; it squinted towards its rear and twitched its ears most thoughtfully; it snorted and finally opened its mouth to bray - but its voice failed it; the awareness that its greatest asset was tied down robbed it completely of the ability to express itself in those noble tones.

"*Allah hu*; he truly does not cry!" shouted the *Bashi-Bozuk*. "Emir, you are the wisest man that I have ever met!"

I departed and went to bed. But below, the pilgrims remained standing for a long time after to see if they had truly witnessed a miracle.

I was awakened early the next morning by the hustle and bustle of the village. More pilgrims arrived, some remained in Baadri, some continued after a short rest to Sheik Adi. The first person who entered my room was Sheik Mohammed Emin.

"Have you looked outside yet?" he asked me.

"No."

"Take a look!"

I went out onto the roof and looked down. A hundred people stood by the donkey and looked at it in astonishment. Someone had told the others what had happened, and when they saw me they stepped away from the house in reverence. I had not intended this! I had simply followed an amusing whim and had no desire to encourage the foolish superstition of these people.

Even Sheik Ali came. He smiled when he greeted me.

"Emir, we have to thank you for a peaceful night. You are a great wizard. Will the donkey cry again if the stone is removed?"

"Yes. The animal is afraid of the night and musters courage through the sound of its own voice."

"Will you follow me to breakfast?"

We went down to the home of the Mistress. Halef and the son of Selek, whom I had designated to be my Kurdish translator, were already there, as well as Ifra, whose face was noticeably unhappy. The *Bei's* wife came in and, with a cheerful expression offered me her hand.

"*Sabah'l kher* - good morning!" I greeted her.

"*Sabah'l kher*!" she answered. "*Keifata ciava* - how are you?"

"*Kangia*! *Tu ciava* - well, and how are you?"

"*Skuker quode kangia* – Well also, may God be thanked!"

"You speak Kurmangji!" cried Ali *Bei* in amazement.

"Only that which I learned from the Pir's book last night," I answered. "And that little is enough."

"Come here and sit!"

First came coffee with *valquapamasi* [honey cakes] and then *quapameh* [roast mutton], which was eaten in wide strips like bread.

With this one drank *arpa*, a kind of thin beer that the Turks call *arpasu* - barley water. Everyone partook of the meal; only the *Buluk-Emini* cowered gloomily apart from us.

"Ifra, why don't you join us?" I asked him.

"I cannot eat, Emir," he answered.

"What is wrong with you?"

"Help, Lord. I have up to now ridden my donkey, beaten it and berated it, have brushed and washed it too little, have often let it go hungry, and now I hear that it is the father of my father. It stands outside and still the stone hangs from its tail!"

One had to pity the *Buluk-Emini* and my conscience was stirred; but the situation was, in truth, so fantastic that I could not control myself and I erupted with laughter.

"You laugh!" he answered reproachfully. "If you had a donkey that was the father of your father you too would shed tears. I am supposed to bring you to Amadijah, but how can I; for I will never again sit upon the spirit of my grandfather!"

"And nor shall you; for it is not possible for anyone to sit upon a spirit."

"What else can I ride?"

"Your donkey."

He looked at me rather confused.

"But my donkey is a spirit, you said so yourself!"

"That was only in jest."

"Oh, you say that only to console me!"

"No, I say it because I am sorry that you took my jest to heart."

"*Effendi*, you truly wish to console me! Why did the donkey run away with me so often? Why did he throw me so often? Because he knew that he was no donkey and that I am the son of his son. And why did the stone help immediately when I did what the soul of the donkey commanded through you?"

"It did not direct me to do anything, I will tell you the reason why it worked. Have you never noticed that the rooster closes its eyes when it crows?"

"I have seen it."

"If you hold its eyes open, by any means you may devise, it will not crow. Have you noticed that the donkey raises its tail when it brays?"

"Yes, he really does this, *Effendi*!"

"Then make sure that it can never raise its tail; and it will bray no more."

"Is that truly so?"

"Truly! Try it tonight when it brays again!"

"Then the father of my father is not really bewitched?"

"No, as I am telling you!"

"*Hamdullillah*!" He cried.

He jumped up and ran outside, tore the stone from the donkey's tail and hurried back to belatedly join in the meal. That he, an underling, was permitted to sit at the *Bei's* table showed me again how communally the *Jesidi* lived with one another.

An hour later I rode out into the bright morning with my translator. Mohammed Emin had preferred to remain behind and to show as little of himself as possible.

"Do you know the Idiz Valley?" I asked my companion.

"Yes."

"Why does it have this name?"

"Because the thieving Kurds had their hiding place there." He replied.

"How long does one have to ride from here to reach it?"

"Two hours."

"I would like to see it. Will you guide me there?"

"As you order, Lord. Shall we ride direct or via Sheik Adi?" He asked.

"Whichever way is the shortest?"

"The direct route; but it is also the hardest."

"We take it nonetheless."

"Will your horse make it? I have rarely seen such a valuable animal, but it is probably more adapted to the plains."

"Today I will test him."

Baadri was behind us. The path - not to be confused with a paved road - rose steeply and then descended just as steeply; but my black stallion put up a good show. The peaks, which initially had been covered with bushes, were now covered with a dark forest and we rode under the leafy and needled boughs.

Finally the path became so dangerous that we had to dismount and lead our horses. It was prudent to examine each foothold before trusting our weight to it. My translator's horse was familiar with this terrain; it stepped with more certainty and seemed to be able to distinguish the dangerous ground from the safe ground. My dark stallion had good instincts and took extraordinarily great care. I was certain that with a little practice he would make a good mountain horse; at least he showed today that he did not tire quickly, whilst the other animal was sweating and blowing.

Two hours had almost passed when we reached a thicket behind which the rocky ground fell away almost vertically.

"That is the valley," my guide said.

"How do we get down?"

"There is only one way down and that leads from here to Sheik Adi."

"Is it used much?"

"No; it is indistinguishable from the rest of the land around here. Come!"

I followed him along the line of the thicket that grew along the rim of the valley, covering it so completely that a stranger without a guide would not have known of its existence. After some time we reached a spot where my guide dismounted. He pointed towards his right.

"Here is where one might reach Sheik Adi, through the forest, but only a *Jesidi* knows how to find the way. Here to the left one can descend into the valley."

He parted the bushes and I now saw a wide valley open before me, the walls of which were almost vertical and only this place afforded a path up or down. We climbed down leading our horses by the reigns. When we reached the bottom I could see the valley in its entirety. It was large enough to accommodate many thousands of people, and the mouths of many caves as well as other signs hinted at its recent occupation. The floor of the valley was covered with a hardy grass that made it possible to conceal herds here, and several hollows had been scooped out of the ground and were filled with enough drinking water for a great many thirsty throats.

We let the horses graze and laid ourselves down upon the grass.

Chapter 24

Before long I commenced a discussion with the comment:

"Nature could not have provided a more practical hiding place."

"It has already been used for that purpose, *Effendi*. The last time the *Jesidi* were hunted, well over a thousand people found safety here. That is why no adherent to our belief will ever betray this place. We never know when we might have need of it again."

"That appears to be the case now."

"I know it. But now it is not a matter of being hunted because of our belief, instead it is a means of plundering us. The *Mutessarif* is sending fifteen hundred men who would attack us without warning; but he will be disappointed. We have not celebrated our feast for many years and that is why whomever can come, will come; that is why we can face the Turk with thousands of fighting men."

"Are they all armed?"

"Every one. You will see for yourself how many times we discharge our weapons during the feast. The *Mutessarif* would not use as much powder for all his soldiers in an entire year as we shall use in these coming three days for our salvos of joy."

"Why are you hunted? Because of your belief?"

"Don't think that, Emir! The *Mutessarif* does not care what we believe in. He only has one goal - which is to be rich, and sometimes the Arabs or the Chaldeans, the Kurds or the *Jesidi* must help to him to achieve that. Or do you think that our belief is so terrible that it must be eradicated?"

That was the point I wanted this young man to concentrate on. From him I could discover what the Pir had not yet told me.

"I do not know," I answered.

"And I suppose that you have not heard much about us either?"

"Very little, and what I have heard I do not believe."

"Yes, *Effendi*, much is spoken about us and much of it is untrue. Have you not discovered anything from my father or from Pali and Melaf?"

"No; at least nothing important; but I think that you can tell me something at least."

"Oh Emir, we do not speak to strangers of our belief!"

"Am I a stranger to you?"

"No. You have saved the lives of my father and his companions and you have warned us of the Turks, as I discovered from the *Bei*. You are the only one that I would offer this knowledge to. But I must tell you that I do not know everything."

"Are there matters that may not be known by all?"

"No. But are there not matters in every household that only the elders alone need to know about? Our priests are our elders."

"May I question you?"

"Ask; but I beseech you not to mention one name!"

"I know; but it is with respect to this that I wish to acquire knowledge. Will you answer me if I avoid the word?"

"As much as I can, yes," he agreed.

This word was the name of the Devil, which the *Jesidi* never utter. The word *Shaïtan* is so taboo to them that they even avoid similar words with great care. When, for example, they speak about a river they say '*nahr*', but never '*shat*', for the latter word almost sounds like the first syllable of *Shaïtan*. The word '*keïtan*' [tassels or thread] is avoided for the same reason. The words '*naal*' [horseshoe] and '*naal-band'* [blacksmith] are eschewed because they are similar to the words '*laan*' [curse] and '*mahlun*' [damned]. They speak of the Devil in reverent terms. They call him *Melek el Kuht* [the Mighty King] or *Melek Ta-us* [King peacock].

"You have another being alongside your good God?" I asked.

"Alongside? No. The being you mean is beneath God. This *kyral meleklerün* [King of the Angels] was the highest of the heavenly beings; but God was his Creator and Lord."

"Where is he now?"

"He outraged God and was banished by him."

"Banished to where?"

"The earth and all the stars."

"Now he is master of those that live in *Jehennah*?"

"No. You believe perhaps that he is eternally unhappy?"

"Yes."

"Do you believe too that God is all-gracious, merciful and compassionate?"

"Yes."

"Then he will also forgive – both men and the angels who sinned against him. That is what we believe and that is why we feel sorry for the one you refer to. For the present he can cause us harm and that is why we do not mention his name. When the time comes and he is returned to his position he can reward man and that is why we do not speak ill of him."

"You honor him? You pray to him?"

"No, for he is God's creature just as we are, but we take care not to offend him."

"What does the symbol of the rooster signify at your services?"

"It does not signify him whom you refer to. It is a symbol of watchfulness. Has *Azerat Esau*, the Son of God not told you of the maidens who awaited their grooms?"

"Yes."

"Five of them fell asleep and could not enter heaven. Do you know the tale of the apprentice that betrayed his master?"

"Yes."

"Even there the rooster crowed. That is why we embrace it as a symbol, so that we might remain watchful and await the groom."

"Do you believe what is written in the Bible?"

"We believe it, although I do not know all of what is written."

"Do you not have a holy book in which your doctrines are written?"

"We have such. It was kept in Baa Sheikha, but I have heard that it was lost."

"What are your holy ceremonial acts?"

"You will learn of them all in Sheik Adi."

"Can you tell me who Sheik Adi was?"

"That I don't know precisely."

"Do you pray to him?"

"No. We honor him only by praying to God at his grave. He was a saint and lives with God."

"What kind of priests do you have?"

"First come the Pirs. This word really means elder or wise man; but with us it means holy man."

"What do they wear?"

"They can wear what they please; but they lead a very pious life, and God gives them the power to heal the body and the soul through their intercession."

"Are there many Pirs?"

"I only know of three at the moment. Pir Kamek is the greatest among them."

"Go on!"

“After them come the Sheiks. They must learn a great deal of Arabic to understand our songs.”

“Are they sung in the Arabian language?”

“Yes.”

“Why not in Kurdish?”

“I do not know. From amongst the Sheiks the watchmen of the Holy Shrine are chosen, they maintain the fire there and serve the pilgrims.”

“Do they have special garments?”

“They wear all white and as a symbol of their office they wear a belt that is red and yellow. After the Sheiks come the Preachers, they are known as *Kawals*. They can play the holy instruments and travel from village to village to instruct the faithful.”

“What are the holy instruments?”

“The tambourine and the flute. The *Kawals* also know how to sing at the high feasts.”

“What do they wear?”

“They can wear all colors, but usually they wear white. But then their turbans must be black so that they can be distinguished from the Sheiks. After them come the Fakirs, who perform the lowliest tasks both at the shrine and elsewhere. They mostly wear dark clothing and have a red cloth across their turban.”

“Who selects your priests?”

“They are not selected, this honor is passed down. When a priest dies without a son to follow then his office is passed to his oldest daughter.”

That was most peculiar, especially in the Orient!

“And who is the highest priest of all?”

“The Sheik of Baadri. You have not yet met him, for he is already in Sheik Adi, to prepare for the feast. Do you have some more questions?”

“Many more! Are your children baptized?”

“Baptized and cut.”

“Are there unclean foods which you are not permitted to eat?”

“We do not eat pork and do not use the color blue, for the sky is so sublime that we do not wish to give it to any earthly things.”

“Do you have a *kiblah*?”

“Yes. When we pray, we turn our face to the place where the sun rises. Even the dead are placed in their graves facing that direction.”

“Do you know the origin of your religion?”

"Sheik Adi, the saint, has taught us. We ourselves came from the lands below the Euphrates. Then our parents migrated to Syria and the Sindshar and finally to this place."

I would have liked to ask more, but a cry came from above and when we looked up we recognized Selek, who was about to climb down to us. Soon he stood next to us and offered us his hand.

"I nearly shot you," he greeted us.

"Us? Why?" I asked.

"From up there I believed you to be strangers and no stranger may ever enter this valley. But then I recognized you. I came to see if the valley needed preparation."

"To take the refugees?"

"Refugees? We will not flee; but I have already told the *Bei* how cleverly you enticed the enemies of the Shammar into that valley where you took them prisoner and we will do precisely that here as well."

"You wish to entice the Turks into this valley?"

"No, but to Sheik Adi; the pilgrims shall stay here during the battle. The *Bei* has ordered it and the Sheik agrees."

He inspected the water and the caves and then asked us if we wished to accompany him on his return journey. The question was superfluous. We led our horses up the path, mounted them at the top and then rode directly towards Baadri. When we arrived there I found the *Bei* to be somewhat excited.

"I received news while you were gone," he said. "The Turks from Diarbekir are already at the Ghomel River, and those from Kerkjuk have also reached that river at the lower reaches of the mountain range."

"Then your scouts are already back from Amadijah?"

"They never reached Amadijah for they had to separate in order to spy on the troops. It has now been proven that the planned attack is meant only for us."

"Is it already known by all?"

"No, for the enemy might discover that we are prepared. I tell you, Emir, I will either die or teach this *Mutessarif* a lesson that he shall never forget!"

"I will remain with you until after the battle."

"I thank you, Emir; but you shall not fight!"

"Why not?"

"You are my guest and God has entrusted your life to me."

"And God can best protect it. Shall I be your guest and let you go into battle alone? Shall your people say of me that I am a coward?"

"That they will never say. Were you not also the guest of the *Mutessarif*? Do you not have his passport in your pocket? And now you wish to fight against him? Must you not also give aid to your friend in freeing his son? And can you not serve me even without killing my enemies?"

"You are right in all you say. I have no desire to kill but perhaps I can ensure that no blood will be spilled."

"Leave that worry to me, *Effendi*! I do not lust for blood, I only wish to repel this tyrant from my people."

"How do you intend to achieve this?"

"Do you know that three thousand pilgrims have already arrived at Sheik Adi? By the start of the feast it will be six thousand and more."

"Men, women and children?"

"Yes. The women and children I shall send into the Idiz Valley, only the men will remain. The troops from Diarbekir and Kerkjuk will join on the path from Kaloni and those that come from Mosul will come up via Jerraijah or Aïn Sifni. They will try to trap us in the Valley of the Saint; but we will climb up behind the shrine and encircle the valley when they have moved in. Then we can defeat them to the last man, if they do not surrender. But otherwise I will send a messenger to the *Mutessarif* and set my demands for their freedom. He will have to answer to the Sultan in Stambul."

"He will report the situation in a different light."

"But he will not succeed in fooling the Padishah; for I have already sent a secret message to Stambul which will arrive before any message he can send."

I had to admit to myself that Ali *Bei* was not only courageous, but also a clever and therefore a careful man.

"And how would you use me?" I asked him.

"You shall join those that I have sent to protect our women and children."

"You are taking your possessions with you?"

"As much as we possibly can. I will inform the people of Baadri today that they should move everything to the Idiz Valley, but secretly, so that my plan will not be betrayed."

"And Sheik Mohammed Emin?"

"He goes with you. You cannot possibly get to Amadijah now, as the way there is no longer open."

"The Turks will have to honor the *Bu-djeruldi* of the Sultan and the *Firman* of the *Mutessarif*."

"But there are people from Kerkjuk with them, and it is quite possible that one of them knows Mohammed Emin!"

While we were still talking, two men entered the house. They were my two old acquaintances Pali and Melaf, who were quite beside themselves when they saw me and kissed my hands joyfully at least ten times over.

"Where is the *Pir*?" asked Ali *Bei*.

"At the grave of Jonas at Kufjunjik. He sent us to tell you that we will be attacked on the second day of the feast, early in the morning."

"Is he aware of the pretext under which the *Mutessarif* will attack us?"

"Two Turks were killed in Malthaijah by a *Jesidi*. He intends to catch the perpetrator in Sheik Adi."

"Two *Jesidi* were killed in Malthaijah by two Turks, that is the truth. Do you see, Emir, how the Turks are? They kill my people in order to justify an attack on us in our own land. Let them come and find what they are looking for!"

I went to my room with my translator and there I commenced my language exercises. Mohammed Emin sat quietly, smoked his pipe, and was amazed that I put so much effort into reading a book and trying to understand a foreign language. I did this for the entire day and well into the evening. The following day passed in the same enjoyable manner.

Whilst occupied with this task I did notice that the inhabitants of Baadri moved their belongings without much fuss; and in another room of the house a huge number of bullets were being cast. I have to add that the *Buluk-Emini's* donkey did not bray once ever since its master tied a stone to its tail as soon as it got dark.

Pilgrims continued to arrive, sometimes by themselves, sometimes with their families and sometimes in larger groups. Many were poor and dependent on the charity of others. Someone would pass by, leading a goat or a fat sheep; richer people would drive one or even two oxen and sometimes a whole herd passed by. These were the offerings that the well-off brought to the holy shrine so that their poorer brothers should not suffer from their shortcomings. While so many came and went: - my *Bashi-Bozuks* and Arnauts remained missing and to this day I have not discovered what happened to them.

On the third day - the first day of the feast - I sat once more with my translator and studied the book. It was still before sunrise. He dictated:

"Shi bu dunya geranra di dunya 'i ashutin, chosh the, seferi ti nav seferi kirin, di her bashereki ditin zinet u chamil, di her konajaki hisa 'i kirin, shi tishti dizi chaber hilanin, shi ne ditiyan pai hilanin, lakin bebini pashija shuchuli, di

basheri chodaya meriv chondekjar. Cheiri ma' in di basheri choda digel munan, jirite shi chandkjarija basheri merivan. Di basheri merivan egerji dibe quenji, dil nabe shi evina mali vala."

I translated:

"It is pleasant to wander throughout the world, to immerse oneself into the world. To complete journey upon journey, to appreciate all the beauties of every city, to find rest in every inn. To take notice of all that is hidden and to ask after all that is unseen; but after all possible efforts you will realize that there is only one city in which man is master. Remaining in his own city and among his own people is better than to rule over a foreign city. Even if it is excellent in a foreign city, the heart never parts from its native flock."

This text was taken from the well-known tale of Iskender, and I was so immersed in the task that I did not notice the entrance of the *Buluk-Emini*.

"Emir!" he called, after he had cleared his throat several times without my having taken notice.

"What is it?"

"Are we going!"

Only now I noted that he was wearing his boots and his spurs, I handed Selek's son the book and jumped up. I had completely forgotten that I needed to bathe and dress in fresh clothes if I wished to visit at the Grave of the Saint in a dignified manner. I took my clothes, went downstairs and hurried out of the village. The creek teemed with bathing bodies and I had to go a considerable distance to find a spot where I believed I would not be scrutinized.

Here I bathed and changed my clothes, a procedure that one cannot often carry out when traveling in the Orient. That is why I felt like a newborn child when I had finished. I was about to leave this spot when I perceived a soft movement in the bushes that grew along the shore of the creek. Was it an animal or a man? We were about to go to war and it could do no harm to investigate. Therefore, without apparent purpose or concern, picking a flower here and there, I moved towards the place where I first noted the movement. I even presented my back to the bush; but suddenly I turned around and leaped into the middle of the scrub. Before me crouched a man. He appeared young and had an almost military air about him, although I noted that he was only armed with a knife. A wide scar crossed his right cheek. He quickly arose and began to retreat but I grabbed his hand and held him fast.

"What are you doing here?" I asked.

"Nothing."

"Who are you?"

"A . . . a *Jesidi*," he answered timidly.

"From where?"

"My name is Lassa and I am a Dassini."

I had heard that the Dassini are one of the noblest families of the *Jesidi*; but he did not look like a 'Devil Worshipper'.

"I asked you what you are doing here?" I repeated.

"I hid because I did not wish to disturb you."

"And what were you doing here before that?"

"I was preparing to bathe."

"Where are your clean garments?"

"I don't have any."

"You were here before me and therefore had the right to remain, instead of hiding yourself. Where did you sleep last night?"

"In the village."

"With whom?"

"With - with - with . . . I do not know his name." He stammered.

"A Dassini does not board with a man he does not know. Come with me and show me your host!"

"I must bathe first!"

"You will do that later. Forward!"

He tried to free himself from my grasp.

"What right do you have to speak to me thus?"

"With the right born of suspicion."

"I might suspect you likewise!"

"Of course! I beseech you to do so. Then you would lead me into the village and it will become apparent who I am."

"Go where you like!"

"That I will do too; but you will accompany me."

His glance rested on my belt; he noted that I had no weapon with me and I could tell that he was considering using his knife. I was not concerned with that right now and so I gripped his wrist harder and wrenched him out into the open.

"How dare you?" he said and his eyes flashed.

"Easily. You are coming with me; *japuk* - at once!"

"Let go of my hand, or else . . .!"

"Or else what?"

"I will use force!"

"Use it then!"

"Here . . .!"

He pulled out his knife and thrust it towards me; but I grabbed his knife hand from below and held that fast also.

"Shame on you; for you do not appear to be a coward!"

I squeezed the hand that held the knife and he dropped it, I retrieved it quickly and seized him by his jacket.

"Now forward, otherwise . . . ! Here, take my clothes and carry them!"

"Lord, don't do this!" He implored.

"Why not?"

"Are you a *Jesidi*?"

"No." I admitted.

"Then why do you want to take me to the village?"

"That I will tell you: You are a Turkish soldier, a spy."

He paled.

"You are wrong, Lord! If you are no *Jesidi* then free me!"

"*Jesidi* or not; forward!"

He struggled under my grip but was forced onward. He was even obliged to carry my soiled clothing. We created something of a spectacle when we arrived at the village and quite a crowd followed us to the home of the *Bei*. He was in the *selamlük*, where I also brought the stranger. Not far from the door, unnoticed by my prisoner, stood the *Bashi-Bozuk*, who looked very surprised when we passed him. He must have recognized the stranger.

"Whom do you bring to me?" asked Ali *Bei*.

"A stranger I found down at the creek. He had concealed himself at a place where he could see the entire village and also the path to Sheik Adi."

"Who is he?"

"He claims that his name is Lassa and that he is a Dassini."

"Then I would know him; but there is no Dassini with that name."

"He tried to stab me when I forced him to come with me. Here he is. Do with him as you please!"

I left the room. The *Buluk-Emini* still stood outside.

"Do you know the man I just brought here?" I asked him.

"Yes. What has he done, Emir? Surely you have misjudged him! He is no thief and no robber."

"What is he then?"

"He is *Kol-Agassi* [surplus infantry staff officer] with my regiment."

"Ah! What is his name?"

"Nasir. We call him Nasir Agassi. He is the friend of *Miralai* Omar Amed."

"Good; tell Halef that he may saddle the horses!"

I returned to the *selamlük* where Mohammed Emin and some of the more important villagers, that were present by chance, had already begun the interrogation.

"How long were you hidden in the bushes?" asked the *Bei.*

"Since this man here began bathing."

"This man is an Emir; remember that! You are not a Dassini and no *Jesidi*. What is your name?"

"I will not tell you!"

"Why not?"

"I have a blood feud up in the Kurdish Mountains; I must conceal who I am and what my name is."

"Since when does a *Kol-Agassi* have a blood feud with the free Kurds?" I asked him.

He became even paler than he had been earlier at the creek.

"*Ko-Agassi*? What do you mean?" He asked spiritedly.

"I mean that I know Nasir Agassi, the confidant of *Miralai* Omar Amed, so well that I will not be fooled."

"You . . . you . . . you know me? *Wallahi*, then I am doomed; this is my undoing!"

"No; it is not your *kismet*. Admit honestly what you were doing here and perhaps nothing will happen to you!"

"I have nothing to say."

"Then you are doo . . ." Ali *Bei* began.

I interrupted the angry *Bei* with a quick wave of my hand and turned to the prisoner.

"Is what you said of a blood feud true?"

"Yes, Emir!"

"Then be more careful in the future. If you promise me to return to Mosul without lingering along the way, and to leave your feud for another time then you are free."

"*Effendi*!" the *Bei* cried with fright. "Remember what we . . ."

"I know what you wish to say," I interrupted him again. "This man is a staff officer of the *Mutessarif*, a *Kol-Agassi*, who will perhaps make general, and you live in friendship and peace with the *Mutessarif*. I am sorry to have troubled this officer; it would not have happened if I had recognized him at once." I turned to the *Kol-Agassi* and asked - "You will promise me to return to Mosul without delay?"

"I promise it."

"Does the feud concern a *Jesidi*?"

"No."

"Then go, and may Allah watch over you, so that the feud should not endanger your person!"

He stood there quite astounded. Just a moment ago he had envisaged his own death and now he was free. He grabbed my hand and cried:

"Emir, I thank you! Allah bless you and your family!"

Then he hurried through the door as though he might have feared that we would yet regret our generosity.

"What have you done!" hissed Ali *Bei*, more angrily than amazed.

"The best that I could do," I answered.

"The best? This man is a spy!"

"That's right."

"And he deserves to die!"

"That's right."

"And you gave him freedom! Did not force him to confess!"

Even the other *Jesidi* were looking darkly at me. I did not let it bother me and answered:

"What would you have discovered from his confession?"

"Perhaps much!"

"Not more than we already know. And besides that man would rather have died than confess."

"Then we would have executed him!"

"And what would have been the consequence of that?"

"There would have been one less spy!"

"Oh, the consequences would have been quite different. The *Kol-Agassi* had certainly been sent to discover if we had any knowledge of the intended attack. If we killed him or held him prisoner he would not have returned and then they would know that we have been warned. But now he has his freedom again and the *Miralai* Omar Amed will be certain that we do not have the slightest idea of the *Mutessarif's* plan. It would be an act of utmost stupidity to allow a spy to go free if one is certain that an attack is pending - so they will think. Am I right?"

The *Bei* embraced me.

"Forgive me, Emir! My thoughts are not as deep as yours are. But I will send a scout after him to ensure that he truly leaves."

"Even that I would not do."

"Why not?"

"He could become suspicious as to why we let him go and what we might have tried to hide from. He is not likely to remain here and besides, enough people are arriving now from whom you can discover if they met him on the road."

Even in this I made sense to him. It was a great feeling to have tied two advantageous events together: I had succeeded in saving the life of a man who was only following orders and at the same time I had thwarted the *Mutessarif*'s plan. With that feeling I went to the home of the Mistress, this really should have been called a kitchen, to partake of breakfast. But before doing so I rummaged through my collection of rarities that had been provided by Isla Ben Maflei and selected a bracelet on which a medallion was fastened.

The little *Bei* was already quite lively. While his mother held him I tried to commit his physiognomy to paper. It was quite good. For all children are similar to one another. Then I put the paper into the medallion and gave the bracelet to the mother.

"Wear this in remembrance of the Emir of the *Nemsi*," I requested of her; "the face of your son is contained within it; the image will remain eternally young, even when he himself has grown older."

She looked at the picture and was quite delighted. Within five minutes she had shown it to the whole household and anyone else present, and I could scarcely save myself from the acts of gratitude that ensued.

After the morning meal we commenced our journey, not with any feeling of joy, but rather in a mood that was grim.

Ali *Bei* had donned his luxurious clothing. He rode with me at the head of our troop, followed by the most respected village elders. Mohammed Emin was of course at our side. He was in a bad mood since our ride to Amadijah had suffered such a delay. In front of us traveled a troop of musicians with flutes and tambourines. Behind them came the women, mostly with donkeys that were laden with carpets, cushions and all sorts of utensils.

"Have you completed your preparations for Baadri?" I asked the *Bei*.

"Yes. Men have been posted as far as Jerajah, they will report the position of the enemy to me."

"You will leave Baadri to the Turks without defense?"

"Of course. They will move through it quietly so as not to warn us too early of their presence."

From now on it became quite noisy around us. Riders who carried out a mock battle rode all around us and from all sides the discharge of rifles thundered without end. Now the path became quite narrow and in places it wound its way so steeply up the mountainside that we had to dismount and lead our horses over the rocks in single file. Only after an hour of strenuous climbing on this path did we reach the peak and from there we could see the lush, forested valley of Sheik Adi.

Everyone that spied the white tower of the shrine fired a salvo and in response an uninterrupted crackle of shots came from below, so that it sounded as though a great infantry battle was in progress, the echo of which resounded from the mountains. Behind us came more people and as we rode down the mountainside we saw many pilgrims lying under the trees to either side of us. They rested here from the strain of the climb and reveled in the sight of the sacred landmark and the wonderful scenery of the mountain - for an inhabitant of the plains this must have been a refreshing sight.

We had not yet reached the shrine when Mir Sheik Khan, the spiritual leader of the *Jesidi* came towards us at the head of many Sheiks. He is called Emir Hajji and is descended from the Ommijaden family. His clan is recognized as the foremost family of the *Jesidi* and is called Posmir or Begzadehs. He himself was a hardy, elderly man of noble bearing, though he appeared unconcerned with his hierarchical nobility; for he bowed before me and then embraced me fervently, just as one would do with his own son.

"*Aaleïk salam u rahhmet Allah. Ser sere men at* - May the peace and compassion of God be with you! You are welcome to me!" he greeted.

"*Chode scogholeta rast init* - May God be with you in your duty!" I answered. "But will you speak Turkish with me? I do not yet fully understand the language of your land!"

"Demand of me what you wish, and be my guest in the house of the one, at whose grave we honor the Almighty and His Grace."

We had of course dismounted on his approach. At a signal from him our horses were taken into care and we - that is Ali *Bei*, Mohammed Emin and I, walked towards the shrine at his side. We first encountered a walled courtyard that was already overflowing with people. Then we came to the entrance of an inner courtyard, which the *Jesidi* enter only after removing their footwear. I followed the example and took off my shoes, which I left at the entrance.

Within this inner courtyard stood many trees, their shade brought cool relief to the pilgrims; thick oleander bushes bristled with blossoms and an enormous vine trellis formed a kind of arbor. To this Mir Sheik Khan led us, and there we seated ourselves. Several Sheiks and Kawals rested beneath the trees and apart from them, we were alone.

In this courtyard stood the actual building of the shrine, which was flanked by two white towers, which contrasted well with the deep green of the surrounding valley. Their roofs were gilded and their sides were interspersed with recesses where light chased the shadows. Above the gateway several figures had been carved and I recognized a lion, a snake, an axe, a man and a comb. The inside of the building, as I later discovered, is divided into three parts, one of which is larger than the other two. This hall is supported by columns and arches and contains a fountain, the water of which is considered to be holy. Children are baptized with this water. The actual crypt of the saint is housed in one of the other two rooms. A great cubic structure rises above this crypt, constructed of clay and covered with plaster. The only decorations here are an eternal flame and an embroidered green cloth that covers the structure.

From time to time the crypt requires restoration; the caretakers of the shrine make little balls from the clay, which are then sold to the pilgrims and taken away as mementos, perhaps even worn as amulets. These clay balls are stored in a vessel that is kept by the aforementioned trellis and are of different sizes: ranging from the size of a pea up to the size of those marbles or glass balls that children love to play with.

In the second chamber is another crypt, but the *Jesidi* appear to be uncertain of who the occupant is.

In the wall surrounding the shrine are many niches that are designed to hold the lights that are lit during a great feast. Buildings that serve as the homes of the attendants surround the shrine. The whole complex is situated in a narrow ravine inside the valley and is surrounded by steep rock on all sides. The entire complex consists of only a few mundane buildings, aside from the shrine, which can accommodate pilgrims. Every tribe or even a large subsection of the same owns such a building that is used exclusively by them.

Outside of the walls a bazaar had been erected. All imaginable kinds of fabrics and wares were hung from tree branches and were offered for sale; a huge variety of fruits and foods were on offer; weapons, jewelry and all sorts of Oriental objects could be had. If it was not for the clothing, I would have thought that I was at home, so joyful and free, so innocent and comfortable was the colorful bustle in the village of the Saint. These so called 'Devil Worshippers' truly gained still more of my sympathy, and I completely agree with what a very understanding Englishman, who had been in Kofau, and whom I later met in Constantinople, said of them:

"The 'Devil Worshippers' are slandered because they are better than their slanderers. If they were more numerous and less dispersed they could become the Germans of Asia, and nowhere has Christianity greater hope of success than with these people. I believe that certain overseas [Protestants] missionaries cast the *Jesidi* in such a false and unflattering light so that they can describe their own small successes as quite significant."

Of course I bridled my curiosity so that it would not become a burdensome prying, and perhaps it was because of this that our discussion was so animated and pleasant, as it would be among family members who have loved and respected each other since their youth. Of course our talk concentrated firstly on the impending attack, but that was soon laid to rest, as it became clear that Ali *Bei* had diligently managed all the important preparations. Then the discussion centered upon Mohammed Emin and myself, on our experiences and current intentions.

"Perhaps you will run into danger and need help," said Mir Sheik Khan. "I will give you a symbol that will ensure the cooperation of any *Jesidi* to whom you show it."

"I thank you! It will be a letter?" I asked.

"No, a *Melek Ta-us*." [See Translation Note Ch 24. 1]

I almost leaped up as though I had received an electric shock. That was the designation of the Devil! That was the name of the beast that, according to the lies that had been spread, stood on the altars of these people during their services and 'extinguished the lights' so that the orgies could commence! And finally it was the name of that seal that was entrusted to every priest who had a special mission, this was what Mir Sheik Khan intended to give to me! And this great, secret word, over which much argument had ensued, he spoke so casually here? I composed myself and with a calm voice asked:

"A *Melek Ta-us*? May I ask what that is?"

With the indulgent expression of a father who was about to instruct his son on the unknown, he answered:

"*Melek Ta-us* is what we call him, whose real name may not be uttered by us. *Melek Ta-us* is also the name of the animal that is, to us, a symbol of courage and watchfulness, and *Melek Ta-us* is the image of the animal that I lend to those whom I trust. I know of all the fables that are told about us; but through your wisdom you will know that I do not need to defend our people against these. I have spoken with a man that has been in many Christian churches. He tells me that there are images of the mother of God, the Son of God and of many Saints. You are even said to employ the image of an eye, that is the symbol of God the Father - and a dove that is the symbol of the Spirit. You kneel and pray at the places where these images are and you never believe that you are praying to the images. We believe rightly of you, and you believe falsely of us. Who is more understanding and who is kinder, you or we? Look at the gate, do you think that we pray to those images?"

"No."

"You see a lion, a snake, an axe, a man and a comb. The *Jesidi* cannot read; That is why it is better that they are instructed through images as to what they need to know. A script they will not understand; but these images they will not forget, for they are seen at the shrine of the Saint. This Saint was a man; that is why we do not pray to him; but we gather at his grave as children gather at the grave of their father."

"He gave you your belief?"

"He gave us our belief but not our customs. The belief lives in the heart, tradition grows from the ground on which we live, and from the lands that encircles that ground. Sheik Adi lived before Mohammed. His teachings also encompass those parts of the Koran that we recognize as good and wholesome."

"I have been told that he performed miracles."

"Miracles are God's work; but when he performs them, he does so through the hand of a man. Look into the hall! There is a fountain that was brought forth by Sheik Adi. He was in Mecca before Mohammed. Even then Zem-Zem was a holy spring. He took the water from Zem-Zem and sprinkled it here on the rocks. At once the rock opened and the holy water spouted forth. So it is told to us. We do not command that this be believed, for the miracle exists without it. Or is it not a miracle when living water flows from the hard, dead stone? To us this is a symbol of the cleanliness of our souls and that is why we believe it to be holy, not because it came from the waters of Zem-Zem."

Chapter 25

Mir Sheik Khan ceased his speech, for the outer gate had opened to permit the entry of a long line of pilgrims, every one of whom carried a lantern. These lamps were a gift of thanks and dedication for the healing of an ill or the escape from some danger. They were meant for Sheik Shems [sun], the shining symbol of God's clarity.

All the pilgrims were well armed. I saw some very strange Kurdish *tüfenks* [flintlocks]. One such weapon had its barrel and shaft bound together with at least twenty strong, wide iron rings, which would make it impossible to aim properly. A second had a kind of bayonet attached that resembled a fork; the two tines were fastened to the side of the barrel. The men gave their vessels to the priests and one by one approached Mir Sheik Khan to kiss his hand; during this process they lowered their weapons or placed them on the ground.

The lamps were used to light the holy village and the entire surrounding area during the evening of the feast. No ordinary oil, or even bitumen and naphtha would be used, for these are considered unclean. Only sesame oil is permitted.

When the procession had passed, some twenty children were baptized and cut, some had been brought from very far away. I stood by and observed these religious acts.

Later I left with Mohammed Emin to wander through the valley. The huge number of torches that were laid out for sale were the most conspicuous. At a guess there were at least ten thousand of them. The traders did good business, their wares were physically ripped from their hands.

As we stood next to a trader of glass and genuine coral wares I saw *Pir* Kamek coming down the mountain path. He was headed towards the shrine and was sure to encounter us on his way; when he did, he stopped.

"Welcome, you guests of Sheik Shems! You will get to know the Saint of the *Jesidi*."

He extended his hands towards us. As soon as he was recognized by the crowd he was surrounded by them; each one trying to touch and kiss his hand and the hem of his robe. He spoke to the gathering; his long white hair streaming in the morning breeze; his eyes shone, and his movements displayed the liveliness of his enthusiasm. The salvos of the arriving pilgrims cracked from above and were answered by salvos from the valley floor. Sadly I could not understand his speech as it was in the Kurdish language. At the end however he began singing a song, which the crowd also took up; the son of Selek, who had just then arrived, translated the first part of it for me:

"Oh gracious and generous God, Who feeds the ant and the crawling snake, Who steers the night and the day, living, highest, the One without cause, Who gives the night darkness and the day light! The wise, ruler of wisdom; the strong, ruler of strength; the living, ruler over death!"

After the song the crowd dispersed and the Pir joined me.

"Did you understand what I said to the pilgrims?"

"No. You know that I do not speak your language."

"I said to them, that I am bringing an offering to Sheik Shems, and they have gone into the forest to gather the necessary wood. If you wish to see the offering, then you are welcome. But now excuse me, Emir; here come the sacrificial animals."

He walked towards the shrine where a long row of animals had been herded together before its walls. We followed him slowly.

"What happens to the animals?" I asked my translator.

"They will be butchered."

"For whom?"

"For Sheik Shems."

"Can the sun eat cattle?"

"No, but the sun will give them to the poor."

"Only the meat?"

"Everything: the meat, the entrails and the hide. Mir Sheik Khan oversees the allotment."

"And the blood?"

"That will not be eaten, instead it will be buried in the earth, for the soul resides in the blood."

This was precisely the Old Testament view that the life of the body was blood and that the soul was in the blood. I understood that here was no pagan offering but a gift that would enable the poor to eat during the feast.

When we reached the shrine, Mir Sheik Khan exited through the gate, closely followed by Pir Kamek, several Sheiks, Kawals and a great number of Fakirs. All held knives in their right hand. The place of sacrifice was encircled by a huge number of warriors, who held their guns at the ready. Mir Sheik Khan threw off his outer clothing, leaped upon the first steer, and thrust his knife with such certainty between the joints of its neck that the animal collapsed and died instantly. At the same time a hundred jubilant voices arose and a great barrage of gun fire erupted.

Mir Sheik Khan stepped back, and Pir Kamek continued the work. It was a strange sight to see this man with snowy white hair and black beard, jumping from one steer to the next, felling each one down the line with a sure thrust of his blade. Not a drop of blood flowed. The Sheiks now came to open the veins in the necks of the fallen beasts and the Fakirs lingered close by with great vessels to catch the blood. [See Translation Notes Ch 25. 1] When this was done, a considerable number of sheep were brought; once again, the first was dispatched by Mir Sheik Khan, but the remainder were then butchered by the Fakirs, who proved to be extraordinarily adept at the task.

Ali *Bei* came up to me.

"Would you like to accompany me to Kaloni?" he asked. "I have to assure myself of the friendship of the Badinans."

"Are you in conflict with them?"

"Could I have chosen my scouts from their ranks if that were so? Their chief is a good friend of mine; but circumstances can arise where one must be more careful then usual. Come!"

We did not have to go far to reach the very large house, built of rough stone, which Ali *Bei* occupied during the time of the feast. His wife was already waiting for us. We found several carpets spread out on an open deck of the building, we seated ourselves here to partake of breakfast. From this place we could almost see the entire valley. People were camped everywhere. Every tree had become a tent.

Over to the right of us was the temple dedicated to the sun [Sheik Shems]. It stood so that the first rays of the morning sun would strike it. When I later entered this temple I found it to have four bare walls and no other devices which could be construed as idols of any kind. Bright water flowed through a channel in the floor, and on the clean whitewashed walls the following Arabian words were written: "Oh Sun, oh Light, oh Life of God!"

Outside the temple sat several families of the rich *kojers* [wandering tribes]. The men leaned against the temple walls dressed in light-colored jackets and turbans and all were festooned with many fantastic weapons. The women were clothed in silken robes and wore their hair in many, flower-entwine plaits that hung down their backs. Their brows were almost completely hidden beneath coins of gold and silver, and large chains of coins, glass beads and cut stones hung from their necks.

Before me a man from Sindshar leaned against the trunk of a tree. His skin was dark brown and his clothes were clean and white. He surveyed his surroundings with a piercing look and from time to time shook his long hair from his face. His gun was a heavy old fuse lock, and his knife blade was fastened to a rough-cut handle; but one could tell that this man could use these weapons skillfully. Beside him his wife sat by the small fire on which she baked barley cakes, and above him, in the branches, two half-naked boys clambered about, they also wore knives in the thin ropes that were wound about their waists.

Not far from him camped several city dwellers, perhaps from Mosul; the men tended their thin donkeys, the women looked pale and exhausted, a picture that spoke of the need, worry and oppression that these people are exposed to.

Then I saw men, women and children from Sheïkhan, from Syria, from Hadshilo and Midiad, from Heïshteran and Semsat, from Mardin and Nisibin, from the region of the Kendali and the Delmamikan, from Kokan and Kojalian, yes, even from the territory of Tuzik and the Delmagumgumuku. Young and old, rich and poor, all were clean. Some had decorated their turbans with ostrich feathers, and others could barely cover their nakedness, but all carried weapons. They associated with one another like brothers and sisters; they shook hands, embraced each other and kissed. Neither women nor girls hid their faces before strangers - it was as though they were all part of a great family that had come together here.

A salvo cracked and I saw how the men went to the shrine individually or in larger groups.

"What are they doing there?" I asked Ali *Bei*.

"They go to fetch their share of the meat from the sacrificial animals."

"Is there a certain person in charge of this?"

"Yes. Only the poor come. They gather according to their tribe or home and their leader accompanies them or they have a certificate from him that they can show."

"Your priests receive no part of the meat?"

"Not from these steers; but on the last day of the feast some more animals are slaughtered, they must be white - completely white, and their meat belongs to the priests."

"Can your priests commit a sin?"

"Why not? They are human after all!"

"Even the Pirs, the holy ones?"

"Even they."

"Even Mir Sheik Khan?"

"Yes."

"Do you believe, that even your great Saint Sheik Adi sinned?"

"Even he was a sinner for he was not God."

"Do you let your sins rest on your soul?"

"No, we remove them."

"How?"

"Through the symbol of cleanliness, through fire and water. You know that we bathed yesterday and today. Through this we acknowledge our sins and promise to put them aside; then they are taken away by the water. And this evening you will see that we cleanse our souls with fire too."

"Do you believe that the soul does not die with the body?"

"How could it die, since it comes from God!"

"How can you prove this to me if I do not believe it?"

"You jest! Is it not written in your *Kitab*: '*Japar-di bir sagh solukü burunuje* - he blew the living breath into his nose'?"

"Good, if the soul cannot die, where does it go after the death of the body?"

"You breathe in again after you have breathed out. Even God's breath returns to him after it has been cleansed of sin. - Let us go now!"

"How far is it to Kaloni?"

"We ride for about four hours."

Below our horses stood ready. We mounted and departed the valley alone. The path led up the steep mountainside and when we reached the summit I saw before me a thickly forested mountain range intersected by many valleys. This land is populated by the great tribes of the Missuri-Kurds, to which the Badinan also belong. Our path led down and then up, sometimes between naked rock and sometimes through thick forest. On the slopes we saw several small villages, but the houses were empty. Here and there we rode through the cold waters of a wild mountain stream that sent its waters towards the Ghomel, which then joined the Ghazir or the Bumadus to eventually flow into the great Zab and finally into the Tigris at Keshaf. Vineyards surrounded the houses and next to these grew sesame, corn and cotton. Their picturesque, almost decorative appeal came from the blossoms of flowers and well-tended fig, walnut, pomegranate, peach, cherry, mulberry and olive trees.

We met no one, for the *Jesidi* that live in this region and as far as Dshulamerik, were already in Sheik Adi. We had ridden for two hours when we heard a voice call to us.

A man stepped from the forest. He was a Kurd. He wore very wide trousers that were not cinched at the bottom and his feet were covered with low leather shoes. His body was covered with a square-necked shirt that hung down to his calves. His thick hair hung in curly strands down to his shoulders. On his head he wore a peculiar and ugly felt cap that had the appearance of a huge spider, the round body of which covered the top of his head and the long legs of which hung backwards and sideward down to his armpits. In his belt he carried a knife, a powder flask and an ammunition pouch, but his gun was nowhere to be seen.

"*Ni, vro'l kjer* - Good day!" he greeted us. "Where does Ali *Bei*, the brave one, mean to ride?"

"*Chode t'aveshket* - God protect you!" the *Bei* answered. "You know me? From what tribe are you?"

"I am a Badinan, Lord."

"From Kaloni?"

"Yes, from Kalahoni, as we call it."

"Are you still living in your houses?"

"No. We have already occupied our makeshift huts."

"Then they are nearby?"

"What makes you think that?"

"If a warrior goes far from his home he takes his gun with him. But you do not have yours with you."

"You have guessed correctly. With whom do you wish to speak?"

"With your chief."

"Dismount and follow me!"

We dismounted and took our horses by the reigns. The Kurd led us deeper into the forest until we reached a strong barrier constructed of felled trees, behind which we saw many huts built from poles, branches and foliage. In this barricade a small opening remained, which served as an entrance. Now we saw many hundreds of children running between the huts and the trees, whilst the adults - men and women - were busy working to enlarge and strengthen the barrier. Atop one of the larger huts sat a man. He was the chief, and had chosen this high place to oversee and more easily direct the work. When he noted my companion, he leapt down and walked towards us.

"*Kjeïr ati; Chode dauleta ta mazen b'ket*- Be welcome; May God increase your wealth!"

With these words he offered Ali *Bei* his hand and summoned a woman to spread a blanket, upon which we might sit. He appeared to ignore me. A *Jesidi* would have shown more courtesy. The same woman, who was certainly his wife, brought three pipes that were fashioned, rather crudely, from the wood of a *injaz* [bitter orange tree], and a young girl brought a vessel in which were *habi tri* [grapes] and *hingiv* [honey slices]. The chief took a cat-skin tobacco pouch from his belt, opened it and laid it before Ali *Bei*.

"*Taklif b' ela k' narek, au, beïn ma batal* - Do not go to any great trouble, that is unnecessary between us!" Ali *Bei* said.

The chief dipped his dirty hand into the honey, pulled out a slice with his fingers and shoved it into his mouth.

The *Bei* stuffed his pipe and lit it. Then he asked the Kurd,

"Tell me if there is friendship between you and I!" he started.

"There is friendship between you and I," the chief confirmed.

"Even between your people and my people?"

"Even between them." The chief agreed.

"Will you ask for my help if an enemy comes to attack you?"

"If I am too weak to defeat them, I will ask for your help."

"And will you help me if I seek it?"

"If your enemy is not my friend, I will do it."

"Is the Governor of Mosul your friend?" Ali *Bei* asked.

"He is my enemy; he is an enemy of all the free Kurds. He is a *kelehsh* [robber], an *iz* [sinner, degenerate], who thins our herds and sells our daughters."

"Have you heard that he plans to attack us in Sheik Adi?"

"So I have heard from my people that serve you as scouts."

"They will come through your land. What will you do?"

"You see this!" He indicated the huts all around with his arm. "We have left Kalahoni and built huts here in the forest. Now we build a wall from behind which we can defend ourselves when the Turks attack."

"They will not attack you."

"How do you know this?" The chief inquired.

"I suspect it. If they are to be successful in surprising us, then they must avoid any battle or discord beforehand. They will therefore move peacefully through your territory. They will perhaps even avoid the open road and come through the forest to reach the heights of Sheik Adi undetected."

"Your thoughts are justified."

"But when they have defeated us, then they will also attack you."

"You will not let yourselves be defeated," the chief said assuredly.

"Will you help me in this?"

"I will. What shall I do? Shall I send my warriors to Sheik Adi?"

"No, for I have enough warriors to defeat the Turks without your aid. You should hide your warriors and let the Turks pass in peace so that they believe themselves safe."

"I should not follow them?"

"No. Yet you may check their rear, so that they cannot retreat. On the second peak between here and Sheik Adi is a pass that is so narrow that only two men can traverse it side by side. If you build an barricade there, you can kill a thousand Turks with just twenty men."

"I will do it. But what do I get in return?"

"If you do not join the battle and I must defeat them alone then you shall receive fifty guns; but if you are brave and fight then I will give you a hundred Turkish guns."

"A hundred Turkish guns!" the chief cried excitedly. He dipped his hand quickly into the honey and pulled out such a huge piece, which he shoveled into his mouth, that I thought he must surely choke on it. "A hundred Turkish guns!" he repeated whilst chewing. "Will you keep your word?"

"Have I ever lied to you?"

"No. You are my brother, my companion, my friend, my ally in battle, and I believe you. I will earn those guns!"

"But you can only earn them if you let the Turks pass by peacefully."

"They shall see none of my men!"

"And if you then impede their retreat, should I fail to surround them and hold them."

"I will not only occupy the pass, I will also block the secondary valleys so that they may move neither right, left, forwards nor back!" The chief said with satisfaction.

"You will do well. But I do not wish much blood to be spilled. The soldiers cannot help that they must obey the Governor; if we are cruel, the Padishah of Stambul is mighty enough to send a great army to destroy us."

"I understand you. A good general must be capable of using cunning as well as force. Then he can defeat a great army with a small *emjerg* [entourage]. When will the Turks come?"

"They will arrange it so that they will reach and attack Sheik Adi tomorrow morning."

"The *ashutin* [attack] shall fall upon them. I know that you are a brave warrior. You will deal with the Turks in the same manner as the Haddedihn-Shammar dealt with their enemies on the plains below."

"You have had word of that?"

"Who has not heard of it? The news of such a heroic deed spreads fast across mountains and valleys. Mohammed Emin has made his *ashiret* [tribe] one of the richest."

Ali *Bei* smiled secretively and then said:

"It is a wonderful deed to take thousands of prisoners without a battle."

"Mohammed Emin would not have managed this deed alone. He is strong and brave; but he had a foreign general with him."

"A foreigner?" asked the clever *Bei*.

He was certainly annoyed by the lack of attention the chief had shown me, and he used this circumstance to shame him. To do this he could not lavish abundant praise himself.

"Yes, a foreigner," answered the chief. "Have you not heard of this yet?"

"Tell me!"

And the Kurd did so in the following manner:

"Mohammed Emin, the Sheik of the Haddedihn, sat before his tent in council with the elders of his tribe. A cloud opened and a rider came down and his horse touched the ground in the midst of them.

"*Salaam aaleïkum*!" the rider greeted them.

"*Aaleïkum sallah*!" answered Mohammed Emin. "Stranger, who are you and where do you come from?"

The rider's horse was as black as night, the rider himself wore body armor and armor on his arms and legs and a helmet of pure gold. Around his helmet a shawl was wound that was woven by the *houri's* of Paradise; for a thousand living stars circled in the weave. The shaft of his lance was of silver, its tip shone like a bolt of lightning, and below it were fastened the beards of a hundred enemies. His dagger flashed like a diamond and his sword could cut iron and steel.

"I am the *Seraskier* [Minister of War] from a far land," answered the glowing one. "I love you and heard not an hour ago that your tribe was to be exterminated. That is why I mounted my horse, which can fly like the thoughts of a man, and hurried to warn you."

"Who is it that wants to exterminate my tribe?" asked Mohammed.

The heavenly one named the enemy.

"Do you know this for certain?"

"My shield tells me all that happens on earth. Here, look!"

Mohammed looked into the golden shield. In the midst of which was a carbuncle five times larger than the hand of a man and in this he saw all his enemies and how they had gathered to move against him.

"What an army!" he cried. "We are doomed!"

"No, for I will help you," answered the stranger. "Gather all your warriors around the Valley of the Steps and wait until I bring you the enemy!"

He gave a sign to his horse, upon which it rose and disappeared from view behind the clouds. Mohammed Emin took up arms and he and his people moved to the Valley of the Steps and encircled it so that the enemy could enter but not escape. The next morning the foreign *jenmeki* [hero] rode up. He shone like the sun and his light blinded the enemy so that they shut their eyes and followed him into the Valley of the Steps. There he turned his shield around and the radiance left him and the enemy opened their eyes and saw that there was no escape from the valley and they were forced to surrender. Mohammed Emin did not kill them; but he took from them a part of their herd and demanded a tribute from them that they must pay each year for as long as the earth exists."

The Kurd told the story in this manner and then fell silent.

"And what happened to the foreign *Seraskier*?" asked the *Bei*.

He said, "*Salaam aaleïkum*! - Then his black horse arose into the clouds and disappeared," was the Kurd's response.

"This story is very fine to hear; but do you know if it really happened?"

"It did happen. Five men from Jelu were in Salamijah at the same time as the Haddedihn who told this tale. They came through here and reported it to me and my people."

"You are right; this story did happen, but differently than you have been told. Do you want to see the black horse of the *Seraskier*?"

"Lord, that is not possible!"

"It is possible for it is nearby."

"Where?"

"There, it is that black stallion."

"You jest, *Bei*!"

"I do not jest, I tell you the truth."

"That horse is magnificent, like none I have seen before, but it is the horse of this man!" He said, indicating me.

"And this man is the foreign *Seraskier*, of whom you have spoken."

"Impossible!"

In his amazement his mouth had opened so wide that one could have made extensive dental observations and perhaps even undertaken an orthodontic procedure.

"Impossible you say? Have I ever lied to you? I tell you again, it is truly he!"

The eyes as well as the mouth of the chief opened wider still; he stared at me like he had lost his reason and then, as though in a dream, his hand reached for the honey, but found the tobacco pouch instead. Without noticing his error, he filled his hand and shoved an enormous portion of this narcotic weed between his gleaming white teeth. I had suspected that this tobacco was something other than regular tobacco and obviously my suspicion was correct; for in that moment the weed produced a reaction in the chief that caused him to momentarily clap his mouth shut and then spray the content into the good Ali *Bei's* face.

"*Katera peghamber* - by the will of the Prophets! Is it truly him?" he sputtered, visibly dismayed.

"I have already assured you!" answered the bespattered *Bei*, whilst cleaning his face with the hem of his clothing.

"Oh *Seraskier*," the chief now turned to me; "*atina ta, inshiallah, keïrah* - May God permit that your visit will bring us luck!"

"You will have luck, that I promise you!" I answered.

"Your horse is here, the black one, " he continued, "but where is your shield with the carbuncle, your armor, your helmet, your lance, your saber?"

"Hear what I tell you! I am the foreign warrior that was with Mohammed Emin, but I did not descend from heaven. I come from a far land, but I am not a *Seraskier* of the same. I do not have weapons of gold or silver, but as you see, my weapons are unlike those you possess, and with these I do not have to fear many enemies. Shall I show you how well they shoot?"

"*Sere ta, Ser babe ta, Ser hemsher ta Ali Bei* - By your head, by the head of your father, by the head of your friend Ali *Bei*, don't do it!" he begged in fear. "You have put aside the armor, the lance, the shield and the sword, so that you can use these weapons, which are perhaps even more dangerous. *Nezanum zïeh le dehm* - I do not know what I should give you; but promise me that you will be my friend!"

"Of what use would it be if you become my friend? In your land there is a saying that states: '*Dishmini be aquil shi yari be aquil jitire* - a friend with wisdom is better than a friend none.'"

"Do I not have wisdom, Lord?"

"Do you not know how one should greet a guest, especially if he comes with a friend?"

"You are right, Lord! You punish me with a proverb; permit me that I answer with another: '*Bejuk lasime thabe 'i mesinan bebe* - the smaller must be obedient to the larger.' Be you the greater; I will obey!"

"Obey first my friend Ali *Bei*! He will be victorious and then the Turkish guns are yours for certain."

"You are angry? Forgive me! *Ser sere men; bu kalmeta ta siuh taksir nakem* - By my head, I will spare nothing to serve you. Take these grapes and eat; take this tobacco and smoke!"

"We thank you," answered Ali *Bei*, who was likewise more used to cleaner fare. "We ate before we came and may not lose any more time in returning to Sheik Adi."

He arose and I did likewise. The chief accompanied us up to the path and again promised that he would fulfill his duty as completely as possible. We then rode back along the same path on which we had come.

[*Note: The book version entitled "Durch die Wüste" – 'Through the Desert' ends and "Durch's Wilde Kurdistan" – 'Through Wild Kurdistan' starts here.*]

As we reached the top of the hill in front of the village where we could overlook the valley of the Saint, we noticed an immense pile of kindling near the house of the *Bei* that was continually being enlarged to by a number of *Jesidi*. Pir Kamek stood nearby and from time to time threw a piece of tar onto the growing pyre.

"That is his *Kurban-kalabalik* [sacrificial pyre]", said Ali *Bei*.

"What will he sacrifice?"

"I do not know."

"Perhaps an animal?"

"Only *Putperestler* [Unbelievers] burn animals."

"Then fruit perhaps?"

"The *Jesidi* burn neither animals nor fruit. The *Pir* has not told me what he will burn, but he is a great holy man and what he does cannot be a sin."

The salvos of the arriving pilgrims from the heights across from us were still being answered by those already in the valley and I noted, when we reached the valley floor, that there was barely room to receive many more people. We left our horses and proceeded to the shrine on foot. There was a spring along the way, which was rimmed with flat stones. On one of these sat Mir Sheik Khan, he conversed with a number of pilgrims of deferential bearing who stood a respectful distance from him.

"This spring is holy and only the Mir, the priests and I may sit on the stones. Be not offended if you must stand!" Ali said to me.

"I will respect your customs." I replied.

As we approached, Khan motioned to those around him and an opening was made for us, allowing us to approach closer to him. He arose and stepped some paces towards us with outstretched hands.

"Welcome on your return! Seat yourself to my right and to my left!"

He indicated his left side to the *Bei*, thus his right side remained for me. I seated myself on the holy stones; I did not notice the slightest discontent from those in attendance. How decidedly different was this to the manners one observed with the Mohammedan.

"Have you spoken with the Chief?" asked Khan.

"Yes, everything is in order. Have you already explained the situation to the pilgrims?"

"No."

"Then it is time to gather the people. Give the command!"

"I am only the regent of the faith and all else is your business. I would never deny you the fame that is your due for the protection of the believers and the victory over the enemy."

Even this was a modesty that one could never expect from a Mohammedan Imam. Ali *Bei* arose and departed. Whilst I was in conversation with Khan I noticed a movement among the pilgrims that spread with every passing minute. The women remained in their places, as did the children, but the men lined up along the brook and the leaders of each tribe, branch or locality formed a circle around Ali *Bei*, who informed them of the intentions of the *Mutessarif* of Mosul. During all this utter silence and quiet reigned, just as at a parade of a European troop. It was quite the opposite of the noisy disarray that one is used to seeing and hearing with Oriental warriors. After a time, in which the leaders informed their men and passed on the orders of the *Bei*, the gathering dispersed in an orderly manner and everyone returned to the places that they had previously occupied.

Ali *Bei* rejoined us.

"What were your orders?" asked Khan.

Ali *Bei* extended his arm and indicated a troop of perhaps twenty men who climbed the path on which we had previously descended.

"See, those are the warriors from Aïram, Haji Dsho and Shura Khan, who know this area well. They move towards the Turks and will inform us of their progress. I have even sent men towards Baadri so that it will be impossible to ambush us. There are still three hours until night falls and that is enough time to move all that is not required here to the Idiz Valley. The men will break camp and Selek will show them the way."

"Will they return by the beginning of the holy service?"

"Yes, that is assured."

"Then they may go!"

After a time a long line of men, who either led their animals or carried their meager belongings themselves trooped past us and disappeared behind the shrine. Shortly they reappeared on a rocky path that could be observed from our location until it disappeared further up the slope in a thick forest.

I then joined Ali *Bei* to partake of a meal. Afterwards the *Bashi-Bozuk* approached me.

"Lord, I have to tell you something!"

"What?"

"A great danger threatens us!"

"Oh! What is it?"

"I am not sure; but the men of the devil have watched me with a terrible gaze that is very frightening. It looks as though they want to kill me!"

Since the *Buluk-Emini* wore his uniform I could easily comprehend the demeanor of the threatened *Jesidi*; but I was absolutely certain that nothing would happen to him.

"That is serious!" I said. "If they kill you who will take care of your donkey's tail?"

"Lord, they will also stab the donkey! Have you not seen that most of the buffalo and sheep that were around here have already been killed by them?"

"Your donkey is safe and you also. You two belong together and no one will tear you apart."

"You promise me this?"

"I promise you!"

"But I was afraid when you were gone earlier. Will you leave here again?"

"I will stay; but I order you to always remain here in the house and not to mingle with the *Jesidi*, otherwise it is impossible for me to protect you!"

That hero whom the *Mutessarif* assigned to me for my protection, departed somewhat assured by my promise. But another warning came from different quarters: Halef had found me.

"*Sihdi*, do you know that we will have war?"

"War? Between whom?"

"Between the *Osmanli* and the devil people."

"Who says this?"

"No-one."

"No-one? You must have heard what we spoke of earlier today in Baadri?"

"I have heard nothing! All of you spoke Turkish and these people speak that language in a dialect that I can not understand. But I have seen a great gathering, after which all the men inspected their weapons. Then they moved their animals and possessions and when I joined Sheik Mohammed on the platform, he too was busy emptying the old load from his pistols and loading them with new shot. Are these not enough signs to say that one can expect strife?"

"You are right, Halef. Tomorrow morning at the break of day the Turks from Baadri and even from Kaloni will attack the *Jesidi*."

"And the *Jesidi* know this?"

"Yes."

"How many Turks?"

"Fifteen hundred men."

"Many of them will die since their plan is discovered. Whom will you assist, *Sihdi*, the Turks or the *Jesidi*?"

"I will not fight at all."

"Not at all?", he replied disappointedly. "Can I not fight?"

"Whom do you wish to support?"

"The *Jesidi*."

"The *Jesidi*, Halef? Those whom you believe will deny you Paradise?"

"Oh *Sihdi*, I did not know them then, but now I like them."

"But they are 'Unbelievers'!"

"Have you not always helped those who were just, without asking if they believed in Allah or another God?"

My worthy Halef, who had wanted to convert me to the Muslim faith, I noted happily, had opened his heart to Christianity. I answered him:

"You will stay with me!"

"Whilst the others are heroic and do battle?"

"Perhaps an opportunity will arise for us to be even more heroic and courageous than they."

"Then I stay with you. And the *Buluk-Emini* too?"

"Him also."

I climbed up to join Sheik Mohammed Emin on the platform.

"*Hamdullillah*, God be praised that you have come!" he said. "I have awaited you like the grass awaits the dew of the night."

"You have remained up here all this time?"

"All this time. No one must recognize me for otherwise I might be betrayed. What news have you discovered?"

I divulged all to him. As I finished he indicated his weapons, which lay before him.

"We will welcome them!"

"You will not require these weapons."

"No? Shall I not defend myself and our friends?"

"They are strong enough. Do you perhaps wish to fall into the hands of the Turks, from whom you recently escaped, or shall a bullet or knife blade meet you so that your son remains imprisoned in Amadijah even longer?"

"Emir, you speak like a clever man but not a courageous one!"

"Sheik, you know that I fear no enemy; it is not fear that speaks from within me. Ali *Bei* demands that we should avoid conflict. Besides, he is certain that it will not come to a battle and I am of the same opinion."

"You think that the Turks will surrender without a fight?"

"If they do not then they will be massacred."

"The Turkish officers are useless, but the soldiers are courageous. They will storm the heights and break free."

"Fifteen hundred against approximately six thousand men?"

"If it is possible to successfully surround them!"

"It will succeed." I assured him.

"Then we must go to the Idiz Valley with the women?"

"You, yes."

"And you?"

"I will remain here."

"Allah kerihm! For what purpose? It would be your death!"

"I don't believe so. I am in *'Giölgeda padishahnün'*, posses the recommendation of the *Mutessarif* and have a *Buluk-Emini* at my side, whose presence should be enough to protect me."

"But what do you plan to do here?"

"To prevent disaster, if at all possible."

"Is Ali *Bei* aware of this?"

"No."

"Or Mir Sheik Khan?"

"Also no. They will find out in plenty of time."

I really had a difficult time trying to persuade the Sheik to accept my proposal. But in the end I succeeded.

"*Allah il Allah*! The paths of men are foretold in the 'Book of Fate'," he said; "I will not dissuade you from your intent, but I will remain at your side!"

"You? That will not work!"

"Why not?"

"The Turks must not find you." I reminded him.

"Neither you."

"I have already explained that I will not be in danger; but for you quite a different lot awaits if you are recognized."

"The end of a mans life is noted in the 'Book of Fate'. If I must die I shall die and thus it is immaterial if it happens here or in Amadijah."

"You wish to rush towards your doom, but you forget that you also involve me."

This appeared to me to be the only method by which I could overcome his stubbornness.

"You? How so?" he asked.

"If I were here alone then my papers would protect me, but if they find you - the enemy of the *Mutessarif*, the escaped prisoner - with me then I have lost that protection. You and I would be done for, both of us!"

He looked at the ground before him in contemplation. I realized why he resisted the retreat to the Idiz Valley, but allowed him time to come to his own conclusion. Finally he muttered in an uncertain voice:

"Emir, do you believe me to be a coward?"

"No. I know that you are courageous and fearless."

"What will Ali *Bei* think?"

"He believes as I do, and so does Mir Sheik Khan."

"And the other *Jesidi*?"

"They know your fame and that you do not flee from any foe. Of that you can be certain!"

"And if my courage is questioned will you defend me? Will you openly say that I went to the Idiz Valley with the women only in deference to you?"

"I will say so to all, everywhere."

"Well then, I will do what you have advised me to do!"

He put the flintlock away in resignation and turned to face the valley that had begun to wrap itself in the shadows of the evening.

Just then the men returned from the Idiz Valley. They formed a single file that dissolved itself in the valley below us.

From the shrine a salvo erupted and at the same time Ali *Bei* came to us with these words:

"The great celebration is starting at the shrine. Never before has a stranger attended it but Mir Sheik Khan has permitted me, in the name of all the priests, to invite you to attend."

That of course was a great honor; but Sheik Mohammed Emin did not accept the invitation:

"I thank you, Lord; but it is forbidden for a Moslem to attend the service of any god other than Allah."

He was a Moslem but still could have worded his reply more diplomatically. He remained behind and I followed the *Bei*.

On exiting the house a unique, indescribable vista opened before us. As far as the valley stretched one could see flickering torches by the waters below, beneath the trees, on every rock above and around the houses and their platforms. Most lively it was around the shrine. The Mir had lit a taper from the Eternal Lamp within the shrine and brought it out into the courtyard. From this taper the Sheiks and Kawals lit their lamps; from those the Fakirs took their flames and now they all stepped into the open where thousands crowded in to cleanse themselves with the holy tongues of fire.

All those who could reach the flames carried by the priests plunged their hands into their midst and then brushed their brows and the region over their hearts. Married men then plunged their hands into the flames a second time to bring the blessing to their wives. Mothers did the same for their children, who did not posses the strength to push their way through the crowd. Thereby a joy and happiness reigned that was not at all offensive.

Even the shrine was illuminated. In every available wall niche a lamp was set and above the courtyards long garlands of flaming lamps were stretched.

Every branch of every tree within the courtyards appeared as an arm of gigantic light, hundreds of torches reached upwards to the peaks of the towers, which looked like two gigantic guardians; their appearance was magical.

The priests now formed two lines and seated themselves in the inner courtyard. On the one side sat the Sheiks in their white garments and across from them sat the Kawals. The latter had musical instruments in their hands, alternately one had a flute and the next a tambourine. I sat next to Ali *Bei* beneath the grapevine trellis. I did not notice where Mir Sheik Khan was.

A cry emanated from within the shrine and the Kawals lifted their musical instruments. The flutes commenced a slow, wailing melody that was accompanied by the soft tapping of the tambourines, which set the beat. Suddenly a long extended four-tone chord sounded, I believe it was a third, fourth and sixth chord, to which a rapid drumming with the fingertips was played on the tambourines, first pianissimo, then piano, louder, ever louder towards fortissimo. Then the flutes joined the two-toned piece, which could not be described in our musical terms, yet the effect was quite pleasant and satisfying.

At the end of this piece Mir Sheik Khan stepped from the inside of the shrine. Two Sheiks accompanied him. One of them carried a wooden frame that was similar to a lectern; this was erected in the middle of the courtyard. The other carried a small bowl of water in one hand and in the other a bowl which contained a burning fluid. These two vessels were placed on the lectern, which Mir Sheik Khan now approached. [See Translation Note Ch 25. 2] He signaled with his hand and the music began anew. The music was an introduction, after which the priests joined in with a monotone hymn. Unfortunately I could not note down the content since that would have been too obtrusive and the actual words have escaped from my memory. The hymn was composed in Arabic and demanded purity, faith and watchfulness.

After this Mir Sheik Khan spoke briefly to the priests. He described in concise words the importance of keeping one's dealings free of every sin, to do good to all men and to keep true to one's faith and to defend that faith against all enemies.

He then stepped back and seated himself among us beneath the vines. One of the priests now presented a live rooster that he tied to the lectern with the aid of a piece of string; the water bowl was placed to its left and the flaming bowl was set down to its right.

The music started again. The rooster sat on the ground oblivious to its surroundings; the soft tones of the flute were lost to him. The tones became louder and he listened. He stretched his head and looked about with bright, clever eyes and noticed the water. Quickly he darted his beak into the vessel and drank. This happy event was acknowledged by a lively, joyful clashing of the tambourines. This sound appeared to stimulate the musical interest of the bird. The rooster cocked his head and listened attentively. In so doing it noticed that it was dangerously close to the flame. It tried to retreat but could not since it was tethered. So annoyed, it raised its stance and brought forth a loud "*Kik-ri-kih*!" which was joined by the flutes and the tambourines. This appeared to be a musical challenge to the rooster. He turned courageously towards the musicians, beat his wings and crowed again. He received the same answer and thus a battle of sound ensued, which finally annoyed the bird so much that he tore free in a moment of rage and fled into the inner sanctum of the shrine.

The music accompanied the heroic deed with the loudest fortissimo; the voices of the priests joined in jubilantly, followed by a finale that used the voices to the musicians instruments as well as those of the singers quite appropriately. At the end of this piece the Kawals kissed their musical instruments.

Was this loud and stormy finale the reason that the Jesidi are mistakenly identified as the deceitful *Cheragh Sonderan*, or *Jerah sonderahn* ['Light Extinguishers'] in the Kurdish language? The religious sentiment of a Christian bristles against the use of this bird, but I did not observe anything immoral in this act. [See Translation Notes Ch 25. 3]

Chapter 26

Now the sale of bullets, the production of which I had noted earlier, was about to commence. But before this began, the priests approached Ali *Bei* and myself and made us a gift of some of them. The *Bei* received seven and I also received the same number. They were completely round and were engraved with an Arabic word with some kind of stylus. Four of my seven lead balls were inscribed with the words '*El Shems*' - the Sun.

The trading took place in the outer courtyard, whilst within the inner walls the instruments and singing could still be heard. I left the shrine. I thought that the valley would provide a wonderful view from the surrounding heights, so I went to fetch Halef to accompany me. I found him seated on the deck of the house with the *Buluk-Emini*. They appeared to be in the middle of quite an animated conversation, for I heard Halef say:

"What? It was a Russian?"

"Yes, a Russian, may Allah cut off his head; for if he had not existed, I would still have my nose! I hacked about me in a rage; but this scoundrel aimed at my head; I tried to avoid him and stepped back. The blow that should have struck my head only struck my . . ."

"Hajji Halef!" I called.

I truly enjoyed being able to interrupt the famous 'Tale of the Nose'. The two leapt to their feet and came towards me.

"You shall accompany me, Halef; come!"

"Where to, *Sihdi*?"

"Up there to the crest, to view the appearance of the illuminated valley."

"Oh Emir, let me accompany you too!" Ifra begged.

"I have no objection, come along!"

We climbed up the valley wall in the direction of Baadri. Along the way we encountered men, women and children carrying torches and lanterns. And all of them greeted and spoke to us with a child-like joy. When we reached the top, an indescribable vista opened before us. A number of Jesidi had followed us to light our way, but I asked them to return or to extinguish their torches. To completely appreciate this view, one had to be surrounded by darkness.

In the valley below flame floated past flame. Thousands of shining points crossed, leaped and ducked, danced, darted and flew about, minute, miniscule at a distance but larger the closer they were to us. The shrine was glowing in the light of the fires and the two towers flared into the dark of the night like flaming hymns. This was accompanied by a dull roaring, an ebb and flow of voices, often interrupted by a loud cry of joy from nearby. I could have remained here for hours, enthralled and feasting my eyes on this spectacular view.

Someone next to me asked a question in Kurdish, “What star is that?”

It was a Jesidi who had spoken.

“Which one?” asked another.

“See the *Rea kadisahn* [Milky Way] there to the right!”

“I see it.”

“Below it a bright star flares. There, again! Do you see it?”

“Now I saw it too. It is *Kjale be sheri* [literally ‘the Old Headless One’ which is the ‘Great Bear’].”

The four stars that form the back of the Great Bear in our naming convention of the constellations are called ‘the Old Headless One’ by the Kurds. They contend that a neighboring star group hides the head. The three stars that form the tail of the Great Bear as we know the constellation (or the shaft or pole of the 'Wagon' as this constellation is also named), are called 'the two brothers and the blind mother of the ‘Old One' by the Kurds.

“*Kjale be sheri*? But it has four stars!” interjected the first speaker. “It must be *Kumikji shiwan* [Venus].”

“It is up higher. There it flares again. Ah, we are crazy; that is south! It must be *Meshin* [Libra].”

“*Meshin* has more stars as well. What do you think it is, Lord?”

The question was directed at me. The phenomenon seemed remarkable to me.

The torches and lanterns cast a glow upwards that made it impossible to discern the stars clearly. But the intermittent flash from across the valley was intense. It was like a will-o'-the-wisp that suddenly flares and immediately disappears. I watched it for a while and then turned to Halef:

“Hajji Halef, hurry down to Ali *Bei* and tell him that he should come up here quickly! It is something very important.”

My servant departed with hurried steps and I walked several paces further, partly to watch the strange ‘star’ and partly to avoid any further questions.

Luckily Ali *Bei* had heard that I had ascended to the rim of the valley and had decided to follow me. Halef met up with him on his way down and led him to me.

“What do you wish to show me, Emir?”

I extended my arm.

"Look steadily there! You will see the twinkle of a star. Now!"

"I see it."

"It is gone now. Do you know it?"

"No. It is too low and does not belong to any constellation."

I stepped up to a bush and cut off some switches. One of them I drove into the ground and then positioned myself several paces ahead of it and directed the *Bei*;

"Kneel directly behind this switch. I will place another switch in line with it and the star. - Did you see it just now?"

"Yes, quite clearly." He replied.

"Where shall I place the switch? Here?" I indicated.

"A foot to the right."

"Here?"

"Yes, that is perfect."

"So! Now we continue to observe!"

"I saw it again just now!" he stated after a short while.

"Where? I will place a further switch."

The star was not in the same place. It was much further to our left.

"How far? Tell me!"

"Two foot from the previous one."

"Here?"

"Yes."

I pushed a third switch into the ground, and Ali *Bei* continued to observe.

"There, I saw it again," he said a moment later.

"Where?"

"Not to the left, now it is to the right."

"Good, that was what I wanted to show you. You may get up now."

The group had observed my conduct were and puzzled, and even Ali *Bei* could not understand the reasoning behind it.

"Why did you need to show me this star?"

"Because it is not a star!"

"What else could it be? A torch?"

"Well, if it were just one torch that would be peculiar in itself, but there are a whole line of torches."

"Why do you think that?"

"It cannot be a star because it sits below the crest of the mountain that lies over there. That there are many torches is obvious from the experiment that we have just conducted. Over there, many people are either walking or riding with torches or lanterns that from time to time flash their light over here."

The *Bei* uttered a cry of amazement.

"You are right, Emir!"

"Who might it be?" I asked him.

"Not pilgrims, for they would come to Sheik Adi via Baadri."

"Then think of the Turks!"

"Lord! Would that be possible?"

"That I do not know, for the lay of the land is not known to me. Describe it to me, *Bei*!"

"Directly from here is the way to Baadri, and here, further to the left is the way to Aïn Sifni. If you divide that way into three parts; follow the first third and you come to the place where the lights are, to your left is the water that flows to Sheik Adi."

"Can one ride beside the water?"

"Yes."

"And in this manner one comes to Sheik Adi?"

"Yes."

"Then a great and mighty error has been committed!"

"How so?"

"You have placed lookouts towards Baadri and Kaloni, but none towards Aïn Sifni."

"The Turks could not come that way. The people of Aïn Sifni would inform us."

"But if the Turks do not come via Aïn Sifni, if instead they cross the Khausser at Jeraijah, then they would be between Aïn Sifni and here, could they then try to reach this valley? If so I believe that they would then be moving in the same direction as those lights. See, they are again moving to the left!"

"Emir, perhaps your supposition is correct. I will dispatch more sentries at once!"

"And I will observe this star more closely. Do you have a man who knows this area well?"

"No-one knows it better than Selek."

"He is a good horseman, he shall guide me!"

We descended as fast as possible. The last part of our discussion was spoken so softly that no one, in particular the *Bashi-Bozuk*, could have heard. Selek was soon located and given a horse, which he, with all his weapons, mounted. Halef was also to come with us. I could depend on him more than any other. Twenty minutes after I first saw the 'star' we raced along the path towards Aïn Sifni. We halted on the next rise. I surveyed the semi-darkness before us and finally saw the flare again. I made Selek aware of it.

"Emir, that is no star, those are no torches either for such would cast a wider glow. Those are lanterns."

"I must get closer. Do you know the area well?"

"I will lead you; I know every rock and every bush. Keep close behind me and keep your horse under control!"

He turned away from the water on our right and we then clambered across rocks and through brush at a trot. It was a terrible ride but after a good fifteen minutes we could distinguish individual lights. And after a second fifteen minutes, during which they disappeared behind a rise before us, we reached the crest and could see quite clearly that there was a long line of lanterns in front of us. Of what this column consisted, we could not determine; but we noted that the line disappeared and that it did not reappear again.

"Is there another hill over there?"

"No. It is flat land," answered Selek.

"Or perhaps a trough, a valley, in which these lights could disappear?"

"No."

"Or a forest . . ."

"Yes, Emir," he interrupted quickly. "Where the lights disappeared there is a small olive grove."

"Ah! You will remain here with the horses and wait for us. Halef will accompany me."

"Lord, take me as well," begged Selek.

"These animals will betray us."

"We will tether them!"

"My stallion is too valuable to leave unguarded. Besides you do not possess the skill of sneaking up on an enemy. They might hear you or even see you."

"Emir, I do know how it is done!"

"Be quiet!" Halef interceded. "Even I thought I knew how to creep into a *duar* to seize the best horse; but when I had to do it for the *Effendi*, I shamed myself like a child! But console yourself, for Allah did not intend that you become a lizard!"

We left our weapons behind and made our way ahead. It was just light enough so that we could easily recognize a man at fifty paces. After about ten minutes a small, dark shape loomed in front of us, the dimensions of which increased with every step we took - this was the olive grove. When we were within about five or six minutes walking distance from the grove we stopped and listened intently. Not the slightest sound could be heard.

"Walk directly behind me so that we appear as one!"

I wore only a jacket and trousers, both of a dark color; on my head I wore a tarbush from which I had unwound the turban cloth. Thus I was not easily distinguishable from the unlit terrain. With Halef it was likewise.

Silently we crept on. Suddenly we heard the sound of breaking twigs. We laid ourselves on the ground and slithered forward. The cracking and creaking sound became louder.

"They are collecting wood, perhaps they intend to make a fire." I said softly.

"Good for us, *Sihdi*!" Halef whispered.

Soon we reached the far edge of the grove. The snorting of animals and the voices of men became audible. We were lying next to a thick bush. I indicated this to Halef and whispered:

"You hide here and wait for me, Halef."

"Master, I cannot leave you, I will follow you!"

"You would betray me. To creep along silently in a forest is more difficult than in an open field. I wanted you along so you could cover my back. You remain here, even if you hear gunfire. If I call you, then you come to me as quickly as possible."

"And if you neither return nor call?"

"Then, after half an hour has passed, you creep forward and see what has happened to me."

"*Sihdi*, if they kill you, then I shall kill them all!"

I ignored this assurance for I was already creeping on, but I had not gotten far before I heard a loud, commanding voice call out:

"*Et atesh* - build a fire and light it!"

The voice came from a distance of perhaps a hundred feet. I could therefore move on unconcerned. I then heard the crackling of flames and soon noted a glow that spread through the trees almost up to my position. This of course would make my intentions more difficult to achieve.

"*Tashlar atesh jewresinde* - put stones around the fire!"
The same voice commanded.

That order must have been followed immediately for the glow diminished at once and I could proceed more easily. I crept from bough to bough and waited behind each until I was sure that I had not been discovered. Luckily the extra care was unnecessary; I was not in an American forest, and the good people that I had before me appeared not to have the slightest idea that someone would have the audacity to eavesdrop on them.

Thus I advanced further until I reached a tree, the roots of which sprouted shoots so plentiful that I anticipated no problem in finding a good hiding place between them. I could wish for nothing better, for nearby sat two men who deserved my closer attention - they were two Turkish officers.

With some care I managed to settle myself between the shoots and could now watch the scene as it unfolded before me.

In the clearing before the grove stood four mountain cannons, or rather two cannons and two howitzers, and at the edge of the wood about twenty mules had been tethered; these beasts were clearly used for transporting the weapons. Usually each cannon would require four or five mules for transportation, one for the barrel, one for the gun carriage and two to four mules had to carry the munitions.

The *topji* [artillerymen] had settled down comfortably; they had stretched out on the ground and talked quietly amongst themselves. But the two officers had a desire to drink coffee and smoke their *Jibuk*; this was why the fire had been lit and a small kettle rested over it on some stones. One of these two heroes was a *Jüs Bashi* [captain] and the other was a *Mülasim* [lieutenant]. The *Jüs Bashi* appeared to be quite unsophisticated. The image of an extremely easygoing and fat German baker came to mind, one who was to play a wild Turk in some amateur theatre production and had, in order to play his part, hired his ensemble from a costume shop for one and a half Marks. It was almost the same with the *Mülasim*. A sixty year old crone, dressed in harem trousers and an *Osmanli* jacket who had inexplicable thoughts of baked fish whilst going to a ball, would look just like him. I felt the urge to step out from behind the tree and surprise them with these flowery words:

"A wonderful good evening, master dolt, I'll announce myself, miss beanpole; what news? Thank you, thank you, I will be so bold!"

Of course the words that I did hear were a lot less comforting. I was so close to them that I could hear everything.

"*Toplerimiz chosh* - our cannons are good!" rumbled the *jus bashi.*

"*Pek chosh* - very good!" wheedled the *Mülasim.*

"*Atar-iz, atar-iz hepsi* - we will shoot, we will shoot them all!"

"*Hepsi* - All!" sounded the echo.

"*Japar-iz kazangdshü* - we will seize much loot!"

"*Jok kazangdshü* - much loot!"

"*Oladshag-iz ji*jid - we will be courageous!"

"*Pek jijid* - very courageous!"

"*Binar-iz* - we will be moved up in rank!" [See Translation Note Ch 26. 1]

"*Jüksek, ghajet jüksek* - high, extremely high!"

"*Tütar-iz sonra tütünü adshemli* - then we smoke Persian tobacco!"

"*Tütünü shirazli* - tobacco from Shiraz!"

"*Ile ijar-iz kawehji arabli* - and drink Arabian coffee!"

"*Kawehji mokkahli* - coffee from Mokka!"

"*Jesidiler gerek olar-lar ölmek hepsi* - all the Jesidi must die!"

"*Hepsi* - all!"

"*Fenalar* - those villains!"

"*Oghanlar* - those rascals!"

"*Na paklar, utanmazlar* - those unclean, those unrepentant!"

"*Kiöpekler* - those dogs!"

"*Öldirar-iz onlari* - we will kill them!"

"*Jarin sabah tiz* - at dawn tomorrow!"

"*Tabiatli, dir doghru* - of course, that is clear!"

I had now seen and heard enough; so I retreated, slowly, carefully at first but then more quickly. I even rose from the ground, an act that caused Halef to wonder when I reached him.

"Who is it, *Sihdi*?"

"Artillerymen. Come we do not have much time!"

"Do we go upright?"

"Yes."

We soon reached our horses, mounted and rode back from whence we came. Of course we covered the distance to Sheik Adi much faster than on the way out. Life there continued on much the same.

I heard that Ali *Bei* was at the Shrine and I met up with him and Mir Sheik Khan in the courtyard of the same. He came to me full of expectation and led me to the Khan.

"What have you discovered?" he asked.

"Cannons!"

"Oh!" the fear in his voice was obvious. "How many?"

"Four small mountain cannons."

"And what is their purpose?"

"Sheik Adi is to be obliterated by them. Whilst the *Askeri* [Infantry] attacks from Baadri and Kaloni, the artillery will play their part down by the water. The plan is not a bad one, for from that position the whole valley can be strafed. The only difficulty would have been bringing the cannons unnoticed over the mountains; and that has been done successfully; they used mules and with their help the cannons can be brought from their camp to Sheik Adi in an hour."

"What do we do, Emir?"

"Give me sixty men on horses right now and some *feneri* [lanterns], and you will have the cannons and their crew in Sheik Adi within two hours!"

"Prisoners?"

"Prisoners!"

"Lord, I will give you a hundred horsemen!"

"Very well, give me eighty immediately and tell them to wait for me by the water."

I departed and joined Halef and Selek, who waited by the horses.

"What will Ali *Bei* do?" asked Halef.

"Nothing, We will do it ourselves, if it is to be done at all."

"What is it, *Sihdi*? You laugh! Master, I know you and can read your face, are we going to get those cannons?"

"Of course! But I would like to get those cannons without spilling a drop of blood, and that is why we are going to take eighty horsemen with us."

We rode to the valley exit where we did not have to wait long for the eighty riders to join us.

I sent Selek and ten men ahead and followed with the rest a short distance behind. We reached the crest without sighting any of our foe. Selek had waited for us there and we dismounted. First I set out some men to act as sentries for our troop; then I left ten men behind with the horses and ordered them not to leave without an explicit order from me. With the remainder I crept towards the grove. We halted at a suitable distance from it and I alone went ahead. Once again I was successful in reaching the tree where I had hidden before. The Turks were settled in separate groups and were talking amongst themselves. I had hoped that they would be asleep, but sleep was the furthest thing from their minds, the anticipation of the forthcoming military action kept them alert. I counted thirty-four men, including the subalterns and officers, and then made my way back to my troop.

"Hajji Halef and Selek, go and fetch your horses! Ride in an arc to the other side of the grove. They will stop you; tell the Turks that you are lost and that you are trying to reach Sheik Adi for the festivities. You will turn the attention of the *Osmanli* from us and onto yourselves. The rest will be our concern. Go!"

I divided the rest of the men and formed them into two single files, the reason for this was to encircle the grove from three sides. I provided the required directions after which we laid ourselves onto the ground and began to creep forwards.

Naturally I was the fastest in this manner of progress. I had reached my tree and had already waited two minutes when the sound of horses' hooves could be heard. The fire was still burning, and so it was possible to see what was going on. The two officers had apparently done nothing other than smoke tobacco and drink coffee during my absence.

"*Sheik Adi kem juwa* - Sheik Adi is a terrible nest!" I heard the captain say.

"*Jum juwa* - exceedingly terrible!" answered the lieutenant.

"*Chalk onda shaïtani etar-lar* - the people there pray to the devil!"

"*Shaïtani; Allah onlari döj-sun de jassilt-sun de* - The devil! May Allah crush and pulverize them!"

"*Bu kylar-iz* - we will do that!"

"*He, onlari jirtar-iz* - yes, we will tear them apart!"

"*Büz bütün* - totally!"

I could follow the conversation up to this point and then the before-mentioned sound of horses' hooves came. The lieutenant lifted his head.

"*Bir kemse gel-yr* - someone comes!" he said.

The captain listened as well.

"*Kim dir olan* - who is it?" he asked.

"*Iki atlilar dirler; onu ishar-im* – I hear two riders."

They arose and the soldiers did likewise. Halef and Selek became visible in the fire's glow. The captain stepped towards them and drew his saber.

"Halt! Who are you?" he shouted at them.

At once the Turks surrounded them. My little Halef looked down at the officers from his elevated position in a manner that indicated to me that his impression of them was similar to the impression that these two had also left on me.

"I asked, who you are!" repeated the captain.

"People!"

"What kind of people?"

"Men!"

"What kind of men?"

"Men on horseback!"

"*Shaïtan sizi jer* - May the devil devour you! Answer properly or you shall receive the *bastinado*! Now, who are you?"

"We are *Jesidi*," Selek now answered in a timid voice.

"*Jesidi*? Ah! From where?"

"From Mecca." Halef answered.

"From Mecca? Allah ill Allah! Are there 'Devil-Worshippers' even there?"

"*Jarisi jük* - Almost five times a hundred thousand."

"*O kadar* - that many! *Allah kerihm*; he permits many weeds to grow among his crop! - Where are you going?"

"To Sheik Adi."

"*Ah, sizi war-benim* - ah, now I have you! What do you want there?"

"A great feast is being celebrated there."

"I know that. You dance and sing for the Devil and pray to a rooster that was hatched in the fires of *Jehennah*. Dismount! *Köle olar-siz* - You are my prisoners!"

"Prisoners? What have we done?"

"*Oghular shaïtanün siz* - You are the sons of the Devil. You must be whipped until your father has departed from you. *Ashaghy atlardan* - Down from your horses!"

He made the first move and both men were bodily dragged from their horses.

"Hand over your weapons!"

I knew that Halef would never obey such a command even under the current circumstances. He searchingly looked towards the fire and lifted his head high enough so that he could see me. Now he knew that he was safe. From the many, soft, rustling sounds behind me I knew that the enemy camp had now been completely surrounded.

"Our weapons?" asked Halef. "Listen, *Jüs Bashi*, allow us to tell you something!"

"What?"

"What we have to say we can only say to you and the *Mülasim*."

"I don't want to hear anything from you!"

"But it is important, very important!"

"What does it concern?"

"Listen!"

Halef whispered some words into the *Jüs Bashi's* ear, the immediate result of which was that the captain took a step backwards and looked at Halef with an impressed gaze. I later discovered what the clever Halef had whispered: "It concerns your money pouch!"

"Is that true?" asked the officer.

"It is true!"

"And you will be discreet about it?"

"As silent as a grave!"

"Swear it to me!"

"How shall I swear?"

"By Allah and the beard of . . . no, you are *Jesidi*. So swear by the Devil to whom you pray!"

"Well then! The Devil knows that I will not say anything later!"

"But he will tear you apart if you lie! Come, *Mülasim*; come you two!"

The four men moved over to the fire; I could hear all of their words.

"Now, speak!" ordered the captain.

"Free us! We will pay you."

"You have money?"

"We have money."

"Don't you know that your money already belongs to me? Everything that you have on you belongs to us."

"You will never find it. We come from Mecca, and whosoever makes such a journey knows how to hide their money well."

"I will find it!"

"You will not find it, even if you kill us and have everything searched meticulously. We 'Devil-Worshippers' have excellent means of making our money invisible."

"Allah is all-knowing!"

"But you are not Allah!"

"I can not let you go free."

"Why not?"

"You would betray us."

"Betray you? How so?"

"Do you not see that we are here to make war?"

"We will not betray you."

"But you are on your way to Sheik Adi!"

"Should we not be?"

"No."

"Then send us to where you desire!"

"Perhaps you wish to go to Baaweiza and wait there for two days?"

"We wish to do so."

"How much do you intend to pay for your freedom?"

"How much do you demand?"

"Fifteen-thousand *piaster* [roughly three thousand Mark] each."

"Lord, we are poor pilgrims. That much we do not have with us!"

"How much do you have?"

"We could perhaps give you five hundred."

"Five hundred? Scoundrel, you try to cheat us!"

"Perhaps we could even scrape together six hundred."

"You will hand over twelve thousand *piaster* and not a *para* less - that I swear to you by Mohammed. If you do not I will have you whipped until you do hand it over. You have said that you have the means to make your money invisible; you therefore carry a great deal of wealth on your persons, and I have the means to make your *piaster* visible!"

Halef pretended to be afraid.

"Lord, can you not make it less costly?"

"No."

"Then we must give it to you!"

"You scoundrels, now I see that you have much money on you! You will not be freed for twelve thousand *piaster*, you will have to pay what I first demanded, namely fifteen thousand."

"Excuse me, Lord, that is too little!"

The captain looked at little Halef, perplexed.

"What do you mean, you scoundrel?"

"I mean that each one of us is worth more than fifteen thousand *piaster*. Permit us to give you fifty thousand!"

"Man, are you crazy?"

"Or a hundred thousand!"

The 'baker'-*Jüs Bashi* was baffled and inflated his cheeks whilst looking at the thin face of the lieutenant:

"*Mülasim, ne sen-der* - lieutenant, what do you say?"

The lieutenant had his mouth open and admitted candidly:

"*Hij, sim hij* - nothing, nothing at all!"

"Same here! These people must be immensely rich!"

He then turned to Halef:

"Where do you keep this money?"

"Must you know this?"

"Yes."

"We have someone that will pay for us, but you can not see him."

"*Allah bizi koruny-sun* - Allah protect us! You refer to the Devil!"

"Should we summon him?"

"No, no, never! I am no *Jesidi*, I do not understand how to talk to him! I would die from fright!"

"You will not be afraid, for this *Shaïtan* comes in the form of a man. Here he is already!"

I had stepped out from behind the tree and with two quick steps stood before the two officers. They dashed apart, one to the left, the other to the right; but since my form did not appear so terrible to them, they stopped and stared at me wordlessly.

"*Jüs Bashi*," I said, "I have heard everything that you said this morning and this evening. You said that Sheik Adi was a terrible nest!"

A heavy gasp was their only response.

"You said that Allah should crush and pulverize the people there."

"Oh, oh!" was the reply.

"You said further that you would kill the rascals, the scoundrels, the unclean and the unrepentant, the dogs; and then you said that you hoped for much loot!"

The *Mülasim* was already half dead from fright and the *Jüs Bashi* could do nothing but moan.

"You hoped to be moved up in rank and smoke tobacco from Shiraz!"

"He knows all!" The fat captain managed to whimper fearfully.

"Yes, I know all. I will 'move' you. Do you know where to?"

He shook his head.

"To Sheik Adi, to the unclean and unrepentant, to those whom you planned to slaughter. I tell you now what a moment ago you said to these two men: *Köle olar-siz* - You are my prisoners!"

The soldiers could not comprehend what was happening; and stood huddled together in a group. A signal I had given along with my last words was enough. The *Jesidi* broke from cover and encircled them. Not one of the soldiers thought to offer the least resistance. They were all too stunned. The officers however came to their senses and made a move for the weapons in their belts.

"Stop, do not offer resistance!" I warned them whilst I pulled my revolver from my own belt. "Any man who reaches for a weapon will be shot!"

"Who are you?" asked the captain.

He sweated heavily. I felt sorry for the brave leader and his Don Quixote like second in command next to him. Their prospects of 'moving up in rank' were now non-existent.

"I am your friend and therefore it is my desire that you not be harmed by the *Jesidi*. Surrender your weapons!"

"But we need them!"

"For what?"

"We need to defend the cannons!"

Such naiveté was without precedent. I burst out laughing. I then consoled them:

"Be unconcerned; we will guard your cannons well!"

Some more words were exchanged, but in the end they surrendered their weapons.

"What will you do to us?" asked the *Jüs Bashi* with concern.

"That depends on how you conduct yourselves. Perhaps you will be executed, perhaps you will receive mercy if you are obedient."

"What shall we do?"

"Firstly, answer my questions honestly."

"Ask!"

"Are there more troops coming behind you?"

"No."

"Are you really the only ones here?"

"Yes."

"Then *Miralai* Omar Amed is a very incompetent man. In Sheik Adi are many thousand of armed warriors and he sends thirty men with four cannons against them. He should have at least sent an *Alai-Emini* with two hundred foot-soldiers along for cover. This *Miralai* thought that the *Jesidi* would be caught and killed as easily as flies. What orders did he give you?"

"We were to move the cannons up to the water unnoticed."

"And then?"

"And then to move along it until we are a half-hour in distance from Sheik Adi."

"Go on!"

"There we were to wait until a messenger arrives. When he arrives we would advance to the valley entrance and fire upon the *Jesidi* with cannon balls, case-shot and grenades."

"The advance we permit you, you will even go further than the valley entrance. But the firing will be done by others."

Now that it had happened, the Turks surrendered themselves to their destiny like true fatalists. They closed ranks and were then escorted by the *Jesidi*. The cannons were loaded onto the mules and followed in behind our troop. Of course we mounted our horses once we returned to where we had left them.

A half-hour from the valley of Sheik Adi I left the cannons under the protection of twenty of our men. This I did in light of the fact that a messenger was expected to arrive from the *Miralai*.

Near the entrance of the valley we were met by a large group of people. The rumor of our expedition had soon spread among the pilgrims, and they had gathered here to discover the result as soon as possible. Because of this, all shooting in the valley had been halted so that a deep silence existed all around. Everyone wished to be alert to the sound of gunfire, in case it had come to a serious battle between the Turks and our party.

The first to approach me was Ali *Bei*.

"Finally you return," he called, relieved, but he continued in a concerned voice: "but without the cannons! And there are people missing from your troop as well!"

"No one is missing and not one is wounded."

"Where are they?"

"With Halef and Selek outside of the valley where I have left the cannons."

"Why?"

"This *Jüs Bashi* told me that the *Miralai* would send a messenger to where the cannons are now located. They were to then advance to Sheik Adi and blanket it with cannon ball, case-shot and grenades. Do you have men that know how to handle these cannons?"

"Enough!"

"Then send them out there. They should exchange their clothes with the Turks, take the messenger prisoner when he arrives and then immediately commence the barrage. This will be our surest sign that the enemy is near and it will also lead to a hurried attack. What will you do with the prisoners?"

"I shall send them away and have them guarded."

"In the Idiz Valley?"

"No. That place may not be seen by anyone who is not a *Jesidi*. But there is a small canyon in which it is possible to hold the prisoners with just a few guards. Come!"

In his house his wife awaited me and served a considerable evening meal. He himself did not stay for he had to manage the exchange of clothes with the prisoners who were then to be led away. Those who received the uniforms of the Turks were trained gunners and soon departed to take over the cannons.

The stars began to fade when Ali *Bei* returned to me.

"Are you ready to go, Emir?"

"Where to?"

"To the Idiz Valley."

"Permit me to remain here!"

"Do you not wish to join in the battle?"

"No."

"Do you not wish to join us to see if we are courageous?"

"I will not join you, rather I wish to remain here in Sheik Adi."

"Lord, what are you thinking!"

"I am thinking that it would be the right thing to do."

"They will kill you!"

"No. I am under the protection of the Sultan and the *Mutessarif*."

"But you are our friend; you have captured their men and artillery, that will cost you your life!"

"Who will tell that to the Turks? I remain here with Halef and the *Bashi-Bozuk*. In this manner I can perhaps do more for you than if I were to fight at your side."

"You may be right, Emir; but when we fire you may be wounded or even killed!"

"I do not believe that, for I will take care not to stand in the way of your shot."

The door opened and a man entered. He was one of the sentries that had been dispatched by Ali *Bei*.

"Lord," he reported to him, "we have retreated, for the Turks are already in Baadri. They will be here within the hour."

"Return and tell your group that they are to remain close to the Turks but that they should remain hidden from their sight!"

We went outside of the house. The women and children moved past us and disappeared behind the shrine. Two messengers ran breathlessly up to us and reported:

"Lord, the Turks left Kaloni some time ago and are marching through the forest. They can be here in an hour."

"Position yourselves on the far side of the first valley and retreat when they arrive. Our people will await you on the crest!"

The messengers returned to their posts and the *Bei* disappeared for some time. I stood by the house and watched the people as they passed by. When the women and children had gone, the men followed, either on foot or on horseback; but the men did not disappear behind the shrine, rather they ascended the heights in the direction of Baadri and Kaloni, in order to leave this valley to the Turks. It was a strange feeling that I felt when I watched these dark shapes pass me by. One light after the next was extinguished; as was one torch after the next, and only the fires at the shrine and the two towers sent a double tongue of flames towards the sky. I was alone here. The *Bei's* relatives were gone; the *Buluk-Emini* was asleep atop the platform overhead, and Halef had not yet returned. Soon I heard the galloping hooves of a horse. Halef rode up to me. As he dismounted a crackling, rending sound and two dull thumps echoed from the lower end of the valley.

"What was that, Halef?"

"Falling trees. Ali *Bei* has ordered the trees to be felled in order to close off the valley and to protect the cannons from an attack by the Turks."

"That is a clever move! Where are the rest of the twenty men?"

"They had to remain with the cannons on the order of the *Bei*, and he has also ordered an additional thirty men for their protection."

"All together fifty men. They should be able to repel an attack."

"Where are the prisoners?" asked Halef.

"Already gone and guarded."

"And these men here go towards battle?"

"Yes."

"And us?"

"We remain here. I do not relish seeing the faces of the Turks when they realize that they have walked into a trap."

This thought appeared to satisfy Halef, as he did not complain about our remaining in Sheik Adi. He may have also thought that remaining here would be more dangerous than joining the combatants.

Chapter 27

"Where is Ifra?" asked Halef.

"He is asleep on the platform."

"He is a *ujkudishi* [sleepyhead], *Sihdi,* and that is probably why his captain gave him that donkey which brays all night. Does he know what is about to happen?"

"I don't believe so. And he shall not know how prepared we are - understand?"

Ali *Bei* returned once more to fetch his horse. He tried few more times to change my mind, but his attempts were also fruitless and in the end he was forced to leave us behind. He did so with the heartfelt wish that nothing untoward would happen to me, and assured me again that he would destroy all fifteen hundred Turks if I were to suffer at their hands. Lastly he begged me to spread out on the platform the large white cloth that hung inside the main room of the house. Whilst it remained visible from the valley rim, it would be a sign that I was well. Should the cloth be removed, he would deem that I was in danger and he would immediately handle the situation accordingly.

He mounted his horse and rode off, the last of all his tribe.

Dawn approached, the sky lightened and if one looked up one could discern the individual branches of the trees. From atop the opposite valley wall the clip-clop of hooves, made by the horse that Ali *Bei* rode, echoed back. Now, that even my translator had departed, I was alone with my two servants in the much-talked about valley of a secretive and enigmatic cult. Alone? Totally alone? Was it truly so, or did I hear steps emanating from the modest yet blessed house of '*El Shems'*?

A tall white figure emerged from the doorway and looked about. He saw me and approached. A long black beard hung down over his chest whilst the hair on his head was as white as snow and cascaded down his back. It was Pir Kamek; I recognized him now.

When he stood before me he asked in a voice that was almost severe; "You still here? When do you join the others?"

"I remain here."

"You stay? Why?"

"Because I will be of more use to your people here than elsewhere."

"That is possible, Emir; but you should go nonetheless!"

"I would ask you the same question: When are you going to join the others?"

"I remain here."

"Why?"

"Have you not seen the pyre over there?" he answered darkly. "It is keeping me here."

"Why is that?"

"Because the time has come for sacrifice, that is why I had it built."

"The Turks will interfere with this!"

"They will bring the sacrifice to me, and today I will celebrate the most important day of my life."

An eerie feeling started to envelop me when I listened to that hollow voice. But I overcame it and asked: "Did you not wish to speak with me about your book today, the one that Ali *Bei* lent to me?"

"Does it give you joy and is it useful to you?"

"Certainly!"

"Emir, I am a poor priest, only three things are mine; my life, my clothes and the book of which you speak. My life I return to the Pure, the Mighty and Compassionate One who loaned it to me. My clothes I leave to the elements in which my body will also be buried and the book I give to you, so that my spirit may speak with my people when times, lands, seas and worlds separate us."

Was this just the flowery, Oriental manner of speech or did he speak these words with a certain foreknowledge of his death? A shiver ran down my back that was difficult to shrug off.

"Pir Kamek, your gift is great; I find it difficult to accept!"

"Emir, I am fond of you. You will receive the book and when your eyes glance at the words written by my hand, then think of the last word that this hand will write in that book, therein is contained the bloody history of the *Jesidi* - the despised and the hunted."

I could not help myself and had to embrace him.

"I thank you, Pir Kamek! I too am fond of you, and when I open your book, your image will step forth and I will hear all the words that your mouth has spoken to me. But now you should leave Sheik Adi for there is still time to do so!"

"Do you see the shrine over there, in which is interred one who was hunted and killed. He did not flee. Does it not also say in your *Kitab* that one must not fear those that can only kill the body? I remain here, for I know that the *Osmanli* can not harm me and if they do kill me, what of it? Must not the dew rise towards the sun? Does not '*El Shems*', the bright one, die each day only to rise again? Is not death the entrance to a brighter, purer world? Have you ever heard a *Jesidi* speak of another's death? They say only that the dead are changed; for neither death nor grave exists, only life, nothing but life. That is why I know that I shall meet you again!"

After these words he walked away quickly and disappeared from sight behind the outer wall of the shrine.

I entered the house and climbed up to the platform. Once there I heard voices. Halef and Ifra were talking.

"All alone?" I heard Ifra ask.

"Yes."

"Where did they go, the many, the thousands?"

"Who knows!"

"And why did they go?"

"They ran away."

"From whom?"

"From you."

"From us? Hajji Halef Omar, I do not understand what you are saying!"

"Then I will explain it to you more clearly: They ran away from your *Mutessarif* and from your *Miralai* Omar Amed."

"But why?"

"Because the *Miralai* comes to attack Sheik Adi."

"*Allah akbar*, God is great, and the hand of the *Mutessarif* is mighty! Tell me if I may remain with our Emir or if I must fight under the command of the *Miralai*!"

"You must remain with us."

"*Hamdullillah*, Praise and thank Allah, for it is good with our Emir, whom I must protect!"

"You? When did you protect him?"

"Always, as long as he remains within the range of my voice."

Halef laughed and replied:

"Yes, you are the man for that! Do you know who the protector of the Emir is?"

"I am!"

"No, it is I!"

"Did not the *Mutessarif* himself deliver him into my care?"

"Has he himself not placed himself under my protection? And who matters more, my *Sihdi* or your *Suzhij* [literally: Nothingness, also nothing, emptiness, void, the most contemptuous expression that a Turk can use] of a *Mutessarif*?"

"Halef Omar, watch your tongue! If I were to mention this word to the *Mutessarif*!"

"Do you believe that I fear him? I am Hajji Halef Omar Ben Hajji Abu Abbas Ibn Hajji Dawuhd al Gossarah!"

"And my name is Ifra, I belong to the courageous *Bashi-Bozuk* of the Sultan and was made *Buluk-Emini* for my heroic deeds! Only one person cares for you, but the Padishah and the whole Osmanian State cares for me!"

"I would truly like to know what benefit you derive from this care!"

"What benefits? - I will list them for you! I get a monthly salary of thirty five *piaster* and each day I receive two pounds of bread, seventeen ounces of salt, one and a half ounces of condiments as well as soap, oil and boot polish!"

"And for that you perform heroic deeds?"

"Yes, many and great ones too!"

"Those I have to see!"

"What? You don't believe me! What happened to my nose then, which I no longer have! That came about in the conflict between the Druse and the Maronites of Jebel Libanon. We were sent there to fight for peace and obedience of the law. In one of the battles I hacked about me in a rage. The enemy aimed for my head. I tried to avoid the blow and stepped back, and that is why the blow did not strike my head but my no . . . ooh, aah . . . what was that?"

"Yes, what was that? A report from a cannon!"

Halef was right, a cannon had been fired, and that had prematurely ended the tale of the little *Buluk-Emini*. Certainly it was the signal that our artillerymen had fired to inform us that the adjutant of the *Miralai* had arrived and had been captured by them. My two servants hurried down from above.

"*Sihdi*, they are shooting!" called Halef, as he attended to the cocks of his pistols.

"With cannons!" added Ifra.

"Good! Fetch our horses and move them to the inner courtyard!"

"And my donkey too?"

"Yes. And then lock the gate!"

I fetched the white cloth myself and spread it atop the platform. I then arranged some blankets and made myself comfortable on top of them, but in such a manner that I would be noticed from below. My two servants later settled themselves not far from me.

In the meantime it had become light and one was able to see clearly. The fog was already rising from the valley, but the torches by the shrine were still burning, a view that was painful to the eyes.

So passed five, even ten minutes of anticipation. Then I heard a horse whinny from this side of the valley, and another and a third answered from the opposite side of the valley. It was clear that the troops advanced simultaneously down into the valley bed. The orders of the *Miralai* were followed in a strict and timely manner.

"They are coming!" said Halef.

"Yes, they are coming!" confirmed Ifra. "Lord, if they think that we are *Jesidi* and shoot at us?"

"Then you push your donkey out, they will immediately recognize it!"

There was no cavalry; the horses that had whinnied belonged to the officers. The hoof-beats of many horses would have been unmistakable. But as time passed, one could hear the sound of an approach and as it came closer one could distinguish that it was made by the feet of many people.

Finally a voice sounded from the shrine and two minutes later we heard the marching step of a column. I moved my head to look down. There were perhaps two hundred Arnauts, wonderful figures with wild faces, led by an *Alai-Emini* and two captains. They moved down the valley in closed rank. Behind them came a band of *Bashi-Bozuk* that dispersed to the right and the left searching out the unseen inhabitants of the valley. A small cavalcade of officers followed them: two *Jüs Bashi*, two *Alai-Emini* [regimental quartermaster or sergeant major], two *bimbashi* [major or battalion commander], one *Kaimakam* [lieutenant-colonel] and some *kol agassi* [staff officers or adjutants]. At the head of this troop was a tall, thin man with an extraordinarily craggy face, outfitted in the richly gold-decorated uniform of a regimental commander.

"That is *Miralai* Omar Amed!" whispered Ifra in an awed voice.

"Who is the civilian at his side?" I asked.

At the leader's side rode a man whose features were most notable. I know that one should not compare a man with a creature of the animal kingdom; but human physiognomy does exist that quite naturally reminds one of specific animal breeds. I have seen faces that have resembled that of a monkey, a bulldog or a cat; certain facial features caused me to think of oxen, donkeys, owls, weasels, proboscideans, foxes or bears. One may be a phrenologist and a physiognomist or not, but one will soon realize, through the application of physiognomy, that the posture, gait, expression, the entire behavior of a certain human has a similarity to a particular species and the ways of the animal of which one is reminded. The face of the man that I now saw had something raptorial about it, it was entirely falcon-like.

"That is the *Makrej* [Head of the Court] of Mosul, the confidant of the *Mutessarif*," answered the *Buluk-Emini*.

What was this *Makrej's* purpose here that he accompanied the troops? I could not contemplate further on this as suddenly the roar of first one cannon, and then another, sounded. A chaotic, confused howling, screaming and shouting arose and I heard the thudding of many feet as though a huge crowd were running towards me. The cavalcade had just halted below my vantage point.

"What was that?" shouted the *Miralai*.

"Two cannon shots!" answered the *Makrej*.

"Quite correct!" mocked the colonel. "Any officer would have had difficulty recognizing this. But, Allah, what is this!"

The Arnauts that had marched past only moments before came running back, screaming and in disarray. Many of them were bloody and torn. But all of them were in the grip of fear.

"Halt!" thundered the colonel. "What happened?"

"We were fired upon with case-shot. The *Alai-Emini* is dead and so is one of the captains; many others are lying there wounded."

"*Allah onlari boza-uz* - May Allah destroy them! Firing on their own people! I will have them all whipped to death. Nasir Agassi, ride ahead and sort these dogs out!"

This order was directed at one of the *Kol Agassi*, who was with his men. He was the very man whom I had surprised at the creek in Baadri and for whom I had later won his freedom. He gave his horse a taste of his spurs and returned after a short while.

"Lord, they are not our men, they are *Jesidi*, it is they who fired the shots. They allowed me to approach so they could shout this fact to me."

"Where are our cannons?"

"They are in the hands of the *Jesidi*; they have fired upon us with them; they took the cannons from the *Jüs Bashi* during the night."

The colonel uttered a terrible curse.

"That scoundrel shall regret this! Where is he?"

"A prisoner, with all his men."

"Prisoner? With all his men? Without having defended himself!"

In rage he rammed his spurs so hard into his horse's sides that his animal rose almost vertically into the air; then he asked further:

"Where are these *Jesidi*, these 'Men of the Devil', these *giaurs* among *giaurs*? I long to capture them, to whip them and to kill them, but none of them can be found! Have they gone? We will find them. But before we do, get back my cannons! The men from Diarbekir have joined us. Send them forward and then send the dogs from Kjerkjuk behind them!"

The *kol agassi* rode ahead and immediately the infantry from Diarbekir started to follow. The colonel and his staff moved aside. The troops marched past him. I could not see more as a curve in the valley hid them from view; but less than a minute later, a cannon roared, a second, a third and a fourth and then the previous scene repeated itself. The survivors and those with minor wounds came running back, they had left their dead and critically wounded behind. The colonel rode among them and chastised them with the flat of his saber blade.

"Stand, you cowards; stand, otherwise I will send you to *Jehennah* with my own hand! *Agassi*, send down the dragoons!"

The adjutant hurried away. The fleeing men gathered themselves and many of the *Bashi-Bozuk* came to report that the buildings were empty.

"Destroy these nests; burn everything, and search for tracks. I have to know where these unbelievers went!"

The time had come for me to be useful, if I was to be useful at all.

"Halef, if something evil befalls me, then remove that white cloth. It will be a sign for Ali *Bei*!"

After these words I arose and was immediately noticed from below.

"Ah," shouted the *Miralai*, "there is one! Come down you son of a dog; I want information!"

I nodded and stepped back.

"Halef, lock the door behind me and let no-one in without my permission. When I call your name, open up at once!"

We both went downstairs and I stepped out of the house alone; the door closed and was locked behind me. At once the officers formed a circle around me.

"*Kurd, sen* - Worm, that you are, answer my questions, otherwise I will have you butchered!" the colonel ordered me.

"Worm?" I asked quietly. "Take this and read!"

He flashed a look of rage at me, but nonetheless snatched the Sultan's *Firman* from my hand. When he saw the seal, he pressed the parchment to his brow, but only lightly and almost with disdain, then browsed through the content.

"You are a Frank?"

"A *Nemje*."

"That's all the same! What are you doing here?"

"I came to study the customs of the *Jesidi*," I answered whilst I took back the passport.

"What for! What has this *Bu-djeruldi* to do with me! Where you in Mosul with the *Mutessarif*?"

"Yes."

"Did you get permission from him to be here?"

"Yes. Here it is."

I handed the second document to him, he read it and returned it to me.

"That is right; but . . ."

He halted, for a clatter of heavy rifle-fire erupted from the opposite side of the valley, and at the same time the fast clatter of horses' hooves could be heard.

"*Shaïtan*! What is that up there?"

This question was partly directed at me and so I answered:

"Those are the *Jesidi*. You are surrounded and any resistance is useless."

He straightened in his saddle.

"Dog!" he roared at me.

"Forget this word, *Miralai*! If you utter it again, I will leave!"

"You will stay!"

"Who will stop me? I will give you all the information you want, but know this, I am not accustomed to placing myself under the command of a *Miralai*. I have shown you under whose protection I stand, and should this not help, I know how to protect myself!"

"Ah!"

He lifted his hand and made to strike me.

"Halef!"

As I shouted this, I pushed myself through the ring of horses; the door opened and just as it was closed and locked behind me, a pistol bullet bit into the wood. The *Miralai* had shot at me.

"That was intended for you, *Sihdi*!" Halef said with concern.

"Come upstairs!"

Whilst we climbed the stairs, we heard confused shouting intermingled with the trampling of horses, and as I reached the top, I saw the rearguard of the dragoons disappear behind the curve of the valley. It was pure madness to send them head-on against artillery that could only have been silenced by an attack from the mountains on their flanks. The *Miralai* was not at all clear about his situation. It was lucky for him that Ali *Bei* wished to spare lives; for above the shrine the Turks stood in dense ranks halfway up the mountain paths, and every bullet fired by the *Jesidi* was bound to hit one or more of them.

The thunder of the cannon erupted anew. The case-shot and the grenades must have been causing terrible devastation among the riders if they were carefully aimed, and this was soon confirmed; for the entire lower section of the valley was soon covered with fleeing riders, running dragoons and riderless horses.

The *Miralai* was utterly frozen with rage and horror; but the realization that the situation had to be handled differently must have dawned on him. He noticed my head as I was looking down and beckoned to me. I arose.

"Come down!"

"What for?"

"I have questions to ask of you."

"And shoot at me?"

"It was not intended for you!"

"Well then, ask! I will answer you from up here; you will hear my words equally well, just as though I stood next to you. But . . ." - and I gave Halef a sign that he immediately understood - " . . . but do you see this man? He is my servant; he has a flintlock in his hands and aims it at you. If just one weapon is aimed at me he will shoot you, *Miralai*, and then I will say as you did, that is: It was not intended for you!"

Halef kneeled close to the edge of the platform and aimed his flintlock at the head of the colonel. The *Miralai's* face changed color, whether from fear or rage, I do not know.

"Put away that weapon!" he shouted.

"It stays!"

"For heaven's sake, I have almost two thousand soldiers here; I can crush you!"

"And I have this one with me; I can send you to your fathers with just one move of my hand!"

"My men would wreak terrible vengeance!"

"Many of them would die before they could successfully enter this house. Besides, the valley is ringed by four thousand warriors, for whom it is but a simple task to annihilate all of you within half an hour."

"How many do you say?"

"Four thousand. Look up towards the valley rim! Do you not see head beside head? There, a man is climbing down and is waving a white turban cloth. It is certainly a messenger from the *Bei* of Baadri, who is to negotiate with you. Permit him safe passage and receive him as custom demands; that would serve you best!"

"I don't need your lecture. Let the rebel come! Where are all the *Jesidi*?"

"Let it be told to you! Ali *Bei* learned that you were to attack the pilgrims. He sent out scouts and had the troops from Mosul, Diarbekir and Kjerkjuk watched. The women and children were delivered to safety. He did not prevent your advance, but instead left the valley and trapped you in it. He is, in number of warriors, superior to you as well as with respect to terrain. He has captured your artillery with its entire ammunition. You are doomed if you do not negotiate in a gracious manner with his messenger!"

"I thank you, *Frank*! I will first handle him and then you. You have the *Budjeruldi* of the Sultan and the *Firman* of the *Mutessarif* and yet you fraternize with their enemies. You are a traitor and will be punished!"

The *Nasir Agassi*, the adjutant, pushed his horse through to the colonel's side and spoke some words with him. The colonel pointed at me and asked:

"It was him?"

"It was. He does not belong with the enemy, he is only their guest and he did save my life."

"We will talk about this further, but now come into that building!"

They rode towards the Temple of the Sun, dismounted before it and entered the same.

In the meantime the negotiator had came down the slope following a straight path, jumping from rock to rock and crossing the brook. He headed towards the shrine and entered. Not a shot was fired; complete silence reigned all about and only the steps of the soldiers could be heard as they came down from the valley slopes where they felt themselves exposed.

Well over half an hour passed. Then the negotiator again appeared outside the shrine, but he was not alone - he was dragged. They had bound him. The *Miralai*, who also appeared at the entrance looked about, saw the pyre and pointed towards it. Ten Arnauts were called for; they took hold of the negotiator and carried him to the wooden pile. Whilst he was held by some, the remainder retrieved their rifles - he was going to be executed.

"Halt!" I shouted at the colonel. "What are your intentions? He is a messenger and therefore an inviolate person!"

"He is a rebel, like yourself. First him, then you, for now we know who ambushed the artillerymen!"

He signaled and the shots cracked; the messenger was dead. But then something happened; a man pushed himself through the ranks of soldiers. It was Pir Kamek. He reached the pyre and kneeled besides the dead man.

"Ah, another!" shouted the colonel and marched towards him. "Stand up and answer me!"

I could not hear more as the distance between us was too great. I saw only the ceremonial gestures of the *Pir* and the angry gestures of the *Miralai*. Then I noticed that the *Pir* put his hands into the pyre and a few seconds later flames where leaping up from it. A realization flashed through me. Dear God, did he mean such a sacrifice, such a penalty, such a vengeance for the murderer of his wife and sons!

The *Pir* was manhandled and pulled away from the pile, but it was already too late to extinguish the flames, for the tar suitably nourished the flames. In the span of hardly a minute they had grown in size and reached towards the sky.

The *Pir* was surrounded and held fast; the *Miralai* appeared to wish to leave. But he returned to the Priest's side. They spoke together, the colonel excitedly but the *Pir* in utter peace and with closed eyes. Suddenly he opened them and threw off the two soldiers that held him and grabbed the colonel. With the strength of a giant he lifted him off the ground and with two leaps he stood before the pyre; one more and they both disappeared in the searing flames which closed around them. Movements within the fire suggested that the two, ordained to die by the flame, were fighting with each other, one to save his life, the other to ensure death.

I felt as though I was plunged into the coldest winter waters. So this was why this day was 'the most important day of his life', as he, the priest, had said to me? Yes, the most important day of one's life is the one when one leaves this life and entrusts oneself to the burning floods of eternity. So this terrible vengeance against the *Miralai* was the 'last word' that his hand was to write in the book, in which was written the bloody history of the *Jesidi* - the despised and the hunted? So this fire was the 'element' in which his body and his clothes were to be buried?

Terrible! I closed my eyes. I did not want to see any more, know anything more; I went down into the room and laid myself on the cushions with my face towards the wall. For a long time it was relatively quiet outside, but then the shooting started anew. This did not concern me. If I were in danger, Halef would surely tell me. I only saw the long white hair, the flowing black beard and the gold-spangled uniform disappear in the fiery vapors of the pyre. My God, how valuable, how immensely precious is the life of a human being, and yet . . . yet . . . yet . . .!

In this manner a considerable amount of time passed; the shooting stopped and I heard steps on the stairs. Halef entered.

"*Sihdi*, you should come onto the roof!"

"Why?"

"An officer is asking for you."

I arose and made my way upstairs. A single glance informed me of the state of things. The *Jesidi* no longer held the heights, they had made their way down towards the valley floor over time. Behind every rock, every tree, every bush one of them was hidden, ready to send their bullets from these safe places. In the lower part of the valley, the *Jesidi* had even reached the valley floor under the protection of the artillery, and had settled themselves behind the bushes by the brook. Only one final thing was left undone: if the artillery were to advance just a little, then with just a few salvos all of the Turks would be eradicated.

Before the house stood *Nasir Agassi*.

"Lord, would you speak with us once more?" he asked.

"What do you have to say to me?"

"We wish to send a messenger to Ali *Bei*, and because the *Miralai*, may Allah grant him entry to Paradise" - he indicated the still smoking pyre – "has killed the messenger of the *Jesidi*, no one among us can go. Will you do it?"

" I will. What should I say?"

"The *Kaimakam* will give you your orders. He is now in command and is in that house. Come over!"

"Orders? Your *Kaimakam* can not order me to do anything. What I do, I do of my own free will. The *Kaimakam* may come and tell me what he wants. This house is open to him and at most one other person. Anyone else that dares approach I will have shot."

"Who besides you is in the house?"

"My servant and a *Khawass* of the *Mutessarif*, a *Bashi-Bozuk*."

"What is his name?"

"He is the *Buluk-Emini* Ifra."

"Ifra? With his donkey?"

"Yes." I laughed.

"Then you are the foreigner who saved the Arnaut officers from the *bastinado* and won the friendship of the *Mutessarif*?"

"I am he."

"Then wait a little, Lord! The *Kaimakam* will come at once."

Truly only a short time passed before the *Kaimakam* came towards the house from the shrine across the way. Only the *Makrej* accompanied him.

"Halef, open the door for them and lead them into the room below. But lock the door again and then return here. If someone comes near the house uninvited, you shoot at him!"

I went downstairs. The two men were of high office, but that made no difference to me; I received them with a calculated manner and indicated that they should be seated. When they had done so, I formulated my question without specifically welcoming them:

"My servant has let you in. Has he told you how to address me?"

"No."

"Here I am called Hajji Emir Kara Ben Nemsi. I know who you are. What do you have to tell me?"

"You are a Hajji?" asked the *Makrej*.

"Yes."

"Then you were in Mecca?"

"Yes. Do you not see the Koran hanging from my neck and the small flask that contains the waters of Zem-Zem?"

"We believed you to be a *giaur*!"

"Did you come to tell me this?"

"No. We beg you to go to Ali *Bei* with our instructions."

"Will you give me safe passage?"

"Yes."

"To me and my servant?"

"Yes."

"What shall I tell him?"

"That he is to lay down his arms and once again be obedient to the *Mutessarif*."

"And then?" I asked, curious as to what was still to come.

"Then the penance that the governor will demand from him will be as merciful as possible."

"You are a *Makrej* of Mosul, and this man is *Kaimakam* and commander of the troops here. It is he who has to impart his instructions to me, not you."

"I am acting as the representative of the *Mutessarif* under his command."

With these words the man with the falcon physiognomy tried to make himself as important as possible.

"Do you have this authority in writing?"

"No."

"Then you count as little as anyone else here!"

"The *Kaimakam* will confirm it!"

"Only a written authority can legitimize you, nothing else. Go and fetch it. The *Mutessarif* of Mosul would only permit a man of knowledge to represent him."

"Is your intention to insult me?"

"No. I am only stating that you are no officer and do not understand matters of a military nature and therefore have nothing to say here."

"Emir!" he shouted whilst glaring at me in rage.

"Shall I prove the truth of my words to you? You are locked in here so that not one of you can escape; it would take less than half an hour and you would be shot down and beyond help. And the way things stand, I should tell the *Bei* that he should down his weapons? He would consider me mad. The *Miralai*, may Allah be merciful and compassionate to him, has led fifteen hundred valiant warriors to their doom. To the *Kaimakam* falls the honorable duty of saving these men from their fate; if he is successful, then he will have behaved as a good officer and a hero. But with pretentious words, behind which lurk fear and betrayal, he will not succeed. I will only talk with him. In military matters only warriors shall have a say."

"Yet still you must listen to me also!"

"I do not see why!"

"There are matters to discuss that concern the law and I am a *Makrej*!"

"Be what you will! You can not show me that authority and that is why we are finished with one another!"

I had a definite aversion towards this man, but I would not have expressed myself so strongly if he had presented himself differently and if I had not harbored the conviction that he carried the majority of the blame for the current situation. Why did this officer of the court join this expedition anyway? It could only be to make the *Jesidi* feel the power of the *Osmanli* by way of the Moslem law once they were defeated.

I now turned to the *Kaimakam*:

"What shall I tell the *Bei*, if he asks me why you attacked Sheik Adi?"

"We were to capture two murderers and the *Jesidi* did not make timely payment of the *haraj* [A tax levied against non-Mohammedans]." He replied.

"The *Bei* will be most surprised at this reason. The murderers you will have to seek among yourselves; that he will make clear to you, and the *haraj* you could have obtained in a different manner. What shall I tell him of your decision?"

"Tell him that he might send me a man with whom I can negotiate the conditions of my withdrawal!"

"And if he asks me for the detail of these conditions?"

"I demand the return of our artillery in the name of the *Mutessarif*. I demand that for every wounded or dead man a reparation price be paid. I demand the payment of the withheld *haraj*, and I demand a sum that I have still to determine for not burning the village."

"*Allah kerihm*, God is merciful! He has given you a mouth that knows well how to demand. You need not tell me more; it is enough. The rest you can tell to Ali *Bei* yourself. I will go to him at once and bring you an answer myself or have an answer sent by messenger."

"Tell him also that he should free our artillerymen and that he must compensate them for their ordeal!"

"This too I will tell him; but I fear that he too will demand compensation for the surprise you created for him. Now we are finished; I will make ready, but I warn you of one thing. If you wreak havoc in Sheik Adi, then the *Bei* will show you no mercy."

I arose. They did the same and left.

I now called Halef and Ifra down to me since they had to saddle the animals. This took but a little time. Then we left the house and climbed into our saddles.

"Wait here, I will return shortly!"

After I spoke these words I first rode a short distance down the valley to see the effect of the artillery with my own eyes. It was a horrifying scene, but one that was moderated by the *Jesidi* who had picked up the wounded Turks and did everything possible to help and comfort them. How different it would have been if the *Osmanli* had been successful in their attack! I turned away despite the victors joyful calls towards me from behind their barricades, I joined up with

Halef and Ifra and rode towards the brook in order to reach the path to Baadri; for on the heights on that side I believed the *Bei* to be positioned.

As I rode past the shrine, the *Kaimakam* with his staff stood before it. He waved at me and I rode towards him.

"Tell the Sheik also that he must pay an compensatory sum for the death of the *Miralai*!"

"I believe that the *Makrej* of Mosul is making a great effort to discover even more demands and I suppose that the *Bei* will demand a considerable atonement for the murder of his negotiator. But I will convey your words to him."

"You have a *Bashi-Bozuk* with you?"

"As you can see!"

"Who has assigned him to you?"

"The *Mutessarif*."

"Do you still need him?"

"Yes."

"We need him too."

"Then fetch yourself an order from the governor. When you show that to me I will release the *Buluk-Emini* to you!"

I rode on and passed many men with grim expressions on their faces. Many a hand twitched towards a dagger, but Nasir Agassi accompanied me until I was safe and then took his leave from me.

Chapter 28

The good byes were short for time was of the essence.

"*Effendi*, will we meet again?" asked Nasir Agassi.

"Allah is all-knowing, even in this, only we do not know."

"You are my savior, I will never forget you and I thank you. If we shall meet again, tell me how I may serve you."

"May God protect you! Perhaps I will see you again as a *Miralai*; then may your kismet be better than that of Omar Amed!"

We shook hands and parted. We would meet again at a time when I thought least about him.

A little distance further up the valley, behind some bushes, we encountered the first *Jesidi*, who had dared to advance this far in order to assure himself of a good aim upon the resumption of battle. He was Selek's son, my translator.

"Emir, are you well?" he called towards me.

"Quite well. Do you have Pir Kamek's book with you?"

"No. I have hidden it in a place where it can come to no harm."

"But if you shall die, then it would be lost!"

"No, *Effendi*. I have made its hiding place known to many others and those would have revealed it to you."

"Where is the *Bei*?"

"Above on the crest, from there one can best see the entire valley. Permit me to lead you!"

He slung his rifle over his shoulder and went ahead. We reached the top and it was interesting to look down from here upon the hiding places where the *Jesidi* stood, sat, squatted and lay, all of them ready to commence hostilities at a signal from their leader. Seeing the situation from this vantage point it was clear that the Turks did not have a chance, if they were not successful in reaching an agreement with their enemies. Here, we stood when Ali *Bei* and I observed the 'star' and now, only some hours later, this small sect, that had dared to do battle with the soldiers of the Sultan, were already turning out to be the victors.

We rode towards the left until we reached a rock that overhung the valley rim. Here sat the *Bei* with his staff that consisted of three barefooted *Jesidi*. He joyfully came towards me.

"I thank the Almighty who has preserved your health and being!" He said warmly. "Did you encounter anything abnormal?"

"No, otherwise I would have signaled you."

"Come here!"

I dismounted and followed him to the ledge. From here one could see everything clearly, the shrine, the *Bei's* house, the battery further down the valley behind the barricade and both of the valley walls.

"Do you see the white spot on my house?" he asked.

"Yes. It is the cloth."

"Had it disappeared, I would have signaled and five-hundred of my men would have stormed down under the protection of the cannons and would have held back the enemy."

"I thank you, *Bei*. Nothing happened to me aside from the *Miralai* shooting at me and missing,."

"That he shall regret!"

"He has already regretted it."

I told him all that had occurred, everything that I had seen, and reported to him the parting words I had received from the *Pir*. He listened attentively and was deeply moved but as I finished he said nothing more than: "He was heroic!"

He then sank into deep thought from which he roused only after some time.

"And what say you? They have killed my messenger?"

"They have executed him, shot him dead."

"Who gave the order for this?"

"Most likely the *Miralai*."

"Oh if he only lived!" he said through clenched teeth. "I had a feeling that this would happen to my messenger. I had told him that I would recommence the hostilities if he had not returned within half an hour. But I will avenge him; I will now give the signal that we are finally earnest!"

"Wait, for I have to talk with you beforehand. The Kaimakam, who is now in command, has sent me to you."

I told him my whole discussion with the lieutenant colonel and the *Makrej*, word for word. As I mentioned the latter, he wrinkled his brow in a dark expression, but he listened to me silently till the end.

"So the *Makrej* is with them! Oh, now I know whom we have to thank for all of this! He is the worst enemy of the *Jesidi*; he hates them; he is their vampyr, their bloodsucker, and he has turned every available murder into a legal reason to attack us and force us to pay a tribute. But my legation which I sent to Stambul will also go to the Anadoli Kasi Askeri [High Court Judge of Oriental Turkey], to present him with a letter from me, written for me by Pir Kamek. They both knew and were fond of each other and the *Pir* was his guest for a long time. He knows how to distinguish a lie from the truth and he will send us help."

"That I wish for you from the depth of my heart. But whom will you send to the Kaimakam? It can not be an ordinary man for he would be outwitted."

"Who will I send you ask? I will send no one. No one at all. Only I will speak with him. I am the head of my people; he is the leader of his, and only we two can make a decision. But I am the victor and he is the vanquished; he should come to me!"

"That is only fair!"

"I will wait for him here. I will give him safe passage; but if he is not here in thirty minutes, Then I will recommence hostilities and not stop until no *Osmanli* remains alive!"

He turned to his adjutants and spoke with them for a short while. Thereupon two departed. One of them picked up a white shawl, laid down his weapons and climbed down to the left where I had ascended earlier; but the other walked to the right along the length of the crest and then descended towards the place where the cannons were located.

Ali *Bei* then ordered some *Jesidi*, who were close by, to erect a tent for us. The necessary materials were already at hand. While they followed the order, I noticed that the barricade below opened. The cannons were brought through the gap and advanced along the brook until they reached the line held by the *Jesidi*, on the valley floor. There, many rocks could be transformed into a new barricade with the aid of some quickly felled trees.

Not twenty minutes had passed since the *Jesidi* were dispatched when the *Kaimakam* approached. He was accompanied by three Turkish soldiers and at his side rode - the *Makrej*. That was not at all clever of him; I perceived that from the dark look with which Ali *Bei* honored him.

The *Bei* entered the tent that had been erected in the meantime and seated himself on the carpet that formed the floor. I received the small group. The three soldiers remained before the tent but the others entered.

"Salaam!" greeted the *Kaimakam*.

The *Makrej* did not greet at all. He as the head of the Sultan's Court of Justice waited for the *Bei* of the 'Devil Worshippers' to welcome him. But the *Bei* did not take any notice of him, neither did he answer the greeting of the lieutenant-colonel. He only pointed at the carpet and said:

"*Kaimakam, komar-sen* - You may be seated!"

The *Kaimakam* seated himself in a dignified manner and the *Makrej* settled himself beside him.

"You have asked us to come to you," the officer started. "Why did you not come to us?"

"You err!" answered Ali *Bei* quite earnestly. "I have not asked you, I have simply informed you that I would blanket the *Osmanli* with case-shot if you did not come here. Is that a request? You ask further why I did not come to you. If I go to Mosul from Sheik Adi, I would search you out and not demand that you make the effort to find me; But you came from Mosul to Sheik Adi and surely know the rules of courtesy that demand you to come to me. Your question, by the way, demands that I make the situation, which we are about to discuss, clear to you. You are a servant of the Sultan and of the *Mutessarif*, an Officer, who by chance, commands a regiment; but I am a free Lord of the Kurds and a General to my warriors. Don't think that your rank is higher than mine . . ."

"I am not a servant of . . . "

"*Sus ol* - Silence! I am accustomed that I am heard till the end, remember that, *Kaimakam*! You have illegally and without prior notice trespassed into my domain, like a thief, like a robber with weapons in your hand. A robber I catch and kill just as it pleases me; but since you are a servant of the Sultan and of the *Mutessarif*, I will, before I exercise my power, reason with you amicably. That you and your people still live is thanks to my leniency and forbearance. Now tell me, who has the right to wait for the other to come to him, you or I!"

Surprise was written all over the *Kaimakam's* face, such a dissertation he had certainly not expected. He thought about how he should answer; but the *Makrej*, across whose falcon physiognomy a seething anger erupted, spoke first:

"Ali *Bei*, how dare you! You call us thieves and murderers, us, who are seated here as the representatives of the Padishah and of the governor! Take care, otherwise you will regret it!"

The *Bei* turned to the officer with complete calm:

"*Kaimakam, kim bu kajyk* - lieutenant-colonel, who is this madman?"

The *Kaimakam* made a fearful gesture.

"Beware your tongue, Ali *Bei*! This *Effendi* is the *Makrej* of Mosul!"

"You jest! A *Makrej* must be in full control of his mental faculties. This *Makrej* of Mosul has talked the *Mutessarif* into a war against me; he would, if he were not mad, never dare to move against me; for he would know what would await him!"

"I do not jest. He is truly a *Makrej*."

"I see that you are neither drunk nor dreaming; that is why I must believe you. But remember that I have granted only that you come to me!"

"He came with me as the representative and emissary of the *Mutessarif.*"

"That is possible, for you are saying so; but can he prove it to me?"

"I say so and bear witness to it!"

"That proves nothing. I trust you; but any other who comes to me in a similar situation must be able to prove that he has the authority and is empowered to negotiate with me; otherwise he runs the risk to be treated in the manner that my messenger was treated by you."

"A *Makrej* can never be in such danger!"

"I will prove the opposite to you!"

He clapped his hands and immediately the *Jesidi*, who had fetched the *Kaimakam*, entered.

"Have you promised safe passage to the *Kaimakam*?"

"Yes, Lord."

"Who else?"

"No one."

"Not the three soldiers who stand outside?"

"No and not to the *Makrej* either."

"Those three will be led away, they are prisoners; and this man, who claims to be the *Makrej* of Mosul, take him as well. He is responsible for the murder of my negotiator."

"I protest!" shouted the *Kaimakam.*

"I know how to defend and avenge myself," threatened the *Makrej*, while he drew the dagger that he had in his belt.

In that same moment Ali *Bei* darted up from his seated position and smashed his fist into the *Makrej's* face with such power that he dropped to the floor backwards.

"Dog, you dare to draw a weapon against me in my own tent! Out, out with him!"

"Stop!" ordered the *Kaimakam.* "We came to negotiate; nothing may happen to us!"

"My messenger came to you to negotiate as well, and yet you have murdered him - executed him as a traitor. Out with this man!"

The *Jesidi* grabbed hold of the *Makrej* and manhandled him outside.

"Then I will go too!" threatened the *Kaimakam.*

"Then go! You will reach your men unharmed; but before you join them, many of them will be dead. Emir Kara Ben Nemsi, step outside and raise your right arm. It is the signal that the cannons shall begin their barrage."

"Stay!" the *Kaimakam* quickly turned to me. "You may not fire."

"Why not?" asked Ali *Bei*.

"It would be murder for we can not defend ourselves."

"It would not be murder, rather it would be punishment and retribution. You wanted to attack us without us having an inkling of it; you came with sabers, flintlocks and cannons to massacre and to obliterate us with case shot. But your cannons are in our hands and now that we are about to treat you in the same manner as you would have treated us, you say, he who fires is a murderer! *Kaimakam*, you may vent your anger, but don't be ridiculous!"

"You will free the *Makrej*!"

"He is the reprisal for my murdered negotiator!"

"You will kill him?"

"Perhaps. It depends how well we agree with each other."

"What do you demand of me?"

"I am prepared to listen to your concessions."

"Concessions? We came to make demands!"

"I have already asked you not to be ridiculous! Firstly tell me what reason you had to attack us!"

"There are murderers among you."

"I know which incident you are referring to, but I tell you that you have been ill informed: not two of our people murdered one of yours, rather three of yours have murdered two of our people. I have already arranged to prove this to you; for the *Kiajah* [head] of that village where this happened will be here with the relatives of the murdered men."

"Perhaps that's a different case"

"There is only this one, but the *Makrej* has twisted the facts. He will not do so again. And if it were, as you claim, then it is not reason enough to attack us in our lands with armed might."

"We had another reason."

"Which?"

"You had not paid the *Haraj*."

"We have paid it. And what do you consider to be the *Haraj* anyway? We are free Kurds; what we pay, we pay of our own free will. We have paid the head tax that everyone who is not a Moslem has to pay for the exemption from military duty. And now you also want the *Haraj*, which is nothing other than the head tax we already paid! And if you were within your right, and if we owed the *Mutessarif* a tax, is that a good enough reason to attack us? Must he attack Sheik Adi now, when there are thousands of people here that do not belong to the realm of Mosul, and who certainly do not owe him anything? *Kaimakam*, you and I, we know precisely what the Governor wants of us; money and spoils. He was not successful in robbing us, and therefore we will speak no further about his reasons. You are neither a jurist nor a tax collector; you are an officer, and that is why I only need to talk to you about your military mission. You shall talk and I will listen!"

"I am to demand the *Haraj* and the murderers from you, otherwise I must, by the order of the *Mutessarif*, destroy Sheik Adi and all villages of the *Jesidi* and execute everyone who offers resistance."

"And to take everything that belongs to the *Jesidi* with you?"

"Everything!"

"That is the order of the governor?"

"That is the order."

"And you will obey it?"

"With all my might."

"Do it!"

He arose to signify that the discussion was at an end. The *Kaimakam* made a move to hold him back.

"What will you do, *Bei*?"

"You will destroy the *Jesidi* villages and rob them, and I, the leader of the *Jesidi* will know how to protect my people. You came unannounced into my territory; you defended that action with lies; you wanted to burn, plunder and murder; you have even murdered my messenger, a deed that is completely against human rights. It therefore follows that I can not look upon you as warriors and must handle you as thieves, and thieves are simply shot. We are finished! Return to your people. At present you are still under my protection; but afterwards you are an outlaw!"

He left the tent and raised his arm. The artillerymen might have long awaited this signal for a cannon fired, and another followed.

"Lord, what are you doing?" cried the *Kaimakam*. "You are ending the cease-fire whilst I am still here!"

"Have we agreed on a cease-fire? Have I not told you that we are done? Do you hear? Those were case-shot . . . and grenades; the same shells that were intended for us; but now they target your people. Allah has judged; the blows meant for the victims now fall upon the perpetrators. You hear the cries of your people. Go to them and order them to destroy our villages!"

The third and fourth salvo truly appeared to have an extraordinary effect; as could be deduced from the wild howling that echoed from below.

"Stop it, Ali *Bei*! Give the signal to cease fire so that we can continue to negotiate!"

"You know the order of the *Mutessarif*, and I know my duty, we are done."

"The *Mutessarif* did not give the order to me but the *Miralai*, and now it is my duty to see that my people are not shot down without defense. I have to try and save them."

"If you will hold fast to that thought then I am prepared to recommence negotiation."

"Then come back into the tent!"

Ali *Bei* unwrapped his turban cloth and waved it to his people below, he then turned and entered the tent.

"What do you demand of me?" asked the *Kaimakam*.

The *Bei* gazed at the floor in deep thought then he answered:

"I am not angry at you and that is why I want to spare you; any agreement we make here would mean your doom, for my demands will be most unfavorable for you. That is why I will only negotiate with the *Mutessarif* himself and you will be blameless."

"I thank you, *Bei*!"

The *Kaimakam* did not appear to be a bad fellow; he was happy that the circumstances had taken such a turn and thus his thankfulness came from his heart.

"But of course I have one demand for you," continued Ali.

"Which is?"

"You consider yourself and your troops as prisoners of war and remain with them in Sheik Adi until I have successfully concluded my negotiations with the *Mutessarif*."

"To that I agree, for I can justify that. The *Miralai* is to blame; he did not proceed with care."

"You therefore surrender your weapons?"

"That is humiliating!"

"Could you keep your weapons as prisoners of war?"

"I declare myself a prisoner of war only insofar that I remain in Sheik Adi and do not attempt to escape until I know what the *Mutessarif* decrees for us."

"An escape would be your doom; it would wipe you out."

"*Bei*, I will be truthful with you and admit that our situation is very grim; but do you know what a thousand men are capable of when they are driven to despair?"

"I know it, but still non of you shall escape."

"But some of you will also fall! And consider that the *Mutessarif* still has an infantry and a dragoon regiment available that remained, for the most part, in Mosul. Add to that the assistance that he can obtain from Kjerkjuk and Diarbekir, from Sulimanijah and other garrisons; add to that the artillery that he still has available and you must admit, that you may be master of the current situation but you will probably not remain so."

"Shall I deny myself the exploitation of victory because I may later be vanquished? The *Mutessarif* may come with his regiments; I will let him know that it will cost you your lives if he attacks me again. And if he has additional aid available to him that is also true in my case. You know that it only requires my call to arms and many a courageous tribe of Kurds will rise against him. But I love peace and not war. Although I have today many *Jesidi* from throughout Kurdistan and the bordering provinces around me and I could easily stir the flames of rebellion among them; but I will not do so if the *Mutessarif* permits me to protect the rights of my people. I will leave you and your troops your weapons, for now; but I have promised my allies rifles and those the governor must deliver."

"Who are your allies?"

"No *Jesidi* betrays his friend. So, you keep your weapons, but you deliver your munitions to me, in exchange I promise you to cater for provisions that you require."

"If I give you the munitions it would be the same as giving you our weapons!"

Ali *Bei* smiled.

"Alright, then you may also keep your munitions; but I tell you; when your people become hungry and plead with me for provisions, then I will provide them in exchange for rifles, pistols, swords and knives. So in that respect you are not prisoners of war, rather we agree on a cease fire."

"That it is, and that I can agree to."

"You see that I am quite considerate. But now hear my conditions: you will remain in the valley of Sheik Adi. You remain there without contact with the outside. You cease all hostilities against my people. You honor our shrine and our homes. The first you may not enter and the last you may enter only with my permission. The cease-fire lasts until you receive an order from the *Mutessarif* and that order must be given to you in my presence. Every attempt at escape, even the escape attempt of a single person, and every act against our agreement lifts the cease-fire immediately. You hold your current position and I hold mine. And in exchange I promise that I will, for the indicated time, cease all hostilities. Do you in agree?"

After a brief reflection and some small additions and explanations, the *Kaimakam* accepted the conditions. He made much intercession for the *Makrej,* demanding his release, but Ali would not relent. Paper was fetched and I composed the contract that both of them signed; one with a signature and the other with his *Bu-kendim* [literally: 'this is me' or 'this is myself' - a symbol that serves as a signature]. The officer then returned to the valley and his three soldiers were permitted to accompany him.

Pali now waited for orders from his superior.

"Would you write a letter to the *Mutessarif* for me?" Ali *Bei* asked me.

"With pleasure! What would you like to convey to him?"

"The present disposition of his troops. And then tell him that I wish to negotiate with him, that I either await him here or meet him in Jerraijah. But he may only be accompanied by at most fifty men and has to abandon all hostile thoughts. The meeting is to take place the day after tomorrow around midday. If he fails to come, I will execute the *Makrej* and let his troops feel their own case-shot. That will also be the case if I notice that he intends to continue these hostilities. Can you write this?"

"Yes."

"I still have to impart some very special orders to Pali, write as fast as possible so that he can depart without delay!"

Some minutes later I sat in the tent with paper resting on my knee, I wrote the letter to the governor in the oriental manner from right to left using my pencil. He would certainly have no idea that it was composed by his protégé. And in less than half an hour Pali, mounted on his horse galloped away on the path to Baadri. -

The festivities of the *Jesidi* had been terribly interrupted but the lament about it was not as great as the joy that they had been successful in diverting a major catastrophe that had been aimed at those gathered at Sheik Adi.

"What about the festivities?" I asked Ali *Bei*. "The *Osmanli* could linger down there for many days, and the *Jesidi* surely would not wait such a long time."

"I will give them a celebration that will be greater than they expected," he answered. "Do you still remember the way to the Idiz valley?"

"Yes."

"You have time, ride there and fetch Mir Sheik Khan, the Sheiks and the Kawals. We will see if the remains of *Pir* Kamek can be found and buried in the Idiz valley."

That of course was a thought that had to find favor among the *Jesidi* and I was exceptionally pleased that I could attend the burial rites of a *Jesidi*. I only took Halef along with me, and the *Buluk-Emini* I left behind.

Although I stated that I knew the way to the Idiz valley, I had never gone there from Sheik Adi but rather from Baadri. The *Bei* obviously believed that I had ridden there via Sheik Adi with Selek's son, and I did not correct him, as it would be a pleasure to see if I could find the valley without truly knowing the way. I could not mistake the general direction and the tracks made days ago by the *Jesidi* had to be a sure sign for me. So I rode along the edge of the valley until I reached a spot above the Shrine. Along the way I passed many *Jesidi* that guarded the slope in a tight group; but then I turned to the left and entered the forest. With a practiced eye it was not difficult to discern the tracks, even from the saddle. We followed them and soon reached the place where my translator and I had previously descended. A guard stood here that had been ordered to turn away every unwelcome person. We dismounted and left our horses there.

As we climbed down the steep slope a rare, lively view presented itself. Thousands of women and children camped below in a picturesque setting. Horses and cattle grazed; sheep and goats clambered among the rocks; but not a sound could be heard, for all talked softly so that the hiding place should not be compromised by a careless sound. Mir Sheik Khan sat by the water with his priests. They welcomed me with great joy; for they had, until then, only heard that the enemies attack had failed, but they had received no detailed information.

"Is the Shrine still standing?" Was the first question the Khan asked of me.

"The Shrine is undamaged, as are the rest of the buildings."

"We heard the shooting. Did much blood flow?"

"Only the blood of the *Osmanli*."

"And our people?"

"I have not heard of a single casualty during the battle. However, two are dead but they did not die in battle."

"Who were they?"

"The Sarraj [saddle maker] Hefi of Baazoni and . . ."

"Hefi of Baazoni? A devout, hard-working and courageous man. Not in battle? How did he die then?"

"The *Bei* sent him to the *Osmanli* as a negotiator and they shot him. I had to witness this without being able to save him."

The priests lowered their heads, folded their hands and remained silent. Only Mir Sheik Khan spoke in a deep, serious voice:

"He is transformed. *El Shems* will no longer light his way, but he wanders under the rays of a higher sun in a land where we shall meet him again. *Orata ölüm ne mozar ne, ajy ne tasa ne; orata ebedi ajyk ile zewk* - there, neither death nor grave exists, nor pain or worry, there is light eternal and bliss; *zira tanry jakin dir* - for he is with God!"

This manner in which the news of the death of a friend was received was moving. Not a harsh word was directed towards the murderer. These priests mourned but did not begrudge the transformation of the dead. Such devotion is unheard of in Islam; it could only result from a Christian ideology that the *Jesidi* had accepted and adhered to.

"And who was the other?" the Khan now asked.

"You will be shocked!"

"A man is never shocked by death for death is *'dost insanün, son günahnun, iptida saadetün'* - a friend of mankind, the end of sin and the beginning of eternal bliss. Who was he?"

"*Pir* Kamek."

Non-the-less they flinched with sudden pain, but no one said a word. Even now Mir Sheik Khan was the first to speak:

"*Ewlija dejishtirmis* - the holy man is transformed. *Chüda bujurdi* - God has ordained it! Tell us of his death!"

I reported in as much detail as I could. They all listened, deeply touched, and then the Khan requested:

"*Kardashlar, fikirimiz ona jakin ol* - Brothers, let us remember him!" [Literally: 'Our thoughts are with him']

They lowered their heads. Did they pray? I do not know, but I saw that the eyes of many filled with tears and that their emotion was thus true and heartfelt. It has been said that only the German possesses that which is named *'Gemüt'* [heart, soul, nature, disposition]. If that were true then the *Jesidi* were very much like the Germans. How it would please me if the divine kindness and clarity of Christianity were permitted to bring light into the shadows of their valleys and bathe the peaks of their mountains in gold!

Only after some time did their contemplation pass back into their usual demeanor so that I could once again talk with them.

"Ali *Bei* has sent me to you to bring you to him. He will attempt to discover if the remains of the holy man permit themselves be found, in which case they may be buried this day."

"Yes, that is an important task that we have to solve. The mortal remains of the *Pir* may not rest in the same place as those of the *Miralai*!"

"I fear that we will not find his bones but rather only ashes!"

"Then let us hurry!"

We started back, that is all the priests and Kawals; but the Fakirs remained behind to keep the Idiz valley under their supervision. As we arrived at the *Bei's* tent above Sheik Adi, the *Bei* spoke with the man whom he had sent to the *Kaimakam* with a request to see if the Turks would permit the priests of the *Jesidi* to examine the pyre. The officer had returned a positive answer and only added one condition, that those people brought no weapons with them.

Ali *Bei* could not accompany the Sheiks since he always had to remain vigilant. I requested that I be permitted to join the group and that request was gladly granted. The most important thing was almost overlooked; namely to take along a vessel to hold the ashes of the 'Holy man'. But when the question arose, it showed that the *Bei* had already considered this.

"Mir Sheik Khan, you know that the famous *Jömlekji* [potter] Rassat of Baazoni made an urn for my father Hussein Bei, that should hold his dust when the time comes to remove him from his *Mezar* [grave], so that he will not be contaminated by the dust of his *Tabut* [coffin]. This *Kilja* [urn, clay vessel] is a masterpiece of that famous potter and probably well suited to hold the remains of a holy man. It is at my house in Baadri, and I have already sent a man to fetch it. It will arrive before your task at the pyre is completed."

This was satisfactory and thus the procession made its way into the valley. We passed the battery and arrived at the place where the 'Holy man' had sacrificed himself and his enemy for the sake of revenge. We saw a heap of ash from which half burned larger stakes of wood protruded. Before it lay the corpse of the executed negotiator. The heat of the fire had destroyed his clothes but not his body. He was removed, a task that made our sense of smell suffer greatly.

The ashes had cooled. From the houses close by, the necessary tools were gathered, and now the careful sifting commenced, inch by inch the blanket of ash was removed. The removal had to be done with such great care that it took considerable time, in the meantime a *Jesidi* arrived with a mule that carried the urn tied on its back. It's form above the base was like an upturned glass screen that we are used to seeing on our lamps and above it rested a lid that was crowned with the image of a sun. On the vessel itself a symbol and some Kurmangji words were emblazoned. The symbol depicted a flying bird with a forked tail and pointed wings. What kind of bird this should be was made clear to me by the words beneath it: *Hajji Hajjik*, the pilgrim among pilgrims. That is; the swallow.

Around the bird and its designation were eight words in the following order:

Speïda

Mezaal **Isterik**

(Picture of the swallow)

Kabirstan **Adef**

(Hajji Hajjik)

Toprash **Azman**

Ross

In the German language these eight words would be:

Morgenröthe [Dawn]

Grabmal [Gravestone] **Stern [Star]**

(Picture of the swallow)

Kirchhof [Churchyard] **Sonne [Sun]**

(Hajji Hajjik)

Erde [Earth] **Himmel [Sky, Heaven]**

Tag. [Day]

The meaning of this inscription is so clear that it is not necessary to provide an explanation. I indicated the bird and asked one of the Sheiks:

"Is the swallow a holy bird among the *Jesidi*?"

"It is a symbol of the earthly pilgrimage. When autumn comes, the swallow moves to more pleasant lands and when the summer of man is over, so he too prepares himself to say goodbye to the mountains in which he has build his nest and passes into a better world. On the other side of the grave, the churchyard and the earth, another day under another star, a purer sun dawns upon the day of heaven that knows not earth and has no night. It is written here on this *Kilja*."

It appeared impossible for me to discern the remains of the 'Holy man' from those of the pyre; but I was mistaken in that assumption. As the ashes had almost been cleared right down to the earth, two formless lumps were exposed upon which the priests focused all of their attention. They appeared not to come to a clear conclusion and Mir Sheik Khan beckoned to me.

It was no simple task to examine the situation; one had to close both mouth and nose. Truly before us were the bodies of the two dead, they were half cooked and carbonized, shrunk to almost a third of their former size and encased in a fairly solid crust that, upon further examination, was composed of ash and those parts of the tar that would not burn.

"These are the dead," I said. "You can thank the tar that you can bury your 'Holy man'."

"But which of them is he?"

"Search him out!"

I wanted to see how astute these men were. They took great pains but were not able to solve the apparently difficult and yet simple problem.

"It is impossible to recognize the *Pir*," the Khan finally admitted perplexed. "We either have to abandon the idea of honoring his ashes or we are forced to place both their bodies into the urn, friend and foe, the holy and the godless. Or do you have better counsel, Emir Kara Ben Nemsi?"

"I know of one."

"And this is?"

"To only place the remains of the *Pir* in the urn."

"But you have just heard that it is impossible to distinguish those from the *Miralai*!"

"That is not difficult! This here is the 'Holy man' and that is the Turk."

"How do you discern that? Can you prove it?"

"With such a certainty that you could only wish for. The *Pir* had no weapons on his person; but the *Miralai* carried a saber, a dagger and two pistols. Do you see the bent pistol barrels and the knife blade stuck to the body? The shafts and the handles are burned. And here, directly beneath him you see the tip of the saber protruding from the ash. This certainly was the *Miralai*."

Now the *Jesidi* wondered how they did not come to that simple conclusion themselves. All, without exception, agreed with my observation and busied themselves with placing the remains of the *Pir* into the urn.

During the entire time, the *Kaimakam* and most of his officers had stayed close by. The corpse of his former superior was left to him and then we returned to the valley crest. There, Ali *Bei* inquired of the Khan his orders in respect of the burial ceremony.

"We have to postpone them until tomorrow," answered the Kahn.

"Why?"

"*Pir* Kamek was the most devout and wisest among the *Jesidi*; he shall be laid to rest honorably and it is too late today do that. I will order a grave marker to be erected in the Idiz valley and that can only be accomplished by tomorrow."

"Then you will require *Duwarji's* [bricklayers] and *Dägerler* [carpenters]?"

"No. We will erect a simple structure of stone that will require no mortar and every man, every woman and every child shall add a stone to it, each according to his strength, so that non of the assembled pilgrims shall be excluded from giving the transformed a fitting memorial."

"But I need the warriors to guard the Turks!" interjected Ali *Bei*.

"They will be relieved; so that there will always be enough to carry out their orders. Let us discuss the shape we shall give to the structure!"

Since I was not required for this task, I searched out my translator in order to receive the manuscript of the dead *Pir*. He had hidden it in a hollow *Thinar* [oak] tree and we settled ourselves nearby where I could practice my language skills without interruption.

The day passed and evening approached. Around the rim of the valley of Sheik Adi many fires were kindled close to each other. It would be impossible for the Turks to escape, even if the *Kaimakam* were to break his promise and use the darkness for such a move. The night passed without any disruption and in the morning Pali returned. The speed and stamina of his excellent horse had shortened the distance between Sheik Adi and Mosul considerably. I had slept in the *Bei's* tent and was thus on hand when the messenger entered.

"Have you met the *Mutessarif*?" Ali asked of him.

"Yes, Lord, late in the evening."

"What does he say?"

"First he was enraged and wanted to have me whipped to death. But then he assembled many of his officers and his *Diwan effendisi* [Gathering of the council] with whom he discussed the matter for a long time. He then permitted me to return."

"Where you present at this discussion?"

"No."

"What answer did you receive?"

"A letter addressed to you."

"Show me!"

Pali produced the letter that was sealed with the great *Möhür mutessarifün* [Seal of the Governor]. Ali *Bei* opened it and gazed at the lines. Inside the larger document lay a smaller open letter; he passed both to me.

"You read Emir! I am eager to learn what the *Mutessarif* has decided."

The letter was composed by the scribe of the governor and signed by the latter. He promised to be in Jerraijah the following morning, accompanied by ten men and he stated the condition that Ali *Bei* too should be accompanied by an equally small number of men. He expected that the reconciliation would be peaceful and requested that the enclosed order be passed on to the *Kaimakam*. The latter contained a very peaceable directive to cease all further hostilities, to spare Sheik Adi and to treat the *Jesidi* like friends. The remark that this order should be read very carefully was added last.

Ali *Bei* nodded his head contently.

Chapter 29

After a small pause, the *Jesidi* chieftain bared his soul:

"We have won and have taught the *Mutessarif* a lasting lesson; do you feel this, Emir? The *Kaimakam* shall receive this letter and tomorrow I will be in Jerraijah."

"Why give the *Kaimakam* this letter?"

"It belongs to him."

"But it is unnecessary, since he has already bound himself to do that what he is now ordered therein."

"He will do it now with greater certainty, once he sees that it is also the will of the *Mutessarif*."

"I must admit to you that this written order arouses my suspicion."

"Why?"

"Because it is unnecessary. And how strange do these last words sound, that the *Kaimakam* should read this order most carefully!"

"That should prove the good will of the *Mutessarif* to us and encourage the *Kaimakam* to be meticulous in his obedience."

"This meticulousness is a matter of course for him and that is why the order appears to be even more superfluous."

"This letter does not belong to me; the governor has entrusted it to my honor and the *Kaimakam* shall receive it."

It was as though fate granted the *Bei* that very opportunity, for just then a *Jesidi* entered and announced:

"Lord, a rider approaches from the valley below."

We stepped outside and after some time recognized the approaching rider as the *Kaimakam*, who came unaccompanied. We awaited him outside the tent.

"*Seni selamlar-im* - I greet you!" he said as he dismounted, first to the *Bei* and then also to me.

"*Chosh geldin-sen, Effendi* - be welcomed, Lord!" answered Ali. "What desire leads you to me?"

"The wish of my warriors who have no bread to eat."

That was spoken without preamble. Ali smiled silently.

"I had expected this. But have you remembered that I only sell bread for weapons?"

"So you said, but you will still take money!"

"What the *Bei* of the *Jesidi* says, that he also knows to keep. You need food and I need weapons. We swap and then both of us are satisfied."

"You forget that we need the weapons ourselves!"

"And you forget that we need the bread for ourselves! There are many thousands of *Jesidi* gathered here, all want to eat and drink. And what do you need your weapons for? Are we not friends?"

"Only until the end of this armistice!"

"Probably even longer than that. Emir, please read the letter from the governor again!"

"Did a letter come from him?" asked the lieutenant colonel eagerly.

"Yes. I sent a messenger that just returned. Read, Emir!"

I read the letter, which I still had with me. I believe the expression of the *Kaimakam* showed disappointment.

"So there will be peace between us!" he said.

"Yes," answered the *Bei*. "And until then you will conduct yourself in a friendly manner as the *Mutessarif's* special orders to you state."

"Special orders?"

"He has included a letter that I should give to you."

"A letter? To me?" cried the officer. "Where is it?"

"The Emir has it. Let it be given to you!"

I was already prepared to hand him the letter; but his haste in reaching for it made me suspicious.

"Permit me to read it to you!"

I read it, but only up to the last remark that had piqued my suspicion. He then asked:

"Is that all? Is there nothing else?"

"Still two lines. Hear them!"

I read to the end but keep an eye on him. For just a fleeting moment his eyes opened wider then normal, but I knew for certain that this sentence had a special meaning.

"This letter belongs to me. Show it to me!"

With these words he quickly reached for it so that I had little time to withdraw my hand that held the letter.

"Why so eager, *Kaimakam*?" I asked, while watching him closely. "Have these lines something so important to tell that you lose your self control?"

"Nothing, they mean nothing; but the letter is mine!"

"The *Mutessarif* has sent it to the *Bei*, and it is up to him alone if you receive it or only be informed of it's content."

"He has already said that I shall receive the letter!"

"Since this paper appears to be so important to you, although you have already heard its content, permit me to examine it more closely."

My suspicion had taken root. Instead of being lifted, it had become a firm belief. I held the paper with its face vertically between my eye and the sun; I could not discern anything out of the ordinary. I felt it, smelled it, but to no avail. Now I held it horizontally so that the sun's rays, falling upon it, would catch my eyes, and there, finally, some marks could be discerned. These marks were ever so faint that only a sharp eye could see them, for they blended with the color of the paper, yet they appeared to be in the shape of symbols.

"You will not get this paper!" I said to the *Kaimakam.*

"Why not?"

"Because it contains secret writings that I will examine."

He changed color.

"You err, *Effendi*!"

"I see it well!" To test him I added: "This secret writing will become readable when I dip the paper into water."

"Do it!" he answered with visible satisfaction.

"Your confident words have betrayed you, *Kaimakam.* I will not dip the paper into water but rather hold it over the flames of a fire."

I had hit the mark; I realized this from the ill-concealed shock that flushed his face briefly.

"Then you will burn and destroy the letter!" he warned.

"Do not worry! An *Effendi* from the Occident knows well how to handle such things."

The *Bei* was most perplexed.

"Do you really believe that this letter contains secret writings?"

"Let a fire be lit, then I will prove it to you!"

Pali was still present. At a hand signal from Ali he gathered together dried twigs and started a fire. I kneeled before it and carefully held the paper over the flames. The Kaimakam quickly leapt towards me and tried to grab the letter from my hands. I had awaited this and with equal speed moved out of his way, he stumbled and fell to the ground. Immediately Ali *Bei* held him down with his knee.

"Stop, *Kaimakam*!" he shouted; "You are treacherous and without honor; you came to me without first seeking my protection, and now you are my prisoner!"

The officer defended himself as well as he could, but we were three against one and many *Jesidi* who were nearby joined us. He was disarmed, bound and moved into the tent.

Now I could complete my experiment. The flames heated the paper to the point of singing it and now the words that were written at the line margins appeared clearly.

"Ali *Bei*, do you see that I was correct?"

"Emir, you are a wizard!"

"No; but I know how one can make such writing visible."

"Oh, *Effendi*, the wisdom of the *Nemje* is great!"

"Did the *Mutessarif* not also understand this magic? There are substances that can be used as inks, which disappear after one has written with them, and means by which such writing can be made visible again. The science that deals with such substances is called chemistry or alchemy. It is more sophisticated in our lands than in yours and we therefore have better means than you do. We know of many kinds of secret writings that are more difficult to discover; the art practiced here is very simple so that no great wisdom is required to make the invisible words visible again. Guess with what these words were written."

"Tell me!"

"With urine."

"Impossible!"

"When you write with the urine of an animal or even a human, then that writing disappears as soon as it is dry. If you hold that paper over a flame, the writing becomes black and you can read it."

"What do these words say?"

"*O bir gün gel-yr-im jen-mek ijin* - I come the day after tomorrow to gain victory."

"Is that true? You are not mistaken?"

"It is clearly written here!"

"Well then, give me this letter!"

He paced up and down several times, quite agitated; then he stopped before me.

"Is this treachery or not, Emir?"

"It is treachery."

"Shall I annihilate this *Mutessarif*? He is within my grasp!"

"You will then have to deal with the Padishah!"

"*Effendi*, the *Urus* [Russians] have a saying that goes: *'Giöj jüksek, thsaar uzak* - the sky is high and the Tzar is far'. So it is with the Padishah. I will be victorious!"

"But you will spill much blood. Have you not said to me that you love peace?"

"I love peace, but one should grant it to me as well! These Turks came to rob us of our freedom and our possession and even our lives; yet I have shown them mercy. Now one weaves new treachery. Shall I not defend myself?"

"You shall defend yourself, but not with the saber!"

"With what else?"

"With this letter. Show it to the *Mutessarif* and he will be vanquished and beaten."

"He will ambush me from behind and take me prisoner if I go to Jerraijah tomorrow!"

"Who stops you from doing the same to him? He is as exposed as you for he does not know that you are aware of his intentions."

Ali *Bei* gazed at the ground before him a while and than answered:

"I will discuss this with Mir Sheik Khan. Will you ride to the Idiz valley with me?"

"I ride with you."

"Before we go I want to render the people below harmless. Do not enter the tent with me but wait here!"

Why should I not enter the tent with him? His hand rested on his dagger and in his eyes was a look of determination. Did he wish to prevent me from hindering him in a rash act? I stood alone for about half an hour and during that time I heard the angry words of a turbulent discussion coming from the tent. Finally he emerged again. He had a paper in his hand and he passed it to me.

"Read! I wish to hear if it is without deceit."

The paper contained a short, measured directive to the officer in charge. It stated that all weapons and munitions were to be handed over to those *Jesidi* whose leader presented this order.

"It is correct. But tell me how you achieved this?"

"I would have ordered the execution of both the *Mukrej* and himself and commenced the cannonade. In an hour we would have been finished with them."

"Now he remains a prisoner?"

"Yes, he and the *Makrej* will be guarded."

"And if his people do not obey?"

"Then I will make my threat a reality. Remain here until I return and you will see if the Turks respect me."

He imparted some orders to his men and then descended to the battery below. Within a space of ten minutes, all *Jesidi* were ready for battle. The marksmen lay in their hiding-places with ready rifles and the artillerymen stood ready by their weapons to commence the barrage. The fortification opened and two hundred *Jesidi* and about thirty mules passed through the gap. The group of animals consisted mainly of those we had captured from the artillerymen. The procession stopped some distance away whilst their leader walked ahead to search out the place where the *Osmanli* officers were located.

From my vantagepoint I could observe everything in great detail. The negotiation took a considerable time. But then the soldiers formed into groups and one by one they marched to where the mules were and there laid down their weapons. Of course this did not go entirely as smoothly as that, especially since the lower ranks were forced to also part with their sabers and pistols; but only empty curses remained since the Turks knew that any real resistance would be ended with case-shot.

Ali *Bei* returned after less than an hour. The mules and their load of weapons followed him, he ordered the mule drivers to take the priceless loot to the Idiz valley. Some warriors likewise brought the *Kaimakam* to safety. He was led to the place where the *Makrej* was lucky enough to enjoy the company of the fat artillery captain and his courageous young lieutenant. He could wait there with these two for some upward movement in rank and in the meantime dream of smoking 'Tobacco from Shiraz'.

We too made ready to depart. Halef rode with us. My *Bashi-Bozuk* was nowhere to be seen; he probably took his donkey for a joyride to relieve his boredom. On the way to the Idiz valley we encountered a long column of returning *Jesidi*. They had added their contribution to the erection of the memorial and should now relieve an equal number of their companions to do likewise. They told us that the construction proceeded speedily.

When we reached the entrance of the valley, a very lively scene opened before us. In the middle of the valley a great number of women were gathered, grinding flour from corn on large flat stones. Others sat by pits that they heated with the aid of fire so that they could bake bread; still others made torches or readied lamps and lanterns that had been brought from Sheik Adi the day before yesterday, for the upcoming ceremony. It was most busy on the upper reaches of the valley where the memorial was being erected. It formed a huge pyramid of rock the rear of which leant against a vertical rock face. The foundation was composed of large stone blocks, the transportation of which had certainly taken a huge expenditure of energy. At the approximate center of the unfinished pyramid a space had been left that had the shape of a sun with twelve rays and in the center of this the urn was to be placed. Many hundreds of men were at work there, hauling stones, or hanging from the rock face like squirrels to see if they could assist in the construction from above.

The priests were likewise busy either assisting in or supervising the construction itself. Mir Sheik Khan sat close by the pyramid. We approached him. Ali *Bei* told him of the events of the day and showed him both of the writings from the *Mutessarif* as well. The Khan sunk into deep contemplation; but he then asked:

"What will you do, Ali *Bei*?"

"You are the eldest and the wisest, I come to you to seek your counsel."

"You say that I am the elder. Old age desires peace and rest. You say that I am the wisest. The greatest wisdom is the though onto the Almighty and the All-gracious. He makes the weak strong; he protects the oppressed; he does not desire that a man spills the blood of his brother."

"Are these Turks our brothers? Those that fall upon our people like wild animals?"

"They are our brothers, although they do not behave like brothers towards us. Do you like a brother that wishes ill for you?"

"No."

"You speak with him in a friendly manner or with strong words, but you do not demand his life. In this manner you should also talk with the *Mutessarif*."

"And if he does not listen to me?"

"The All-merciful gave man understanding in order that he may think and a heart so that he might feel. He who does not consider the words of another and he who does not feel the feelings of his brother, he has denied and deserted the Merciful, and then, only then may the wrath and punishment descend upon him."

"Mir Sheik Khan, I will proceed according to your words!"

"Then I repeat my question: What will you do?"

"I will go with ten men to Jerraijah, but I will have enough warriors follow me to take the *Mutessarif* prisoner. But before that, today even, I will send scouts to Mosul, Kufjunjik, Telkeïf, Baaweiza, Ras ul Aïn and Khorsabad, who will inform me of his plans in time. I will speak to him with care and then with sternness, if he still does not hear me, then he has no respect for me, then I will show him his secret message and give the signal to capture him. While I am with him, my men will encircle Jerraijah. He can not escape me."

"Perhaps he will send scouts as well to determine how you prepare for this meeting with him."

"He will discover nothing for my people will depart during the night, not on the road to Baadri, but to the right, almost towards Bozan. They will be by the stream to the west of Jerraijah in the morning."

"And who will be in command at Sheik Adi during your absence?"

"Would you do it?"

"I will."

That sounded so simple. Here the worldly ruler of the *Jesidi* passed his power to the spiritual ruler without the least bit of jealous emotion, without all mistrust and a second thought. "Would you?" asked one. "I will," answered the other. How would the words 'Culture Clash' sound in one of the dialects of these 'Devil Worshippers'!

Now the provisioning of the captive Turks in Sheik Adi was discussed, followed by the discussion of the ceremony scheduled for later today. Meanwhile I wandered from group to group to try my language skills with one or another. Suddenly behind me someone approached panting and in a breath snapping voice called:

"Move aside, *Sihdi*!"

I turned around. It was Halef, who exerted his entire bodily strength to roll a mighty rock before him.

"What are you doing with that?" I asked with amazement.

"My contribution to the monument."

"Will they take it? You are, after all, no *Jesidi*!"

"Most willingly! I have asked."

"Then I too shall fetch a stone!"

Not far from where we were lay a considerable boulder. I laid down my weapons, removed my outer garment and proceeded to move it. It was accepted by the Sheiks with much gratitude and after I had engraved my name with my dagger, it was hauled into place with ropes to a position directly above the sun shaped space.

Meanwhile Ali *Bei* had completed the purpose of his visit. He desired to return and asked me if I would accompany him or if I wished to remain.

"How can I best view the ceremonies?"

"If you come with me," he answered. "The urn will be moved to the Idiz valley from Sheik Adi this evening by the glow of torches and lanterns."

"I thought it was already here!"

"No. It stands by a cool water in the forest and will first be brought to the Shrine."

"Despite the Turks?"

"They can not hinder us."

"Then I ride with you."

"You have spare time till the evening. Will you do me a favor?"

"Gladly, if I am able!"

"You know that I have promised rifles to the chieftain of the Badinan-Kurds. Can you find the place where his huts are?"

"Quite easily. In any case, one does not have to ride all the way there since he wanted to occupy the path and the secondary valleys. And incidentally it is about time to provide him with some news."

"Will you take this upon yourself?"

"Yes."

"And bring him his rifles?"

"If you entrust me with this task!"

"He shall receive a hundred rifles as well as ammunition. Three mules may carry these. How many men do you wish to accompany you?"

"Is an attack or some other hostility to be expected?"

"No."

"Then give me ten warriors. I will also take Mohammed Emin with me, he just now descends from above."

I discovered previously that the Sheik of the Haddedihn had gone hunting. I had not met up with him over the past days. He wanted to be seen as little as possible so that his presence would not be mentioned, and he had probably still not come to terms with his prejudice of the 'Devil Worshippers'. Therefore it was a pleasure to him that he could depart with me at once.

Only a short time passed and the Mules were packed and our little procession started to move. First we headed towards Sheik Adi and then we veered to the left to join the path to Kaloni. My guess proved to be correct; we met a group of Badinan-Kurds on the first rise behind Sheik Adi and were led by them to their chieftain, who welcomed me, this time with great respect. I had to remain with him and partake of a meal that his wife prepared for us. He was quite satisfied with the rifles and was especially pleased with the *Kaimakam's* saber that Ali *Bei* had sent along as a special present to him. Mohammed Emin discovered that he liked the Badinan-Kurds so much that he decided to remain with them and await my return although he did not understand a word of Kurdish. I did not try to dissuade him since the Turks could still notice his presence in Sheik Adi and then the purpose of our ride into the mountains could be compromised. I therefore returned without him.

The day had almost passed when I returned to Ali *Bei* and reported to him about the Badinan-Kurds. I commented that the Turks had moved more to the center of the valley and that the Shrine was quite accessible.

"When do the ceremonies begin?" I asked the Bei.

"As soon as it is dark. Take along your guns; there will be much shooting."

"Give me one of yours. I have to preserve my bullets which I can not easily replace."

I was truly curious about these burial ceremonies to which I was to bear witness. It was quite possible that before me, no European had ever seen, much less attended, the burial of a 'Devil Worshipper'. I sat near the rim of the valley and looked down until the shadows of the night descended. Then suddenly the watch fires flared and at the same time a double pyramid of lights rose over the Shrine, exactly like on the first evening I had spent in Sheik Adi. Both doors of the Shrine were overhung with lamps.

"Come!" Ali Bei encouraged me, as he and some so favored mounted their horses.

The *Bashi-Bozuk* remained behind. Halef accompanied us. We rode down into the valley and reached the Shrine that was now completely bathed in light. The plaza before it was encircled by a double row of armed *Jesidi* so as to deny every Turk entrance. Only Mir Sheik Khan and his priests were in the Shrine itself; to others, except Ali *Bei* and myself, entrance was denied. In the inner courtyard stood two, closely coupled mules, which carried a kind of rack across their backs on which the urn was fastened. Around these two animals the priests had formed a circle. At our appearance they commenced to slowly sing in a monotone in which the words '*dacha denim* - I surrender my soul' were oft repeated. After that the mules were watered from the holy well and given a handful of corn, to indicate that who they carried had a long journey before him. Mir Sheik Khan now signaled with his hand, the meaning of which I did not understand, and then a second song started softly and harmoniously. It had four verses that started with the words: '*Tu Chode delaine, kef minim* - You love God, enjoy the peace'. Unfortunately I understood too little Kurdish, to comprehend and remember it all.

When the song was finished the Khan made another sign. He took up the lead position; two Sheiks took hold of the mule's reigns; behind them the other Sheiks and Kawals followed in pairs, Ali *Bei* and I joined them. The procession started and when it exited the Shrine, it was welcomed by a salvo from those who had weapons.

Immediately hundreds of shots cracked from above and hundreds more carried the message that we had started towards the Idiz valley.

We slowly ascended the heights. As we reached the path to the valley, a magical vista unfolded. The *Jesidi* had formed a guard of honor from Sheik Adi all the way to the Idiz valley; the two ranks were about thirty paces apart. Every one of these men carried a torch and a gun, and every one of these joined behind us and fired their rifle. In this manner they formed a procession that grew longer with every passing moment and with every salvo. The light of the torches lit the dark forest, which was mainly composed of tall oaks, with indescribable tints of color, and the thunder of the salvos echoed from the forest depth without interruption.

But the spectacle that awaited us when we reached the valley was truly magnificent. It appeared like a massive volcanic crater in which gigantic flames blazed and in which thousands of ghostly will-o'-the-wisp floated about aimlessly. A multitude of voices shouted a welcome to us and in a space of several seconds all lights arranged themselves on both sides of the valley. The large, wide basin was as bright as day. But the largest and brightest light emanated from two gigantic fires burning to either side of the pyramid. Their flames were fed by the material of two large pyres and were leaping high up the naked wall of the valley,. A 'sweet horror' enveloped me, one that was both depressing and also agreeable to the human heart. It felt like something was reached in, past the borders of our private little world inside.

We moved down into the valley, through the swirling ocean of torches and stopped before the memorial. In its sun shaped opening stood two priests whose white garments made a lively contrast to the dark rock behind them. High above many men had positioned themselves, holding the ropes that were to lift the urn.

As soon as the mules had reached the front of the pyramid, the guns fell silent; an utter stillness settled over the valley. The urn was unloaded and fastened to the ropes. Another rope was fastened under the base of the urn and served to hold the fragile container away from the rocks. Mir Sheik Khan signaled and the ropes were pulled upwards. The urn swung higher and higher and finally reached the sun shaped opening. The priests took hold and pulled it inside. They then positioned it, grabbed hold of the ropes and let themselves be lowered.

Now the Khan signaled that he would speak. He made a short speech. His slow and clear, yet loud, words rang across the entire valley and although I understood little of it, I felt deeply moved by these extraordinary proceedings. When he had ended, a choir of priests commenced a joyful song, of which I could only understand part of a single refrain: '*Ro debee* - the sun rises.' At the last tone, all raised their hands and a massive salvo, unlike I had ever heard before, cracked.

And with that the official ceremonies were completed. But now life began to stir. There is nothing that I could use to compare to this night in the Idiz valley. This night of flaming torches shining upwards and lighting the skyward reaching cliffs. This night of questions and pain among the despised and outcast. This night among the confessors of a form of worship the basis of which rose from the dissatisfaction of those that wandered in ignorance and yet sought out the light that shone for those Sheiks of this land in which I now found myself. Who made a pilgrimage to Bethlehem for the purpose of acknowledging their faith before the crib: 'We have seen your star in the Orient and came to pray to you.'

I sat with the priests long past midnight, then the torches where extinguished and the fires collapsed. Only the two flames by the monument still burned, as I wrapped myself in my burnoose beneath a tree in the search of sleep. There above stood the urn with the remains of the 'Holy man'. This *'Merd-el-Shaïtan'* was the most enlightened among all his people of this faith, and yet he had not been able to find the right way to the truth.

How lucky are those, whose cradle already stands by this path and yet how difficult is it for them to recognize and cherish this fortuitous event! I closed my eyes and I was finally able to sleep; but I dreamt of fire-lit processions and salvos, of pyres and urns from which climbed skeletons that danced around me, a Christian. They wanted to grab hold of me; but *Pir* Kamek appeared and warded them off me and said:

"He has a holy *Kitab* in which it is written: *'Oghuljikler, sizi oranizde sewyn-iz* - Children, love one another!'" . . .

This is the last chapter that Elaine edited before her death.
Her remains,
Like that of the Holy man in this chapter,
Now rest in an urn.
Her eyes will no longer see the fruits of her labor.
But her love, her strength and her perseverance live on,
In my memory.

Karl May's Oriental Odyssey will be completed.
In your memory
Sleep peacefully my sweet
Elaine.

Chapter 30

Prester John, before God and our Lord Jesus Christ, Merciful King of Kings, to Alexios Komnenos, Governor of Constantinople. Health and a happy conclusion.

Our Majesty has become aware that you have heard of our splendor and that you have been informed of our greatness. What we would like to know is whether you adhere to the true belief, in particular a belief in our Lord Jesus Christ.

If you desire to know of our magnificent greatness and our might as well as the extent of our lands, then know and believe without doubt that we are Prester John, the servant of God. That we exceed all the riches under heaven and that in respect of honor and might, we are greater than all the kings of the earth. Seventy Kings pay us tribute. We are a devout Christian and we protect and support with charity every poor Christian who seeks refuge and mercy in our domain. We have made an oath to visit the grave of our Lord with a great army and to do battle against any enemy of the cross of Christ, to chastise them and to honor his holy name, as is proper for the glory of our Majesty.

Our splendor reigns over the three Indies and our occupation extends to the furthest reaches of the India, in which the body of the Holy Apostle Thomas rests. From there across the wilderness, which extends to the rising sun, and back towards the sunset, to Babylon, the abandoned, yes, even to the tower of Babel.

Seventy-two provinces obey us, some of those provinces are Christian, and each has its own King. Yet all these kings pay us tribute. Elephants, Dromedaries and Camels can be found in our lands, and almost all kinds of animals that exist under heaven. Our lands run with milk and honey. In one part of our domain no poison can do harm; in another grow all kind of peppers; in yet another, hyenas are so plentiful that they are like the trees of a forest, and snakes are in our entire domain. There is even a sea of sand without water. Three days of journey from this sea are mountains, from which rivers of stones descend. Near these mountains is a desert between arid hills. Beneath these flows a subterranean stream to which there is no access, this stream fills a great river, and people of our domain enter it to find gems in great quantity. Further across from the river live ten tribes of Jews, who, although they claim to have their own King, are nonetheless our servants and pay us tribute.

In another one of our provinces, near the hot zone, there are worms that are called Salamander in our language. These worms can only live in fire and weave a cocoon about them just like the silk worms. From these cocoons our palace ladies spin threads and our clothes are the proof of it. But they can only be cleansed in a bright flame.

At the head of our army, thirteen, gold with gemstone encrusted, crosses are carried. But if we ride without heads of state, only one cross is used that is not adorned with neither figures or jewels so that we think of our Lord Jesus Christ. So that all people know that we carry the King of Kings before us, we also carry a silver urn filled with gold.

Every year we visit the body of the Holy Daniel who is in the desert near Babylon. Our palace is of ebony and of acacia wood and can not be damaged by fire. At each end of the roof are two golden apples and in each apple are two carbuncles, so that the gold may shine by day and the carbuncle may shine by night. The great doors are of sardonyx mixed with horn, so that anyone carrying poison can not enter. The smaller doors are of ebony. The windows are of crystal. The tables are of gold and amethyst, and the pillars that carry them are of ivory. The room in which we sleep is a wondrous masterpiece of gold, silver and every kind of gemstone. In it incense burns continually. Our bed is of sapphire. We also have the most beautiful women. Every day we entertain thirty thousand people, aside from the occasional visitors. And all these draw daily from our resources to tend to their horses and for other uses. Whilst every month we are served by seven kings who in turn are served by sixty-five Dukes and they are served by three hundred and sixty-five Earls. In our hall dine daily twelve Archbishops to our right and twenty bishops to our left, as well as the patriarch of Saint Thomas, the protopapas of Salmas and the Archiprotopapas of Susa, in whose city the throne our fame and the emperor's palace is located. Abbots, that number the days of a year, manage the spiritual duties for us in our chapel. Our cupbearer is a primate and a King. Our housemaster is an Archbishop and a King. Our chamber servant is a bishop and a King. Our marshal is an Archimandrit and a King. And our chef is an abbot and a King; but we take a lower rank and a humble name, so that we show our great humility."

Such reads the extract of a letter that the famous, but perhaps historically questionable, Tartar King Prester John wrote, or allegedly wrote, to the Greek emperor. Whether the letter was real or not, it contains, apart from some amusing peculiarities that are founded in the erroneous views of the previous centuries, facts and details that have been substantiated by Marco Polo, Sir

John Mandeville and other travelers and researchers. And I was jovially reminded of these as I now stopped on the eastern height of Sheik Adi and looked towards morning, where the mountains of Surgh, Zibar, Haïr, Tura Ghara, Baz, Jelu, Tkhoma, Karitha and Tijari lay.

In the valleys that lie between them, live the last remnants of this Christian sect that once belonged to that Tartar King. In his time they were mighty and influential people. The seats of their churches were scattered across the entire Asian continent, from the coast of the Caspian Sea to the Seas of China and from the most northern borders of Scithia [Skythien] to the furthest southern reaches of the Indian sub-continent. They were the advisors of Mohammed and his successors. The Christian reminiscences of the Koran are mostly taken from their books and teachings. But with the fall of the Caliph, their might also crumbled, and with a tremendous speed; for their inner, spiritual constitution lost the divine purity that lends its might to an unconquerable disposition. Under the rule of Kassan, the son of Arghun and nephew of the famous emperor of Baghdad, Hulaku Khan, the rout against them had already begun. But then the great Tamerlan attacked them without mercy. He pursued them with a ravenous rage, destroyed their churches and delivered all those who did not manage to escape into the impassable mountains, to the sword. The great-nephews of these survivors still live today, in places that can only be compared to castles. They are all that remains of the once mighty Assyrian people, who now constantly see the sword of the Turk and the dagger of the Kurd dangle above them, and lately had to suffer atrocities that raise the hairs at the nape of one's neck in their retelling. The greater part of the guilt can be attributed to those overseas missionaries, that gave their schools and houses of worship the appearance of fortifications and thereby awoke the distrust of the local wielders of power. With this and similar careless acts they have damaged not only their work but also their followers.

On my ride to Amadijah I also came, quite expectedly, into villages that were occupied by these Chaldean Christians; reason enough to think about that letter which detailed the past in such a lively manner. Once minister and advisors to Princes and Caliphs, they are now, unless they have returned to the folds of the Catholic Church, without inner and outer strength. Thus men like the infamous Beder Khan *Bei* and his ally Abd el Summit *Bei* could wage a terrible butchery among them, without finding the slightest resistance. And yet the difficult terrain in which they lived provided them with the most successful defense.

How exceedingly manlier had the *Jesidi* acted!

After the night of the flames in the Idiz valley, Ali *Bei* rode to Jerraijah, apparently only accompanied by ten men. But shortly before his departure he had send a considerable number of warriors towards Bozan.

The *Mutessarif* arrived with an equally strong entourage, but Ali *Bei* had discovered from his scouts, that between Scio Khan and Ras ul Aïn a considerable troop had been assembled, that was to advance on Sheik Adi that same day. On receiving this intelligence he simply had the *Mutessarif* surrounded and taken him prisoner. To regain his freedom, the *Mutessarif* was forced to abandon all treacherous plans and accept the *Bei's* suggestions peacefully.

It followed then that the interrupted festivities of the *Jesidi* were recommenced with a joy that was probably never before or since seen in Sheik Adi.

After the conclusion of these festivities I wanted to begin the journey to Amadijah, but I discovered that Mohammed Emin twisted his ankle in the Kaloni Mountains and so I was forced to wait three weeks for it to heal. But I did not let the highly welcome opportunity pass to enhance my familiarity with the Kurds.

Finally the Haddedihn let me know through a messenger that he was ready to depart and so I had arisen early this day to meet him at the abode of the chieftain of the Badinan Kurds. My farewell from the *Jesidi* was heartfelt and I had to promise, on my return, to spend a few days with them. Although I had declined to be accompanied, Ali *Bei* could not be dissuaded to at least bring me as far as the camp of the Badinan to also say a farewell to Mohammed Emin.

We kept to the eastern slopes of Sheik Adi and reminisced about the happenings of the last weeks. What would the next days bring? The further we climbed towards the northeast, the wilder the inhabitants of the mountain became, and they knew no farming and only existed through robbery and the raising of cattle. Ali *Bei* may have read my thoughts.

"Emir, you proceed on difficult and dangerous paths," he commented. "How deep do you go into these mountains?"

"Firstly to Amadijah."

"You will have to got further."

"How so?"

"Your task in Amadijah may or may not succeed, then your only remaining option is to flee. The way that the son of Mohammed Emin would choose to return to his Haddedihn is known, and it will be watched. How do you intend to proceed?"

"I will have to be guided by the circumstances. We could go south and down the Zab Ala or escape on horseback along the Akra-River. We could also go north, across the mountains of Tijari and Maranan-Dagh, then on to Khabur and ford the Tigris, so that we reach Sindshar after crossing the salt plain."

"In that case we will not see you again!"

"God guides the thoughts and steps of men; to him all is known!"

We rode on. Halef and the *Bashi-Bozuk* followed us. My stallion had made full use of the interlude. He had earlier only eaten *Balahat*-dates and now had to get used to other food, it seemed to me that he had gained quite a bit of muscle flesh and desired to show his overabundance of his strength, I thus had to clamp him roughly between my thighs. Besides, I was also anxious to discover how he would prove himself when it came to crossing the snowy mountains of Kurdistan.

Soon we arrived at the camp of the Badinan and were welcomed happily by them. Mohammed Emin was ready for travel, and after we had talked, eaten and smoked for an hour we departed. Ali *Bei* shook everyone's hand and mine last. In his eyes was a tear.

"Emir, do you believe, that I care for you?" he asked movingly.

"I know it; but I too part from you melancholically for you have touched my soul."

"You depart and I remain; but my thoughts will accompany you, my wishes will settle in the tracks of your feet. You have said farewell to Mir Sheik Khan, but he has given me a blessing that I am to lay upon your head at the moment of our parting. God be with you and remain with you for all time and on all your paths; may his wrath be felt by your enemies and his mercy by your friends! You go towards great danger and Mir Sheik Khan has promised you his protection. He sends you this *Melek Ta-us* that it may serve you as a talisman. I know that you do not consider this bird an idol but a symbol that identifies you as our friend. Every *Jesidi*, to whom you show this *Ta-us*, will offer his service and his life to you. Take this gift but never entrust it to another, for it is only meant for you! And now, farewell and do not forget those who love you!"

He embraced me, quickly mounted his horse and rode off without looking back. I felt as though a part of my heart went with him. It was a great, mighty gift that Mir Sheik Khan had given to me through him. How much argument had been made on the existence of this *Melek Ta-us*! And here I had this enigmatic symbol in my own hand. It was an unusual trust that the Khan had bestowed on me, and it was clear that I would only use this device in the direst need.

It was of copper and depicted a bird that spread its wings for flight, below it the Kurmangji-word *'Hemjer'*, that is 'Friend' or 'Compatriot', was engraved. A silken cord was attached so that it could be fastened around the neck.

The Badinan desired to accompany us for a while, I had to permit it, but made it conditional that they return upon reaching the village of Kalahoni. This village is some four hours distance from Sheik Adi. Its houses are almost exclusively built of stone and are situated in-between the vineyards like gigantic bird nests high above the riverbed of the Gomel. Their durable appearance comes from the huge stone blocks that serve as door lintels and also as the cornerstones of these structures.

Here we said farewell and then the four of us rode on.

On a very steep path that was difficult on our horses, we reached the small village of Bebozi, which sits on the peak of a considerable height. There is a Catholic Church, for the inhabitants are Chaldeans who have been converted to that religion. They welcomed us in a friendly manner and we received food and drink without payment. They wanted to provide me with a guide; but since I declined this, the way to the next village was described to me with such great care that we could not possibly err.

The path firstly led us along a crest and through a forest of dwarf oaks and then descended into a valley in which lies Cheloki. In this village we rested briefly and I took the *Bashi-Bozuk* aside:

"*Buluk-Emini*, listen to what I say to you!"

"I hear, Emir!"

"The *Mutessarif* of Mosul has ordered you, to cater for everything that I need. Up to now you have not been of use to me; but from this day forth you will do your duty."

"What shall I do, *Effendi*?"

"Tonight we will stay in Spandareh. You ride ahead and make certain that everything is prepared for my arrival. Do you understand me?"

"Very well, Emir!" he answered with the dignity of his office. "I will hurry and when you arrive the whole village will greet you with joy."

He kicked his heels into his donkey's flank and rode off.

It is not far to Spandareh from Cheloki, yet night was already coming when we reached this great Kurdish village. It derives its name from the large number of poplars that grow there; for Spidar, Spindar and also Spandar is the Kurmangji word for white poplar. We asked for the home of the Kiajah, but received only a grim look instead of an answer.

I had asked my question in Turkish; I now repeated it in Kurdish and thus I asked for the *Malkoe-gund*, which means village elder. This immediately made the people more amenable. We were led to a large house where we dismounted and entered. In one of the rooms a loud discussion was taking place, which we could hear quite clearly. I stood still and listened.

"Who are you, you dog, you coward?" shouted an angry voice. "*A Bashi-Bozuk* you are, that rides a donkey. That is an honor for you, but a disgrace for the donkey; for the one it carries is more stupid than it is. And you come here to drive me out!"

"And who are you, hey?" answered the voice of my brave Ifra. "You are an Arnaut, a cutthroat, a scoundrel! Your mouth is like the mouth of a frog; your eyes are that of a toad; your nose is like a *Chyjar* [cucumber], and your voice equals the cry of a quail! I am a *Buluk-Emini* of the Sultan; and what are you? A *Khawass*, a simple *Khawass*, nothing else."

"Blast you, I turn your face towards your back if you are not silent! What is my nose to you? You don't have one at all! You say that your master is a great *Effendi*, an Emir and an Occidental Sheik? One only has to look at you and one knows who he is! And you come here to oust me?"

"And who is your master? A great Occidental *Effendi* as well, so you say? But I say to you that in the entire Occident there is only one great *Effendi* and that is my master. Remember that!"

"Listen," a third voice uttered quietly and seriously; "You have announced two *Effendies* to me. One has a letter from the *Onsul* [Consul] of the Franks, that has been countersigned by the *Mutessarif*; that counts. But the other is *Giölgeda padishahnün*; he has writings from the Onsul, the Sultan and the *Mutessarif* and even has the right to the *Dish-parassi*; that counts even more. The latter will stay with me; for the other I will have another house prepared. One will receive everything free of charge; but the other will pay for everything."

"That I will not tolerate!" the voice of the Arnaut said. "What goes for one goes for the other too!"

"Listen, I am the *Nezanum* [head, leader] and master here; what I say, goes, and no foreigner dictates to me. *Söjle-dim* - I have spoken!"

I now opened the door and entered along with Mohammed Emin.

"*Ivari 'l kher* - Good evening!" I greeted. "You are the master of Spandareh?"

"That I am."

I indicated the *Buluk-Emini*. “This man is my servant. I have sent him to you to request your hospitality. What have you decided?”

“You are the one who is under the protection of the Sultan and have the right to the *Dish-parassi*?”

“I am he.”

“And this man is your companion?”

“My friend and companion.”

“Do you have many people with you?”

“Just this *Buluk-Emini* and another servant.”

“*Ser sere men at* - You are welcome to me!” He arose from his seat and offered us his hand. “Sit next to my fire and enjoy my home! You shall have a room that is suitable for your needs. How high do you estimate *your Dish-parassi* to be?”

“For both of us and my servant, may it be a gift to you. But for *this Bashi-Bozuk* you will pay five piaster [one Mark]. He is a representative of the *Mutessarif*, and I do not have the right to deny it for him.”

“Lord, you are considerate and kind; I thank you! You shall not be left wanting for your comfort. But permit me and this *Khawass* to leave for a moment!”

He meant the Arnaut. That one had listened to us with a dark mien; and now he raged:

“I will not leave; I demand the same right for my master!”

“Then stay!” the Nezanum said simply. “But if your master does not find any accommodation than it will be your fault.”

“Who are these men that claim that they are under the protection of the Sultan? Arabs they are, who rob and steal in the desert and play at being Lords here in the mountains ... “

“Hajji Halef!” I called loudly.

The little servant entered.

“Halef, this *Khawass* dares to revile us; if he utters just one more word that I disapprove of, I will place him into your hands!”

The Arnaut, who was armed to his teeth, looked down at Halef with open hostility.

“I should fear this dwarf, I, who ... “

He could not speak further for he already lay flat on the ground and the little Hajji was kneeling on him with a dagger twitching in his right hand whilst his left was clasped tightly around the Arnaut's throat.

"Shall I, *Sihdi*?"

"For now it is enough; but tell him that his life is forfeit if he commits another hostile act!"

Halef let him go, and he arose. His eyes flashed with angry guile but he did not dare to make another move.

"Come!" ordered the village elder. "You will accept the allocated accommodation?" then elder asked.

"Yes, for now. But when my master arrives I will send him to you and then it will be decided who will sleep in your house. And he will also pass judgment over me and this servant of these two Arabs!"

They departed together. During their absence, one of the sons of the *Nezanum* acted as our host and soon it was said that the place where we should sleep had been prepared for us.

We were led into a chamber in the middle of which two soft beds had been prepared with the means of some carpets; in the midst of these the evening meal had been served. This had happened with such speed that it was obvious that the elder did not count among the poorer inhabitants of the village. His son sat down with us but did not partake of the meal; perhaps it was proof of the respect in which we were held, at least we could imagine such. The woman and a daughter of the leader attended to our needs.

First off, we were handed sherbet. We drank it from very lovely *Finjani ferfuri* [Porcelain bowls], they are a rarity here in Kurdistan. Then we received *Valquapamasi*, wheat bread fried in honey, to that the imperative *Findika* [salad made from the delicate pistachio leaves] did not fit quite well. That was followed by a young *Bizihn* [roasted goat] with rice balls, that swam in the juices of the same, along with *Bera ash* [literally: millstones - a very solid biscuit in the form of a millstone], that completely explained the name. Two little roasts that formed the transition were very appetizing to me. They were roasted to a 'crisp' brown perfection; I certainly believed them to be pigeons. They were really delicious, but they had a taste that was somewhat foreign.

"Is this *Kewuk* [pigeon]?" I asked the young man.

"No. It is *Barjemik* [bat]," he answered.

Hmm! A right beautiful gastronomic surprise! The leader entered. On my invitation he seated himself next to us and partook of the meal. All throughout the meal fragrant *Fistik* [Mastix] [See Translation Note Ch 30. 1] burned on a tin plate. Now that the master of the house was present, the main dish was served. It contained *Quapameh*, roast mutton in sour cream, and it was served with *Pirinj*

[Rice], that was boiled with *Pivaz* [onions]. When we had satiated ourselves with it, the leader beckoned. A covered vessel was brought that he received with an important mien.

"Guess what this is!" he invited me.

"Show it!"

"This is a dish that you do not know. It is only made in Kurdistan where there are strong and courageous men."

"You are making me inquisitive!"

"Whoever eats of it, his might is doubled and he does no longer fear any enemy. Smell it!"

He lifted the lid a little and let me sniff the aroma.

"Such a roast is only available in Kurdistan?" I asked.

"Yes."

"You err; for I have already eaten this meat many times."

"Where?"

"With the Urus and other people, but particularly in a land that is called America. There this animal grows much larger and is even more dangerous and much wilder than here."

"It is you who err; for only here in Kurdistan does this beast exist."

"I have never been in Kurdistan, yet I already know this meat from its aroma; thus I must have already eaten it in other lands."

"What kind of animal is it?"

"Its is a *Hirj* [Bear]. Am I right?"

"Yes truly, you know it!" he exclaimed full of wonder.

"I know it better than you think. I have not yet peeked inside this vessel, yet I wager that it is the meat of the *Nanuhk* [paw] of the bear!"

"You have guessed it! Take and eat!"

Now the hunting tales began. The bear is quite abundant in Kurdistan, but he is by far not as dangerous as the great fearsome beast of North America. Along with the steamed bear paws came a thick purée of dried *Hermeh* and *Eruhks* [Pears and Plums], that was followed by an armored dish, namely boiled crabs, that were accompanied by a side dish that appeared foreign and complicated to me. I thus desired to be enlightened and the wife of the leader was prepared to provide me with information:

"Take *Kundir* [pumpkin] and cook it until it is mush," she said. "Add *Shukir* [sugar] and *Rune kehl 'e* [melted butter], stir in clear *Panir* [cheese] and cut *Sir* [garlic] and add some crushed *Tu* [mulberries] and softened kernels of *Guli roshyan* [sunflower] to it. Then you have a dish that has no equal!"

I tried the unequaled mix of pumpkin and sunflower, cheese, sugar, butter, mulberries and garlic and discovered that the taste of this dish was not as terrible as the ingredients suggested. The end of the meal was comprised of dried *Sev* and *Sherabi* [Apple and Grapes], to which *Racki* was sipped. And finally the tobacco pipes came into play.

Whilst we lit the strong, rough and poorly fermented tobacco of Kelekowa, a boisterous conversation could be heard from below. The leader went to investigate, and since he left the door open we could hear every word that was spoken.

"Who is there?" he asked.

"What does he want?" I heard another voice ask in English.

"He asks, who it is," answered a third voice also in English.

"What is Turkish for: I?"

"*Ben.*"

"Well! *Ben*!!!" was shouted at the host.

"*Ben*?" the host asked. "What is your name?"

"What does he want?" asked the rattling voice that was so well known to me, that I arose in surprise.

"He asks, what your name is."

"Sir David Lindsay!" the voice shouted.

In the next second I was standing next to him on the floor below. Yes, there he was, lit by the fire of the *Aryuhn* [hearth]. There was the high, gray top hat, the long thin face, the wide mouth, the Sierra-Morena-Nose, the bare, dry neck, the wide collar, the gray checkered necktie, the gray checkered vest, the gray checkered frock, the gray checkered trousers, the gray checkered spats and the dust gray boots. And truly, in his right hand he carried the famous hoe that had the noble purpose of excavating 'Fowling-bulls' and other ancient artifacts!

"Master Lindsay!" I cried out.

"Well! Ah, who is it? Oh - ah - it is you?!"

He opened his eyes and mouth even wider than before and looked at me in amazement as though I were a man risen from the dead.

"How do you come to Spandareh, Sir?" I asked almost as amazed as he.

"I? Well! I rode!"

"Naturally! But what do you seek here?"

"I? Oh! Hmm! You and 'Fowling-bulls'!"

"Me?"

"Yes! Will explain. But first squabble!"

"With whom?"

"With mayor, with leader of this village. Terrible fellow!"

"Why?"

"Does not want Englishman, wants Arabs! Miserable! Where is the fellow, him?!"

"Here he is," I answered indicating the elder who had come closer.

"Squabble with him, reason with him!" Lindsay ordered the translator who stood next to him. "Quarrel, scold, very loud and much!"

"Permit me, Sir, to take over," I said. "The two Arabs that annoy you will not be in your way. They are your best friends."

"Ah! Where are they?"

"I am one and the other is Mohammed Emin."

"Moh - - - ah! Emin - - ah! Where?"

"Upstairs. Come with me!"

"Well! Ah, extraordinary, immense, inconceivable!"

He did not resist as I pushed him up the narrow stairs, the translator and the Arnaut wanted to follow but I turned them back. The two Kurdish ladies were quite shocked by the gray checkered apparition; they cowered into the furthest corner. But Mohammed Emin, who was normally a serious man, laughed out loud as he spied the dark crater that was formed by the wide open mouth of the Englishman.

"Ah! Good day, Sir, Master Mohammed! How do you do?"

"*Mash Allah*! How did this *Inglis* get here?" Mohammed asked.

"That we will discover."

"Do you know this man?" The master of the house asked.

"I know him. He is the same stranger who sent his *Khawass* earlier to arrange to stay with you. He is my friend. Have you arranged accommodation for him?"

"If he is your friend then he shall stay in my house," came the answer.

"You have room enough for so many people?"

"For guests, that are welcome, there is always enough room. He may be seated and partake of the meal!"

"Sit down, Sir," I said to Lindsay, "and let us know what thought enticed you to leave the grazing lands of the Haddedihn and come to Spandareh!"

"Well! But first provide."

"What?"

"Servants."

"They may cater for themselves, for that is their task."

"Horses."

"They will be provided for by the servants. Well then, Master?"

"Hmm! Was tedious, terribly boring!"

"Have you not excavated?"

"Much, a great deal."

"And found something?"

"Nothing, zilch, nothing at all! Terrible!"

"Go on!"

"Yearning, horrible yearning!"

"For what?"

"Hmm! You, Sir!"

I laughed.

"So, because of yearning for me!"

"Well, very well, yes! Not find 'Fowling-bulls', you not there so I go."

"But Sir, we had decided that you stay until we return!"

"No patience, could not stand it!"

"There would have been enough conversation!"

"With Arabs? Pshaw! They could not understand me!"

"You had a translator!"

"Gone, away, absconded."

"Ah! The Greek, this Kolettis escaped? But he was wounded!"

"Hole in the leg, it healed. Scoundrel was gone early in the morning!"

"Then of course you could not have made yourself understood. How did you find me?"

"Knew that you headed for Amadijah. Went to Mosul. Consul provided a passport; Governor signed it, arranged translator and *Khawass*. Went to Dohuk."

"To Dohuk? Why the detour?"

"War with Devil men; could not get through. From Dohuk to Duliah and from Duliah to Mungeyshi. Then to here. Well! Found you. Very good, wonderful!"

"But what now?"

"Stay together, adventure, excavate! Send 'Fowling-bulls', Traveler-Club, London, yes!"

"Right, Master Lindsay! But now we have other things to do."

"What?"

"You know the reason that leads us to Amadijah!"

"Know it. Good reason, courageous reason, adventures! Fetch Master Amad el Ghandur. Will help!"

"I believe that you will not be of much use to us."

"Not! Why?"

"You only understand English."

"Have translator!"

"Do you want to make him privy to this secret? Or perhaps you have already spoken with him about it?"

"Not a word!"

"That is good, Sir, otherwise we would have been placed into a tremendously risky situation. I have to openly admit to you that I would have wished to meet up with you much later."

"You? Me? Well, away! Believed that you were my friend! But not this, so away! Travel to ... to ... to ... "

"To where the pepper grows, nowhere else! It is self evident that you are my friend and that I am yours also; but surely you must see that you could only endanger us!"

"Endanger? Why?"

"You are too noticeable!"

"Well, no longer noticeable! What must I do?"

"Hmm, that is a highly delicate affair! I can't send you back; I can't leave you here; I will have to take you along; there really is no other solution!"

"Great, very good!"

"But you have to listen to us."

"Listen? Well, will do it!"

"You dismiss your translator and your *Khawass*."

"Must go, to the devil, yes!"

"And your clothing must go!"

"Go? Ah! Where?"

"Away, totally. You must dress like a Turk or a Kurd."

He gave me an indescribable look, as though I had dared him to go and devour himself. His oral grimace would have been entirely capable of that.

"Like a Turk? Like a Kurd! Horrible, dreadful."

"There is no other way!"

"What to wear?"

"Turkish pantaloons or black and red Kurdish leggings."

"Black and red! Ah, good, very good! Black and red checkered!"

"If you like. How do you want to appear? As a Turk or a Kurd?"

"Kurd."

"Then you will have to wear black and red; those are the Kurdish traditional colors. So Kurdish trousers, a vest and a shirt that is worn over the trousers."

"Black and red?"

"Yes."

"Checkered?"

"If you like! It has to cover you from the neck to the ankles. Then a frock or a coat over that."

"Black and red?"

"Of course!"

"Checkered?"

"If you like! Then a turban of gigantic size, as is worn by the elegant Kurds."

"Black and red?"

"As well!"

"Checkered?"

"If you like!"

"Followed by a belt, socks, shoes and weapons ... "

"Black and red?"

"No objection!"

"And checkered?"

"I don't care if you have your entire face checkered with black and red!"

"Where do we buy these clothes?"

"I have no idea. We will only find a bazaar in Amadijah. But perhaps a trader can be found here, for Spandareh is a large village. And ... you have money, lots of money, right?"

"Much, very much, well! Will pay for everything!"

"I will ask."

I turned to the leader:

"Is there an *Urubaji* [tailor or garment seller] here?"

"No."

"Is there a man that can ride to Amadijah and fetch some clothes for this foreigner?"

"Yes, but the bazaar will only open early tomorrow morning, and the garments will arrive much later."

"Or is there a man that could lend us some clothes till we reach Amadijah?"

"You are my guest; I have a new *Panbukah* [Suit made of woolen cloth]; I will gladly lend it to you."

"And a turban too?"

"No-one here has two turbans; but a cap you can obtain easily."

"What kind?"

"I will give you a *Kulik* [a cap of felt made from goat hair], that will fit him."

"What color is it?"

"Its is red and has black bands."

"Then I request of you to gather everything together early tomorrow morning. You designate a man who will accompany us, whom we shall compensate. We will give him the suit in Amadijah to return to you. But I desire that nothing is said about this!"

"Both of us, my man and I, will be silent!"

Now the evening meal commenced for the Englishman. He received our leftovers that had been refurbished. He not only displayed a healthy appetite but also appeared to be genuinely hungry; for a great part of the meal that was placed before him, disappeared between his long yellow teeth. With silent satisfaction I noted that he too was served that little roast which I had believed to be pigeon. He did not leave even the smallest bone. Later a finely decorated wooden plate was set before him, among other things, that contained a small serving in the form of a beef steak, that had such a beautiful aroma that even my own appetite was stimulated once again despite my being quite satiated. I had to know what this was.

"*Sidna*, what lovely food is this?" I asked the wife who served the Englishman.

"It is *Jekurjek* [grasshopper]," she answered.

"And how is it prepared?"

"The grasshoppers are roasted, crushed and laid into the earth until they begin to smell. Then I fry the dough in *Dune zeitun* [olive oil]."

Not bad! I decided that it was most important to relay this recipe to my dear 'Master Fowling-bull' as soon as possible. I descended the stairs to see to the horses whilst he was still eating. They were well catered for. Halef, the translator, the *Buluk-Emini* and the Arnaut stood close by. They were deeply involved in a squabble that immediately ceased when I approached.

"What are you quarreling about, Halef?" I asked of him.

He indicated the Arnaut.

"This man dishonors you, *Sihdi*. He has threatened to murder you and I, because I have thrown him to the ground at your command."

"Let him talk! He will do nothing."

The Arnaut placed a hand on his pistol and shouted:

"Silcncc, Man! Or you will mcct this, your scrvant in *Jehennah* this day?"

"*Jit-i, ker, werujem, ti szi szlep* - Be quiet, dog! I believe you are totally blind!" I answered him in his language. "Do you not see the danger to which you submit yourself?"

"What danger?" he asked incredulously.

"*Male ti pucshke ne gajaju dobo* - Those pistols don't shoot so well!" I answered whilst pointing at his weapons.

"Why?"

"*Buduji um-e-m öno bölje* - because I can do it better!"

At the same time I pointed my revolver at him. I had learned enough of the violence of these Arnaut soldiers to take even such a little incident seriously. An Arnaut cares little for the life of a fellow human being. He shoots a man down for the sake of a sip of water and then bends his own head for the sword of his executioner with the same demeanor. We had insulted this *Khawass*; at least one shot could be expected of him. Yet he removed his hands from his pistols and asked in amazement:

"You speak the language of the *Shkiperia* [that is what the Albanian call their land]?"

"As you can hear!"

"Are you a *Shkipetar*?"

"No."

"What else?"

"I am a *Nematz* [German], and I tell you that the people of *Nemacshka* [Germany] know how to deal with your kind."

"You are only a *Nematz*? No *Majar*, no *Rusz*, no *Szrbin* [Serb] and no *Turcshin*? *Obictz-i jawo-wraga* - Go to hell!"

He lifted a pistol with lighting speed and squeezed off a shot. If I had not kept a keen eye on the barrel of the pistol, the bullet would have entered my brain; but I ducked quickly and the shot went over my head. Before he could fire the second barrel, I had rushed him pinned his arms to his side.

"Shall I shoot him, *Sihdi*?" asked Halef.

"No. Bind him!"

To pull his arms to his back, I had to release him momentarily. He made full use of the moment, tore himself free, and ran. In the blink of an eye he was gone between the trees that separated the buildings. All present hurried after him, but they returned soon without having seen him.

The crack of the shot had enticed the others to come.

"Who fired, Sir?" asked Lindsay.

"Your *Khawass*."

"At who?"

"At me."

"Ah! Terrible! Why?"

"Because of vengeance."

"A real Arnaut! Did he hit you?"

"No."

"Shoot him, Sir; immediately!"

"He absconded."

"Well; let him go! No damage!"

Of course he was quite correct. The Arnaut did not wound me, why should I thus thirst for his blood? Surely he would not return, and a treacherous attack was likewise unlikely. The Englishman, now that he had found me, did not need him or the translator and so the translator was paid off with the understanding that he would leave Spandareh early tomorrow morning and return to Mosul.

The rest of the evening we spent with the Kurds in lively conversation that ended with a dance that was dedicated to us. We were invited to come into the courtyard. It was a square that was surrounded by a low roof, on which all the men present had seated themselves. They laid, squatted and kneeled in various artistic poses, whilst some thirty women gathered in the courtyard for the dance.

They formed a double circle, in the middle of which stood the main dancer who swung a lance. The orchestra was comprised of a flute, a kind of violin and two tambourines. The lead dancer gave a loud shout that was the signal to commence the dance. His art consisted of complex arm and foot movements that always started from and ended in the initial position. The circle of women copied each movement. I did not believe that this simple dance had a purpose or that it was symbolic; but yet the women, with their multi-edged turban caps, from which long veils descended down their backs, and the uncertain flicker of the burning torches, the whole presented a beautiful sight.

When this dance was concluded, the men made their approval known via a loud murmur, I pulled forth an armband and called the daughter of the leader, who had served our meal, over to me. The band was made of yellow pieces of glass and had the deceptive appearance of smoky, semi-transparent amber, which is so expensive and much desired in the Orient. In a German *Kitsch* store I would have paid fifty or sixty pennies for the band; but here I would create such joy, which would be of far greater worth to me.

The girl came to me. All the men had heard that I had called her to me, and knew that it regarded praise. I just had to try to honor the politeness of my parents.

"Come here, you loveliest daughter of the Missuri Kurds! The light of *Shefag* [rosy dawn] dances on your cheeks, and your face is as lovely as the *Kelch Sumbul* [Hyacinth]. Your long locks carry the aroma of *Hauch Gulilik* [Flower], and your voice sounds like the song of the *Bulbuli* [Nightingale]. You are the child of hospitality, the daughter of a hero, and will be the bride of a wise Kurd and a courageous warrior. Your hands and your feet have delighted me just like a drop satiates one who thirsts. Take this *Bazihn* [armband], and think of me when you adorn yourself with it!"

She flushed with joy and with embarrassment and did not know how to answer.

"*Az khorbane ta, Hodia* - I am yours [literally: 'Your offering'], oh Lord," she finally lisped.

That is the traditional greeting of a Kurdish woman and girl towards a noble man. Even the village elder was so joyful that his daughter received such notice that he forgot the oriental restraint and let the gift be passed to him in order to examine it.

"Oh how lovely, how valuable!" he cried and let the armband pass around the circle. "That is amber, such good, such splendid amber, the Sultan has non-better for his pipe! My daughter, your father could not give you such a marriage gift, like this Emir has given to you. From his lips sounds the voice of reason, and from the hairs of his *Simbehl* [mustache] drips mercy. Ask him if he permits to be thanked as a daughter thanks her father!"

She blushed even more than before; but she asked non-the-less:

"Do you permit it, Lord?"

"I permit it."

She bent over me, since I was sitting on the ground, and kissed me on the lips and on both my cheeks; then she quickly danced away.

I was not surprised by this display of gratitude, for I knew that with the Kurds it was permitted that girls even greeted their acquaintances with a kiss. To a nobleman such a familiarity would have been an insult, and that is why the perception of my kindness doubled as I permitted to receive a kiss. The village elder immediately voiced such.

"Emir, your mercy enlightens my house as the light of the sun that warms the earth. You have blessed my daughter so that she might remember you; permit me that I too give you a remembrance so that you might not forget Spandareh!"

He lent over the edge of the roof and shouted the word *'Dojan'* [falcon] into the courtyard below. At once a happy barking was heard; a door was opened, and I noted that those standing below made room for a dog so that it could ascend the stairs and come to us. Only a moment later it stood next to the elder and caressed him. It was one of those valuable yellow-gray and extraordinarily large and strong Afghan hounds that are called *Slogi* in India, Persia, Turkestan and all the way to Siberia. With the Kurds this rare breed is called *Tazi*. They run down the flighty gazelle; they often catch the wild donkey on their own, match the fast as the wind *Jiggetai*, and are fearless of the panther and the bear. I had to admit that the sight of this animal awakened a lively admiration within me. It was as a dog as valuable as my stallion that deserved this same rating among horses.

"Emir," the elder said, "the dogs of the Missuri Kurds are famous across all of our mountains. I have raised many *Tazi*, of which I could have been proud; but none was equal to this one. It is yours!"

"*Nezanum*, this gift is so valuable that I can not possibly accept it," I answered him.

"Do you wish to insult me?" he asked seriously.

"No, that I do not want to do," I began. "I only wanted to say that your kindness is greater than mine. Permit it that I accept this *Tazi*, but also permit me to give you this little bottle!"

"What is it? A scent from Persia?"

"No. I bought it at the Beith Allah in the holy city of Mecca and it contains water from Zem-Zem."

I loosened it from my neck and passed it to him. He was so mightily astounded that he forgot to reach for it. I thus laid it into his lap.

"Oh Emir, what are you doing!" he finally cried with delight. "You bring the most delightful gift into my house, a gift that Allah has lent to the world. Are you seriously giving this to me?"

"Take it; I give it to you gladly!"

"Blessed be your hand and may luck always be on your path! Come here, you men, and touch this bottle so that the goodness of this great Emir may also shine upon you!"

The bottle passed from hand to hand. With it I had bestowed the greatest joy possible. As the immense delight of the elder abated somewhat, he again turned to me:

"Lord, this dog is now yours. Spit into its mouth three times, and take him this night under your mantle when you sleep, then he will never leave you!"

The Englishman had watched everything without understanding much of the goings on. He now asked me:

"Gifted Zem-Zem, Master?"

"Yes."

"Well! Away with it! Water is Water!"

"Do you know what I got for it?"

"What?"

"This dog."

"How? What? Inconceivable!"

"Why not?"

"Too valuable. Know these dogs! This one is worth fifty pound!"

"Much more. But it still belongs to me."

"Why?"

"Because I have gifted that armband to the village elder's daughter."

"Horrible fellow! Colossal luck! First, horse from Mohammed Emin, nothing to pay and now Afghan hound as well! Not so lucky I. Not found a single 'Fowling-bull'. Awful!"

Even Mohammed admired the dog, and I would have happily believed that he was a little jealous of me. I had to admit it. I was very lucky.

Shortly before going to bed, I checked on the horses once more. The leader met me there.

"Emir," he asked quietly, "may I ask you a question?"

"Speak!"

"You go to Amadijah?"

"Yes."

"And still further?"

"That I do not know."

"There is a secret to it?"

"You guess there is?"

"I guess it."

"Why?"

"You have an Arab with you that is careless. He drew back the sleeve of his garment and exposed his tattoo to my eyes. He is an enemy of the Kurds and an enemy of the *Mutessarif*; he is a Haddedihn. Have I seen correctly?"

"He is an enemy of the *Mutessarif*, but not an enemy of the Kurds," I answered.

This man was trustworthy; I could not lie to him. It was certainly better to trust him than to tell him untruths that he would not believe anyway.

"The Arabs are always enemies of the Kurds; but he is your friend and my guest; I will not betray him. I know what he seeks in Amadijah."

"Speak it!"

"Many days have passed since the warriors of the *Mutessarif* led a prisoner though my village. They stopped at my house. The prisoner was the son of the Sheik of the Haddedihn and he was destined to be a prisoner in Amadijah. He had such a resemblance to your friend, like a son to a father."

"Such resemblance occurs very often."

"I know, and I will not rob you of your secret; but one thing I will say to you: When you return from Amadijah then stop at my house, no matter whether day or night, in secret or openly. You are welcome to me, even if the young Arab, of whom I spoke, is with you."

"I thank you!"

"You need not thank me! You have given me the water from the Holy Zem-Zem; I will protect you in every peril and danger. But if your path leads in another direction, then you must fulfill one request for me."

"Which is?"

"In the valley of Berwari there is the Gumri palace. There lives the son of the famous Abd el Summit *Bei*; one of my daughters is his wife. Greet them from me. I will provide you with a symbol so that they know that you are my friend."

"That I will do."

"Tell them of any request that your heart desires; they will gladly fulfill it, for no worthy Kurd loves the Turks nor the *Mutessarif* of Mosul."

He returned to the house. I knew what this brave man intended. He had guessed our intention and desperately wanted to be of service to me. I now went to sleep and took the Afghan hound with me. When we awoke the next morning, we were told that the Englishman's translator had already departed Spandareh. He had chosen the road to Bebozi.

I had slept in the same chamber as Mohammed Emin; but another room had been prepared for the Englishman. He now entered our chamber and - was greeted by light laughter. No one could imagine the image that the brave Master Lindsay presented to us. He was completely clad in black and red from neck to foot, of course not as yet checkered, and the Kurdish cap on his tall and pointy head, sat there like an overturned coffee sack, from which hung long bands like the tentacles of a polyp.

"Good morning! Why the laughter?" he greeted us seriously.

"For joy at your extraordinarily amusing exterior, Sir."

"Well! I am happy!"

"What are you carrying under your arm?"

"Here? Hmm! A packet I think!"

"I see that of course. What does it contain?"

"It's my Hat-box."

"Ah!"

"Have wrapped up the hat, the spats and the boots too. Well!"

"You could have left everything here!"

"Here? Why?"

"You wish to burden yourself with useless trifles?"

"Useless? Trifles? Ghastly! Will need them again!"

"But not immediately."

"We return to this place?"

"That is doubtful."

"There! Hatbox will come along! Self-evident!"

The wide garment hung loosely on his skinny body like an old rag hangs on a scarecrow. But that did not bother him. He took his seat next to me in a dignified manner and said confidently:

"Now I am Kurd! Well!"

"A real genuine one!"

"Famous, excellent! Splendid adventure!"

"But one thing is still missing!"

"What?"

"The language."

"Will learn."

"That does not go so quickly, and you don't want to betray us, then you are forced to choose between two alternatives."

"Which alternatives?"

"Either you are held to be dumb ... "

"Dumb? Dumb? Terrible! Never!"

"Yes, for dumb or even deaf and dumb."

"Sir, you are crazy!"

"Thank you! But it remains the same. So, either you are considered dumb or you have taken an oath ... "

"Oath? Well! Nice thought! Interesting! What kind of oath?"

"Not to speak."

"Not to speak? Not a word? Ah!"

"Not a single one!"

"Not a syllable?"

"None! But only if we are watched. If we are alone you can talk to your hearts content."

"That's good! Not at all bad! Will make an oath! When does it start?"

"Immediately upon leaving Spandareh."

"Well! Agreed!"

After the morning coffee we received all kinds of provisions; we then mounted our horses. We took our leave from all the inhabitants of the house, apart from the host, as well as the others that had gathered. The host had a horse saddled and would accompany us a part of the way.

Behind Spandareh there was a very difficult, almost impassible, path that led up the Tura-Ghara Mountains. One almost needed feet like a chamois to make it up this rocky path, but we reached the crest successfully. Here the leader halted his horse and took a packet from his saddlebag.

"Take this and give it to my daughter's husband, if you should make for Gumri. I have promised her a Persian cloth and her husband a *Dizgin* [reign] like that of the *Pir Mani* Kurds for his *Mehin* [mare]. If you deliver these then they will know that you are my friend and bother and they will take you in as they would me. But I yet desire for your sake that you might return to me."

He indicated the rider who had followed us and who had stopped by Halef and the *Bashi-Bozuk*.

"This is the man who will return the suit of the foreigner to me. To him you may also give the parcel if you know that your path does not lead to Gumri. And now we part! *Aaleïk sallam, u rahhmet Allah* - May the peace and mercy of Allah be with you!"

We embraced and kissed. He then proffered his hand to the others and departed. I had become to know him as a man that I continue to respect and I still wish him well to this very day.

Chapter 31

We rode on. The path led downhill into the valley of Amadijah. This valley is carved from sandstone and is cut by many ravines, in which flow rushing forest steams. All their waters run into the Zab. The ravines and the general terrain are covered with a thick forest of oak that delivers a considerable harvest of oak apples [See Translation Note Ch 31. 1] that provide a lucrative trade for the local inhabitants. On the plain, are a great number of Chaldean villages, that are either desolate or deserted, or just sparsely populated since the Chaldeans prefer to escape into the surrounding mountains to avoid being oppressed by the Turk and the rapacious attack of the Kurdish tribes.

We rode through this terrain towards our goal and the oak trees reminded me of home.

"May I speak?" Lindsay asked softly.

"Yes. We are unobserved."

"But the Kurd behind us?"

"Does not count."

"Well!"

"Village named Spandareh?"

"Yes."

"How did you like it?"

"Very much. And you, Sir?"

"Wonderful! Good host, good hostess, fine meal, good dance, splendid dog!"

The last word caused me to look down at the dog that trotted next to my horse; I had been careful to tie it to my stirrup with a length of rope. Besides, the dog had already formed a friendship with my horse and appeared to know with certainty that I was its new master. It looked up at me attentively with its large and clever eyes.

"Yes." I answered. "Everything was good, in particular the food."

"Excellent! Even pigeon and beef steak!"

"Hmm! You really believed it to be pigeon?"

"Well! Why not?"

"Because it wasn't."

"Wasn't? Not pigeon. Was one!"

"Was not!"

"What else?"

"It was an animal, that zoologists have given the Latin name of *vespertilio murinus* or *myotis*."

"No zoologist. Don't know Latin!"

"This 'pigeon' is normally called a bat."

"Ba ... "

He stopped. His taste buds and digestive nerves were overtaxed by the sound of that word, so that his mouth formed a trapezoidal and perennial cave opening in which one could undertake a wonderful journey of discovery. Even his nose appeared to join in sympathy, for it's tip turned that white color of which a poet should have said: "I know not, what does it portend, that I should feel so sad!"

"Yes, bat it was, Sir. You have eaten a bat."

He stopped his horse and stared up into the blue sky.

Finally I heard a loud clap; his mouth finally shut, and I guessed that his ability to form words had returned.

" ... at!!!"

With this part of the interrupted syllable he concluded the previously commenced 'Ba ...'; then he reached across to me and grasped my arm.

"Sir!"

"What?"

"Don't forget the courtesy a gentleman is due!"

"I have not forgotten it in respect of you?"

"Very much, I say!"

"How so?"

"How could you claim that Sir David Lindsay eats bats!"

"Bats? I have only spoken of one."

"Same thing! One or many, the injury is the same. You will give me satisfaction! Well!"

"You have already had it!"

"I have? I had? Ah! How?"

"You have received a kind of satisfaction that should be quite sufficient for you."

"What kind? Know of none!"

"I too have eaten bat; and even Mohammed Emin."

"Too? You and him? Ah!"

"Yes. Even I thought it to be pigeon. But as I asked, I discovered that it was bat."

"Bat has skins!"

"Were cut away."

"So, really true?"

"Really."

"No joke, no fun?"

"Seriously!"

"Horrible! Oh! Will get colic, cholera, typhus, oh!"

He pulled a truly cholera induced face; I had to show some pity:

"Do you feel unwell, Sir?"

"Quite! Yes!"

"Can I help?"

"Quick! How?"

"Via homeopathic means."

"You have one? I truly feel unwell! Poorly! What means?"

"*Similia Similibus*."

"Again zoological? Latin?"

"Yes. Latin it is; more of the same. And zoological it is too, namely grasshoppers."

"What! Grasshoppers?"

"Yes, grasshoppers."

"For feeling ill? I shall eat them?"

"You shall not eat them, rather you have already eaten them."

"Already eaten? I?"

"Yes."

"Silly! Stupid! Impossible! When?"

"Last night."

"Ah! Explain!"

"You said earlier that the beefsteak was very good."

"Very! Exceedingly good! Well!"

"It was no beefsteak."

"Non? No beefsteak! Am Englishman! T'was!"

"Was not! I asked."

"What else?"

"Was grasshoppers fried in olive oil. We Germans call these delicate jumpers 'Heupferde' [literally: hay horses] at times."

"Heu - - -"

As before, the word stuck halfway, but this time he managed to control the frank expression of his mouth, instead he clamped his lips together with such force that the previous over extension was compressed to a thin line. So tight were they that either corner of his mouth could easily have squeezed off an ear lobe. And the nose was so dismayed over the disappearance of the congenial opening that the tip bent down as if to see if the loss of it could be remedied.

Finally the mouth took on its former dimensions; the *'restitutio in integrum'* came about and the lips let go from each other.

" ... pferde!"

In this manner he voiced the continuation of his interrupted "Heu ... ", and the tip of his nose rose up with satisfaction.

"Yes, you have eaten 'Heupferde'."

"Ah! Terrible! But have never tasted them!"

"Do you know for certain what they taste like?"

He made movements with his arms and legs as if he desired to turn on his own axis whilst remaining seated on his horse.

"No, at no time, never!"

"I assure you, they were grasshoppers. They are roasted and crushed; then laid into the earth until they get *'haut gout'*, and then they are fried in the oil of the tranquil olive. I have received the recipe from the wife of the village elder and therefore know precisely what I am talking about."

"Shocking! Get stomach cramps!"

"Are you content with your 'Satisfaction'?"

"Have you eaten 'Heupferde' as well?"

"No."

"No? Why not?"

"Because I was not served any."

"Only I?"

"Only you alone; certainly a respectful gesture to you, Sir!"

"Did you know?"

"Not at first. But whilst you were eating, I asked."

"Why not tell me at once?"

"Because you certainly would have done something that would have insulted the host."

"Master, wants to deny me that! Yes! Deceit! Malice! Malicious pleasure! Will battle with you, box or ... "

He ceased, for a shot cracked and a bullet tore a shred from my turban.

"Down, stand behind the horses!" I cried.

At once I was down from my horse and not a moment too soon, for a second shot cracked and the bullet whistled over my head. With a quick movement I loosened the rope that I had tied to the dogs collar.

"*Sert* - Hold fast!"

The dog only gave a short bark that almost sounded as if it acknowledged my order and then it shot off into the undergrowth.

We were in a ravine the sides of which were thickly covered with young oak trees. To enter this thicket myself was too dangerous as we would be exposed to the weapon of the unseen sniper. We thus sought protection behind the bodies of our horses and listened.

"*Mash Allah*! Who could that be?" asked Mohammed Emin.

"The Arnaut," I answered.

We heard a cry closely followed by the loud barking call of the dog.

"*Dojan* has the culprit," I said as calmly as possible. "*Buluk-Emini*, go and fetch him!"

"*Allah illa Allah*! Emir, I stay; there could be ten or even a hundred and then I would be done for!"

"And your donkey would then an orphan, you coward! Look after the horses! Come!"

We penetrated the hard undergrowth and did not have to go far. I had been correct; it was the Arnaut. The dog did not stand but rather lay upon him and in such a manner that I wondered at the extraordinary cleverness of the animal. For the Arnaut had drawn his dagger in order to defend himself against his attacker, the dog therefore had more than one task. Therefore it had pulled the Arnaut down and was thus able to lie on his right arm so that he could not move it. At the same time he had him by the throat, although softly, yet so that the Arnaut was doomed if he made the slightest move.

I took the dagger from the hand of this treacherous coward and then the lone pistol from his belt; the other, spent, was lying on the ground; he had obviously dropped it when the dog attacked.

"*Geri* - Back!"

On this order *Dojan* let go of the Arnaut. He arose and reached for his throat involuntarily.

"Damn, you murderer! Shall I knock you down?"

"*Sihdi*, command it and I shall hang him!" begged Halef.

"Pah! He did not hit anyone of us. Let him go!"

"Emir," Mohammed said, "he is a wild animal that has to be rendered harmless!"

"He shot at me and will not have another opportunity. Get going, scoundrel!"

In no time he had disappeared among the undergrowth. The dog wanted to follow him immediately, but I held it back.

"*Sihdi*, we have to follow him; he is an Arnaut and remains a danger to us!" Halef cried.

"Where will he be a danger to us? In Amadijah? There he can't let himself be seen for I will have him charged."

Mohammed and even the Englishman protested bitterly, but I returned to the horses and mounted. The dog followed me without being bidden; I noted that I did not need to tie him and my trust in him would soon be confirmed.

Towards midday we reached a small village by the name of Bebadi; it appeared very poor and had, what I considered to be, Nestorian inhabitants. We rested briefly and had difficulty in finding food and a drink of sherbet.

A cone shaped mountain loomed before us, atop which perched Amadijah. We reached it very soon. To the right and left of the path that led upwards, we noted orchards that appeared to be well cared for; the city itself did, however, not make much of an impression on us. We rode through the gate that was quite dilapidated and only tentatively repaired. Some ragged Arnauts stood about to ensure that no enemy attacked the city. One of them grabbed the reigns of my horse and another the reigns of the horse of the Haddedihn.

"Halt! Who are you?" he asked me.

I indicated the *Buluk-Emini*.

"Don't you see that we have a soldier of the Sultan with us? He will answer you."

"I have asked you, not him!"

"Get away, stand aside!"

With these words I reared my horse up; it made a jump, and the man fell to the ground. Mohammed followed my example and we rode on. But behind us we heard the cursing of the Arnauts and the bickering of the *Bashi-Bozuk* who squabbled with them. A man approached us who wore a long Kaftan and had an old rag wound about his head.

"Who are you, man?" I asked him.

"Lord, I am a *Jehudi* [Jew]. What do you command of me?"

"Do you know where the *Mutesselim* [Commandant] lives?"

"Yes, Lord."

"Lead us to his *Serai*!"

The more confident one acts in the Orient, the more respectfully one is treated. Besides, this man was a Jew, that is, one who was tolerated in Amadijah; he would not dare to rebel. He led us through a number of lanes and bazaars, which strengthened my opinion of the city's decay.

This important border fort appeared to be very neglected. There was no life in the streets and shops; only a few people passed us by and those that we saw appeared to be ill and had such a painful appearance that they served as the living examples of that well known sickness of this city.

The *Serai* did not deserve the title of 'palace' by its outward appearance. It was more a poorly renovated ruin, before its entrance there was not even a guard. We dismounted and handed the reigns of our horses to Halef, the Kurd and the *Buluk-Emini*, who had caught up with us. After the Jew had received a *Baksheesh*, for which he thanked us profusely, we entered.

Only after we had wandered through some halls did we finally see a man, who quickened his pace once he spied us.

"Who are you? What do you want here?" he asked in an angry voice.

"Boy, change your tone, otherwise I will teach you some manners! Who are you?"

"I am the *Nazarji* [overseer] of this palace."

"Is the *Mutesselim* available?"

"No."

"Where is he?"

"Out riding."

"That means he is at home and partakes of the *Kef*!"

"Do you wish to command him on what he may or may not do?"

"No; but I do command you to tell me the truth!"

"Who are you that you speak to me so? Are you an infidel, that you dare to enter the palace of the Commandant with a dog?"

He was right, for next to me stood the Afghan hound, and he watched us with eyes that clearly indicated that he awaited my sign to leap on this Turk.

"Place guards at the gate," I answered him; "then no one will gain entrance without permission. At what time can I speak with the *Mutesselim*?"

"At dusk."

"Good. Tell him that I will come!"

"And when he asks me who you are?"

"Then tell him that I am a friend of the *Mutessarif* of Mosul."

He became embarrassed; but we returned and mounted our horses and searched for accommodation. Such was easily found, for we noted that many houses were empty; yet it was not my intention to secretly take possession of one.

Whilst we rode on and inspected the buildings a giant, warlike figure, approached us. The man walked with his legs wide apart like an Osterland twelve spanned horse drawn cart. [See Translation Note Ch 31. 1] His velvet jacket as well as his trousers was covered in gold braid; his weapons were not invaluable, and from his *Jibuk*, which he smoked with great self-confidence, hung, as I later counted, fourteen silken tassels. he stopped at our side to admire my stallion with the look of a connoisseur. I stopped and greeted him.

"*Sallam*!"

"*Aaleïkum*!" he answered with a proud nod of his head.

"I am a stranger here and do not desire to speak with a *Birkaji* [an ordinary man]. Permit me to make some inquiries of you!" I said at least as proud as he was.

"Your tone of voice tells me that you are an *Effendi*. I will answer your question."

"Who are you?"

"I am Selim Agha, the commander of the Albanese, that defend this famous fort."

"And I am Kara Ben Nemsi, a protégé of the Padishah and emissary of the *Mutessarif* of Mosul. I am in search of a house in Amadijah, one in which I can rest for a few days. Can you recommend one?"

He permitted himself a motion of military respect and said:

"Allah bless your Highness, *Effendi*! You are a great Lord, who must be accommodated in the palace of *Mutesselim*."

"The overseer of the palace has sent me away, and I ..."

"Allah crush this creature," he interrupted me. "I will go and tear him to pieces!"

He rolled his eyes and waved about with both his arms. This man was apparently only a braggart of the ordinary kind.

"Let the man be! He shall not have the honor to have guests that pay him a rich *Baksheesh*."

"*Baksheesh*?" asked the hero. "You provide much *Baksheesh*?"

"I take care not to be miserly."

"Oh, then I know of a house in which you can live and smoke like the *Shah-in-Shah* of Persia. Shall I lead you?"

"Show it to me!"

"He turned and paced ahead. We followed. He led us though a number of empty bazaar lanes until we reached a small open space where we stopped.

"This is the *Meidan jüjelikün*, the 'Place of the Great'," he explained.

This place might have had many qualities but 'Great' it was not, and that is probably why it had received such a pretentious name. That I was in a Turkish city I could see quite clearly; for some twenty masterless dogs roamed this *Meidan jüjelikün*, and most of them were mangy. At the sight of my dog these curs began a furious howling, but *Dojan*, like a Pasha in the presence of beggars, did not give them the slightest attention.

"And here is the house that I mean," the Agha added.

He indicated a building, the frontage of which took up one entire length of the square and did not at all look too bad. It had many *Pengjeri* [windows], that were fitted with wooden bars and all around the flat roof ran a balustrade, certainly a great luxury in this land.

"Who lives in this house?" I asked.

"I myself, *Effendi*," he answered.

"And who owns it?"

"I."

"Have you bought or rented it?"

"Neither. It was the property of the famous Ismaïl Pasha and has been empty until I took possession of it. Come, I will show you everything!"

This valiant commander of the Arnauts certainly had developed a liking for my *Baksheesh*. Yet his offering was most welcome to me, since his position made it possible for me to get information about all I desired to know. We dismounted before the house and entered. In the passage squatted an old woman that was peeling onions and chewed the discarded skins with tears in her eyes. From her appearance she was either the great grandmother of the eternal Jew, or the aunt of Methuselah, bypassed by death.

"Listen, my sweet Mersinah, I bring you men!" he addressed her in a very loving tone.

She could not see us for the tears in her eyes and thus she wiped them away with the onion in her hand, which doubled the flow of her tears.

"Men?" she asked in a voice that emanated from her toothless mouth, a voice that sounded dull, like that of a poltergeist.

"Yes, men, that will live in this house."

She threw the onion down and sprang from the floor with youthful speed.

"Live? Here in this house? Are you crazy, Selim Agha?"

"Yes my dearest Mersinah, you will be the *Meichaneja* [hostess] of these men and you will serve them."

"Hostess? Serve? *Allah kerihm*! You have become truly mad! Don't I already have to work day and night just to get done with you alone! Send them away, away at once; I order you!"

He was a little embarrassed; that was obvious. The 'Sweet and lovely' Mersinah appeared to wield a mighty scepter here.

"Your work shall not increase, my dove. I will arrange a *Kyzla* [girl, serving wench], that shall serve them."

"A *Kyzla*?" she asked, and her voice was no longer dull and emotionless, rather it was screeching and snapping, as though this rosy mouth of this lovely dove had transformed into a beak that could trill like a clarinet. "A *Kyzla*! And I suppose a young and beautiful *Kyzla*, hey?"

"That will depend on these men, Mersinah."

She placed her hands on her hips, a movement that has pretty much the same meaning in the Orient and in the Occident, she then took a deep breath. That was a sign that she needed a considerable amount of air to get her message across to the gathering of men.

"On these men? On me it will depend! I am the mistress of this house! Here I alone give the orders! Here I decide what will happen, and I order you to get rid of these men! Do you hear me, Selim Agha? Away, immediately!"

"But these are not just men, my one and only Mersinah!"

Mersinah, which in German means 'Myrte' [Myrtle], again wiped her eyes and looked at us very carefully. I too was somewhat amazed at the Agha's statement. If we were not just men, what were we?

"No," he answered. "They are not just men, rather *Effendies*, great *Effendies*, that stand under the protection of the Sultan."

"What do I care about the Sultan! Here I am the grand mistress, the mistress *valide*, and what I say, that ... "

"But listen already! They will provide a very good *Baksheesh*!"

In the Orient, the word *Baksheesh* has a magical quality; it also appeared to have that same power in this circumstance. The 'Myrte' lowered her arms slowly and tried to smile, but it looked more like a derisive grin, and then she turned to Master David Lindsay:

"A great *Baksheesh*? Is that true?"

Sir David shook his head and pointed to me.

"What is wrong with him?" she asked me. "Has he gone mad?"

"No," I answered. "Be told what we are, you soul of this house! This man, whom you just asked, is a very holy pilgrim from Londonistan; he dug deep into the earth with the hoe that you see here, to eavesdrop on the conversations of the dead, and he has made an oath not to speak a word until he has obtained permission."

"A pious man, a holy man, a wizard?" she asked with fear in her voice.

"Yes. I warn you, do not insult him! This other man is a leader of a great people far to the west of here, and I am an Emir of those warriors that revere women and provide *Baksheesh*. You are the Sultana of this house. Permit us to look it over, to see if we can live in it for a few days!"

"*Effendi*, your speech creates the aroma of roses and carnations; your mouth speaks more wisely and more cleverly than the mouth of this Selim Agha, who always forgets to say the right things, and your hand is like the hand of Allah, that distributes blessings. Do you have many servants with you?"

"No, for our arms are strong enough to protect us. We only have three companions: a servant, a *Khawass* of the *Mutessarif* of Mosul and a Kurd, who will depart Amadijah this very day."

"Then you are welcome to me! Look about my house and my garden, and if you approve of it, then my eye will shine and watch over you!"

She wiped the 'watchful' and 'shining' eyes once again and gathered the onions from the floor so that they would not be in our way. The brave Agha of the Arnauts appeared to be happy with this turn of events. First he led us to a room which served him as his home. It was quite large and only contained a lonely old carpet that was used as a sofa, bed, stool and table. On the walls hung some weapons and tobacco-pipes, on the floor stood a bottle and nearby were some empty eggshells.

"I bid you welcome, my Lords," he said. "Let us drink the drink of friendship!"

He bent over to pick up the bottle and the eggshells, and then handed each of us the latter. He then poured the liquid into the eggshells. It was *Raki*. We drank from the hen fashioned goblet, but he placed the bottle to his lips and did not remove it until he was certain that the sharp, sulfuric drink contained therein could do no more chemical harm. Then he took the shells from our hands and sucked at whatever we had left behind, contented he then placed them carefully on the floor.

"*Kendim ijad eter* - my own invention!" he said proudly. "Are you amazed that I have no glasses?"

"You prefer this pretty discovery to glasses," I answered.

"I prefer it because I have no glasses. I am the Agha of the Albanese and I receive as my salary and keep a monthly sum of three-hundred-and-thirty piaster [66 Mark]; but I already waited eleven month for this money. *Allah kerihm; Padishah kendisi onu kullar* - God is merciful, and the Sultan needs it himself!"

Thus it was no wonder that the word *'Baksheesh'* had such a deep meaning to him.

He led us around the house. It was built with space in mind, but it too was in decay. We took four rooms, one for each of us and one for Halef and the *Bashi-Bozuk*. The price for the rooms was minimal, five piaster, that is one Mark, per week.

"Do you wish to see he garden?" he asked.

"Of course! Is it beautiful?"

"Very nice, so lovely, like the gardens of paradise! You will see all kinds of trees, herbs and grasses, of which I have no knowledge. By day it is blessed by the sun and by night by the moon and the stars. It is wonderful!"

"Does it also rain on your garden?" I asked in amusement.

"When it rains it also receives its due; yes, it has even snowed on it at times. Come and see!"

In the courtyard was a shed that we rented for our horses. It too cost one Mark. The garden measured roughly forty paces square and was thus very unimpressive. I saw a crippled cypress and a wild apple tree. The 'all kinds of herbs and grasses' were just wild *Kendir* [hemp], wild *Madanos* [parsley] and some notoriously poor daisies. But the greatest wonder of this garden was bed in which grew *Soghani* [onions], *Sarmysak* [garlic], *Kedilan* [catnip], a gooseberry bush, some hops and some faded violets that starved in loving harmony next to each other.

"*Bir güzel bagje* - a lovely garden! Is it not?" the Agha asked, whilst he blew a mightly cloud of tobacco smoke from his lips.

"*Güzel-zorli* - immensely wonderful!" I answered.

"*Pek bereketli* - very fruitful!"

"*Ghajet bereketli*- exceedingly fruitful!"

"*Ile jok güzel dikekler* - and many beautiful plants! No?"

"*Syz sajyjü* - without number!"

"Do you know who worked wonders here?"

"Who?"

"The loveliest rose of Kurdistan. Have you ever heard of Esma Khan, who, in beauty has never been surpassed by anyone?"

"She was the wife of Ismaïl Pasha, the last male heir of the Abbassinian Caliph?"

"Yes; you know. She held the honorary title 'Khan', as did all women of this enlightened family. He, that is Ismaïl Pasha, was besieged by Injeh Bairakdar Mohammed Pasha; that one broke through the walls of the palace and it was then overrun and taken. Then Ismaïl along with Esma Khan were transported to Baghdad as prisoners. She once lived and bloomed here. Emir, I wish she would still be here!"

"Did she also plant the parsley and the garlic?"

"No," he answered quite seriously; "Mersinah, my housekeeper planted those."

"Then thank Allah, that instead of Esma Khan you have the sweet Mersinah at your side!"

"*Effendi*, at times she is quite bitter!"

"You should not grumble about that, for Allah distributes his gifts in various ways. And that you should breathe the aroma of this 'Myrte', that is surely written in the book of fate."

"So it is! But tell me if you wish to rent this garden, Emir!"

"How much do you ask for it?"

"You pay me ten piaster [two Mark] per week for it. Then you can all go into the garden and think of Esma Khan as often as you wish!"

I hesitate with my answer. The rear wall of a building in which I had noted two rows of small holes bordered the garden. It appeared to me exactly like a prison. I had to discover more:

"I do not think that we will rent this garden."

"Why not?"

"Because I am bothered by that wall."

"This wall? Why, *Effendi*?"

"I do not like being that close to a prison."

"Oh, the people that are in there can not disturb you. Their holes are so deep that they can not reach the little windows at all."

“Is this the only prison in Amadijah?”

“Yes. The other one collapsed. My *Jaush* [sergeant] guards the prisoners.”

“And you believe that this will not disturb me?”

“You will not see them nor hear a sound from them.”

“Then I will give you the ten piaster. You therefore should receive the sum of thirty-five piaster for one week from us. Permit me to pay you for the first week immediately!”

His whole person smiled with delight at the offer. The Englishman noted that I put my hand into my pocket in order to pay. He shook his head, pulled out his own purse and handed it to me. He could endure a little lightening of his purse; that is why I took three *Mahbub-Zechin* from it and gave them to the Agha.

“Here, take! What is left over is a *Baksheesh* for you.”

That was more than double of that which he should have received and thereore he pulled a very delightful face and said with great respect:

“Emir, the Koran says: 'Who gives double, him Allah will bless a hundred fold'. Allah is your debtor; he will richly repay you!”

“We will need carpets and pipes for our rooms. Where can one borrow these, Agha?” I asked him.

“Lord, if you provide just two more gold pieces then you will receive whatever your heart desires.”

“Here you have them!”

“I hurry to bring you what you need.”

We left the garden. In the courtyard stood Mersinah, the soul of this palace. Her hands were blackened with soot. She stirred a vessel of rendered butter with her finger.

“Emir, will you take the rooms?”

As she asked the question it might have come into her head that her finger was not an integral part of the pot it had stirred; she thus pulled it out and wiped it on her extended tongue.

“I will keep them, and the shed as well as the garden.”

“He has already paid for it all,” remarked the Agha emphatically.

“How much?” she asked.

“Thirty-five piaster for the first week.”

Of the *Baksheesh* the rogue said nothing. Did he also stand under the *Papist* [slipper, 'slipper hero', henpecked] of his 'Myrte' in this respect? I took another *Mahbub-Zechin* [about five Mark] from the purse and gave it to her.

"Here, take this, you pearl of hospitality! That is the first *Baksheesh* for you. If we are happy with you, you will receive more."

She grasped at the coin with great speed and slipped it into her girdle.

"I thank you, oh Lord! I will be watchful that you will be as happy in my house as you would be in the lap of the patriarch Ibrahim. I see that you are the Emir of courageous warriors, who revere women and provide *Baksheesh*. Go up to your rooms! I will prepare strips of *Pirinj* for you, with plenty of rendered butter!"

With those words she stuck her finger thoughtlessly, and perhaps driven by 'old habits make tradition', back into the pot and she began to stir anew. Her offer was a very affable one, but ... yuck!

"Your kindness is great," I answered, "but we do not have the time to accept it, as we have to leave immediately."

"But it is your wish that I prepare meals for you, Emir?"

"You said already that you had to work day and night just to provide for the Agha alone; we must not burden you further. Besides, it is expected that we will be invited for a meal quite often, and if that is not the case, then we will have our meals fetched from a *Jemegiji* [provider of food]."

"But the meal of honor you may not refuse!"

"Well, then boil us some eggs; we may not eat anything else today."

That was the only reasonable fare one could enjoy from the hands of the delicate 'Myrte'.

"Eggs? Yes, you shall have them, *Effendi*," She answered zestfully; "but when you eat them, preserve the shells, for Agha Selim uses them as cups, and this careless lout is so thoughtless that he breaks them all."

We returned to our rooms for a short while, in which the Agha soon appeared with blankets, carpets and pipes, which he had 'borrowed' from the respective dealers. They were new and therefore clean so that we could be happy with them. Then Mersinah appeared with the lid of an old wooden box that served as a display plate. On it were the eggs, which were to be our meal of honor. Next to them were some half burned dough paddies and - even the famous butter pot, surrounded by some eggshells that contained some dirty salt, roughly ground pepper and very dubious caraway seeds. Knives or egg spoons were of course absent.

We were polite enough to invite Mersinah to partake of this Epicurean welcome meal, and it was soon dispensed with. She thanked us profusely for the unexpected honor that was extended to her and returned, along with her 'delightful dishes' [See Translation Note Ch 31. 3], to the kitchen. The Agha arose as well.

"Do you know, Lord, where I will go now?" he asked.

"I will soon hear it."

"To the *Mutesselim.* He shall discover what a noble Emir you are, and how the palace overseer has treated you."

He perfected his official appearance by wiping the rendered butter, of which only he and Mersinah had partaken, from his mustache before departing. Now we were alone.

"May I speak, Sir?" asked Lindsay.

"Yes, Master."

"Buy clothes!"

"Now?"

"Yes."

"Red checkered?"

"Of course!"

"Then we will go to the bazaar!"

"But I don't speak! You must buy, Sir. Here is money!"

"Do we only buy clothes?"

"What else?"

"Some dishes, that we use and then, wisely, can make a present of to the Agha or the housekeeper. Also tobacco, coffee and other such things that we can not do without."

"Well; pay for it all!"

"We will make use of your purse and then settle our accounts with one another afterwards."

"Pshaw! Pay for everything! Settled!"

"Do I come along?" asked Mohammed.

"If you like. But I think that it would be better if you are seen as little as possible. In Spandareh you have been identified as a Haddedihn, not even considering that you look so much like your son as the village elder has testified."

"Then I remain behind!"

We lit our *Jibuks* and departed. The hallway was filled with smoke, and the 'Myrte' coughed in the kitchen. When she noticed us she came towards us briefly.

"Where are our men?" I asked her.

"With the horses. You are going?"

"We go to the bazaar to buy a few things. Don't let yourself be distracted, you protector of the kitchen. Your water is running over."

"Let it run, Lord. The meal will still be made!"

"The meal? Do you cook it in that large vessel?"

"Yes."

"Then it is certainly not only for you and Selim Agha?"

"No. I have to cook for the *Sealer* [prisoners]."

"Ah! The prisoners next door?"

"Yes."

"Are there many of the unfortunate ones in that house?"

"Not quite twenty."

"Are they all from Amadijah?"

"Oh no. There are quite a few Arnaut soldiers, who chose the wrong path, some Chaldeans, a Kurd, some inhabitants of Amadijah and even an Arab."

"An Arab? But there are no Arabs here about!"

"He was brought from Mosul."

"What do they get to eat?"

"Flat bread, which I bake and then around midday, or later in the afternoon, as it pleases me, a warm meal."

"Consisting of what?"

"Flour stirred into water."

"Who brings it to them?"

"I myself. The Sergeant opens the holes for me. Have you ever seen a prison, Emir?"

"No."

"If you desire to see it, then you only have to ask me, I will take you along with me."

"But the Sergeant would not admit me!"

"He will admit you, for I am his mistress."

"You?"

"Yes. Am I not the mistress of his Agha?"

"That is true! I will consider if it is proper for a dignified Emir to visit a prison and to give a good *Baksheesh* to those who permit it."

"It is proper, Lord; it is very proper. You perhaps desire to let your mercy shine on those prisoners so that they may buy some treats or tobacco from me which they will otherwise not get!"

Nothing would be dearer to me than the discoveries I would make there; but I was careful enough to avoid asking detailed questions through which I could easily come under suspicion. Halef, the *Buluk-Emini* and the Kurd from Spandareh were called to accompany us and then we departed.

The bazaars were deserted. As soon as we found a coffeehouse where the drink did not taste of burnt barley, we discovered the reason for the lack of liveliness in Amadijah. Despite the high and free mountain location of this city, it is quite unhealthy. During the warmer seasons of the year, a creeping fever occurs. The inhabitants depart the city and make for the neighboring forests where they live in summer homes called *Jilaks*.

After we had finished the mysterious drink and stuffed our pipes anew, we headed off to barter for clothes. The host of the coffee shop had described the place, where we could find what we desired, for us. The barter was concluded with the silent assistance of the Englishman and he was obviously content with the deal. He received a completely red and black checkered garment for a reasonable price. Then the rest of our needs were catered for and all was sent to our accommodation along with our servants. The Kurd was given a full, pearl encrusted, tobacco pouch as a present, which he accepted with pride, and which he fastened to his belt so that it might substantiate his manly dignity to all who saw it.

I now walked through the city in the company of just the Englishman in order to familiarize myself with it, and I was convinced that this, once so important border fort, which the Turks still consider important to this day, could easily be taken by a handful of dedicated Kurds. The few soldiers that we met appeared hungry and sick with fever and the defenses were in such a state that they did not deserve the name.

When we returned home, the Agha was waiting for me.

"Emir, I already wait a long time for your return."

"Why?"

"I am to bring you to the *Mutesselim*."

"Bring?" I asked smiling at the emphasis on that word.

"No, rather accompany you. I have told him everything and even wagged my fist under the nose of the palace overseer. Allah protected him, otherwise I would have strangled him or even killed him!"

He rolled his eyes and bent his ten fingers like tongs whilst speaking these words.

"What does the Commandant say?"

"Emir, shall I tell you the truth?"

"I expect it!"

"He was not happy of your visit."

"Ah! Why not?"

"He does not like strangers and rarely accepts visitors."

"Is he a recluse?"

"No. But as a Commandant he receives, aside from his free accommodation, a monthly income of six-thousand-seven-hundred-and-eighty piaster [1356 Mark], as he, like the rest of us, has not received any pay for the last eleven months, he is at a loss as to what he should eat and drink. Can he thus be happy to receive important visitors?"

"I will visit and speak with him, but I do not come for a meal!"

"That will not do. He has to receive you in the proper manner and that is why has asked the ... the ... "

He became embarrassed.

"The ... the ... the what??"

"The Jews ... , asked the Jews to come and loan him five-hundred piaster. He will need those to buy what is necessary for your visit."

"And have they loaned that sum to him?"

"*Allah illa Allah*; they did not have such a sum as they already had to give him everything before. Now he borrowed a sheep and much more to go with it. That is very bad, especially for me Emir!"

"Why for you?"

"Because I have to loan him the five-hundred piaster or ... or ... "

"Or ... or ... Well?"

"Or ask you if you ... you ..."

"Continue, Agha!"

"If you are rich. Oh, Emir, I would not have a single para, if you had not paid me today! And from that I had to give Mersinah thirty-five piaster!"

To entertain me, the *Mutesselim* had to borrow five hundred piaster, which would be the same as making him a gift of that sum! Roughly a hundred Mark. Hmm, I was, thanks to the money I discovered in the saddlebags of Abu Seïf's animal, quite well off, and for our purpose, the well-being of the *Mutesselim* was of great advantage. Five hundred piaster I could certainly spare, and Master Lindsay could supply as much again since he would gladly spend this, to him, a minimal sum for an adventure. Thus I went to the Englishman's room and the Agha had to wait for my answer.

Sir David was busy changing his clothes. His face beamed with delight.

"Master, how do I look?" he asked.

"Like a true Kurd!"

"Well; good, very good! Excellent!"

"But how wind turban?"

"Give it to me!"

His hand had never held a turban cloth in his lifetime. I placed the cap on his beaming head and wound the black and red cloth artistically around it. In this manner I constructed a huge turban, as is worn by the noble men in this land. Such a headdress often has a diameter of four feet.

"Well then, now the Kurdish Lord is complete!"

"Excellent! Marvelous! Wonderful adventure! Free Amad el Ghandur! Pay for everything; pay very well!"

"Are you serious, Sir?"

"Why shouldn't I be serious?"

"I of course know that you are well off and that you know the best time to use it ... "

He looked at me quickly and searchingly before he asked:

"Want money?"

"Yes." I simply replied.

"Well; shall have it! For yourself?"

"No. I hope that you have not come to know me in that manner!"

"That's right, Sir! Then for whom?"

"For the *Mutesselim.*"

"Ah! Why? What for?"

"This man is very poor. The Sultan owes him eleven month of back pay. For that reason he has certainly made use of the well-known system of exhorting money from every Turkish officer and every citizen. Now no one has any money left and no one can loan him any. That is why my visit puts him into an awkward situation. He has to receive me in a hospitable manner and does of course not posses the means with which to achieve this. That is why he has borrowed a sheep and other things along with it and asks, underhandedly, if I am rich enough to loan him five-hundred piaster. Of course this is a Turkish custom and one can not expect to have such a loan repaid. But since it is very necessary for us to encourage his friendly demeanor, I have decided ..."

He interrupted me with a dismissive gesture.

"Good! Shall have a hundred pound note!"

"That is too much, Sir! According to the current exchange rate in Constantinople, that would be eleven thousand piaster! I will give him five-hundred piaster and ask that you add the same sum. He should be happy with that."

"A thousand piaster! Too little! Have given the Arab Sheiks silken garments! Want to see him too. If I can come will pay for everything; you pay nothing!"

"That is fine with me."

"Then tell Agha, he should let us do!"

"And what will we do?"

"Buy presents on the way."

"But not too much, Sir!"

"How much? Five-thousand piaster?"

"Two-thousand is more than enough!"

"Well; two-thousand then! Done!"

I returned to the Agha.

"Tell the Commandant that I will visit him with one of my companions!"

"When?"

"Shortly."

"Your name he already knows; what other name shall I tell him?"

"Hajji Lindsay-*Bei*."

"Hajji Lindsay-*Bei*. Good! And the piaster, Emir?"

"We ask permission to bring him a present."

"Then he has to give you one in return!"

"We are not poor; we have all that we need, and would be most pleased if he gives us nothing more than his friendship. Tell him that!"

He departed confidently and appeased.

Within five minutes the Englishman and I sat on our horses; I had impressed upon him not to speak a single word. Halef and the *Buluk-Emini* followed us. The Kurd had been sent back to Spandareh with the garments and many greetings. We rode through the bazaar where we bought embroidered things along with a ceremonial dress and a beautiful purse, in which the Englishman placed twenty gold *Mejidje* each worth a hundred piaster. In such matters, my good Master Lindsay was no scrooge; I had discovered this quite often and to my advantage.

We then rode to the Commandant's palace. Before it stood some two hundred Albanese on parade, led by two *Mülasim* under the command of the brave Selim Agha. He drew his *Sarras* and commanded:

"*Ajagda duryn dykkatli* - stand straight!"

They made a concerted effort to follow that command, but managed only a kind of serpentine line that tapered off into a very curved tail.

"*Jalghy! Islik jaryn:* - Music! Pipes!"

Three flutes began to wail. A Turkish *Trempete* [drum] rattled a roll that sounded like the grinding of a coffee mill.

"*Daha giöre! Kuwetlirek!* - Louder, more forceful!"

The good Agha rolled his eyes in step with the swiftest motion of Melzel's metronome; the musicians aped him, and during this artistic, and for us amusing, reception we rode through the gate and dismounted. Two lieutenants came running and held our stirrups. I dipped my hand into my pocket and gave each a silver ten-piaster piece. They received it with satisfaction, without their honor, as officers, having been offended. The Turkish subaltern officer is to this day, particularly in remote garrisons, a servant of his immediate superior. And thus used to being treated as such.

To the Agha I gave the gifts and the purse.

"Announce us, and give the Commandant these gifts!"

"He marched ahead in a dignified manner and we followed. The *Nazarji* of the palace stood by the door. He now received us quite differently than before. He crossed his arms over his chest and bowed deeply and mumbled humbly:

"*Bendeniz el öpir; aghamin size selami wer* - Your servant kissed your hand; my Lord commends himself to you!"

I walked past him without answer, as though I did not notice him. And Lindsay did likewise. I must admit that my Master 'Fowling-bull', despite the screaming colors of his dress, made a respectable impression. The clothes fitted as though they had been made for him, and the knowledge that he was a rich Englishman, gave his posture a confidence that was quite proper for this situation.

The overseer, despite having been ignored, took the lead and led us up the stairs and into a room that appeared to serve as the reception area. Here the officers of the Commandant sat on tattered carpets. They arose as we entered and greeted us respectfully. Most of them were Turks and some were Kurds. The latter, at least in dress, made a better appearance than the first who appeared to find themselves in much poorer circumstances. A Kurd stood by the window, one had to immediately recognize him as a free mountain man. He looked out at the mountains with a dark, impatient mien. One of the Turks approached me:

"Are you Emir Hajji Kara Ben Nemsi, who is awaited by the *Mutesselim*?"

"I am he."

"And this *Effendi* is Hajji Lindsay-*Bei*, who made an oath of silence?"

"Yes."

"I am the *Bash Kiatib* [court stenographer] of the Commandant. He begs you to wait a moment."

"Why? I am not accustomed to wait and he knew that I was coming!"

"He has an important engagement that will be concluded soon."

What kind of important engagement this was I was soon to discover. A servant rushed from the *Mutesselim's* room and returned after a short while with two tins that were missing their lids. The larger held tobacco and the smaller some roasted coffee beans. The Commandant had only been able to fetch these important necessities after the receipt of our gift. Before the servant's return, the Agha exited the *Mutesselim's* room.

"*Effendi*, please be patient another moment! You may then enter!"

The Kurd by the window turned to him:

"And when may I finally enter?"

"You will be presented this day."

"This day? I have been here before this *Effendi*, and before all these others. My case is important and I have to depart this day!"

Selim Agha rolled his eyes.

"These *Effendies* are an Emir and a *Bei*, but you are just a Kurd. You come after them!"

"I have the same right as they, for I am the ambassador of a brave man who is likewise a *Bei*!"

The candid and fearless nature of this Kurd was much to my liking, even though his complaint was indirectly aimed at me. But the Agha appeared to be most annoyed for he rolled his eyes anew and answered:

"Your turn will come later and perhaps not at all. If you don't like it, you can go! You do not even know the smallest necessities that are expected before one is permitted to approach a great and influential man!"

Ah, the Kurd had forgotten the smallest 'necessity', namely the *Baksheesh*. But he was not intimidated and answered thus:

"Do you know what the necessity of a Berwari-Kurd is? It is this saber!" With these words he slapped the hilt of the aforementioned weapon. "Would you like a taste of it? The *Bei* of Gumri sends me; it is an insult to him, that I am continually passed over and that I have to carry keep on waiting, and he will know how he must answer this insult. I go!"

"Halt!" I shouted.

He was already by the door. Was this *Bei* of Gumri the one to which the elder of Spandareh had advised me to go? That was an excellent opportunity to announce myself favorably.

"What do you want?" he asked roughly.

I walked over to him and extended my hand.

"I wish to greet you, for it is the same as if the *Bei* hears my greeting."

"Do you know him?"

"I have not yet met him, but I have been told about him. He is a courageous warrior that deserves my respect. Will you relay a message to him from me?"

"Yes, if I can."

"You can. But first let me prove to you that I know how to honor the *Bei*: You shall see the *Mutesselim* before me."

"Are you serious?"

"One never jests with a courageous Kurd."

"Do you hear that?" he turned to the others. "This foreign Emir has learned what it means to be courteousness and respectful. But a Berwari also knows this custom as well." Again turning to me, he added: "Lord, I thank you; you have delighted my heart! But I will gladly wait until you have spoken with the *Mutesselim*."

Now he extended his hand to me. I shook it.

"I suspect that you will not have to wait long. But tell me if you have enough time to visit me after you have spoken with the Commandant!"

"I will come and then ride a little faster afterwards. Where are you staying?"

"I stay with this Selim Agha, the colonel of the Arnauts."

He nodded and stepped back for the servant opened the door to permit Lindsay and myself to enter.

The walls of the room into which we stepped was covered with old scratched wallpaper, at the far end of the room was a dais about a foot high, that was covered by a carpet. The Commandant sat on it. He was a tall, thin man. He had a sharp-featured face that had aged well before its time. His gaze was veiled and did not encourage trust. He arose at our entrance and indicated that we should both be seated, one on each side of him. For me this was easy; but Master Lindsay struggled to bend his legs into a position that the Turks call the 'resting the limbs'. He who is not used this will soon find that his lower extremities go numb, so that one is forced to arise. I therefore had to ensure, for the sake of the Englishman, that the discussion did not last too long.

Chapter 32

"*Chosh geldin demek; ömriniz jok ola* - You are welcome to me; may your life be long!" the Commandant greeted us.

"As long as yours," I answered him. "We have come from far away to tell you that we are happy to see you. May God's blessings reside on your house and may every task you undertake, succeed!"

"I too wish you well and success in all that you do! What is the name of the land of your birth, Emir?"

"Germanistan."

"Does it have a great Sultan?"

"It has very many Padishahs."

"And how many warriors?"

"If the Padishahs of Germanistan gather their warriors together, then they would see many millions of eyes looking at them."

"I have not yet seen this land, but it must be a great and famous land for you stand under the protection of the Sultan."

This was of course a hint to legitimize myself. I did so immediately:

"Your word is just. Here is my *Bu-djeruldi* of the Padishah!"

"He took it, pressed it to his brow, his lips and his breast before reading it.

"Your name is other than Kara Ben Nemsi in this document!"

Ah, that was fatal! The fact that I kept the name that Halef had given me could prove dangerous here; but I gathered my wits and quickly replied:

"Would you care to read the name that is written in the document?"

He tried, but it would not succeed. And he stumbled fatally over the name of my origin.

"You see!" I explained. "No Turk can correctly read, much less pronounce a name from Germanistan; no *Mufti* and no *Mullah* can do it, for our language is very difficult and is written in a script that is different to yours. I am Hajji Kara Ben Nemsi; that I will prove to you with the letter that the *Mutessarif* of Mosul has addressed to you and given to me."

I handed him this letter. When he had read it, he was satisfied and returned the *Bu-djeruldi* to me with the customary ceremony.

"And this *Effendi* is Hajji Lindsay-*Bei*?" he then asked.

"Such is his name."

"From what land is he?"

"From Londonistan," I answered, avoiding the familiar name of England.

"He has made an oath not to speak?"

"He is silent."

"And he can perform magic?"

"Listen, *Mutesselim*, one should not speak of magic, and least of all to someone one does not know."

"We will get to know each other, for I have a great liking for magic. Do you believe that one can make money?"

"Yes, money can be made."

"And that the stone of the prophets does exist?"

"One does exist, but it is not in the earth, rather it is buried in the hearts of men and it can not be brought forth with trickery."

"You speak very gloomily; but I see that you are an authority on magic. There is white and black magic. Do you know both?"

I could not help myself and answered jovially:

"Oh, I know of many other arts too."

"There are more? Which?"

"A blue, a green and a yellow, a red and a gray. This Hajji Lindsay-*Bei* was first an adherent of the gray checkered, but now he took on the black and red."

"One sees this by his dress. Selim Agha has told me that he has a *Kazma* [hoe] with him with which he digs in the earth to learn the language of the dead."

"That is right. But let us not speak of that today. I am a warrior and an *Effendi*, but no *Choja* [schoolmaster], that instructs others."

The brave Commandant had sucked all provincial sources of assistance dry and now he sought his salvation in magic. It was not my purpose to enhance his superstition, but under the current circumstances, I had no compulsion to dispute his belief. Perhaps the famous hoe of my Master 'Fowling-bull' had given him the idea to converse with me on the subject of magic? That was possible as well. Besides, my last words made an impression on him, he clapped his hands and had the coffee and pipes brought in.

"I heard that the *Mutessarif* had a battle with the *Jesidi*?" He began another subject.

This too was dangerous for me, but I did not know how to avoid it. It started like an examination: 'I heard!' And yet, as the Commandant of Amadijah, he must know more details than just rumors. I therefore walked in his footsteps:

"I too have heard of it." And in order to sidestep one of his questions, I added: "He would have beaten them, and now the rebellious Arabs are most likely next in line."

He listened to me and looked at me searchingly.

"From what do you suspect this, Emir?"

"He spoke to me of it himself."

"Himself? The *Mutessarif*?"

"Yes."

"When?"

"When I was with him, of course."

"What gave him that idea?" he inquired without being able to hide a look of distrust.

"Certainly because he trusted me and was willing to discuss the campaign with me."

"Which?"

"Have you ever heard of politics and diplomacy, *Mutesselim*?"

He smiled in a superior manner.

"Would I be Commandant of Amadijah if I were not a diplomat?"

"You are very right! But why don't you show me that you are one?"

"Was I not diplomatic?"

"Very."

"What do you mean?"

"Because you have asked me in such a direct manner that I was astonished. There are matters that I may not speak of and you could only have discovered the detail of these matters through very clever questioning."

"Why may you not speak to me of such? The *Mutessarif* keeps no secrets from me!"

"You had to ask me about the incident; is this not proof that the *Mutessarif* was more open with me than with you. Why did I come to Amadijah when I was involved in a matter concerning his attack on the Arabs?"

"That is impossible!"

"Its is very possible! I will tell you this much in confidence; the governor will send me to the grazing lands of the Arabs upon my return from Amadijah. I shall secretly study the terrain so that I can advise him."

"Is this true?"

"I tell you this in confidence, therefore it is true."

"Then you are a great *Inanji* [friend] of the *Mutessarif*!"

"Apparently!"

"And you have influence with him!"

"If that were the case, I could not claim it. Otherwise any influence I had, I could easily loose."

"Emir, you make me concerned!"

"Why?"

"I know that the mercy of the *Mutessarif* does not shine upon me. Tell me if you are truly his friend and confidant!"

"He has told me of things that he would not tell others, he even told me of his attack against the *Jesidi* beforehand; whether I am his friend is a question to which you should expect no answer."

"I will test you, to see if you truly know more than others!"

"Do it!" I answered confidently, although I felt doubt creep into my being.

"Against which particular Arab tribe is the attack intended?"

"Against the Shammar."

"And which sub-tribe of the same?"

"The Haddedihn."

Now his sharp-featured face assumed a sly expression.

"What is the name of their Sheik?"

"Mohammed Emin. Do you know him?"

"No. But I heard that the *Mutessarif* has taken him prisoner. He surely has spoken to you, his confidant, about it. Especially since he intends to send you to these Arabs!"

This good man truly made an effort to be diplomatic! But I laughed him in the face.

"Oh *Mutesselim*, you really concoct a difficult test for me! Is Amad el Ghandur so old that he could be mistaken for his father, Mohammed Emin!"

"How can I mistake them if I have never seen either of them before!"

I arose.

"Let us end our conversation! I am no *Genji* [boy], to be fooled about with. But if you desire to see the prisoner, then go down to the prison; the Sergeant will show him to you. I only tell you this: Keep his identity secret and don't let him escape! As long as the future Sheik of the Haddedihn is in the hands of the *Mutessarif*, he can make demands of the Arabs. Permit me to leave!"

"Emir, I did not wish to insult you. Stay!"

"I have other things to do this day."

"You must remain for I have ordered a meal to be prepared!"

"I can eat in my room and I thank you. Besides, there is a Kurd outside that has to speak with you urgently. He was here before me and although I offered him to precede me, he was polite enough to refuse."

"He is a messenger from the *Bei* of Gumri. He can wait!"

"*Mutesselim*, permit me warn you of making an error!"

"What error?"

"You treat this *Bei* like an enemy or like a man that one does not have to respect or fear!"

I noted that he tried hard to control the boiling rage within him.

"Do you wish to teach me, Emir, you whom I hardly know?"

"No. How could I possibly dare to teach you, as you are much older than I am! Besides, as we spoke of magic, I have proved to you that I considered you as one of the wise and not one whom I could teach. But a young man may give advice to an elder!"

"I know how to handle this Kurd. His father was Abd el Summit *Bei*, who made much trouble for my predecessor and particularly Selim Zillahi!"

"Should his son be equally troublesome to you? The *Mutessarif* needs his troops for his move against the Arabs, and a part of his troops must always be ready for the *Jesidi*, who he can not trust. What will he say if I tell him that you handle the Berwari Kurds in such a manner that he may have to fear an uprising from them if they knew that the governor is in no position to subdue them? Do as you please *Mutesselim*. I will neither teach nor advise you."

This argument astounded him; that much was obvious.

"You mean I should receive this Kurd?"

"I say again, do as you please!"

"If you promise me that you stay for a meal, I will permit him to enter in your presence."

"Under such a condition I can remain as my departure was out of consideration for him so that he would not have to wait any longer."

The *Mutesselim* clapped his hands and a servant emerged from a side door. The servant was commanded to let the Kurd enter. When the Kurd entered, he did so proudly and spoke his greeting with a simple *'Salaam'*, without bowing.

"You are a messenger from the *Bei* of Gumri?" asked the Commandant.

"Yes."

"What message has your Lord for me?"

"My Lord? A free Kurd does not have a Lord. He is my *Bei*, my leader in battle, but not my master. Only the Turks and the Persians know this word."

"I did not call you so that you can argue with me. What message do you have for me?"

The Kurd might have guessed that I was the cause of his shortened wait. He looked at me with understanding and answered very seriously and slowly:

"*Mutesselim*, I had a message for you; but since I had to wait such a long time, I have forgotten it. The *Bei* must send you another messenger who might not forget his message if he does not have to wait as long!"

The last words he spoke when he was already at the door; then he was gone. The Commandant looked perplexed. Such a thing he had not expected, and I thought that no European ambassador could have handled this better than this common, young Kurd. My legs twitched with the desire to hurry after him so that I could acknowledge the esteem in which I held him. Even the *Mutesselim* wanted to run after him, but obviously not with the same intention.

"Scoundrel!" he shouted whilst leaping from his seated position. "I will ... "

He reconsidered and remained standing. I calmly stuffed my *Jibuk* and lit it.

"What do you say to that, Emir?"

"That I expected it to come to this. A Kurd is neither a hypocritical Greek nor a devious Jew who does not even bend when he is kicked. What will the *Bei* of Gumri do now and what will the *Mutessarif* say!"

"You will inform him?"

"I will be silent, but he will see the results."

"I will have this Kurd called back!"

"He will not come."

"I will not be angry with him!"

"He will not believe you. There is only one person who might convince him to return."

"Who is that?"

"I am that person."

"You?"

"Yes. I am his friend; perhaps he will hear my voice."

"You are his friend? You know him?"

"I have met him for the first time in your anteroom. But I spoke with him as one speaks to a man who is the messenger of a *Bei*, and that has surely made him my friend."

"But yet you do not know where he has gone to!"

"I know it."

"Where is he? Gone from Amadijah. His horse was below."

"He went to my rooms, for I have invited him."

"You have invited him? He shall partake of a meal with you?"

"I will receive him as my guest; the main thing is that I will entrust him with a message to his *Bei*."

The *Mutesselim* became more and more astounded.

"What kind of message?"

"I thought you were a diplomat? Ask the *Mutessarif*!"

"Emir, you speak in riddles!"

"Your wisdom will soon solve them. I will be candid with you and tell you frankly that you made an error in not heeding my warning and refusing my advice, at least permit me to correct this error and allow me to send a peaceful message to the *Bei* of Gumri!"

"I may not know the message?"

"I will tell it to you in confidence, although it is a diplomatic secret: I have to send him a gift."

"A gift? From whom?"

"Of course I may not say that, but perhaps you can guess if I tell you that the officer and Master from whom it comes lives to the west of Amadijah and much desires that the *Bei* of Gumri has no thoughts of hostility against him."

"Lord, now I know that you are truly the confidant of the *Mutessarif* of Mosul; for the gift can only come from him, you may admit it or not!"

The man was weak minded and quite unsuitable for his office. I later discovered that he was a creature of his predecessor who was elevated from *Nefus Emini* of Zillah in little Asia to *Mutesselim* of Amadijah. My visit with this Commandant had taken a remarkable turn. Whatever he considered me to be I could only guess, but not claim with certainty; and yet the strange direction of our conversation made me say things from which he could have easily deduced the purpose of our presence here. He certainly did not have the right stuff to be a village elder, much less a *Mutesselim*; and yet I secretly regretted the embarrassment that he would suffer because of the success of our mission. The possibility of saving him from that would have been welcome, but impossible.

The continuation of our conversation was postponed as food was being served. It consisted of some pieces of the 'borrowed' mutton and a very meager Pillau. The Commandant partook of it ravenously and forgot to speak altogether; when he was satiated, he asked:

"You will really meet with this Kurd?"

"Yes; I believe he will keep his word."

"And send him back to me?"

"If you wish to see him, yes."

"Will he wait for you?"

This was a gentle indicator that was not founded in my lack of hospitality but rather in the concern that the messenger would also loose his patience with me. That is why I answered:

"He will soon depart and that is why it is advisable that I do not tire him. Do you permit us to leave?"

"Under the condition that you promise me to again come tonight as my guest."

"I promise. When do you desire us to come?"

I will let you know though Selim Agha. Besides, you are always welcome to me whenever it pleases you to come."

Our meal had thus not taken up much time. He accompanied us in the most congenial manner right up to the gate. There our companions waited with our horses.

"You have a *Bashi-Bozuk* with you?" asked the Commandant.

"Yes, as my *Khawass*. The *Mutessarif* offered me a greater entourage, but I am used to protect myself."

He now admired my stallion.

"What a horse! Have you bought it or raised it?"

"It was a gift."

"A gift! Lord, whoever gave you this gift was a prince! Who was it?"

"Even that is a secret; but perhaps you shall meet him soon."

We mounted our horses and Selim Agha roared an order to his soldiers of the guard who had patiently waited for us:

"*Silahlarile nishanlaryn* - aim your guns!"

They did so but not a single one of the flintlocks formed a coherent line in respect to each other.

"*Jalghy, shamataji kylyn* - Music, make noise!"

As before the whine and coffee grinding commenced.

"*Hepsi herbiri halan atyn* - all fire at once!"

Oh dear! Hardly half of these murderous weapons had the courage to make a sound. The Agha rolled his eyes. The holders of these confused shooting implements rolled their eyes and furiously worked at the mechanisms of their front-loaders. But only after we had already turned the next corner we heard a soft, intermittent report that one could only assume was the result of yet another wad being hurled from the barrel of these ancient flintlocks.

When we reached our accommodation, the Kurd sat on the carpet in my room and smoked my tobacco from one of my pipes. That made me happy for it proved that our opinions on hospitality were one and the same.

"*Kheïr att, hemsher* - Welcome, friend!" I greeted him.

"What, You speak Kurdish?" he asked happily.

"Only a little, but we shall try!"

I had given Halef the order to find some food from some street vendor and therefore could dedicate myself entirely to the *Bei* of Gumri's messenger. I too lit a pipe and settled myself next to him.

"I have let you wait longer than I intended," I started; "I had to partake of a meal with the *Mutesselim*."

"Lord, I gladly waited. The lovely maiden that is your hostess had to pass me a pipe and then took of your tobacco. I knew your intention and thus I knew that you would not be angry."

"You are a warrior of the *Bei* of Gumri; what is mine is yours. I must also thank you for the delight you have brought me when I was with the Commandant."

"What delight?"

"You are a youth, but you acted like a man when you gave him your answer."

He laughed and said:

"I would have spoken differently if I had been alone with him."

"More severely?"

"No, rather more mildly. But since a witness was present, I had to defend the honor of him who sent me."

"You have achieved your purpose for the *Mutesselim* desires that you return and complete your assignment."

"I will not give him that satisfaction."

"Not even for me?"

He looked at me.

"Do you desire this?"

"I ask it of you. I have promised him that I will deliver his plea to you."

"Do you know him? Are you his friend?"

"I have never seen him before and today was my first time with him."

"Then I will tell you what kind of man he is. Actually I best describe this man if I say no more about him other than that the *Saliahn* [wealth tax] now hardly brings twenty thousand piaster into Amadijah, and that he does not have the right to it as he should have. It has been taken from him. The Sultan rarely listens to a complaint; but he had to hear this one for it screamed towards heaven. He plundered from the inhabitants so much that they even remained in the mountains during winter and did not dare to return to the city. Now the whole district is impoverished, and hunger is a steady guest of the people. The *Mutesselim* always needs money and borrows. Whoever is not willing to lend, suffers and fears his wrath. Besides, he is a cowardly being who is only courageous against the weak. His soldiers go hungry and freeze because they do not receive food or clothing. Their guns he has exchanged for poorer models so that he can benefit from the profit, and when the powder for the two canons that defend the fort arrives, he will sell it and keep the money."

That was a typically Turkish business! I no longer had to wonder at the highly effective weapons display that I had witnessed.

"And how is it with your *Bei*?" I inquired.

"Not good. Many Kurds are coming to the city to either buy or sell produce. For these the Commandant has introduced a high tax that the *Bei* will not endure. The Commandant also imposes his authority over us, which is not his right. Two Kurds came to Amadijah a little while ago to purchase lead and powder, at the gate a tax was demanded for these items. This has never happened before; they did not have enough money to pay the tax that was even higher than the price of the already quite expensive wares, so they were thrown into prison. The *Bei* demanded their freedom and agreed that the lead and powder could be confiscated; but the *Mutesselim* did not agree. He demanded the confiscated wares, the tax, a penalty as well as costs for the search and the prison costs so that twenty piaster grew into a hundred-and-forty. He will not let the men go unless this is paid and then he adds an additional ten piaster to it each day they remain in prison."

"And you wanted to speak to him in this respect?"

"Yes."

"Should you pay that sum?"

"No."

"Only negotiate? That would lead to nothing."

"I should tell him that we make a prisoner of every man from Amadijah who enters our territory and that we will hold them until both of our men are returned to us."

"In other words a reprisal! That will not make a great impact for it means nothing to him if an inhabitant of Amadijah is your prisoner or not. And then you have to consider that from such action a considerable conflict could easily erupt. The best thing would be if these men could somehow escape."

"The *Bei* says that as well; but escape is not possible."

"Why not? Is the guard that diligent?"

"Oh, the guard is not a problem. A Sergeant and three men, they would be overpowered easily; but they could raise an alarm that could be far more dangerous."

"Dangerous? Hmm!"

"The main thing is that it is impossible to escape that prison."

"Why?"

"The walls are thick and the entrance is locked by two doors that are armored with iron. The prison backs against the garden of the Agha of the Arnauts; every unusual noise could alarm him and that could be dangerous. We have to forgo any thoughts of escape."

"Even if you find a man who is prepared to assist you?"

"Who would that be?"

"I!"

"You Emir? Oh, that would be good! And I would thank you greatly! The two men are my father and my bother."

"What is your name?"

"Dohub. My mother is from the Kurdish tribe of the Dohubi."

"I have to tell you that I am a stranger here myself and that I am not certain how to affect the escape; but your *Bei* was recommended to me and even to you I am well disposed. I will investigate tomorrow how best to approach this task."

Behind this assurance hid of course just a little self-interest. It was quite possible that we would have need of the *Bei* of Gumri's support and that could best be obtained if we took his people under our protection.

"You therefore recommend that I should go to the *Mutesselim*?"

"Yes, go to him and try your luck at negotiating once again; I have tried to soften him, perhaps he will let your kin go of his own free will."

"Lord, have you really done this?"

"Yes."

"How did you begin this?"

"To tell you this would be too much; but I will write down a few words to the *Mutessarif* that could be of value, if you follow my advice."

"What advice do you give me?"

"Do not speak of reprisals. Tell him that if he does not release the prisoners this very day, you will ride to the *Mutessarif* of Mosul and tell him that the Berwari-Kurds will rise up in revolt. And in passing you should mention that you will ride through the territory of the *Jesidi* and will speak with Ali *Bei*, their commander."

"Lord, that is too much and much too daring!"

"Do it all the same; I advise you and I have my reasons. He keeps the prisoners mainly because he wants to exhort money that he has much need of; but now that reason is diminished for we have made him a present of many piaster."

"Then I will go to him!"

"Do so immediately. But then return to me so that I can give you my message for your *Bei*!"

I wrote the following Turkish words on a page from my notebook: "Permit me, to impress upon your heart the request of this Kurd and avoid angering the *Mutessarif*!" After I added my name, I handed it to Dohub who hurried away.

I had the audacity to consider myself an influential man. I acted adventurously, that is true; but the opportune events had, as one might say, placed me before a pole and boosted me half way up; should I slide down again and forgo the prize if it was almost entirely within my reach?

Halef returned and brought a huge assortment of cold foods and fruit so that we would be well provided for an entire week.

"Very plentiful, Hajji Halef Omar!" I said.

"*Allah akbar;* Allah is great, *Sihdi*, but my hunger is greater. Do you know that I and the little Ifra have eaten nothing since this morning in Spandareh?"

"Then eat! But serve up a good portion for my guest that he does not depart hungry from me. Do you have wine?"

"No. You have become a true believer and still want to enjoy the drink of the infidels! *Allah kerihm;* I am a Moslem and should ask for wine in Amadijah?"

"Then I will fetch some myself. You understand!"

"No, *Sihdi*, you shall not; but many people only speak Kurdish here, a language I don't understand and I only know a little Turkish. Therefore I can only buy things that I know the name of."

"In Turkish 'wine' is called *Sharab* and in Kurdish *Sherab*; that is easy to remember. Master Lindsay will want some too, go and fetch it!"

He departed. As the door opened I heard the scolding voice of Mersinah mixed with the conciliatory voice of a man, Halef returned at once.

"*Sihdi*, there is a man below whom the mistress will not let pass."

"Who is it?"

"An inhabitant of Amadijah whose daughter is sick."

"What does that have to do with us?"

"Forgive me, *Sihdi*! When I was buying bread, a man ran into me and nearly knocked me over. I asked him what his hurry was and he told me that he was seeking a *Hekim* [doctor] because his daughter had suddenly fallen ill and might die. I advised him that if he could not find a doctor that he should come to you, and now he is here."

"That was silly, Halef. You know that I no longer have that little apothecary, the content of which I used for cures by the Nile!"

"Oh, *Sihdi*, you are a great scholar and can cure the sick even without those kernels you once had."

"But I am not a doctor!"

"You can do everything!"

What could be done? Halef had once again exaggerated my abilities and no doubt his memory of that substantial *Baksheesh* had most likely attributed to it. Now it was I who had to bite into the already plucked apple.

"The mistress is more clever than you, Halef! But go and fetch the man!"

He went and soon returned with the stranger whose brow and beard dripped with sweat. He was a Kurd; one recognized that from the *Tolik* [a lock of hair that falls across the brow] that peeked from his disheveled turban; yet he wore Turkish garments.

"*Sallam*!" he greeted breathlessly. "Oh Lord, come quickly, otherwise my daughter will die, she already speaks of heaven!"

"What is wrong with her?"

"She is possessed by an evil spirit who intends to kill her."

"Who says this?"

"The old Turkish *Hekim*, that I fetched. He has hung an amulet around her neck but he reckons that it will not help her."

"How old is your daughter?"

"Sixteen years."

"Does she suffer from cramps or fainting spells?"

"No, she has never been ill until today."

"What does the evil spirit do to her?"

"He has invaded her mouth and she complains that he is scratching her throat; then he enlarges her eyes that he may see outside through them. Her mouth is red and her face too and now she lies there and speaks of the wonders of heaven and what she can see there."

Quick help was imperative, as this was certainly some kind of poisoning.

"I will see if I can help you. Do you live far from here?"

"No."

"Is there another doctor in town besides the old *Hekim*?"

"No."

"Then come quickly!"

We hurried ahead. He led me through three lanes and then into a house the exterior of which suggested something about the owner's status. Whoever owned this house could not be numbered among the poor. We passed through two rooms and entered a third. On a low cushion a girl lay on her back, completely straight. By her side knelt some weeping women, and nearby squatted an old man who had removed his turban and mumbled loud prayers towards the patient.

"Are you the *Hekim*?" I asked him.

"Yes."

"What ails the patient?"

"The devil has possessed her, Lord!"

"Ridiculous! If the devil was inside of her, she would not speak of heaven."

"Lord, you do not understand! He has denied her food and drink and has made her faint."

"Let me see her!"

I pushed the women aside and knelt next to the girl. It was a very lovely girl.

"Lord, save my daughter from certain death," wailed one of the women, "and we will give you all we possess."

"Yes," confirmed the man who had fetched me. "Everything, you shall have everything, for this is our only child and our life."

"Save her," a voice said from the back of the room; "and you shall be rich and beloved by God!"

I looked into the direction from which the voice emanated and spied an old woman whose appearance made me shiver. Her years might have numbered a hundred; her body was bent over severely and she appeared to be of just skin and bones; her frightfully gaunt face gave the impression of a grinning skull, but from her crown hung two heavy, white plaits almost down to the ground.

"Yes, save her, my great grandchild!" she repeated, whilst she raised her folded, dried out hands in a pleading gesture that exposed the rosary that dangled there. "I will kneel and beg the merciful mother of God that you might succeed."

A Catholic! Here among the Turks and Kurds!

"Pray," I answered quite touched; "I will see if she can still be helped by human intervention!"

The sick girl lay there with lively, open eyes; but her pupils were quite dilated. Her face was deeply infused with blood, her breath and her pulse were too fast, and her throat moved with a cramp-like heaving. I did not ask when the illness had manifested itself; I was a lay person, but I was certain that she had swallowed belladonna or *'stramonium'*.

"Has your daughter retched?" I asked the man.

"No."

"Do you have a mirror?"

"A small one here."

"Pass it to me!"

The old *Hekim* laughed hoarsely:

"The bad spirit will not let himself be seen in that glass!"

I did not answer him, rather I let the meager light of the already setting sun that still penetrated through the window fall onto the mirror and reflect on the girl's face. The blinding beam caused no reaction in the dilated pupils.

"When did your daughter last eat?" I asked.

"I do not know," answered the father. "She was here alone."

"Where?"

"Here."

"No bad spirit has entered her, rather she has ingested an *Aghy* [poison]!"

"*Allah il Allah!* Is that true, Lord?"

"Yes."

"Don't believe it!" warned the *Hekim*. "The devil is inside her."

"Silence, you old fool! Do you have lemons about?"

"No."

"Coffee?"

"Yes."

"Can you get oak-apples?"

"Those grow in our forests. We have some in the house."

"Quickly make a very strong, hot coffee and boil the oak-apples in the same water. Also send someone to fetch some lemons!"

"Ha, he wants to feed the devil with oak-apples, lemons and coffee!" the *Hekim* cried in astonishment and horror whilst he clapped his hands together.

In the absence of something more appropriate, I stuck my finger into the girl's mouth, hoping that I could induce her to vomit. I took the precaution to protect my finger from her teeth with the aid of my knife hilt, which I placed between her teeth. After some effort the experiment succeeded, although my efforts were painful for the girl. I repeated it, but the emptying was not sufficient.

"Is there a *Ejzaga* [Apothecary] nearby?" I asked since I needed something to encourage vomiting.

"In the same lane."

"Come quickly, guide me!"

We left and my guide stopped before a small shop.

"Here lives the *Attar* [dealer in herbs]!" he said.

I entered the small *Budika* and found myself surrounded by a chaotic jumble of useful as well as useless things. Rancid pomades, pipe-stems, old dried out plasters and tallow, rhubarb and brown sugar in a box, coffee beans. As well as lime-blossoms, peppercorns and crushed chalk, senna leaves in a tin and on top of it some 'honey'; wire-nails, ginger and blue vitriol. Soap, tobacco, salt, eye-glasses, vinegar, *Charpie*, *Spiessglanz*, ink, hemp seeds, lead crystal [Gallizenstein], yarn, gum, valerian, buttons and buckles, tar, pickled walnuts, umbellifer [Teufelsdreck] and figs. … Everything was resting here peacefully side by side -, next to -, under -, over - and amongst each other, and in the midst of it all sat a dirty little man, that appeared as though he had tried all these ingredients both internally as well as externally. What havoc had this *Attar* already wreaked!

For my needs I could only use blue vitriol but I took a little bottle of spirit of ammonia as well. After we returned, the first worked quite well on the patient. Then I gave her strong coffee with lemon juice and then a brew made from oak apples. I then impressed upon her relatives, that in order to prevent a possible blockage or stroke, to keep her from sleep by shaking her, sprinkling her with cold water or passing the ammonia under her nose, and I promised to return soon.

This treatment was probably not the best, but I did not know any better, and - it worked. Since the immediate danger had now passed, I could concentrate on other things. I looked around the room and saw a basket in the far corner that was still partially filled with mulberries. Between them I saw a number of - belladonna berries.

"Do you want to see the bad spirit that invaded the patient?" I asked the *Hekim*.

"One can not see a spirit. And even if that were possible, you could not show it to me, because you don't believe in it. If the girl does not die, then it is because of my amulet."

"Have you not seen me take your amulet from her neck at once? Here it lies, I will open it."

"You may not!" he screamed whilst gripping my hand quickly.

"Let go, old man! My hand is stronger than yours. Why should I not open it?"

"Because there is magic within. You will immediately be possessed by the same spirit that possessed the girl!"

"We will see!"

He wanted to prevent it but I opened the squares of calf leather that had been sewn together - and between them I found a dead fly.

"An innocent insect! Don't make me laugh." I laughed all the same, whilst I dropped it to the floor and squashed it. "Now where is this spirit that should posses me?"

"Just wait, it will come!"

"I will show you the devil that is responsible for this illness. Look here! What is this? You, a *Hekim* must know these berries!"

I held a belladonna berry under his nose and he was shocked.

"Allah be merciful! That is a *Ölüm kires* [literally: Cherry of Death]! Whoever eats this must die for they can not be saved!"

"Well, the patient has eaten of these fruits; that, I have seen in her eyes. Whoever eats of these, their eyes enlarge; remember that! Now put on your turban and get out of here, otherwise I will make you partake of these cherries of death, and make you hope that a *Sin-ek* [fly] will save your life!"

I took some cherries in my hand and made towards him. He crushed his turban onto his bald shaven head and with a true fear of death ran from the house without taking leave.

Those present realized that I was correct. Even without my words, it was evident to them what had happened to the girl. They thanked me in such a reverent manner that I could only end it by my own quick departure. But I left them my advice to call me immediately if the girl's condition worsened.

When I returned to my rooms, I met up with Mersinah who burst from the kitchen with threatening motions of the huge spoon she held in her hand. Closely behind her flew a great, wet dishrag that had been aimed so superbly that when it caught up with her small, tangled *knackwurst* plaits, it wrapped itself lovingly around her venerable head. And then the angry voice of Hajji Halef Omar followed from the thus profaned shrine:

"Wait, you old dragon!" he shouted; "You shall yet make good on my coffee!"

She unwound the wet embrace of the dishrag and balled it up with the obvious intent to send it back from whence it came when she spotted me.

"Oh, Emir, how good it is that you come! Save me from this furious man!"

"What is the matter, oh rose of Amadijah!"

"He claims to have found my coffee in his tin and his in my bag."

"And that is probably true?"

"True? I swear to you by Ayesha, the mother of all Saints, that I have not touched his tin!"

"So, you great grandmother of liars and scoundrels!" it sounded from the kitchen. "You did not come across our coffee, of which two-hundred *Drem* [one and a third pound] cost twenty-five good piaster? I will prove otherwise to my *Sihdi*!"

He came from the kitchen, in his right hand he held the newly purchased coffee tin and in the left a great, open paper bag.

"*Sihdi*, you know the coffee of Harimah?"

"You know that I do."

"Have a look where it is!"

I carefully and intently scrutinized the content of the tin as well as the bag.

"It is in both, but mixed with bad beans and dried shells."

"You see well, *Effendi*! I have bought good Harimah coffee and this mother and great-grandmother of robbers and thieves brews only bad coffee, mixed with shells. Do you now see that she has messed with my tin!"

"*Sihdi*, you are a mighty warrior, a great scholar and wisest of all judges," the 'Myrte' retorted whilst she swung her dishrag uncomfortably close under the Hajji's nose. "You will punish this father of scoundrels and this son of liars!"

"Punish?" shouted Halef quite amazed. "As well!"

"Yes." she decided with certainty. "For it was he who interfered with my bag and swindled me. Only he could have mixed the coffee to discredit me and my house!"

"Oh, you paragon of all thirty-nine vices!" Halef growled angrily; "You dare to call me a thief? Me? If you were not a woman I would ... "

"Stop, Halef, don't quarrel, for I am here and I will pass fair judgment! Mersinah, you claimed that this Halef Omar has mixed the two kinds of coffee?"

"Yes, Emir!"

"Then he has contributed to this difficult case. Now do your part and separate the two kinds! I will soon come and see if it has been done and make my judgment."

She opened her mouth to tell me that she was inclined to object or to claim dispensation, but Halef managed to speak first:

"But that has to happen quickly for we need the coffee urgently!"

"Why?" I asked.

"Because you have guests upstairs!"

"Who?"

"Three Kurds, that await your return. The one that visited you before is with them."

"Then quickly fetch some more coffee!"

I hastily climbed the stairs for the other two Kurds could only be the erstwhile prisoners. This assumption was soon confirmed. As I entered the room, Dohub arose and spoke:

"Here is the Emir who has saved you! Oh *Effendi*, the *Mutesselim* has read your words and returned my father and brother to me!"

"Did you tell him that you would go to Mosul?"

"Yes, your advice was good, for at once the Commandant became friendly and when I handed him your letter, he read it and called for Selim Agha who had to bring the prisoners."

"What about the tax and the penalty?"

"He dismissed both, but kept the powder and the lead. Emir, tell us how we can thank you!"

"Do you know the *Nezanum* of Spandareh?"

"Oh, very well! His daughter is married to our *Bei*, and he often comes to Gumri to visit both of them."

"He is also my friend. I was with him until early this morning and he asked me to visit your *Bei* if I came to Gumri."

"Come, Lord, come to us. Your welcome shall be better than if the *Mutesselim* or the *Mutessarif* came!"

"Perhaps I will come; but many days may yet pass. The *Nezanum* has given me a package that I should give to your *Bei*. It should not remain here long and that is why I ask you to take it with you to Gumri. Relay my greetings to the *Bei* and tell him that I am his friend and wish him all the best and success!"

"That is your message that you wished to give to us?"

"Yes."

"It is not enough, Lord!"

"Perhaps you can grant me a favor later."

"We will do it. Only come and demand your desire from us!"

"Would you protect a friend of mine, one that is hunted by the *Mutesselim* and flees to you?"

"The Commandant would never see him!"

I turned to the eldest of the other two on whose face one could read the privations that they experienced during their interment.

"Do you know who else was imprisoned with you?"

"No," he answered. "I was thrown into dark hole that hardly received any light, and I could see and hear little."

His son had the same experience.

"Is the Sergeant that guarded you a mean man?"

"He never spoke to us. The only human voice that we heard was that of an old and dirty hag who brought us food."

"What are the paths to Gumri like?"

"You first have to descend into the valley of Berwari and do so on a path that is so steep that you can not ride but rather have to lead your horse by its reigns. That valley is thickly covered with oak trees and there are villages that are inhabited in part by Kurds and by Nestorian Chaldeans. You will also pass through an arid plain, which we call *Newdasht* and which contains the Kurdish village of Maglano; then you will reach the Kurdish hamlet of Hajis, where only a few families live. You must then cross over many waterways that all flow towards the Zab, then you see Gumri from afar, as it is built on a high rocky outcrop that stands alone in the plain."

After these important questions I invited them to a meal. The two released prisoners indulged ravenously, which indicated to me that the old Mersinah had surely been responsible for their meals. Halef brought coffee, a drink that the Kurds had sorely missed, and so it was with the tobacco, which they smoked afterwards.

Finally they departed, just as Selim Agha entered to tell me that the *Mutesselim* was ready to receive me. They said their good-byes in the most heartfelt manner and impressed upon me once again that I should come to Gumri. Dohub took the package of the village elder along with him, and I was certain that I had made myself new friends upon whose help I could depend in my hour of need.

Next I visited my patient and was happily welcome in the anteroom of her parents.

"How is your daughter?" I asked them.

"Oh, much, much better already, Lord," answered the man. "Your wisdom is almost greater than our gratitude, for she can once again speak coherently and has told us that she did indeed eat of the cherries of death. And your mercy is still greater than we deserved or anticipated; for I have discovered that you are not a doctor that comes to the sick for money, but rather a great Emir who is the beloved of the Sultan and a friend of the *Mutessarif*."

"Who says this?"

"The whole city knows it. Selim Agha is do full of praises for you; the *Mutesselim* has welcomed you with a parade and at your order he even had to free some prisoners. One said it to another and soon we heard it too."

"Are you a child of this city? I see that you are really a Kurd!"

"You have guessed correctly, *Effendi*. I am a Kurd of Lizan and moved to Amadijah for a short time because I did not feel safe in my hometown."

"Not safe? Why?"

"Lizan is in the territory of Tijari and is mostly inhabited by Nestorian Christians. They have suffered great oppressions, so that of late they have decided to rise up and take vengeance. Since I am no Christian but a Mohammedan, I have sought to find a safe haven and so I conduct my business here in peace until the danger has passed."

"What kind of business to you have?"

"I buy up the oak-apples and send them to the Tigris, from there they are shipped further."

"You are a Moslem and yet the old mother, that I saw, is a Christian. How did that come about?"

"Emir, that is a story that saddens both my wife and I. Her ancestor was a famous *Melek* [King, Prince] of the Tijaris and he accepted the teachings of Christ, the crucified. His wife, the ancestor that you have seen, did likewise. But his son was an adherent of the prophet and separated from his father. The father died and his son, who had lost the dignity of a *Melek*, did too in his time. He had lost everything because of the prophet, despite his father being the richest Prince of the land. His children remained poor too, and when I married my wife, the grandchild of that old woman, she hardly possessed a dress to cover her nakedness. But we loved one another, and Allah blessed us; we became rich."

"And the ancestor?"

"We had never seen her until she came to us in Lizan. Her years counted to well over a hundred, and she believed that she would soon die, so she desired to see the children of her children one last time. Since that time, she has visited us twice yearly; but we do not know from whence she comes nor to where she goes to."

"Have you not asked her?"

"Only once, but she did not answer and disappeared for a long time. Ever since then I have never asked again. She is now at our daughter's side. Do you wish to see her?"

"Yes; come!"

The patient was considerably better. The redness had almost totally disappeared; her pulse was weak but even and she was able to speak more coherently than before when she fantasized under the influence of the berries, albeit with some exertion. Her pupils were no longer dilated but she still had difficulty swallowing. She looked at me full of curiosity and extended her hand so that she could thank me.

I advised to continue the administration of coffee and lemon juice and also a hot bath for her feet; then I was ready to depart. The frail body of the ancient one arose from the end of the bed where she had cowered.

"Lord." she said, "I had thought you a *Hekim*, forgive me that I promised you payment!"

"The joy of saving the life of your great-grandchild is payment enough."

"God has blessed your hand, Emir. He is mighty in weakness and merciful in strength. How long does the girl still have to convalesce?"

"Some days should be enough to overcome her weakness."

"Emir, I live, but not in my body, rather I live in the body of this child. I have died many, many years ago; but I arose again in those that I desire to see protected from every mar of the body and the soul. You have not only saved her life but also my own and you do not know how good that is for many that you neither know nor will ever see. You will come again?"

"Yes, tomorrow."

"Then I need not tell you more now."

She turned and resumed her previous position. She spoke so gloomily and she was even an enigma to her relatives. I wished I had the time to solve this riddle. Since I had been invited to a meal with the *Mutesselim*, I had to decline to partake of what was offered to me here, just as I was ready to depart this house.

When I arrived at the Commandant's palace, he had already had a gathering of officials and officers around him. It was to be a great soirée. I was led to the place of honor by his side. We were in a large room that was something like a small ballroom. There was enough space to mill about freely, yet everyone remained motionless in their designated place and smoked a pipe or drank the coffee that was being passed around, all the while they conversed in a whisper with their immediate neighbor. But when the *Mutesselim* spoke a loud word, everyone lowered their head and listened intently as one would do before a mighty emperor.

Even my discussion with him was conducted quietly. After some broad discussions on various subjects he said:

"I have heard that you healed a girl today that was possessed by the Devil. My *Hekim* has seen him enter her; he demands that I send you away because you are a wizard."

"Your *Hekim* is a fool, *Mutesselim*! The girl had eaten a poisonous fruit and I gave her something that counteracted the poison. There never was a Devil nor a spirit to speak of."

"Then you are a *Hekim*?"

"No. You know who and what I am! But in the west, far from Stambul, where I was born, everyone knows more about sicknesses than your *Hekim* does who thinks he can scare away the Devil with a dead fly."

That was inconsiderate and perhaps even a little courageous: but it would not harm these people if someone came along and shook their misguided belief in their own magnificence.

Chapter 33

The *Mutesselim* acted as though he had not heard my rebuke and asked further:

"Then you are acquainted with all kinds of ills?"

"All!" I answered very self-assured.

"And you can make all kinds of elixirs?"

"All!"

"Are there such elixirs that a good Muslim may not drink?"

"Yes."

"Which are these?"

"The *Paksitz* [unclean], that are fashioned from ingredients, the taste of which, the Prophet has forbidden. For example, pigs fat and wine."

"But wine is also a medicine?"

"Yes, a very important one."

"When would it be drunk?"

"For certain sicknesses of the blood and nerves, as well as for digestion and as a tonic or a stimulant."

Again the conversation halted. Those present began to whisper to each other and after a while the *Mutesselim* turned to me and whispered as well:

"*Effendi*, I am sick, very sick!"

"Ah, is that so! May Allah return your health to you!"

"Perhaps he will, for I am good Muslim and a true and pious adherent of the Prophet."

"What ails you?"

"I have already asked many doctors; all of them say that I suffer from a certain sickness of the blood and the nervous system, as well as poor digestion."

I could hardly contain myself so that I would not laugh at him. So this was the reason for this strange line of questioning that danced around the real issue like a 'Cat around a hot dish'. The issue then involved a little begging on his part.

"Have the doctors given you something?"

"Yes, but what they gave me did not help. These men were not as clever and educated as you. Don't you think that I am in need of some stimulant and a tonic?"

"I am certain of it."

"Would you provide me with such?"

"I may not."

"Why not?"

"The Prophet forbids it."

"The Prophet did not desire that the 'True Believers' die of an illness that effects the blood and the nerves. Have you read the Koran carefully?"

"Very carefully."

"Then tell me if you have found a single medicine that is forbidden therein!"

"None!"

"You see! So, will you give me a stimulant?"

"I do not have the ingredients from which to prepare it."

"You jest, for you have them!"

"How would you know this?"

"Your servant has bought them from a Jew today."

Ah, the *Mutesselim* had us watched! He already knew that my little Hajji had bought some wine for the Englishman. We had to be careful if our plan was to remain secret.

"More is required then my servant purchased," I answered.

"A little is better than nothing at all. Since I am quite weak you may not mix too many things together. Would you send me an ordinary dose?"

"Alright; you shall have it!"

"How much?"

"A full *Ilaj-shishe* [medicine bottle]."

"Emir, that is too little! I am Commandant and a very tall man; the bottle will be empty long before the whole body has been treated. Surely you appreciate this?"

"I see it, that is why I will send you a big bottle."

"One? Does a patient only take medicine once?"

"Well then you shall have two bottles!"

"Let me take the medicine once daily and for two weeks!"

"*Mutesselim*, I believe that would make you too strong!"

"Oh, Emir, you do not have to fear that."

"Then we shall try it for one week!"

"But one request you will grant me."

"And that is?"

"A *Mutesselim* should not let his subordinates know that he suffers from weak nerves or poor digestion."

"That is quite right!"

"Then you will pack the medicine quite well, so that none will know the content of the bottles."

"I will fulfill your wish."

"Do you suffer from weak nerves as well, Emir?"

"No. Why should I suffer from such?"

"Because you had such medicine bought for you."

"It was not for me."

"For whom then? For the silent Hajji Lindsay-*Bei*?"

"You said before that a *Mutesselim* should avoid letting anyone know that he is in poor health. Other men have to avoid this too."

"Or perhaps it was for the third man who is seldom seen? He must be quite ill since he never leaves his room!"

That sounded like an interrogation. He wanted to know about Mohammed Emin.

"Yes, he is quite ill," I answered.

"What kind of illness does he have?"

"A sickness of the heart."

"Can you heal him?"

"I hope so."

"I regret that you could not bring him along due to his ill health. Is he a friend of yours?"

"A very good friend."

"What is his name?"

"He asked me not to mention it to you yet. You know him quite well and he desires to surprise you."

"Ah!" he said full of curiosity. "A surprise? When?"

"As soon as he is feeling better."

"How long will that take?"

"A few more days."

"Perhaps I should visit him if he can not come to me?"

"Such a visit would excite him too much. A sickness of the heart can be life threatening; as you probably know quite well?"

"Then I must wait."

Again he descended into silence; after a while he began anew:

"Do you know that you are an enigma to me?"

"You are one to me as well."

"How so?"

"Because you see me as an enigma. Tell me if any one has ever dared to be as open, as sincere or as fearless in speech with you as I have been!"

"That is true, *Effendi*! I would not advise anyone else to try it! But you are an Emir, you stand in the shadow of the Padishah and have been well introduced by the *Mutessarif*; from you I suffer this."

"And yet, despite all this fearlessness, I am an enigma to you?"

"Yes."

"I will help you solve this riddle. Ask me!"

"Above all I wish to know how you came to be under the protection of the Sultan and what the Sultan thinks of me and what plans he has for you and me. But there is not enough time for this today. We will speak again tomorrow, when we are alone."

That was fine with me. And now too the conversations around us ceased for a *Medah* [a teller of stories] had been allowed to enter, the Commandant had engaged him for the entertainment of his guests. The pipes were freshly stuffed and lit. The cups were filled and then all listened intently to the words of the *Medah*.

He took his place in the middle of the room and recited his stories with a lamenting sing-song tone. He told of Abu-Szaber, the crooked mouthed schoolteacher, of the love slave Ganem, of Nureddin Ali and Bedreddin Hassan, stories that had been told many of thousands of times before. For his service he was paid two piaster and was then dismissed.

The *Mutesselim* arose, a sign that the amusing soirée was over. Brilliantly worded courtesies were exchanged, the guests bowed to each and sundry and were happy to have successfully survived the Commandant, the Emir Hajji Kara Ben Nemsi, the tobacco, the coffee and the *Medah*. I had the great joy of being taken home by Selim Agha, arm in arm.

"Emir, permit me to link arms with you!" he begged.

"You have it!"

"I know that I should not, for you are a great Emir, a wise *Effendi* and beloved of the prophet; but I like you and you have to consider that I am not an ordinary Arnaut, but rather a very courageous Agha, who would defend this fortress against fifty-thousand enemies."

"I know it. I like you too. Come, let us walk!"

"Who is that?"

He indicated a shape that had lent against a wall and had flitted past us before disappearing into the darkness of the street. I recognized the man. It was the Arnaut who had ambushed us, but I chose not to mention this now.

"Probably one of your Arnauts."

"Yes, but I don't think I have seen his face before."

"The light of the mocn may deceive."

"Do you know, Emir, what I wanted to say to you?"

"What?"

"Hmm! I am sick."

"What is wrong with you?"

"I suffer from a nerve and blood disorder."

"Selim Agha, I believe you have eavesdropped!"

"Oh no, *Effendi*! But I could not avoid overhearing your conversation with the *Mutesselim*, as I sat right next to him."

"But yet so far from him that you had to strain your ears!"

"Shall one not hearken when it concerns a tonic?"

"And surely you do not hope to get one from me!"

"Should I ask the old *Hekim*? He would give me dead flies!"

"Would you want it in a *Ilaj-shishe* or in a large bottle?"

"You would advise some large bottles!"

"When?"

"Now, if it pleases you!"

"Then let us hurry to get home!"

"Oh no, Emir, for there Mersinah would interfere. She should never know that I have poor digestion!"

"But she should know for she prepares your meals."

"She would drink the medicine instead of me. I know of a place where one can drink this elixir in peace and safety."

"Where?"

"*Effendi*, such a place is always with a Jew or a Greek. Have you never noticed that?"

"Very often. But you will be seen and then the whole city will know that you can not entirely trust your inner workings!"

"Only we two will see one another. This Jew has a room from which one can not even see the moon."

"Then come! But let us take care that we are not seen."

Here was another assault on my purse! Besides, I was quite amused to get to know the Agha as a Muslim, to whom the wine but not the medicinal properties of the blood of the grape were forbidden. A little indiscretion and tipsiness could be an advantage to me.

After we had passed through some narrow lanes we stopped before a poorly maintained house, the main door of which just lent against the frame. We entered the dark passageway and Selim clapped his hands together. At once a bent shape with a truly Jewish countenance came from one of the rooms and shone a light into the Agha's face.

"It is you, Highness? Abraham's God, I am used to welcome just yourself into my house every day, with delight and very great servility! But when I saw the two of you rather than just yourself, I was frightened already!"

"Open up, you old crone!"

"Open up? What? The room, which shall it be, the smaller or the larger one?"

"The small one!"

Am I also assured that this man, who has the honor to accompany you to my house, is a man whose mouth does not speak of things that I offer out of charity? And yet these things may not be mentioned for otherwise the mighty *Mutesselim* would severely punish me already?"

"You are quite safe. Open up, or I will open it myself!"

The old crone pushed aside some boards, behind which a door was hidden. It led into a small room. A tattered mat of raffia and some moss cushions that served as a sofa covered the floor.

"Should I light the lamp?"

"Of course!"

"What would the gentlemen like to drink?"

"Same as always!"

He now lit the two lamps and for the first time the Jew could now see me better as I no longer stood behind Selim.

"*Katera Musa* [by the Will of Moses], that is a great *Effendi* and a great war hero! He is clad with so many glistening *Silahs* [weapons], wears the golden Koran around his neck and has a *Simbehl* [mustache] like *Jehoshuah*, the conqueror of the land of Canaan. To him I may not bring the usual, rather I must go into the furthest corner of the cellar where a drink is buried that can not be had by just anyone."

"What drink is that?" I asked.

"Its is a wine from *Türbedi Haidari*, from a land that no one knows and where the grapes are like apples and their juice can topple the walls of a whole city."

"Bring a bottle!" Agha ordered.

"No, bring two mugs! You must know that the wine of *Türbedi Haidari* is stored in great earthenware amphora and is only drunk from small mugs."

"You know it?" asked the Jew.

"I have drunk it often."

"Where? Where is this land?"

"The name you mentioned is the name of a city that is located in Terbijan in Persia. The wine is good and I hope that you knew how to handle it. What is the price?"

"You are a noble Lord; you shall have it for almost nothing. You shall pay thirty piaster for the mug."

"That is almost for nothing? Bring two mugs, so that I can taste it. Then I will decide how much I will pay for it!"

He went to fetch it. In the corner were some pipes and a box of tobacco. We seated ourselves and selected a pipe each. They did not have a mouthpiece. I pulled mine out of my pocket and screwed it into place, then I tried the tobacco. It was a good Persian blend.

"What is in the other half of the house, Selim Agha?" I asked.

"A spice shop and a coffee shop. In the back is an Opium den and a wine bar for the public; but here only noble men may enter," he explained with a self-satisfied grin.

I had to admit that I was pleased with the prospect of this wine. It is a red, thick and exceptionally strong natural drink of which three sips would be enough to give anyone not used to it quite a rush. Selim loved to partake of Noah's drink, but I was convinced that one mug of this wine was more than enough to overwhelm him.

The host returned with two mugs, each of which easily held a liter. Hmm, poor Selim Agha! I tasted it. The wine had suffered during transport but it was drinkable.

"Well, Highness, how is it?" asked the Jew.

"It is such that I give you twenty piaster for the mug."

"Lord, that offer is too small, much to small! For twenty piaster I will take this wine back and bring another."

"In the land where it is prepared, I would pay no more than four piaster for this. You see that I wish to pay you well, but if that is not enough for you then take it back!"

I stood up.

"What shall I bring for whom?"

"Nothing! I only drink this for twenty piaster, a drink that you would even give me for fifteen. If I don't get it then I will go and you can drink it yourself."

"Then his Highness, the Selim Agha will drink it."

"He will leave with me."

"Give me twenty-nine!"

"No."

"Twenty-eight!"

"Good night, old crone!"

I opened the door.

"Come, *Effendi*! You shall have it for twenty piaster already, for it is an honor to see you in my house."

The barter was completed and certainly only to the satisfaction of the Jew who departed with an ill concealed grin after he had received the money from me. The Agha tried a little sip and then took a larger one.

"*Allah illa Allah! Wallah, Billah, Tallah*! Such I have never had before. Do you think that it is good for a poor constitution such as mine, Emir?"

"Very good!"

"Oh, if the 'Myrte' only knew!"

"Does she also suffer from the same affliction as you?"

"A very thirsty one, *Effendi*!"

He took another considerable drink and then a third.

"No wonder," I said. "She has many worries, much work and many other things to do."

"Not for me; Allah knows it!"

"But for your prisoners."

"She brings them their daily ration of bread and flour with water."

"How much does the *Mutesselim* give your for each prisoner?"

"Thirty para daily."

In other words, approximately fifteen Pfennig! And of that at least half stuck to Selim's hands.

"And what do you receive for watching them?"

"Two piaster daily, which I never receive. It is no wonder that I have never tasted such a wonderful medicine before?"

He took another gulp.

"Two piaster? That is very little, since the prisoners would certainly be a lot of work."

"Work? None at all! Why should I make an effort for these scoundrels? I go down to the jail once a day and check if anyone has died."

"And when exactly do you do this?"

"When it suits me."

"Even at night?"

"Yes, if I forgot to go during the day and I am already out. *Wallahi*, now I remember that I have not yet been there today!"

"My arrival has distracted you."

"That is true, *Effendi*."

"Then you must go and check?"

"That I will not do."

"Why not?"

"These scoundrels are not worth my efforts!"

"Right! But will you make light of your respect?"

"What respect?"

"You are an Agha, an elite officer. Your Arnauts and your non-commissioned officers should fear you! No?"

"Yes, that they should. By Allah, they must!" he asserted.

"Even the Sergeant in the jail?"

"Even he. Of course! This *Mazir* is a particularly rebellious dog. He should fear me most of all!"

"Then you have to watch him well, even surprise him occasionally, to see if he carries out his duties in a timely manner, otherwise he will never fear you!"

"That I will do; yes, by Allah, I will!"

"If he is certain that you do not check on him then he probably sits at a *Kaweji* [coffee server] or ogles some dancer and laughs at you."

"He should dare that! I will surprise him, tomorrow or even still tonight. Emir, will you come with me and surprise him?"

I took care not to show uncertainty by questioning if I had even the right to enter the prison; instead I acted as though my accompanying him would be an honor.

"Is it worth it that such a scoundrel sees the face of an Emir?"

"You do not accompany me for his sake, but for mine."

"Then I also expect to be receive the honor that is due to an Emir and an *Effendi* who has studied the law!"

"That goes without saying! It will be as though the *Mutesselim* himself were accompanying me. You shall inspect the prison."

"Then I will go with you, for I am certain that this Arnaut will not consider me to be a *Khawass*."

He only had a little left in his mug and I had kept pace with him. His eyes had become smaller and the tips of his mustache were quite scraggly.

"Shall we have another mug brought, Selim Agha?" I asked him.

"No, *Effendi*, if it is alright with you. I thirst to surprise this *Mazir*. We will come here again tomorrow!"

The Sergeant was just an excuse, in reality the good Agha felt the danger of the wine from *Türbedi Haidari*. He put aside his pipe and arose a little unsteadily.

"How was the tobacco, *Effendi*?" he inquired.

I guessed the reason and thus answered:

"Bad. It causes headaches and dizziness."

"By Allah, you are right. This tobacco weakens the blood and the nerves, yet one came here to strengthen them. Come let us go!"

"Must we let the Jew know of our departure?"

"Yes."

He clapped his hands together. It was a sign; then we stepped out of the house and into the street. This short wine tasting had been advantageous for me.

"Come, Emir, give me your arm! You know that I like you!"

It was less due to his liking for me and more because of the weakness of his 'system' that was the cause of his offer; for when we breathed the fresh air, he demonstrated his penchant for the fatal acrobatic error in which one mistakes the nadir for the zenith.

"Mohammed was a clever man, what say you, Emir?"

He asked so loud that a man who was passing stopped in his tracks to scrutinize us.

"Why?"

"Because he has not forbidden medicines. If he had done so, one would have to make ink from grapes. Do you know where the prison is?"

"Behind your house."

"Yes; you are always right, Emir. But where is our house?"

That of course was a question that was difficult to answer, if the answer is not to be as stupid as the question.

“Right in front of the prison, Agha.”

He stood still, or rather tried to stand still whilst he looked at me in surprise.

“Emir, you are also a very bright man, just like the old Mohammed; no? But I tell you, that bad tobacco has rushed to my brain so that I see the prison to my right and to my left as well. Which is the real one?”

“None of the two. There, to your right is an oak tree and that above and to the left is a cloud.”

“A cloud? *Allah illa Allah*! Permit me to hold you a little better!”

The valiant Agha led me and had a peculiar obsession with taking some involuntary steps of the kind that one refers to as 'shooting a lark' in some areas of Germany. Thus we made good progress and finally I was successful in steering us to the building, which I believed to be the prison, although I had never seen it from this frontal vista.

“Is this the *Zindan* [prison]?” I asked him.

He pushed the turban back into the nape of his neck and looked about.

“Hmm! It looks familiar. Emir, is there no-one around we can ask? I had to hold so tight that my eyes were spinning, and that is bad; for these houses leapt past like a galloping caravan.”

“I see no one. But this must be it!”

“Let us try!”

He fumbled around in his belt sash for something that he could not find.

“What are you looking for?”

“The key to the prison door.”

“Do you have it?”

“Always! Give me a hand and see if you can find it!”

I searched and found the key immediately. It was easy enough to find for it was so large that it could have been loaded with number zero bear shot.

“Here it is. Shall I unlock the door?”

“Yes, come! But I think you will not find the hole in the lock for your 'system' has suffered much.”

The key fitted and soon the door creaked on its hinges.

“We found it!” he said. “These sounds I know quite well. Let us enter!”

“Shall I lock the door again?”

“Of course! One has to be careful in a prison.”

“Call the guard!”

"The Sergeant? Why?"

"He shall shine a light for us."

"Would not think of it! After all, we want to surprise that scoundrel!"

"In that case, you have to speak more softly!"

He wanted to go ahead, stumbled and would have fallen if I had not grabbed hold of him with both hands.

"What was that? Emir, we did enter the wrong building after all!"

"Where is the Sergeant's room? Is it on this level?"

"No, upstairs."

"And where are the stairs, in front or in the back?"

"Hmm! Where! In front, I think. From the door it should be six to eight steps."

"Right or left?"

"Well, where am I? Here or there? Oh Emir, your soul can not endure this medicine well; for you have stood me a kilter, the floor is not straight, it goes uphill!"

"Now then! The door is behind you; this is your right and this is your left. On which side are the stairs?"

"To the left."

We carefully went that way, and soon my questing foot actually touched the first step.

"Here are the stairs, Agha!"

"Yes, there they are. Don't fall, Emir! You have never been in this building; I will lead you with great care."

He hung heavily on my arm so that I had to literally carry him up these unfamiliar steps.

"We've reached the top. Now where is the Sergeant's room?"

"Speak softly; I hear well! The first door to the right is his."

He pulled me along, but straight ahead and not to the right; I managed to turn him and felt for the door which, once found, I carefully examined by touch.

"I feel two bolts, but no lock."

"There isn't one."

"The bolts are pushed shut."

"Then we are in the wrong house after all."

"I will open them."

"Yes, do that, so that I know where I am!"

I opened the heavy bolts. The door opened outwards and we entered.

"Is there a light in this Sergeant's room?"

"Yes. A lamp and a lighter is in a recess on the left wall."

I lent against the wall and searched. The recess and the things it contained were discovered and soon I had the lamp lit.

The room was small and narrow. A raffia mat lay on the floor; it served as the only furniture. A broken beaker, a pair of torn shoes, a slipper, an empty water jug and a whip were strewn around the floor.

"Not here! Where is this man?" asked the Agha.

"He could be with the Arnauts that also guard this place."

He took the lamp and swayed ahead but bumped into the doorframe.

"Don't push, Emir. Come, hold this lamp; I rather lead you, otherwise you could easily push me down the stairs. I like you and I am your friend, your best friend. That's why I advise you to never ever drink this Persian medicine again. It makes you quite forceful!"

I did indeed need to be quite forceful to get him down the steps without injury. When we reached the indicated door, it too was locked, and when we had opened it, we found this room empty as well. It was more like a stable than a room in which men lived and this sadly hinted that the prisoner's accommodation would be much worse.

"Gone too! Emir, you were right. These scoundrels have absconded from their post. But they shall learn to fear me. I will see to it that they receive the bastinado; yes, I will even see them hanged!"

He tried to roll his eyes, but was not able to manage it; the wine worked more strongly with the passing of time; and they fell shut.

"What do we do now?"

"What do you think, Emir?"

"If I were in you, I would wait, to greet the Arnauts in the manner they deserve."

"This, of course, I will do. But where do we wait?"

"Down here or upstairs."

"Here. I will not climb the stairs again; you are too heavy for me, *Effendi*. Look at how you sway! Sit down!"

"I thought we wanted to inspect the prison?"

"Yes, that we wanted to do," he said in a tired voice. "But those people are not worth it. They are a bunch of rogues, thieves, robbers, Kurds and even an Arab, who is the worst of all."

"Where is this fellow?"

“Right next door, because he has to be guarded most of all. Now sit down!”

I settled next to him even though the floor was just hard pounded clay and quite filthy. The Agha yawned.

“Are you tired?” He asked me.

“A little.”

“That's why you yawn. Sleep till they return. I will wake you. *Allah illa Allah*, you have become quite weak and undependable! But I will make myself as comfortable as possible.”

He lay down, rested his elbow on the floor and put his head onto his hand. Complete silence surrounded us and after a little while his head slid completely off his hand - the master of the prison was asleep.

How often had I read and been angered by this very novelist’s touch that a prisoner was freed when the guard was under the influence of alcohol. And now, because of such an influence, I was in fact in control of the fate of all the prisoners. Should I open the door and the gate for the Haddedihn? That would not have been very smart. We were not prepared to leave the city immediately. There were guards at the city gate and they would surely be suspicious. The entire blame would fall upon the poor Agha and I would be labeled as the perpetrator, which would be a great danger for me or at least create many complications later on. It would certainly be better to make the prisoner disappear in a manner that was inexplicable. It was now within my power to avert all suspicion from me. I therefore decided to speak with the Haddedihn now and to facilitate the escape only then when we were sufficiently prepared.

The Agha lay on the floor and snored loudly, his mouth was agape. I shook him by his shoulder, first softly then more roughly. He did not awake. I then took the lamp and left the room, softly closing the door behind me. I also gently pushed one of the bolts shut, so that I would not be surprised. I had noted before that all the doors were without locks and were only fitted with two bolts. I therefore did not need to search for a key.

It was a weird feeling to stand here alone, holding a lamp, the light of which could not dispel the gloomy darkness. But I was ready for anything. If an urgent situation were to arise, then I would have desperately tried to escape with the prisoner. I pulled back the bolt and opened the door wide, leaving it open so that I could listen for any sound once I was inside.

Yes, it was a hole that I saw! Immediately beyond the door, there was a drop of about two ells and there were no steps to facilitate a descent. The room was roughly four paces long and two paces wide and there was no sign of daub or a wooden or clay floor. Above, close to the ceiling, was one of those holes that I had spotted from the garden earlier today. I saw nothing else in this hole besides a 'beaker' of water, which one might have set before a dog and the prisoner.

He had been lying on the damp and musty earth but arose when I entered. Eyes hollowed and emaciated, he appeared as one half dead, yet his bearing was proud and his eyes flashed angrily as he asked me:

"What do you want? Can't I even sleep?"

"Speak softly! I am not one of your guards. What is your name?"

"Why do you ask?"

"Speak more softly, for no one should hear us. What are you called?"

"That you should know!" he answered, but in a softer voice than before.

"I guess so, but I want to hear who you are from your own lips."

"I am called Amad el Ghandur."

"Then you are the one that I seek. Promise me to be calm when you hear what I will tell you!"

"I promise!"

"Mohammed Emin, your father is close by."

"*Allah il Al* ... !"

"Silence! Your call could betray us!"

"Who are you?"

"A friend of your father. I came to be a guest of the Haddedihn and have fought by your father's side against your enemies. I heard that you were a prisoner and we came to free you."

"Allah be praised! But I can not believe it!"

"Believe it! See that window, it leads to a courtyard that abuts to the garden of the house where we are staying."

"How many men are you?"

"Just four. Your father, I, a friend and my servant."

"Who are you and who is this friend?"

"Leave that till later for now we must hurry!"

"Away?"

"No. We are not yet prepared and I came here by chance without the slightest preparation. Can you read?"

"Yes."

"But there is not light enough."

"Around midday there is enough light."

"Then listen. I could take you out of here immediately, but that would be too dangerous; but I assure you that it will not take long before you are freed. I do not yet know how we will accomplish it; but when you hear a stone fall through that window, then pick it up, a paper will be tied to it that will tell you what you should do."

"Lord, you give me back my life; for I had almost given up hope! How have you discovered that I had been taken to Amadijah?"

"A *Jesidi*, that you met at the water, told me."

"That is right," he answered quickly. "Oh, now I see that you speak the truth! I will wait but greet my father for me!"

"I will do it this day. Are you hungry?"

"Very!"

"Can you hide bread, candle and matches?"

"Yes. I will dig a hole in the earth with my hands."

"Here, use my dagger for that. It is useful in many cases to have a weapon. But it is valuable to me so hide it well!"

He hastily grabbed it and pressed the blade to his lips.

"Lord, may Allah remember this in your hour of death! Now I have a weapon, now I will be free even if you can not come!"

"We will come. Do not act hastily; that could be dangerous for you and your father."

"I will wait a whole week. If you have not come, I will act on my own."

"Good! If I can, I will bring you food, candle and matches through that window this very night. Perhaps we can talk with each other as well. If possible you shall even hear the voice of your father. Now take care, I must go!"

"Lord, give me your hand!"

I stretched it towards him. He clasped in both of his so tightly that it hurt.

"Allah bless this hand for as long as it moves and when it is folded in the sleep of death then may your spirit ascend to paradise and rejoice at the hour in which you became my angel! Now go so that nothing happens to you!"

I bolted the cell door and softly made my way back to the Agha. He still slept and snored and I seated myself next to him. I probably sat there for about an hour when I heard steps that stopped before the gate. I quickly pulled the door to and shook the Agha awake. This was not an easy task, especially since it had to be done quickly. I stood him up. He stared at me in amazement.

"You, Emir? Where are we?"

"In the prison. Pull yourself together!"

He looked about in a daze.

"In the prison? Ah! How did we get here?"

"Remember the Jew and the medicine; remember too, the Sergeant whom we wanted to surprise!"

"The Sar... *Mash Allah*, now I know! I have slept. Where is he? Is he not back yet?"

"Speak softly! Do you hear? They are standing by the gate and talking with one another. Wipe the sleep from your eyes!"

The good Selim looked terrible; but at least he was able to stand upright without swaying. And now, as the gate was being locked, he took up the lamp, kicked open the door and stepped into the passage. I followed him. The culprits froze with fear as he marched towards them.

"Where do you come from, you dogs?" he raged at them.

His voice sounded like thunder in the long narrow space.

"From the *Kaweji*," the Sergeant answered haltingly.

"From the *Kaweji*! While you should be on duty here! Who gave you permission to leave your post?"

"No one!"

The men shook with fear; I felt sorry for them. Their carelessness had been to my advantage. Despite the small flame of the lamp I saw how horribly the Agha rolled his eyes. The tips of his mustache quivered and with seething rage he balled his hand into a fist. But he might have felt that he was not quite steady on his feet yet and thus he thought of something better.

"You will get your punishment tomorrow!"

He placed the lamp on a step and turned to me:

"Or do you perhaps you wish that I judge them immediately, Emir? Do you wish that I have one whip the other?"

"Delay it till the morning, Selim Agha! They can not escape it."

"I will obey your will. Come!"

He opened the door and again locked it behind us.

We walked home where the 'Myrte' awaited us.

"Where you long with the *Mutesselim*?" she asked suspiciously.

"Mersinah," he answered, "I tell you that we were invited to stay till the early hours of the morning; but I knew that you were at home alone and that is why I had to decline the hospitality of the Commandant. I do not wish that the Russians cut off your head. There will be war!"

She clapped her hands together in fear.

"War? With whom?"

"The Turks, Russians, Persians, Arabs and Kurds. The Russian are four hours march from here at Serahru with a hundred-thousand men and three-thousand cannons."

"Oh Allah! I die; I am already dead! Do you have to fight as well?"

"Yes, polish my boots tonight! But tell no one. This war is still a state secret and the people of Amadijah should only discover it tomorrow, when the city is encircled by the Russians."

She staggered back and sat down listlessly on the first available pot nearby.

"Tomorrow morning already! They will really be here in the morning?"

"Yes."

"And they will shoot?"

"A great deal!"

"Selim Agha, I will not polish your boots!"

"Why not?"

"You shall not help to lead this war; you shall not be shot!"

"Good! I prefer that, for then I can go to sleep. Good night, *Effendi*! Good Night, my sweet Mersinah!"

He left. The flower of the house looked after him, perplexed; then she asked me:

"Emir, is it true that the Russians are coming?"

"That is still a little uncertain. I believe that the Agha has taken the circumstances a little too seriously."

"Oh, you drip balsam into my wounded heart. Is it impossible to keep them away from Amadijah?"

"We will see. Have you separated the coffee into the two kinds?"

"Yes, Lord. It was a terrible task; but this terrible Hajji Halef Omar did not let me rest till it was done. Do you want to see?"

"Show me!"

She brought the tin and the paper bag and I assured myself that she indeed had been diligent.

"And what is your verdict, Emir?"

"The verdict is in your favor. Since your delicate hands have touched the beans so often, they shall be yours. Also the dishes that I bought today shall be yours; but the glasses I give to the stout Selim *Bei*."

"Oh *Effendi*, you are a righteous and wise judge. You have more grace than I have pots, and this aromatic coffee is proof of your splendor. May Allah turn the heart of the Russians so that they do not come and shoot you. Do you think that I can sleep peacefully tonight?"

"That you can; I assure you!"

"I thank you for rest is the one thing that a plagued woman can enjoy!"

"Do you sleep down here, Mersinah?"

"Yes."

"But not in the kitchen rather out in front?"

"Lord, a woman belongs in the kitchen and sleeps in the kitchen too."

Hmm! That was a problem. Besides, the Agha's joke was most inopportune. The 'Myrte' would probably not fall asleep quickly tonight. I climbed the stairs, but instead of going to my room I went to the Haddedihn's. He had already settled himself for sleep but awoke immediately. I told him of my adventure in the prison and he was full of wonder.

We packed some food, candle and matches and crept to one of the empty rooms on the upper level of the house. It only had a window, or rather a square opening that was shuttered. The shutter was slightly ajar and when I looked out I could see the flat roof that shielded the surrounds of the small courtyard just five feet below me. We climbed out and from there down to the courtyard. The door there was locked; we were thus alone and we made for the garden in which once the fair Esma Khan had reposed. Only a wall separated us from the prison, an outstretched hand could reach the top.

"Wait," I begged of the Sheik. "For safety's sake I will determine if we are truly unobserved."

I swung myself on top of the wall and softly dropped to the ground on the other side. From the first little window hole on the ground floor I saw light. That was the room in which the Agha had slept. And now the Arnauts were probably sitting there unable to sleep because of their fear. The next window hole belonged to the cell in which Amad el Ghandur's waited for us.

I examined the narrow courtyard without finding anything suspicious, even the door that led to it from the prison was locked. I now returned to the wall behind which the Haddedihn stood.

"Mohammed!"

"How goes it?"

"All is safe. Can you make it over the wall?"

"Yes."

"But quietly!"

He did.

We flitted across the courtyard and stood beneath the little window that I could almost reach with my outstretched hand.

"Bend down, Sheik, support yourself against the wall and place your hands on your knees!"

He did so and I climbed on his back, which was almost level. I stood and my face was directly in front of the hole that led into this dungeon.

"Amad el Ghandur!" I spoke into the hole and quickly turned my head to listen.

"Lord, is it you?" it echoed from below.

"Yes."

"Is my father there too?"

"He is here. He will first lower you food and candle at the end of a string and then he will speak with you. Wait; he will be here soon."

I climbed off the Arabs back.

"Was I heavy?"

"One can not hold such a position for long for it is uncomfortable."

"Then we will do it differently since you would not speak with your son just briefly: You kneel on my shoulders and I can stand upright and hold that position for as long as you need."

"Did he hear you?"

"Yes. He asked for you. I have a string in my pocket with which you can lower the package."

The string was attached and I bent and clasped my hands to form a step into which Mohammed placed his foot and he then climbed up onto my shoulders. After that, I placed my hands onto his knees so that he would not slip, and thus he kneeled on my shoulders as surely as he would on the flat earth. He lowered the small packet and then spoke softly yet eagerly with his son, of the conversation I could only hear Mohammed Emin words. Occasionally the Sheik asked me if he were too heavy. He was a tall, strong man and thus it was a relief to me when he finally leapt to the ground some five minutes later.

"Emir, he has to come out of there; I can not wait."

"We must leave now. Go on ahead; I will make certain that our tracks will not be found."

"But the ground is as hard as stone!"

"Precaution is better than negligence."

He went ahead and I soon followed after him. In a short time we had retraced our steps and were back in the Sheik's room.

He immediately wanted to discuss the plan that would free his son with me; but I advised him to sleep on it and crept from his room.

The next morning I visited my patient; she was out of danger. Her mother was alone with her, at least I did not see anyone else. Then I proceeded to wander through some of the streets to find a place where we could get past the city wall and reach freedom without having to pass through the city gate. I found such a place but it could only be passed by people on foot and not with horses.

When I returned to the house, Selim Agha just arose from his bed.

"Emir, now it is day," he reckoned.

"It has been day for some time," I answered.

"Oh, I mean that one can now speak better than yesterday about our matter."

"Our matter?"

"Yes, ours. You were there. Shall I report it or not? What do you think, *Effendi*?"

"In your place I would not."

"Why?"

"Because it will be better if it is not spoken of that you were in the prison last night. Your people must have noted that you were somewhat unsteady on your feet and they could easily mention this during their cross examination."

"That is true! When I woke last night, my clothes looked very rumpled and I had to rub for ages to wipe off the dirt. It is a wonder that Mersinah did not see this! So you think that I should not proceed with the charge?"

"Yes. You can give those people a warning and your mercy will blind them like a sunbeam."

"Yes, *Effendi*, I will give them a terrible lecture first!"

His eyes rolled like an overhead room fan. Then suddenly they stood still and his face took on a softer expression.

"And then I will be as merciful as a Padishah, who holds sway over the life and property of millions of people."

He made to depart but stopped at the door for outside a rider had dismounted and I heard a familiar voice ask:

"Sallam, Lord! Are you perhaps Selim Agha, the commander of the Albanians?"

"Yes, I am he. What do you want?"

"Does an *Effendi* live with you who is called Hajji Emir Kara Ben Nemsi and who has two other *Effendies*, a servant and a *Bashi-Bozuk* with him?"

"Yes. What about him?"

"Permit that I speak with him!"

"Here he is."

Selim stepped aside so that the man could see me. It was Selek, the *Jesidi* from Baadri.

"*Effendi*," he cried joyfully, "permit that I greet you!"

We shook each other's hands and I noted that he rode one of Ali *Bei's* horses and it literally steamed. Obviously he had ridden it very fast. It was reasonable to assume that he had a message for me and that it was very important that I get it.

"Lead your horse into the courtyard and come upstairs!" I said to him.

When we were settled in my room and we were alone, he pulled a letter from him belt.

"From whom?"

"From Ali *Bei.*"

"Who wrote it?"

"Mir Sheik Khan, the head priest."

"How did you find my accommodation?"

"I asked for you as soon as I reached the city gate."

"And how do you know that I have two *Effendies* with me? When I was with you there was just one accompanying me."

"I discovered that in Spandareh."

I opened the letter. It contained some interesting and good news that referred to the *Jesidi* and one bad piece of news that concerned me.

"What? Ali *Bei's* legation had such success?" I asked. "Anadoli Kasi Askeri [High judge of the Turkish Asiatic Empire] accompanied them back to Mosul?"

"Yes, Lord. He loves our Mir Sheik Khan and began a thorough investigation. The *Mutessarif* will be removed from office and another will take his place."

"And the *Makrej* of Mosul fled?"

"It is so. He was guilty of all the deeds the *Mutessarif* committed. Some very bad things were brought to light. For eleven month no local governor received the necessary funds and no commander and no soldier received their pay. The humiliation of the Arabs that was ordered by the high counsel had been ignored for he pocketed the sums for that very purpose himself. And still much more. The *Khawassen*, who should have taken the *Makrej* prisoner, came to late; he had absconded. That is why all *Beis* and *Kieijahs* of the region were given the order to take him prisoner as soon as he showed himself. Anadoli Kasi Askeri believes that he has fled to Baghdad for he has a friend there who was once a *Weli* [viceroy]."

"That is probably a wrong guess! The fugitive probably fled to the mountains where he will be hard to catch and would rather run to Persia than to Baghdad. The traveling funds would be easily obtained along the way. He is the high judge and all the lower courts funds are at his disposal."

"You are right, *Effendi*! Last night we discovered that he was in Alkosh on the morning of the preceding day and in the evening he was already in Mungeyshi. It would appear that he desires to come to Amadijah but via a detour as he fears the places of the *Jesidi* he attacked."

"Ali *Bei* is right in thinking this and that his arrival here will cause me great difficulties. He will indeed prove to be a hindrance to me and I can unfortunately not prove that he is a fugitive."

"Oh Emir, Ali *Bei* is clever. When he heard the news about the *Makrej* he ordered me to saddle his best horse and to ride all night so that I would reach Amadijah before the *Makrej* would, just in case that this was his intention. And when I left Baadri he gave me two letters that he received from Mosul. Here they are; you shall see them and decide if you can use them."

I opened and read them. One was a letter from Anadoli Kasi Askeri to Mir Sheik Khan, in which the dismissal of the *Mutessarif* and of the *Makrej* was mentioned. The other contained orders for Ali *Bei*, namely to take the *Makrej* prisoner and to transport him to Mosul as soon as he showed himself in that region. Both had the signature and the great seal of Kasi Askeri.

"These letters are indeed quite important to me. How long can I keep them?"

"They are yours entirely."

"So on the evening on the day before yesterday, the *Makrej* was in Mungeyshi?"

"Yes."

"Then he could arrive here today and I will only require these letters this day. Can you wait that long?"

"I wait for as long as you command, Emir!"

"Then go two doors down! There you will meet some friends, namely Hajji Halef and the *Buluk-Emini*."

The news that the *Makrej* might come to Amadijah caused me concern at first; but as soon as I had the letters in my possession, that concern evaporated and I could calmly await the event. Yes, I even believed that the dismissal of the

Mutessarif might lead to the release of the Haddedihn, but I thought otherwise when I read that the animosity towards the Arabs was not the private affair of the *Mutessarif* but by the order of the council.

In the afternoon the 'Myrte' entered my room.

"*Effendi*, do you want to come with me to the prison?"

That was desirable, but I had to first speak with Mohammed Emin. Therefore I said:

"I don't have the time now."

"But you have promised me and said that you will permit the prisoners to buy some things from me!"

The rose of Amadijah apparently placed a great importance on the profit that this little trade might bring.

"I will keep my word; but unfortunately I shall only be available in a quarter of an hours time."

"Then I wait, Emir! But we can not go together!"

"Is Selim Agha there?"

"No. He is on duty with the *Mutesselim*."

"Then order the Sergeant to open the gate for me. In that case you can go ahead and I will follow."

She departed with a happy expression on her face. She apparently thought the possibility, that the Sergeant might not permit me entry since I did not have the right, or the permission of his superior, not worth considering. Of course I immediately went to Mohammed Emin and told him of my forthcoming visit to the prison. I advised him to be prepared for an escape and to secretly arrange to buy some Turkish clothing for his son with the help of Halef. Then I lit one of my *Jibuk* and walked with solemn steps along the narrow streets. When I saw the prison I also saw that its gate was open. The Sergeant stood beneath its lintel.

"*Sallam*!" I greeted briefly and with dignity.

"*Sallam aaleïkum*!" he answered. "Allah bless your entrance into this house, Emir! I have to thank you greatly."

I entered and he locked the gate behind me.

"Thank me?" I asked indifferently. "What for?"

"Selim Agha was here. He was furious. He wanted to have us whipped, but finally he said that we should have mercy because you have pleaded for us. Be so good as to follow me."

We climbed the stairs, which I so painfully searched for and climbed with the Agha last night. In the passage stood Mersinah with a tin cauldron that held a floury brew that appeared to have been made from dishwater and bits of her bedding, and on the floor lay the bread that she had baked with her tender hands. Once it too had been this floury brew, but though fire and attached bits of charcoal it had taken on a more solid appearance. Beside it stood the Arnauts, with empty vessel in their hands, vessels that looked like they had been picked from some pile of broken crockery. They bowed almost to the ground and respectfully remained silent.

"Emir, do you command that we shall begin?" asked the 'Myrte'.

"Yes."

Immediately the first cell door was opened. The cell I saw also was a hole, but the floor was level with the passage. A Turk lay within. He arose and did not honor us with even a glance.

"Give him two portions, for he is an *Osmanli*!" ordered the Sergeant.

The man received two ladles full of the brew in a largish dish, as well as a piece of bread. A Turk was also in the next cell and he received the same portion. The inhabitant of the third was a Kurd.

"This dog gets only one portion, for he is a man from Balahn [A village of the Kazikahn Kurds]!"

This was a very delightful arrangement! I desired to give this fellow a clap around the ears. He used this principle during the entire meal allocation. When the prisoners on the upper level had been provisioned, we descended to the lower level.

"Who is in here?" I asked.

"The worst kind. An Arab, a Jew and two Kurds of the tribe of Bulamuh. Do you speak Kurdish, Emir?"

"Yes."

"You may not wish to speak with the prisoners?"

"No; for they are not worth it!"

"That is true. But we can not speak Kurdish and not Arabic either, and these dogs always have something to say."

"Then I will speak with them."

That was exactly what I desired; only I had not believed that I would be doing the guards a favor.

The cell of one of the Kurds was opened. He stood right next to the door. The poor devil was obviously hungry; for as he received his ladle of brew he begged that he might receive a larger piece of bread than usual.

"What does he want?" asked the Sergeant.

"Some more bread. Give it to him!"

"He shall have it since you ask for him."

Then came the Jew. I was silent, for he could speak Turkish. He had many complaints, which, from my point of view, were quite well founded; but he was ignored.

The second Kurd was an old man. He only begged to be brought before a judge. The Sergeant promised it to him and laughed at the same time.

Finally the last cell was opened. Amad el Ghandur squatted in a corner far below and appeared to have no desire to move, but when he saw me he arose.

"Is that the Arab?" I asked.

"Yes."

"Does he not speak Turkish?"

"He does not speak at all."

"Never?"

"Not a word. That is why he does not receive a warm meal either."

"Shall I try to talk with him?"

"Try it!"

I stepped closer to him and said:

"Do not speak to me!"

Of course he remained silent.

"You see, he does not answer!" the Sergeant said angrily. "Tell him that you are a great Emir, and then he might talk!"

Now I knew that the guards truly did not understand Arabic; and even if they could, the dialect of the Haddedihn was foreign to them.

"Be ready tonight," I said to Amad. "Perhaps it will be possible for me to return."

He straightened, so that he stood upright and proud, without betraying the slightest facial expression.

"Even now he does not say anything!" shouted the Sergeant. "Well, then he shall not receive any bread either since he does not even answer the *Effendi*."

The inspection of the pits was complete. Now I was shown around the remainder of the building. I permitted this although it had no purpose. Finally we were finished and Mersinah looked at me with an inquisitive expression.

"Can you make coffee for the prisoners?" I asked her.

"Yes."

"And give them bread as well, a fairly large serving?"

"Yes."

"How much will it cost?"

"Thirty piaster, *Effendi*."

In other words, it would cost roughly two Taler. The prisoners would receive little more than one Mark from this. I pulled the money from my belt and handed it to her.

"Here. But I desire that they all benefit from this."

"They shall all have something, *Effendi*."

I gave the old one and the Sergeant fifteen piaster each and each Arnaut received ten piaster, a gratuity that they surely had not expected. So they shook off their amazement with extraordinary expressions of thanks, and when I left the prison, they still executed the deepest bows even after I had already stepped into the lane and turned my back on them.

When I got home I searched out Mohammed Emin. I met Halef who was with him for he had brought the clothes for Amad. This he had done without being noticed, as neither the Agha nor Mersinah had been around.

I described my prison visit to the Haddedihn.

"So it will be tonight!" he said happily.

"If it is possible," I added.

"But how will you accomplish this?"

"I will, if the circumstances bring nothing better, try to get the key from the Agha and ... "

"He will not give it to you!"

"I will take it! Then I wait until the guards sleep and open Amad's cell."

"That is too dangerous! They will hear you."

"I don't think so. They have not slept last night and thus they will be very tired. I have also given them a *Baksheesh*, I am certain that they will exchange it for some *Raki*, and that will ensure their sleep. Besides I have carefully observed and noted that the lock of the gate can be opened noiselessly. If I take a little care, it will succeed."

"But if you are caught?"

"Then I still will not worry. As far as the guards are concerned, I have an excuse. And if they saw me with the prisoner, well then some action would need to be taken, and quickly."

"And where will you take Amad to?"

"He will immediately leave the city."

"With whom?"

"With Halef. I will now ride with him beyond the city walls to find a location that may serve as a hiding place. Halef will remember the way and lead your son there."

"But the guards at the city gate?"

"They will not see either of them. I know of a place where one can get past the wall."

"We should also come along immediately!"

"We will remain here for some days so that no suspicion falls upon us."

"But Amad will be in great danger during that time for the whole surrounding area will be searched."

"I have even thought of that. Not far from the city gate the rocks on which Amadijah stand drop off sharply and form a ravine into which few men would dare to descend. To that place we will bring Amad's old clothing which we tear up and scatter. These rags will be found and it will be assumed that he has fallen into the ravine during the night of his escape."

"Where does he change his clothes?"

"Here. And his beard will have to be shaved immediately."

"Then I shall see him! Oh, Emir, what joy!"

"I will make one condition, you must both be very quiet."

"That we will be, certainly. But our hostess will see him come; for she is always in that open kitchen."

"That you will prevent. Halef will inform you when Amad is coming. Then you will go downstairs and prevent our hostess from seeing him. That is not difficult, and in the meantime my servant will lead him to your room which you will keep locked until I return."

I now saw that Halef had brought out the horses and left the room. Outside I discovered that the Englishman's door was open. He beckoned me to come into his room and then asked:

"May I speak, Sir?"

"Yes."

"Heard horse. Go for a ride? To where?"

"Out of the city."

"Well; will come along!"

"I was thinking of a ride into the forest. You would be forced to crawl with me through the undergrowth."

"Will crawl!"

He was ready in no time. His horse was also saddled and soon we rode out of the city gate that led towards Asi and Mia. It was like the Kurd Dohub had told me. The path was so steep that we had to lead our horses. Incidentally, we had not been detained at the gate, as the same Arnauts who had been on parade in my honor were on duty there and thus knew who I was.

We had descended to the valley floor, if we were to turn to the right, we would have encountered the *Jilaks* of the citizens of Amadijah who had withdrawn to the mountains. That is why we turned left and into the forest. It was not so thick that it interfered with our riding and so we reached a clearing within fifteen minutes where we dismounted and settled ourselves on the grass.

"Why lead us here?" asked Lindsay.

"I am searching for a suitable place to hide Amad el Ghandur."

"Ah! Free soon?"

I explained the plan to him.

"Splendid!" he reckoned. "Nice and dangerous! Grab! Box! Shoot! Well; will join in!"

"Oh, Master, you could not be of much use to me!"

"No? Why? Knock everyone down who stands in our way! Am free Englishman! Yes!"

"Well, let us see! Above us to the left is the place where the city wall can be crossed. Therefore we must find a hiding place somewhere in this area. Do you want to help find one?"

"Very much!"

"Then let us separate. You go straight ahead and I go down this way. Whoever finds a good spot will fire one round from their pistol and waits until the other comes."

Halef remained with the horses and we proceeded to search. The forest was getting thicker but I searched for some time without finding a suitable spot that would offer real security. Then I heard a shot to my left. I made my way in that direction and soon heard the crack of a second shot quite close to me. The Englishman stood by some undergrowth from which four massive oaks reached towards the sky. He was barefoot and had dispensed with his outer clothing. Even his gigantic red checkered turban lay on the ground.

"Have shot twice. Could have missed me, the echo in the forest is deceptive. Found hiding place?"

"No."

"Have one."

"Where?"

"Guess! Will never guess!"

"Will see!"

He was barefoot and half-undressed; he thus must have done some climbing and the hiding place must be in one of those oak trees. But these were so massive that they would have been impossible to scale. Yet next to them grew a slim pine and it entwined its umbel like crown in the far-reaching branches of the oak tree. Pretty high up, the trunk of the pine leant against one of the oaks' bigger branches so that one could reach the oak quite easily, and above that, in the trunk of the oak, was a hole.

"I've got it, Sir!" I said.

"Where?"

"Up there. The trunk is hollow."

"Well; found it! Was already up there."

"You climb pretty well?"

"Like a squirrel! Yes!"

"But the whole tree is probably hollow!"

"Quite!"

"And whoever enters the hole up there, falls and can't get out again."

"Right! Can't get out."

"Then this is not a good hiding place!"

"Hiding place is good, very good. Only need to make sure that nothing falls down."

"And how?"

"Ah, You don't know? Hmm, Master Lindsay smart fellow! Nice adventure! Splendid! Want to pay, pay well! Cut stout poles and wedge into hole, crosswise. Much moss here. Lay that on top. Then can not fall down. Hiding place finished! Nice country house! Magnificent Villa!"

"You are right! How large is the diameter of the hollow?"

"Roughly four foot. Further down even bigger. Can you climb?"

"Yes. I will have a closer look at this find."

"Don't climb empty handed. Take poles at once!"

"That is, of course, more practical. There are more than enough oak poles here."

"But how will we get them up there? Climbing as well as carrying? That won't work!"

"I have my lasso with me. It comes along on all my travels for such a thing is quite useful."

"Well; then we cut!"

"But with care, Master! First we must be sure that we are alone. Our discussion in English would be quite meaningless to anyone around here; it would not have betrayed our intentions. But before we act we have to be certain of our situation."

"Then seek! Will make poles in the meantime."

I did a circuit and assured myself that we were unobserved; then I helped the Englishman who was quite chuffed with himself, to build a 'villa' up in the tree. We cut a dozen saplings of somewhat more than four foot in length from amid the shrub, but in such a manner that our work would go unnoticed. Then I unwound the cloth that served as my belt from around my waist, beneath it I carried the lasso wound around my body. It was long enough to reach the first branch of the pine. Whilst the Englishman tied the poles to the eight-times plaited and unbreakable leather strap, I took the other end between my teeth and climbed up the tree. Any clothes that might restrict me, I had of course discarded. When I reached the first branch, I pulled up the bundle. Lindsay climbed up after it and so we brought the 'poles' to the opening where we tied them. I explored the hollow. It had the indicated width and grew larger the further it descended, it reached all the way to the ground.

We now started to wedge the poles into place to make a floor. That had to be done with care so that Amad would not crash to the ground. With the aid of our knives and some exertions we accomplished this. The floor was solid and safe.

"Now moss, straw and leaves - up with the lasso!"

We climbed down and soon gathered what we needed. We tied it into my *Haïk* and into Lindsay's outer garment and after two trips up and down, the hollow was transformed into a comfortable and soft hiding place in which one could rest safely.

"Worked valiantly," the Englishman reckoned, while he wiped the sweat from his brow. "Amad will live well. Now fetch food, drink, pipe and tobacco and the divan is complete!"

We made our way back to Halef, he was worried about us as we had been gone for such a long time.

"Master Lindsay, now you remain with the horses for I must show Hajji Halef Omar this hiding place!" I said.

"Well! But return soon! Yes!"

"Can you climb?" I asked Halef, when we reached the oak.

"Yes, *Sihdi*. I have relieved many palms of their dates. Why?"

"That is quite a different art of climbing. Here we have a clean trunk, there is no support and also no climbing loop as one would use for picking dates. Do you see that hole in the trunk of the oak, just above the branch?"

"Yes, *Sihdi*."

"Climb up there and inspect it! You have to go up the pine and then along the branch of the oak."

He tried it and low and behold, he did rather well.

"*Effendi*, that is a small house," he said when he had climbed down. "You probably just finished building it?"

"Yes. Do you know where the Fort of Amadijah is from here?"

"There, up towards the left."

"Then listen to what I tell you! I believe that I can spring Amad el Ghandur from the prison tonight. He must leave the city this very night and you shall lead him."

"Lord, the guards will see us!"

"No. There is a place where the city wall is so damaged that you can easily leave the city without being seen. I will show you the place on our return. But the important thing is that despite the darkness of the night you must find this place, for the Haddedihn should hide in that hollow above us until we come to fetch him. That is why you will take the path up to the left of us so that you familiarize yourself with the way you need to follow tonight. Memorize the terrain well. Once he is safely settled, you must ensure that you return to our quarters unseen; for no-one may know that one of us has left the city."

"*Sihdi*, I thank you!"

"What for?"

"For allowing me to do something by myself; for I have had to stand by and watch for a long time."

He started on his way and I returned to Lindsay. When I approached I saw him lying on the mossy ground and looking up at the sky.

"Wonderful in Kurdistan! Just the ruins are missing!" he said.

"There are ruins enough here, even if they are not many thousands of years old like by the Tigris. Perhaps we are forced to search out places where you can convince yourself of the existence of such ruins. From the valleys of Kurdistan the smoke of burning villages and the smell of rivers of spilled blood has risen towards heaven. We are in a land where life, freedom and possessions are more endangered than in any other. Let us wish that we will not be convinced of this through our own experience!"

"But want to be convinced, Sir! Will have adventure! Want to do battle, box, shoot! Will pay."

"For that there may be enough opportunity without payment, Sir; for directly beyond Amadijah is the Turkish border and beyond that are the lands of the Kurds who are only thought to be taxable and under the high council's influence by name. There our passports do not afford us the slightest protection; yes, it might even be that we are treated as enemies just because we enjoy the recommendation of the Turks and of the Consuls."

"Then not show!"

"Of course. When faced with these half-wild, violent hordes one must be inclined to win their hospitality. An Arab might have an ulterior motive when he takes a stranger into his tent; but never a Kurd. And if that were the case and there is no other possibility of escape then one seeks the protection of the women; for then one is secure."

"Well, will let myself be protected by women! Wonderful! Very good idea, Master!"

Perhaps an hour later Halef returned. He was certain that he could find the hiding place even at night without problem as soon as he was successful in leaving the city unseen. The purpose of our outing was thus achieved and we returned to Amadijah. I made sure that we passed the place where the wall was damaged.

"This is the place that I mentioned, Halef. When you go out later, you might examine this breach in detail, but in such a manner that you are not noticed."

"I will do that as soon as possible, *Sihdi*," he answered; "for soon it will be evening."

The day had indeed progressed when we reached our accommodation. I did not have the opportunity to rest from our ride for Selim Agha welcomed me at the door:

"*Hamdullillah*, Allah be thanked that you finally return!" he said. "It was painful waiting for you."

"Why?"

"The *Mutesselim* has sent me to fetch you."

"For what purpose?"

"I do not know."

"And you can not guess either?"

"You shall speak to an *Effendi* that arrived recently."

"Who is it?"

"The *Mutesselim* has forbidden me to tell you."

"Pah! The *Mutesselim* has no secrets from me! I knew long ago that this *Effendi* would come!"

"You knew? But it was a secret!"

"I will prove it to you that I know this great secret. It is the *Makrej* of Mosul, who came."

"Truly, you knew!" he cried in amazement. "But he is not alone with the *Mutesselim*."

"Who else is there?"

"An Arnaut."

Ah, I guessed who that was and thus said:

"Even that I know. Do you know this man?"

"No."

"He has no weapons on his person."

"*Allah akbar*; that is right! *Effendi*, you know everything."

"At least you see that the *Mutesselim* is not the man who can hide anything from me."

"But Lord, they must have spoken badly of you!"

"Why?"

"I must be silent about that."

"Good, Selim Agha, I now see that you are my friend and that you hold me dear!"

"Yes, I care for you, Emir; but my duty demand that I obey."

"Then I tell you that I will yet give you orders this very day that you obey as though they were spoken by the Commandant himself! How long has the *Makrej* been here?"

"For almost two hours."

"And so long you have also waited for me?"

"No. The *Makrej* came alone, very secretly and without an entourage. I was with the Commandant when he entered. He said that he came secretly because it concerned very important matters that no one should even suspect. They discussed a little more and the Commandant mentioned you and your companions. The *Makrej* had to know you for he became attentive and the *Mutesselim* had to describe you. 'It is he!' the *Makrej* then shouted and requested of the Commandant that I be sent from the room. Afterwards I was called and given the order to fetch you and ... "

"Well, and ... "

"And ... Emir, it is certainly true that I care for you and that is why I desire to tell you. But will you betray me?"

"No. I promise you!"

"I had to take some Arnauts with me to occupy the square so that your companions could not escape. And some of my Arnauts are even waiting at the palace for you. I shall arrest you and put you into prison."

"Ah, that is quite interesting, Selim Agha! Then you probably already have one of your pits made ready for me?"

"Yes. You will be placed into the cell next to the Arab and I had to place some straw mats into the cell; for the *Mutesselim* said, you were and Emir and should be handled better than the other scoundrels!"

"I am truly indebted to him for this consideration. Should my companions also be placed into the cells?"

"Yes, but I have no specific orders regarding them yet."

"What does 'Myrte' say about this?"

"I have told her. She is sitting in the kitchen and is crying her eyes out."

"The poor thing! But you mentioned an Arnaut?"

"Yes. He was there even before the *Makrej* came, and he spoke with the *Mutesselim* for a long time. I was then called and questioned."

"About what?"

"If the black and red *Effendi* did not even utter a word in his rooms."

"What was your answer?"

"I told the truth. I have not heard the *Effendi* utter a single syllable."

"The come. Let us go!"

"Lord, I should bring you, that is true; but I like you. Would you not rather flee?"

This brave Arnaut truly was my friend.

"No, I do not flee, Agha; for I have no reason to fear the *Mutesselim* nor the *Makrej*. But I will ask you to take along another man besides me."

"Who?"

"The messenger who came to find me."

"I will call him; he is in the courtyard."

In the meantime I stepped into the kitchen. Mersinah crouched on the floor and looked quite depressed. A sight that truly touched me.

"Oh there you are, *Effendi*!" she cried as she jumped to her feet. "Run, run! I have ordered the Agha to let you escape."

"Be thanked for this, Mersinah! But I will stay."

"They will imprison you, Lord."

"We will see!"

"If they do that, *Effendi*, then I will weep until I die and will cook the best soups in existence for you. You shall not hunger!"

"You will not have to cook anything for me, for no-one will imprison me; I assure you."

"Emir, you return my life to me! But they can do it still and then they take everything away from you. Perhaps you may wish to leave me your money and all other things that are dear to you? I will take care of everything and not say a word."

"I believe you, you guardian angel of this house; but such a precaution is unnecessary."

"Then do as you please! Go now and may Allah and his prophets protect you!"

We departed. As I marched across the square I noted that behind the doors of some buildings the Arnauts, that Selim had spoken of, were hiding. Certainly this was a serious affair. Soldiers were even posted in the passage, on the stairs and also in the anteroom of the palace. I was almost worried.

The Commandant was not alone in his room; two lieutenants sat at the doorway and even Selim Agha did not withdraw but rather sat down.

"*Sallam aaleïkum*!" I greeted as nonchalantly as possible despite the situation in which I now found myself.

"*Aaleïkum*!" the Commandant answered somewhat reserved whilst he indicated that I should seat myself on a carpet some distance from his side.

I did as if I had not seen nor understood this and sat down by his side as I had done earlier.

"I sent for you," he started, "but you did not come. Where were you, *Effendi*?"

"I was out riding."

"Where to?"

"Outside of the city."

"What did you want there?"

"To exercise my horse. You know that a noble animal must be well cared for."

"Who was with you?"

"Hajji Lindsay-*Bei*."

"He who was made the oath not to speak?"

"The same."

"I have heard that he does not keep his oath very well."

"So!"

"He speaks."

"So!"

"Even with you."

"So!"

"I know that for certain."

"So!"

These repetitive utterances of 'So!' caused this good man some embarrassment.

"You must know this too!" he said.

"Who has told you that he speaks?"

"One who has heard him."

"Who is this?"

"An Arnaut who came today to accuse you."

"What did you do?"

"I sent for you."

"Why?"

"To interrogate you."

"*Allah illa Allah*! So because of an accusation made by a villainous Arnaut you send for me, me an Emir and an *Effendi*, to interrogate me, like you would a villain like him! *Mutesselim*, Allah bless your wisdom so that it does not fully escape you!"

"*Effendi*, ask God to preserve your own wisdom for you will need it!"

"That almost sounds like a threat!"

"And your words sounded like an insult!"

"After you have insulted me. Let me tell you something, *Mutesselim*. Here in this revolver are six bullets and in this other one are equally as many. Speak and tell what you have to tell me; but consider that an Emir from Germanistan is no Arnaut and that such a man will not allow himself to be compared with one! If my companion does not keep his oath, of what concern is it to an Arnaut? Where is this man?"

"He is in my service."

"Since when?"

"Since a long time."

"*Mutesselim*, you do not speak the truth! This Arnaut was not in your service yesterday. He is a man of which I will yet speak more. If Hajji Lindsay-*Bei* speaks, then it is matter he has to reconcile with his conscience, but it is of no concern to another!"

"You would be right if I knew this only from him."

"What else?"

"He is the friend of a man who is under my suspicion."

"Who is this man?"

"You are that man!"

I pretended to be amazed.

"I! *Allah kerihm*, God is merciful; he will surely be merciful to you also!"

"You have spoken with me of the *Mutessarif* and said that you were his friend."

"I told you the truth."

"And yet it not true!"

"What! You claim that I lie! Then I can not remain here any longer. I will give you the opportunity to prove this insult."

I arose and made as if to leave the *Selamlük*.

"Stop," shouted the Commandant. "You stay!"

I turned to face him.

"Are you ordering me?"

"Yes."

"Have you that right?"

"Here you are under my authority and if I order you to stay then you will obey!"

"And if I do not stay?"

"Then I will force you! You are my prisoner!"

Both of the lieutenants arose; even Selim Agha did so, but so slowly and reluctantly that I could not miss it.

"Your prisoner? Are you serious? *Sallam*!"

I again turned and made for the door.

"Hold him!" he ordered.

The two lieutenants grabbed me, one on each arm. I stopped and laughed, first into the face of the one on my right and then also into the face of the one on my left; then they flew one after the other, across the room and landed on the floor in front of the *Mutesselim.*

"There you have them, *Mutesselim.* Pick them up! I tell you that I will go when it suits me and no Arnauts of yours shall stop me! But I will stay, for I have yet to speak with you. But I only do so to prove to you that a *Nemje* does not fear a Turk. So ask the other questions you have of me!"

The good man had never experience such resistance; he was used to having everyone bow deeply before him and now he appeared unsure of what to do next.

"I tell you," he finally commenced, "that you are not a friend of the *Mutessarif.*"

"Yet you have read his letter."

"And you have fought against him!"

"Where?"

"At Sheik Adi!"

"Prove it!"

"I have a witness."

"Let him come!"

"I will fulfill your wish."

Chapter 34

On a hand signal from the *Mutesselim*, the Agha left the room.

Some moments later he returned with - the *Makrej* of Mosul. That one did not even honor me with a glance, rather he passed me and sat in the place I had previous occupied, and took hold of the tube from the water pipe which stood close by.

"Is that the man of whom you spoke earlier, *Effendi*?" the Commandant asked him.

He briefly looked in my direction with disdain.

"It is him."

"You see?" the Commandant turned to me. "The *Makrej* of Mosul, whom you must know, is witness to you battling against the *Mutessarif*."

"He is a liar!"

The judge now stared hard at me.

"Worm!" he hissed.

"You will soon get to know this worm!" I answered calmly. "I say it again: You are a liar, for you have not seen me take up arms against the troops of the *Mutessarif*!"

"Then others have seen it!"

"But not you! And the Commandant has said that you yourself have seen it. Name your witnesses!"

"The *Topjis* [artillerymen] have spoken of it."

"Then they too have lied. I have not fought against them; not a single drop of blood has been spilled. They have surrendered themselves and their weapons without battle. And then, when you were besieged in Sheik Adi, I have advised the *Bei* to show mercy, so that you have to thank me for not being massacred. Do you wish to claim that this is proof that I am an enemy of the *Mutessarif*?"

"You have attacked the artillery and taken it!"

"That I admit to gladly."

"But you will answer for that in Mosul."

"Oh!"

"Yes. The *Mutesselim* will take you prisoner and send you to Mosul, you and all who are with you. There is only one way by which you may save yourselves."

"And that is?"

He waved his hand and the three officers left the room.

"You are an Emir from Frankistan, for the Nemsi are Franks," the *Makrej* commenced. "I know that you are under the protection of your consul, and that we may not kill you. But you have committed an act that demands the death penalty. We have to send you to Mosul and then to Stambul, where you will certainly receive your punishment."

He paused. It appeared that it was not easy for him to find the right words.

"Go on!" I encouraged him.

"But you once were protected by the *Mutessarif*; and even the *Mutesselim* has received you as a friend, therefore these two do not wish it that you are treated badly."

"May Allah remember them for that in their last hour!"

"Yes! Therefore it is possible that we do not follow this matter to its natural conclusion if ... "

"Well, if ...?"

"If you tell us how much the life of an Emir from Germanistan is worth."

"It is worth nothing."

"Nothing? You jest!"

"I speak quite earnestly. It is worth nothing."

"How so?"

"Because Allah may also call an Emir to him at any minute."

"You are right; all life is in the hands of Allah; but life is a property that one should protect and preserve!"

"You do not seem to be a good Muslim, otherwise you would know that the fate of mankind is written in the book."

"And yet man can throw away his life if he does not follow the book. Do you wish to do this?"

"Well alright then, *Makrej*. How highly do you value your own life?"

"At least ten-thousand piaster."

"Then the life of a Nemje is worth ten-thousand times more, namely one million piaster. How come that a Turk's life is worth that much less?"

He looked at me in amazement.

"Are you such a rich Emir?"

"Yes, since I posses such an expensive life."

"Then I believe that you would value your life at twenty-thousand piaster here in Amadijah."

"Of course!"

"And the life of Hajji Lindsay-*Bei* equally high."

"I agree."

"And ten-thousand for the third."

"That is not too much."

"And your servant?"

"He is but an Arab, yet he is a brave and trustworthy man who is worth as much as any of the others."

"Then you say he is also worth ten-thousand piaster?"

"Yes."

"Have you totaled the sum?"

"Sixty-thousand piaster. Right?"

"Yes. Do you have that much money on you?"

"We are very rich *Effendies*."

"When do you wish to pay?"

"Never!"

It was quite comical to see the look on the faces of these two men who first looked at me and then at each other. The *Makrej* then asked:

"How do you mean that, *Effendi*?"

"I mean that I come from a land in which there is justice. With the *Nemsi* a beggar is worth as much as a king when standing before a judge. And if the Padishah of the *Nemsi* commits an offense then he is punished with the instruments of the law. No one can buy his life for there are no judges that are villains. But the *Osmanli* have no other law besides their purses and so they haggle with justice. I can not pay for my life if I deserve to loose it."

'Then you will loose it!"

"I don't think so. A *Nemje* does not haggle for his life, but he knows how to defend it."

"*Effendi*, to you a defense is impossible!"

"Why?"

"Your guilt is proven, and you have already admitted it."

"That is not true. I have not admitted to any guilt, rather I have admitted that I have taken possession of your cannons. And that is not a deed for which I would be punished."

"That is what you think. You therefore reject our offer of mercy and pity?"

"I do not need pity."

"Then we must arrest you."

"Try it!"

Even the Commandant presented a well-meaning proposal to me; but since I did not listen, he clapped his hands and the three officers reappeared.

"Take him away!" he ordered them. "I hope, *Effendi*, that you will not refuse to go with them. There are enough people outside to make any resistance impossible. You shall be treated well during your imprisonment here and ... "

"Silence, *Mutesselim*!" I interrupted him. "I would like to see the man who has the courage to overpower me. A *Nemje* would handle you five in three seconds, and your feverish Arnauts run before my gaze; of that you can be certain! That I would be well taken care of as your prisoner is self-evident; for that is governed by your ulterior motive. I will not be sent to Mosul, for it serves no purpose to the *Makrej*; he only desires that I pay a ransom for he needs the money to escape across the border."

"Across the border?" asked the *Mutesselim*. "How shall one interpret your words?"

"Ask him yourself!"

He looked at the *Makrej* who suddenly changed color.

"What does he mean?" he asked him.

"I do not understand him!"

"He understands me quite well," I replied. "*Mutesselim*, you have insulted me; you want to arrest me; you have made me an offer that will have serious consequences for you if I spoke of it. Both of you have threatened me; but now I shall take a weapon into my own hands after I have seen how far you dared to go. Do you know who this man is?"

"The *Makrej* of Mosul."

"You err. He is no more; he was dismissed."

"Dismissed!" he cried.

"Damn you!" the *Makrej* swore. "I will throttle you."

"Dismissed!?" shouted the Commandant a second time partially in fear and partially as a question.

"Yes. Selim Agha, I told you before that I would give you an order this very day that you will obey. Now you shall hear it: Arrest that man and place him into the very pit that was readied for me! He will then be sent to Mosul."

The good Agha amazed by this, first looked at me and then at the other two; but did not make a move to comply with my order.

"He is mad," the *Makrej* said whilst he arose.

"You are mad yourself for daring to come to Amadijah. Why did you not come directly instead of going via Mungeyshi? You see that I know all. Here, *Mutesselim*, is the proof that I have the right to demand his arrest!"

I handed him the letter that was sent to Ali *Bei*. He first looked at the signature.

"From Anadoli Kasi Askeri?"

"Yes. He is in Mosul and demands the extradition of this man. Read!"

"It is true!" he said quite amazed. "But what about the *Mutessarif*?"

"He too has been dismissed. Read now the second letter!"

I handed it to him and he read it.

"*Allah kerihm*, God be merciful to us! Great things are happening!"

"They are happening indeed. The *Mutessarif* is dismissed, the *Makrej* likewise. Do you also want to be dismissed?"

"Lord, you are a secret agent of Anadoli Kasi Askeri or perhaps even of the Padishah!"

"Who I am is unimportant; but you see that I know everything and now demand that you carry out your duty."

"*Effendi*, I will do so. *Makrej*, I can do nothing else; it is written here; I must arrest you!"

"Do it!" the *Makrej* answered.

A dagger flashed in his hand, in no time he had crossed the room, passing by me, and escaped through the door. We hurried after him and were in time to see him being wrestled to the floor. Selek, who had accompanied me, kneeled on the *Makrej* and tried to get the dagger away from him. Escape was now impossible for him. He was disarmed and brought back into the *Selamlük*.

"Who is this man?" asked the Commandant as he indicated Selek.

"He is the messenger who was sent to me by Ali *Bei* of Baadri. He will return there and you should permit him to accompany the transport. For then we will be sure that the *Makrej* can not escape. But I will hand you yet another prisoner."

"Who, Lord?"

"Let the Arnaut who accused me come!"

"Fetch him!" he ordered.

One of the lieutenants went to fetch the man who was not aware that the turn of events was no longer in his favor.

"Ask him," I said, "where his weapons are!"

"Where are they?"

"They were taken from me."

"Where?"

"Whilst I slept."

"He lies, *Mutesselim*! The Mutessarif assigned this man to Hajji Lindsay-*Bei*; he had shot at me and then fled; on our way, he ambushed us and fired two shots in our direction from a thicket in the forest, but these missed their mark. My dog held him but I was merciful and forgave him, letting him go. But we took his weapons, which my *Khawass* still has in his possession. Shall I have the witnesses to these events brought to prove that I speak the truth?"

"Lord, I believe you! Arrest this dog and throw him into the most secure pit that the prison has to offer!"

"Lord, do you order me to take the *Makrej* with me at once?" asked Selim Agha of the Commandant.

"Yes."

"*Mutesselim*, let him be bound first." I reminded him. "He has tried to escape once and will try to do so again."

"Bind him!"

They were both led away and I remained alone with the Commandant. The events had so strained and fatigued him that he collapsed onto the carpet.

"Who would have thought!"

"Obviously not you, *Mutesselim*!"

"Lord, forgive me! I did not know of these matters."

"Certainly the Arnaut had met with the *Makrej* beforehand and they had come to an agreement, otherwise he would not have dared to appear before us for we had grounds to have him punished."

"He shall never shoot at another person! Permit me to provide you with a pipe!"

He causes a *Nargileh* to come and lit the pipe with his own hand. Then he said in almost servile tones:

"Emir, do you believe that I was serious?"

"What?"

"That I would have taken money from you?"

"Yes."

"Lord, you are mistaken! I aligned myself to the will of the *Makrej* and would have returned my share to you."

"But I would have been permitted to flee?"

"Yes. You see that I desired only the best for you!"

"That, you would not have been permitted to do if the accusation against me were proven."

"Will you think more on this matter?"

"No, if you act in a manner that allows me to forget it."

"You shall not think on it again, Emir. You shall forget as you have already forgotten another matter."

"Which one?"

"The medicine."

"Yes, *Mutesselim*, that I have indeed forgotten; but you shall receive it this day; I promise you!"

A servant came.

"Lord, a *Bash Jaush* [Sergeant-Major] is outside," he reported.

"What does he want?"

"He comes from Mosul and says that his message is very important."

"Send him in!"

The non-commissioned officer entered and handed a letter bearing a large seal to the Commandant; it was the seal of Anadoli Kasi Askeri; I recognized it immediately. He broke it open and read. Then he informed the man that he would have an answer ready in the morning.

"Lord, do you know what it says?" he asked me when the soldier had departed.

"A letter from the high judge of Anadolian?"

"Yes. He writes to me of the dismissal of the *Mutessarif* and of the *Makrej*. The latter I shall send to Mosul as soon as he shows himself here. I will hand him over to the *Bash Jaush* in the morning. Shall I mention you in my reply?"

"No. I will write myself. But do send a sufficient guard along!"

"It shall not be lacking for another important prisoner shall also go along."

I was startled.

"Which one?"

"The Arab. Anadoli Kasi Askeri orders it and says that the son of a Sheik shall be sent to Stambul as a hostage."

"When does this transport depart?"

"In the forenoon. I will immediately commence to write my reply."

"Then I shall not detain you any longer."

"Oh *Effendi*, your presence is most dear to me!"

"And your eye is to me like the eye of a best friend; but your time is valuable; I may not impose upon it."

"But you come back early tomorrow morning?"

"Perhaps."

"You shall be present when the transport departs to see that I have thought of everything!"

"Then I will come. *Sallam*!"

"*Sallam*! May Allah lead you!"

When I reached our accommodation a joyful cry greeted me:

"*Hamdullillah*, *Effendi*, you live and are free!"

It was 'Myrte'. She took hold of both my hands and sighed deeply:

"You are a great hero. Your servants and the foreign messenger have said so. If you would have been taken prisoner you would have destroyed the whole palace and perhaps Selim Agha too."

"Not him, but everyone else; of that you can be sure!" I answered amused.

"Yes. You are like *Kelad*, the strong one. Your beard goes left and right like that of a panther and your arms are like the legs of an elephant!"

Of course that was meant to be more than figuratively. Oh 'Myrte', how you have assassinated the dark blond decoration of my face and the symmetry of my indispensable limbs! I had to be equally polite:

"Your lips speak verses like a poet, Mersinah, from them torrents of sweet honey run like from a full pot; your words are like a balm upon a swelling, and the sound of your voice will not be forgotten by anyone who has ever heard it. Here, take five piaster to buy *Khol* for your eyes and *Henneh* for the rosy nails of your hands. My heart wished to rejoice at the sight of you so that my soul will become young and my eye delight in the grace of your gait!"

"Lord," she cried, "You are more courageous than Ali, wiser than Abu Bekr, stronger than *Simsah* [Samson] and more beautiful than *Hosseïn*, the Armadener! Command what I should roast for you; or do you prefer something cooked or baked? I do anything that you demand of me, for with you, joy has come into my house and blessings have poured over the threshold of my door."

"Your kindness touches me, oh Mersinah; I can not repay it! But I neither hunger nor thirst when I see the gleam in your eyes and the color of your cheeks and the lovely picture of your hands. Has Selim Agha come?"

"Yes. He has told me everything. Your enemies are vanquished. Go upstairs and console your companions who are much worried about you!"

I went upstairs.

"Finally return!" the Englishman said. "Great worry! Wanted to get you! Lucky that you are here!"

"You were in danger?" even Mohammed asked.

"Not much. It is passed now. Did you know that the *Mutessarif* has been dismissed?"

"Of Mosul?"

"Yes, and the *Makrej* too."

"So that is why Selek came?"

"Yes. Has he not told of it when we had ridden out in the afternoon?"

"No. He is a quiet one. But Amad might now be freed, for only the *Mutessarif* has held him prisoner!"

"I too hoped this but the situation is much worse. The Sultan approves of the Turkish action against you, and the high judge of Anadolian has ordered that your son is to be moved to Stambul as a hostage."

"*Allah kerihm*! When should he be moved?"

"Tomorrow, before noon."

"We ambush his transport on the way!"

"As long as we still have hopes of freeing him through a ruse no human life shall be harmed."

"But we only have this one night!"

"That time is enough."

I then turned to the Englishman:

"Sir, I need wine for the *Mutesselim*."

"This fellow? Would not be worth the wine! Should drink water! Coffee, chamomile, valerian and buttermilk!"

"He has asked me to get him some wine!"

"Rogue! But may not drink it! Is Mohammedan!"

"The Muslims like to drink it as much as we. I desire to preserve his good will for as long as we need it."

"Good! Shall have wine! How much?"

"A dozen. I give half and you the other."

"Pshaw! Don't buy half of the wine. Here is money!"

He handed me his purse without caring how much I might take from it. He was a gentleman and I a poor devil.

"How does it go?" he asked. "We free Amad?"

"Yes."

"Today?"

"Yes."

"How?"

"I go and drink wine with Selim Agha and try ..."

"Drinks wine too?" he interrupted me.

"Passionately."

"Nice Muslim! Deserve a hiding!"

"It is precisely this penchant that gives us the advantage. He will become intoxicated and then I remove his prison keys unnoticed. I help the Arab escape to his father where he will change his clothes. Then Halef will lead him to the 'villa' that you have built for him."

"Well! Very nice! What do I do in all this?"

"First of all watch. When I bring him I will make a sign by the corner over there. I will caw like a raven that was disturbed in its sleep. Then Halef hurries down to open the door and to keep the hostess in the kitchen. You join Mohammed at the stairs, welcome Amad and lead him upstairs. He dresses and you wait till I come."

"You leave again?"

"Yes. I have to return the keys to Selim Agha, so that no suspicion is aroused."

"Difficult thing for you! If you are discovered?"

"I have a fist and if that is not enough I also have weapons. Now let us all eat our evening meal."

Mohammed was also carefully instructed during our meal. Halef brought the wine and had to pack it well.

"You carry this to the *Mutesselim*," I told him.

"He wants to drink it, *Sihdi*?" he asked in amazement.

"He shall use it how he sees fit. You give him this package personally and to non-other and tell him that it is I who sends him this medicine. And listen! When I go with Selim Agha then you follow secretly and remember the exact house into which we enter! If I am needed for anything you will come and fetch me."

"And where in the house will I find you?"

"You walk along the passage roughly eight paces from the front door and knock on the door to your right, I will be in the room beyond. If the host, who is a Jew, should see you - you tell him that you are looking for a foreign Emir who drinks from the mug. You understand?"

He departed carrying his parcels.

Mohammed Emin was in very exited state. Even at the Valley of the Steps, when he had captured his enemies, I had not observed him like this. He had armed himself with all of his weapons and had even loaded his flintlock with a fresh load. This should not amuse me. The heart of a father is a sacred thing; I too had a father at home, who worried and often made great sacrifices on my behalf, thus I could understand this well.

Finally Selim Agha came back from the *Mutesselim*. He ate his evening meal in the kitchen and then we secretly made our way to the house of the Jew.

Yesterday Selim Agha had learned the effect the strong wine had on him, so tonight he was more careful. He now sipped it quite slowly.

We may already have been sitting here for three quarters of an hour, and still the wine had no effect on the Agha, other than his becoming quieter and dreamier and finally he slouched into a corner, deep in thought. I was just about to goad him into drinking up and to order another two mugs when someone knocked on the door.

"Who is that?" asked the Agha.

"That must be Halef."

"Does he know where we are?"

"Yes."

"*Effendi*, what have you done!"

"But he does not know what we are doing here."

"Don't let him come in!"

It was a good idea that I prepared Halef! That he came to fetch me was proof that something out of the ordinary had happened. I opened the door and stepped into the passage.

"Halef!"

"*Sihdi*, is that you?"

"Yes. What is it?"

"The *Mutesselim* came."

"That is a problem; that could spoil everything. Go. We follow soon. But remain at the door of my room so that I can call you when I need you!"

I returned to the small room.

"Selim Agha, it was lucky that I told the Hajji where we were. The *Mutesselim* has come to your house and waits for you."

"*Allah illa Allah*! Come quickly, *Effendi*! What does he want?"

"Halef did not know."

"It must be important. Hurry!"

We left the wine and walked home at a rapid pace.

When we arrived there, the Commandant sat in my place of honor, the magical light from the red paper lantern illuminated him and he sucked on my *Nargileh*. He was, as soon as he saw me, courteous enough to arise.

"Ah, *Mutesselim*, you are here in my room! Allah bless your entry and be content at my side!"

But of course my private wish did not quite agree with this courteous phrase.

"Emir, forgive me that I came unannounced. The mistress of this house, to whom Allah has given a face like no other, said I should. I did want to speak with Selim Agha!"

"Then permit me that I remove myself!"

He was now forced to ask me to stay if he did not want to go against all Turkish customs.

"Stay, Emir, and be seated. And Selim Agha may seat himself as well; for you may know what I am about to ask of him."

Now my reserve pipes had to be brought out. During the lighting of these I carefully watched the Commandant. The red light of the lantern did not permit me to see his facial expression clearly, but his voice appeared to have that certain quality that indicated that his tongue has lost some of its nimbleness.

"What do you think, *Effendi*? Is the *Makrej* an important prisoner?"

"I think so."

"I do too. That is why the very thought that it may be possible for him to escape causes me great concern."

"But yet he is securely locked up!"

"Yes. But that does not give me enough assurance. Selim Agha, I will not sleep this night and I will yet go to the prison another two or three times to make certain that he really still is in his pit."

"Lord, I will do this for you!"

"Then certainly you will see him, but not I, and thus I still can not sleep. I will go myself. Give me the key!"

"Do you know Lord, that you wound me?"

"I do not wish to wound you, rather I want to reassure myself. Anadoli Kasi Askeri is a strict man. I would be awarded the silken cord [garrote] if I allowed this prisoner to escape."

And with this turn of events, the execution of our plan was impossible! Was there no other solution? I decided quickly. Either by wine or by force! Whilst the

Agha still made proposals to his superior I arose and stepped into the corridor where Halef stood.

"Bring some of the best tobacco, here is some money; go to the house from which you fetched me and ask the Jew for some of the wine from *Türbedi Haidari*, that I drunk earlier."

"How much shall I bring?"

"A vessel that holds ten mugs of the size used by the Jew. He will loan you such vessel."

"Do I bring this drink of the Devil into your room?"

"No. I will get it from your room. But the *Bashi-Bozuk* may know nothing of this. Give him this *Baksheesh*. He may go out and stay out as long as he likes. He can go to the guards and show himself to the *Bash Jaush* with whom he will ride tomorrow. Then we are rid of him!"

When I entered my room again, the Agha was just handing the key to the Commandant. The latter stuck it into his belt and said to me:

"Do you know that the *Makrej* was rebellious?"

"Yes. He first wanted to bribe the Agha and then even sought to take his life."

"He will rue this!"

"And," added Selim, "when I ordered him to empty his pockets, he refused."

"What did he have in them?"

"Much money!"

"Emir, to whom does this money belong?" the Commandant asked me expectantly.

"You have to receive it."

"That is right. Let us go!"

"*Mutesselim*, you wish to leave me?" I asked. "Do you wish to insult me?"

"I am your visitor but not your guest!"

"I had not known that you were coming. Permit me to stuff your pipe with a tobacco that is seldom smoked here."

Just then Halef entered and brought the tobacco; it was the kind that Master Lindsay smoked; the Commandant was sure to find it to his liking. Besides, I was determined that he would not leave my room against my will. Luckily it did not come to that for he accepted the stuffed pipe I handed him. But during our continued discussions, I noted that he eyed the door expectantly. He was waiting for coffee. Therefore I asked:

"Have you received the medicine, Lord?"

"Yes, I thank you, *Effendi*!"

"Was it enough?"

"I have not yet counted."

"And not sampled either?"

"A little."

"How was it?"

"Very good. But I have heard that a very sweet one exists too!"

The good Agha knew precisely what we were talking about. He smiled and looked at me with eyes that sparkled with temptation.

"A very sweet one exists," I answered.

"But it is rare?"

"No."

"And medicinal?"

"Very much. It is like the milk that flows from the trees of paradise."

"But it can not be had in Amadijah?"

"I can prepare some everywhere, even in Amadijah."

"And how long will it take to prepare it?"

"Ten minutes. If you wait that long then you shall taste of the drink that the *Houris* passed to Mohammed."

"I wait!"

His eyes sparkled with delight, but the eyes of the worthy Selim Agha sparkled with greater delight still. I left the room and used this moment to go to Mohammed Emin.

"Emir, it is futile to go on!" he greeted me.

"No, rather now it begins!"

"But you will not get the key now!"

"Perhaps I will not need it. Just be patient."

And then Lindsay crept into the room.

"Took from my tobacco! Who smokes it?"

"The Commandant."

"Very well! Drinks my wine, smokes my tobacco! Wonderful!"

"And why shouldn't he?"

"Should stay at home! Not mess with the escape!"

"Perhaps he makes it possible. I have sent for more wine."

"Again?"

"Yes. For Persian wine. Knocks down an elephant. Sweet as honey and strong like a lion!"

"Well! Drink Persian too!"

"Have seen to it that you will get some of it. I will guide these two towards happiness and then we shall see what can be done."

I then went into the kitchen and made sure a fire was lit. Before that had started to burn properly, Halef returned. He brought a large vessel of the dangerous drink. I filled a pot with it and set it over the fire, leaving it in the care of Mersinah. Then I returned to the Englishman. "Here is the Persian wine! But get me some glasses, they are in your room."

When I entered my room again, the two Turks looked at me full of expectation.

"I bring the medicine, *Mutesselim*. First try it cold. And then you shall discover how it entices the heart when it is tasted hot."

"Tell me truly, *Effendi*, is it wine or medicine!"

"This drink is the best medicine that I know of today. Drink it and tell me if it rejoices your soul!"

He tried it and then tasted it once more. A transforming glow spread across his sharp, yet dull facial features.

"Have you invented this tonic yourself?"

"No, rather Allah gives it to those he loves most of all."

"Then you believe that he loves us?"

"Certainly."

"I know that you are beloved by the prophets. Do you have more of this tonic?"

"Here. Drink!"

I topped up his glass.

His eyes sparkled with greater delight than before.

"*Effendi*, what is *Ladakia*, *Djebeli* and tobacco from Shiraz against such a medicine! It is better than the finest coffee aroma. Will you give me the recipe of how it is prepared?"

"Remind me of this and I will write it down for you before I depart Amadijah. But the jug is here. Drink! I have to go to the kitchen to prepare the other medicine."

I deliberately went down the stairs very quietly and carefully opened the kitchen door a little. I was right! There by the pot stood the 'Myrte' and she bailed the already hot wine from the pot with a small Turkish coffee cup which she emptied unceasingly between her wide open lips. After each completed motion, she clapped these together with a satisfied and hearty smack.

"Mersinah, don't burn your teeth!"

Thus startled she dropped the cup and turned around.

"Oh, *Sihdi*, it was an *Öremjek* [Spider, Garden spider] that had dropped into the pot and I wanted to fish it out!"

"And then you poured this spider into your mouth?"

"No, *Effendi* only the little drops that clung to the spider."

"Give me that little pot there!"

"Here, Emir!"

"Fill it with this drink!"

"For whom?"

"For yourself."

"What is it, Emir?"

"It is a medicine that a Persian *Hekim* invented to make the old young again. Who drinks enough of it, to him is given bliss and who drinks of it unceasingly has eternal life!"

She thanked me profusely with flowery phrases and I took the rest of the wine upstairs. The two 'wine enthusiasts' had moved closer to each other despite their difference in rank and appeared to have a quite pleasant discussion.

"Do you know, *Effendi*, what we are arguing about?" the Commandant asked of me.

"I did not hear it!"

"We argued about whose system suffers most, his or mine. Who is right?"

"That I will tell you: For whom the medicine is most effective, his system has suffered the most."

"Your wisdom is greater than we can comprehend. What have you got in that pot?"

"It is *Ijki ijkilerin* [The Drink of all Drinks], for none is its equal."

"And you desire that we shall taste it?"

"If you wish, I will pour it for you."

"Give me!"

"Me too, *Effendi*," begged the Agha.

Both of them had already that, which a *'Spiro-Zoologe'* [maître de chai] would call a 'bug', yes, it already appeared to be a considerable stag-beetle that clearly indicated its intention to transmute into that well known 'four handed' sloth. It was only hot wine that they had tasted, without any spices, but it had transported them close to the state, so aptly described by the words *'Seid umschlungen, Millionen!'* [Beethoven's Ode to Joy - 'Be embraced, you millions!'] They already shared their drink from just one glass, and the *Mutesselim* tenderly wiped some spilled drops of that magnificent medicine from his Agha's forest of a beard. The conversation that went along with that was one that can be expected of two people to whom the 'valiantly battle of full tankards' is quite new; that is; both fantastic and plain gibberish. Even I, who only pretended to drink, was drawn into this; for the *Mutesselim* embraced me again and again and the Agha trustingly draped his arm around my neck.

The Agha arose to fetch a new candle for the red lantern. He arose without a problem, but then he stretched out his arms and his knees started to quiver uncertainly like someone who is on skates the very first time.

“What is wrong with you, Agha?” asked the Commandant.

“Oh, Lord, I am getting the *Baldyr jekmish* [cramp in the calf]. I believe I have to sit down again!”

“Sit! I will help you!”

“Do you know of a remedy?”

“A very good one. Sit!”

The Agha resumed his seat. The Commandant straightened himself somewhat and asked with loving condescension:

“In which calf is the cramp?”

“In the right.”

“Give me your leg then!”

The Agha extended it towards him and his superior began to pull and tug at it with all his might.

“*O jazi*k - oh woe, Lord; I believe that is the left after all!”

“Then give me that one!”

Selim stretched his other ambulatory limb towards the Commandant, and this 'assistant in the hour of need' pulled at it with all his bodily strength. It was both comical and touching to see that a superior officer, who was used to have others do the smallest things for him, pull and pummel his subordinate's calf in such a brotherly manner.

“Good! I believe it is gone now!”

“Then stand up and try it!”

Selim arose and this time really tried hard. He stood stock straight. But walking was a different matter! I could see that for him it was just like it was for a bird that was ready to try the air for the very first time.

"Try to walk!" commanded the *Mutesselim*. "Come; I will support you!"

He wanted to arise with the usual speed, but lost his balance and quickly resumed his previous position. But he knew how to help himself. He placed a hand on my shoulder and stood up. He then spread his legs wide apart to get a more stable posture and stared at the red lantern in a most perplexed manner.

"Emir, your lantern is falling!"

"I believe it is hanging quite firmly!"

"It is falling, and the paper is burning. I already see the flames!"

"I don't see anything!"

"*Mash Allah*! I see it fall and yet it remains hanging! Don't sway so, Selim Agha, otherwise you will fall down!"

"I do not sway, *Effendi*!"

"I see it very well!"

"You are swaying yourself, Lord!"

"I? Agha, I am much worried about your system. Your nerves are pushing you to and fro, and your digestion has sunk into your legs. You shake your arms and roll your head as though you wish to swim. Oh, Selim Agha, this medicine was too magnificent and too strong for you. It will throw you to the ground!"

"Lord, you are mistaken! What you say of me is true for yourself. I see your feet dance and your arms flap. Your head is spinning around. *Effendi*, you are very ill. May Allah send you assistance that your blood system is not totally devastated!"

That finally was too much for the *Mutesselim*. He balled his hand into a fist and threatened:

"Selim Agha, take care! Who says that my system is not in good order, I will have him whipped or even locked up! *Wallah*! Have I received the key?"

His hand reached for his belt and found what he was searching for.

"Agha, get ready to accompany me! I will now inspect the prison. Emir, your medicine is truly like the milk of paradise; but it has turned your stomach; you head strives towards the floor. Do you permit us to leave?"

"If it is your will to visit the prisoners then I may not interfere with the fulfillment of your duty."

"Then we go. We thank you for the goodness that you allowed us to taste this day. Will you prepare more medicine soon?"

"As soon as you desire."

"The hot one is much better than the cold, but it penetrates the legs and marrow and pushes the bones about. Allah preserve you and grant you a peaceful rest!"

He made for the Agha and took him by the arm. They started for the stairs and I followed them. They stopped at the top of the stairs.

"Selim Agha, you go down first!"

"Lord, this honor belongs to you!"

"I am not proud; as you well know."

The Agha carefully placed one foot and then the other on the step and held onto the railing with both hands. The *Mutesselim* followed him. It did not go quite so easily, as the stairs were unfamiliar to him.

"*Effendi*, are you still there?"

"Yes."

"Do you know that it is customary to accompany a guest to the door?"

"I know it."

"But you are not accompanying me!"

"Then permit me to do this!"

I took him by the arm and supported him. Now it went a little better. Once down by the door he stopped to breathe deeply.

"Emir, this *Makrej* is actually your prisoner as well," he stated.

"If one considers it, yes."

"Then you too must assure yourself that he is still there!"

"I will accompany you."

"Then come, give me your arm!"

"You have two arms, *Effendi*," the Agha said; "give me your arm too!"

Both men hung heavily upon my arms, but their state of drunkenness still allowed them some control over themselves. Their gait was uncertain, yet we made good headway. The lanes were dark and deserted. Not a single soul passed us by.

"Your Arnauts will be frightened when I arrive," the *Mutesselim* said to the Agha.

"And I with you!" the Agha bragged.

"And I with you!" I finished.

"Is the Arab still there?"

"Lord, do you believe that I let such people escape?" asked Selim Agha quite indignant.

"I will also see to him. Did he have money too?"

"No."

"How much do you think that the *Makrej* carries on his person?"

"I do not know."

"He must hand it over. But, Selim, your Arnauts should not be present then."

"Then I will order them to go."

"And if they listen?"

"I will lock them up."

"Good. But when we are gone they will talk with the prisoners."

"They remain locked up."

"That is good. This money belongs into the *Mutesselim's* coffer and the Agha of the Arnauts receive a very nice *Baksheesh* from him."

"How much, Lord?"

"That I do not know yet, for first I will have to see how much he has on his person."

We had reached the jail.

"Open up, Selim Agha!"

"Lord, you have the key yourself!"

"Yes, so I have!"

He reached into his belt and pulled out the key in order to open the door. He tried but could not find the keyhole.

This I had anticipated.

"Permit me, *Effendi*, that I unlock it for you!"

I took the key from his hand and unlocked the door, took the key from the lock, stepped into the passage and put it back into the lock on the other side.

"Enter. I will lock up!"

They entered. I did as though I locked the door but quickly turned the key the other way again and then rattled the door pretending to see if it was truly locked.

"It is shut tight. Here is the key, *Mutesselim*!"

He took it. The Arnauts came from the furthest cell, carrying lamps.

"Is everything in order?" asked the *Mutesselim* with dignity.

"Yes, Lord."

"No one escaped?"

"No."

"Not even the Arab?"

"No."

"But the *Makrej*?"

"Not even he," the Sergeant answered these most intelligent questions.

"You are lucky, you dogs. Otherwise I would have you whipped to death. Remove yourselves to your room! Selim Agha, lock them in!"

"Emir, would you do this?" Selim asked me.

"Certainly!"

That was good. The Agha took one of the lamps and I led the people to their room.

"Why are we being locked up, Lord?" asked the Sergeant.

"The prisoners are being interrogated."

I waited for them to enter the cell and then shut the bolts. After that I descended the stairs. Since the Commandant and the Agha had already gone, the main door lay in darkness. I darted across to it and opened it so that it was just leaning to. Then I quickly followed them.

"Where is he?" I heard the *Mutesselim* ask.

"Here."

"And where is the Haddedihn?" I asked in order to prevent the opening of the other door first; for I had to see to it that the door to the Arab's cell was opened before any other.

"Here beyond the second door."

"Then open it!"

The Commandant appeared to agree with my demand. He nodded and Selim unlocked the cell.

The prisoner had heard of our loud arrival and stood upright in his pit. The *Mutesselim* stepped closer.

"You are Amad, the son of Mohammed Emin?"

He did not receive an answer.

"Can't you speak?"

Only silence followed.

"Dog, one knows how to open your mouth! You will be sent away tomorrow!"

Amad did not utter a single syllable, but instead watched my face closely so as not to miss any meaningful expression. I therefore let him know that he should be vigilant by rapidly raising my eyebrows; then Selim bolted the door again.

Now the other door was opened. The *Makrej* lent against the wall of his cell. His eyes watched us full of expectation.

"*Makrej*, how do you like it?" asked the Commandant with a little irony that was probably due to the wine.

"May Allah wish that you were in my place!"

"May the Prophet prevent that! Your fate is a terrible one!"

"I am not afraid!"

"You have tried to kill this Agha."

"He deserves death!"

"Have tried to bribe him."

"He is stupidity personified!"

"Have tried to pay him immediately."

"That fellow deserves to be hanged immediately!"

"Perhaps your wish could be fulfilled," the Commandant said cleverly. His face was aglow with the hope of booty and from his 'wine tasting'.

"How?" the *Makrej* snapped. "Do you speak earnestly?"

"Yes."

"You wish to barter with me?"

"Yes."

"How much do you want?"

"How much do you have?"

"*Mutesselim*, I need my travel money!"

"Then we will be so cheap that we leave you some."

"Good, then let us bargain. But not in this pit!"

"Where else?"

"In a room that is for people and not for rats."

"Then come up!"

"Give me your hand!"

"Selim Agha, you do it!" said the Commandant, who did not appear to trust his balance.

But the Agha had the same concern and nudged me in the ribs as he said:

"*Effendi*, you do it!"

So as not to delay matters further, I reached down, took the *Makrej* by the hand and pulled him up.

"Where to?" I asked.

"In the guardroom," answered the Commandant.

"Shall I leave the door open or ... ?"

"Just push it to!"

I busied myself with the door, planning to wait until the three of them entered the guardroom, but that did not work as the Commandant was waiting for me. I had to think of another plan.

The *Makrej* entered first followed by the Commandant who carried the lamp, then the Agha and I entered last. Once inside the guardroom, this order disintegrated and opportunity presented itself where a quick bump into the Agha cause the latter to bump into the elbow of the Commandant and knock the lamp from his hand.

"Agha, what are you doing!" shouted the Commandant.

"It was not I, Lord!"

"You bumped into me! Now it is dark. Fetch another lamp!"

"I will get one from the Arnauts," I interjected and left the room. I locked the door behind me, opened the door of the neighboring cell by drawing back the bolts.

"Amad el Ghandur!"

"Lord, is that you?"

"Yes. Climb up quickly."

He made it to the top with my help and I bolted the door again.

"Do not talk, rather hurry!" I whispered.

I took hold of him and led him to the main gate of the prison, went outside with him and pulled the gate to.

The fresh air almost drove him back inside. He was very weak.

I took him by the hand, we hurried on, around a couple of corners, and then we stopped at the third. His lungs labored loudly.

"Pull yourself together! There is my abode and there your father awaits you."

I made the previously agreed signal of a croaking bird and immediately I saw a light come through the opening door of the house.

We hurried across the square. Halef stood by the door.

"Inside, quickly!"

I now hurried back. I reached the prison barely two minutes after we had left it, opened the gate and stepped into the darkness and then made for the stairs that I now knew quite well. I few seconds later I returned to the guardroom.

"You were gone a long time, *Effendi*!" stated the *Mutesselim*.

"The guards wanted to know why they were locked up."

"You should have given them a clap around the ears instead of an answer! Why did you lock us in?"

"Lord, you had a prisoner with you!"

"You are cautious, Emir; and you did right. Put the lamp down and let us begin!"

It was clear that the Commandant had no intention to let the prisoner go in exchange for payment. His fear that the *Makrej* would not pay willingly led him to this cunning plan. But this cunning was deceitful, a treachery and at the same time a great mistake. Both of them were under the influence of alcohol; the *Makrej* could overpower them, take the key from them and flee, and the locked up Arnauts would have been powerless to help them.

"Now tell us, how much money do you have on you!" the Commandant began.

"Rather tell me how much you want from me!"

"I can only tell you that if I know that you can pay it."

"Try!"

"Will you pay three-thousand piaster?"

"That is too much," the Makrej said quite reserved.

"Then you pay four-thousand."

"Lord! You are raising the price!"

"*Makrej*, and you are trying to lower it! A *Mutesselim* does not need to haggle. If you don't agree, I will go higher still."

"But I do not have it. Two-thousand is all I could give!"

"Your hand is closed, but you would gladly open it. Now I demand five-thousand!"

"Lord, I will give you the three-thousand you asked for!"

"I said five!"

The *Makrej* looked at the Commandant with a furious gaze, and the fear for his money was clearly written upon his face. Yet the concern for his freedom was still greater.

"Dc you promise that you will let me go if I pay?"

"I promise it to you."

"Swear it to me in the name of the Prophet!"

"I swear it!"

The Mutesselim spoke these words without a second thought. The *Makrej* had unfortunately phrased his request so that it had a double meaning.

"Then count!"

He reached into his pocket and pulled forth a package that was wrapped in a silken cloth. He opened it and began to count out the money, whilst the Agha's eyes glowed.

"Is it correct?" he asked once he had finished.

The *Mutesselim* counted it and then said:

"These are *Kaime* [like the *'Sehim'* a kind of paper money] with the value of five-thousand piaster. But you must know that this money does not have the right value. The Pound Sterling, if paid in *Kaime*, is now worth one-hundred-and-forty instead of one-hundred-and-ten piaster, and thus you have to add another two-thousand piaster on top!"

"Lord, consider that the *Kaime* attracts six percent interest!"

"That was the case long ago, but only for a part of this money; yet the Sultan did not pay the interest even for that. Put on another two-thousand."

"Lord, that is unjust!"

"Good! Then return to your pit!"

Sweat was breaking out on the *Makrej's* brow.

"But it is not two-thousand!"

"How much then?"

"One-thousand-three-hundred-and-sixty-three."

"That is immaterial! What I have said, stands. You pay another two-thousand!"

"Lord, you are as terrible as a tiger!"

"And greed will yet kill you!"

Grimly the *Makrej* counted anew.

"Here, take it!" he said finally whilst drawing a deep breath.

Again the *Mutesselim* checked the count, pushed the paper money together and pocketed the stack.

"Its right!" he said. "Thank the Prophet that he turned your heart to reason for otherwise I would have demanded far more!"

"Now let me go!" demanded the *Makrej* whilst he folded the silken cloth around the remaining money.

The Commandant looked at him with a well-played amazement.

"Let you go? Yes, but only after you have paid!"

"But I just have!"

"Yes, you paid me, but you have not paid this Agha of the Arnauts!"

"*Allah illa Allah*!" the prisoner cried angrily. "You have only demanded five-thousand piaster!"

"Allah has darkened your senses. Why did you not ask for whom these five thousand piaster were meant? They were meant for me. The Agha has yet to receive his share."

"How much?"

"As much as for me!"

"Lord, *Shaïtan* is talking through you!"

"Pay, then he will be silent!"

"I will not pay!"

"Then you return to your pit!"

"Oh, Mohammed, oh, you Caliphs, You have heard his oath! *Shaïtan* has already possessed him; he will consume him!"

"The lamp oil is running low. Will you pay or not?"

"I will give him a thousand!"

"Five-thousand! Don't haggle or else I will go higher!"

"I don't have that much!"

"You have it. I have seen that it is sufficient."

"Then I pay ... "

"Shall I demand six-thousand?"

"You are a tyrant, yes, you are *Shaïtan* himself!"

"*Makrej*, we are finished with one another!"

He slowly and carefully arose.

"Wait!" cried the prisoner. "I will pay!"

Obviously his freedom was worth more to him than his money. He started to count afresh whilst the Commandant seated himself again. The content of the package was truly sufficient; and only a few notes remained.

"Here it is," he said, "and may Allah damn whoever takes it!"

"And you have spoken wisely, *Makrej*," answered his earlier compatriot and opponent very calmly. "This Agha of the Arnauts will not take this money."

"Why not?"

"For it is only five-thousand. You have forgotten to add the additional two-thousand to it."

The *Makrej* moved as though he was about to pounce upon the Commandant; but reconsidered.

"I have no more than these three notes."

"The I will lock you up. Perhaps you will then remember that you have more money on you. Come!"

The *Makrej* appeared to choke, then he reached into his pocket and produced a bag which he held so that only he could see its content.

"Then I will try to see if I can scrape it together! Your heart is like stone and your soul has transformed into a rock. Here I have only some pieces of silver and some gold *Mejidje* among them. You shall have the latter if they are enough."

He placed the notes onto the ground and then very slowly added one gold piece after another to the growing pile.

"Here, now I am poor, for I have just forty piaster left and these I must keep so that I will not starve!"

I had to admit that I felt sorry for that man; but I realized that he would have to part even with his last penny. It appeared as though the sight of the money had completely sobered the *Mutesselim*. And even the Agha appeared free of the influence of alcohol. The latter hastily reached forward to take possession of the pile.

"Stop!" the Commandant ordered him. "I will hold onto this money for a little while."

He pushed the pile together and pocketed it.

"Now I am finally free!" said the *Makrej*.

The Commandant shook his head in utter amazement.

"Free! Have you paid?"

"Have your senses departed from you? You have just pocketed the money!"

"My money and that of Selim Agha. But this Emir has received nothing!"

"And he should not receive anything!"

"Who says so? He is here and must be paid!"

"But he holds no sway over me!"

"Has he not caused you to become a prisoner? You have a fever, *Makrej*, otherwise you would realize that he has actually more right than both of us together."

"He shall receive nothing!" shouted the tortured man in utter rage. "He gets nothing for I have no more, and I would not give him any piaster and not a single para, even if I carried millions upon my person!"

"You still have money!"

"Forty piaster, as I have already stated!"

"Oh *Makrej*, how I pity you! Do you believe that I can not discern the sound of gold from that of silver! Your bag is still full of golden *Mejidje*, to a value of at least one-hundred-and-fifty piaster, and your belly has such a circumference that you could scrape together far more than you need to pay the Emir. You have provided yourself quite well with travel funds!"

"You are mistaken!"

"Show me your bag!"

"It belongs to me!"

"Then keep it, but pay up!"

The *Makrej* squirmed like a worm at the inconsiderate demand of this avaricious man. It was a disgusting scene, but it shed a very clear light upon the circumstances of the Turkish government, in particular within those provinces that were furthest from the reach of the Padishah.

"I can't!" the *Makrej* declared adamantly.

"Then follow us to your pit!"

"I will not go. I have paid you!"

"We will know how to force you."

"Then give me back my money!"

"It belongs to me. Remember that you are my prisoner and that I am obligated to take from you all that you carry on your person!"

"I would even pay this sum if I had it!"

"You have it. And even if the content of your bag is insufficient, I have spied a nice watch on your person and your fingers are adorned with sparkling rings that are worth far more than what I still demand from you."

"It remains with me, I can not! I will give five-hundred piaster to this man who is my greatest enemy."

His eyes flashed at me with the greatest possible hatred. I could not doubt his animosity toward me.

"Then this is your final word?" asked the Commandant.

"Yes."

"Then come! Follow us!"

He arose decisively and so did the Agha.

I had stood by the door and now moved aside to let the *Mutesselim* pass through first. The key was visible in his belt. The eyes of the prisoner flared briefly, he leapt forward, tore the key from the Commandant's belt and pushed him into the Agha so that both tumbled to the ground and almost took me with them, he made for the door and hurried down the dark passage. The lamp had fallen over and we were enveloped in darkness.

"After him!" shouted the Commandant.

The *Makrej* would have made it if he had kept his head and shut the door behind him and bolted it. There had been enough time for that for both men were so entangled in one another that I, in order to follow him quickly, had to push them back from the door so that I could exit.

I heard the key rattle in the lock. The fact that I had already unlocked the door was the *Makrej's* undoing. He tried to turn the key with all the might that his despair could muster, but never tried to open the door itself. But the bolt could yet falter. Now I was there and grabbed hold of him. He turned his frustration upon me and with forethought grabbed at my belt. I felt that and reached downwards. He managed to get hold of my knife and in pulling it from the scabbard, he managed to wound me with a cut across the back of my hand. It was so dark that I could not see his movements. I therefore held him as firm as I could with my left hand whilst I found his shoulder with my right and moved outward and down along his arm until I reached his wrist and grabbed it also. I was just in time, for he intended to strike.

In the meantime the other two arrived amidst shouts and curses. The Commandant grabbed hold of me.

"Let go, *Mutesselim*, it is I!"

"Do you have him?"

"Yes. Quick! Lock the door and light a lamp. He can not escape us!"

"Can you hold him by yourself, Emir?" asked the Agha.

"Yes."

"Then I will fetch a lamp!"

The Commandant locked the door but did not dare to approach us. I had managed to maneuver the prisoner against the far wall, but could not force him to the ground as I still held his hand with the knife and had to protect myself from it. But I held him fast for a long time until finally the Agha returned with a lamp. He first had to fetch more oil from the Sergeant's cell. Now he placed the lamp on the lower step of the stairs and came closer.

"Take the knife," I begged him.

He pulled it from the *Makrej's* grasp and now that I could again use my hand. I grabbed the *Makrej* by his garment close to his neck. He tried to prevent it but I quickly bent down, grabbed his legs and whilst his hands flayed at thin air I pulled his legs from beneath him so that he lost his balance and fell to the floor.

"Bind him!" I said.

"With what?"

"With his belt."

They did so. He lay there, still and silent, and allowed it to happen. After this great struggle, a feeling of being powerless had overtaken him.

"Hold his legs!" the Mutesselim ordered the Agha.

The Commandant now emptied everything from the prisoner's pockets; finally he pulled the rings from his fingers and pocketed the lot. The Agha then grabbed hold of the prisoner's legs and dragged him to his cell where he slid him into the pit. The cell was then locked. Now Selim had to mount the stairs to free the guards and impress upon them the greatest need for vigilance.

"Take their gate key from them!" shouted the Commandant. "Then no-one can open up and they can't either."

Selim did so and we then left the prison.

Chapter 35

The *Mutesselim* stopped outside. He was now completely sober in what he said:

"Agha, I will prepare a complete inventory of all the *Makrej* had on his person; for I will have to send everything to Mosul along with him. You will sign it, so that I can prove that I have written the truth, in case he should get the idea to claim that he had more!"

"When shall I come?" asked Selim.

"At the usual time."

"And you will keep the key?"

"Yes. Perhaps I will come once more during the night. Good night, Emir! You were of great assistance to me this day and you will tell me how I can show you my appreciation."

He departed and we returned to our abode.

"*Effendi*!" the Agha mused.

"What?"

"I had seven-thousand piaster on the ground before me!"

"And you are happy?"

"Greatly!"

"Let them be given to you!"

"I? Have them given to me? Do you know what will happen tomorrow?"

"Well?"

"He will prepare a statement, in which will be noted that the *Makrej* had a thousand piaster on his person, and I will sign it. The rest, the watch and the rings, he will keep and for this I will receive the great sum of a hundred piaster."

"And you will be happy with that too!"

"I will be angry onto death!"

"Will the *Bash Jaush* receive the statement?"

"Yes."

"Then you will receive a larger amount."

"And who shall give it me?"

"Either the *Mutesselim* or I."

"I know that you have a merciful heart. Oh *Effendi*, if you only had a tiny drop of your medicine left!"

"I still have some. Do you desire it?"

"Yes."

"I will bring you some from the kitchen."

The door to the house was not locked. In the kitchen 'Myrte' was lying on some old tatters that served as her rags during the day and her bed at night, there she slept the sleep of the righteous.

"Mersinah!" shouted the Agha.

She did not hear him.

"Let her sleep," I begged him. "I will bring you the medicine and then you may rest, you will need it."

"Allah knows that I have earned it!"

Upstairs, all the participants in the escape were gathered in the Haddedihn's room. They all talked to me at once in a loud wave of words so that I had to order them to be quiet. First I took care of the Agha and assured myself that he went to sleep; then I returned to them.

Amad el Ghandur had dressed in his new clothes and his father had shaved and bathed him. Now he looked totally different from how he had appeared in his cell earlier. The resemblance to his father was undeniable. He arose and approached me.

"Emir, I am a Beni Arab and not a chattering Greek. I have heard what you have done for my tribe and for me. My life belongs to you, even all that I posses!"

That was spoken simply but the words came from his heart.

"You are still not completely safe. My servant will take you to your hiding place."

"I am ready. We were only waiting for you."

"Can you climb?"

"Yes. I will manage to make it to the hiding place despite my having become weak."

"Here you have my lasso. If your strength leaves you, then Hajji Halef Omar may climb ahead and pull you up. Do you have weapons?"

"There they lie; my father has bought them for me. Here is your dagger. I thank you!"

"And food?"

"Everything is packed."

"Then go! We will fetch you soon."

The Sheik's son and Halef left the house with great care, and soon I too crept out. I had all of Amed's old clothes in my arms. I made it to the edge of the ravine unnoticed, tore his *Haïk* into tatters and hung them from the edge and onto the branches of the undergrowth that was there.

When I returned home, I was pulled into the room of the Englishman. He wore an angry frown.

"Come in and sit, Sir!" he growled. "Terrible mess! Miserable here!"

"Why?"

"Sit with these Arabs and don't understand a word! My wine is gone, my tobacco is gone and I too am empty! Yes!"

"But I am at your service to tell you everything!"

I had to abide his will although I craved for sleep. But I would have had to await Halef's return anyway, and so it happened that the day was already dawning.

"How is it?" asked Master Lindsay. "Reached the villa alright?"

"With some exertion!"

"Well! Halef has torn clothes. Here, Halef, *Baksheesh*!"

The Hajji did not understand the English words but certainly understood the last word of the sentence. He stretched out his hand and received a one-hundred piaster coin.

"Buy new coat; tell him, Sir!"

And so this eventful night was over and I could get a few hours of sound and dreamless sleep at last. I did not wake by myself but was instead woken by a frantic voice:

"*Effendi*! Emir! Wake up! Quickly!"

I looked up from my bed. There stood Selim Agha, with neither jacket nor turban. His hair hung loosely and disheveled across his face; his mustache bristled upwards to meet it in horror, and the wine he had consumed was visible in his bleary eyes, which he tried to roll with little success.

"What's up?" I asked nonchalantly.

"Arise! Something terrible has happened!"

Bit by bit I managed to elicit that the *Mutesselim* had discovered the young Arab's escape and that he was now in a terrible rage. The frightened Agha pleaded with me to accompany him to the prison and to try to pacify the *Mutesselim*.

We were on our way shortly. The *Mutesselim* waited for the Agha at the prison gate. He did not even think to greet me, but instead grabbed Selim by the arms and dragged him into the corridor where the frightened guard stood shivering.

"You luckless one, what have you done!" he roared at him.

"I, Lord? Nothing, I have done nothing at all!"

"That is precisely your crime, that you have done nothing, nothing at all! You have not been watchful!"

"Where should I have been watchful, *Effendi*?"

"Here in the prison of course!"

"But I could not enter!"

The *Mutesselim* stared at him. This thought had apparently not yet dawned on him.

"I did not have the key!" added the Agha.

"No key ... ! Yes, Agha, that is true, and that is also lucky for you, otherwise you would have suffered terribly. Come here, and look down into the pit!"

We marched down the passage. The cell door was open and in the pit … nothing could be seen - other than the pit itself.

"Gone!" reckoned the Agha.

"Yes, gone!" raged the *Mutesselim.*

"Who has opened the door for him?"

"Yes, who? Tell me, Agha!"

"Not me, Lord!"

"And not me either! Only the guards were here."

The Agha turned to these now.

"Come here, you dogs!"

They came closer, hesitantly.

"You opened the door for him!"

The Sergeant dared to answer:

"Agha, non of us have touched the bolts. We only have to open the cell doors in the afternoon when the meal is served so not a single one was opened at all."

"Then I was the first who opened this door?" asked the Commandant.

"Yes, *Effendi*!"

"And when I opened, the pit was empty. He escaped. But how could he get out? Last night he was still there; now he is gone. During the time in-between only you were here. One of you have let him out!"

"I swear by Allah, that we did not open this door!" stated the quivering Sergeant.

"*Mutesselim*," I interceded, "these people did not have the key to the main gate. If one of them let the prisoner out of his cell, then he must still be in the building."

"You are right; I had both keys," he admitted. "We will search everywhere and everything."

"And send the guard to inspect the walls and the ravines around the city too. If he has left the city, it is certain that he did not do so via the city gate, but rather via the city wall and I am certain that some trace of that could be found. His clothing has suffered much whilst he was in this pit, it was stained with mould and was so rotten that it would certainly not have survived a trek across stones and rocks."

"Yes," he ordered one of the Arnauts, "hurry to the guard and bring them my order that they are to search the city."

Now the careful search of the prison building started and continued for a whole hour. Of course no sign or trace of the escaped prisoner was found. Just when we were ready to leave the prison, two Arnauts came carrying some shreds of cloth.

"We found this outside by the ravine," reported one.

The Agha took the pieces and examined them.

"*Effendi*, this is part of the prisoner's cloak," he informed the *Mutesselim*. "I know it well!"

"Are you certain?"

"As certain as I am of my beard."

"Then he did manage to escape from the building after all!"

"But he must have fallen into the ravine," I added.

"Let us go and see!" he ordered.

We left the prison and made our way to the place where I had torn apart and scattered the cloak. When I saw this place in daylight I was amazed that I had not fallen into the ravine myself during the hours of darkness. The *Mutesselim* scrutinized the terrain.

"He fell and is surely dead. From down there, there is no resurrection! But when did he escape?"

Of course this question remained unanswered despite the Commandant's attempt to solve this puzzle over the following hours. He was furious and raged at anyone who approached him, and so it was no wonder that even I avoided him. But despite this, I was not bored for I had plenty to do. First of all a horse was purchased for Amad el Ghandur and then I visited my patient whom I had neglected until now.

Before the door of the house stood a saddled mule; it was meant to carry a woman. The father was in the front room and welcomed me joyously.

I found my patient sitting up; her cheeks were already slightly rosy and her eyes were free of any trace of her accident. Her mother and her ancestor stood by her bed. The latter was dressed in her traveling clothes. Over her white dress she wore a black cape-like garment, and over her head she wore a black veil that hung down her back. The girl stretched out her hand to me immediately.

"Oh, I thank you, *Effendi*, for now it is certain that I will not die!"

"Yes, she will live," said the old one. "You are God's tool and the tool of the Holy Virgin, to preserve a life for me, a life which is dear to me, dearer than everything on this earth. I may not offer you wealth, for you are a great Emir, who has everything that he needs; but tell me how I should thank you, *Effendi*!"

"Thank God instead of me, then your gratitude will be directed to the right place; for it is he who has saved your grandchild!"

"I will do this and I will also pray for you, Lord, and the prayer of a woman who has already departed from this world, will be heard by God. How long do you remain in Amadijah?"

"Not much longer."

"And where will you go?"

"That shall be known by no-one, for there may be reasons to keep it quite. But I can tell you that will I ride towards the sunrise."

"Then you will go to the same region to which I will travel, Lord. My beast already waits outside. Perhaps we may never see each other again; for that reason take the blessing of an old woman that may give you nothing more, and also could not give you anything better! But a secret I will tell you, for it could be of use to you. Dark days are coming from the east, and it is possible that you will experience one of them. If you have the need or you are in danger at a place between Ashiehtah and Gunduktha which is the last village of Tkhoma, and no-one can help you, then say to the first person that you meet that *Ruh 'i kulyan* [Kurdish: Spirit of the Cave] will protect you. If he does not listen to you then go on until you find someone that will aid you."

"*Ruh 'i kulyan*? 'The Spirit of the Cave'? Who carries this strange name?" I asked the centenarian.

"No one will be able to tell you."

"But you speak of him and can surely give me some information?"

"*Ruh 'i kulyan* is a being that no-one knows. He is sometimes here, sometimes there, wherever someone is in need who deserves to have his plea fulfilled. In many villages there is a special place where once can speak with him at certain times. Those that are in need go there around midnight to tell him what they desire. He then gives counsel and comfort, but he also knows how to threaten and to punish and many a mighty man does what is desired of him. He is never spoken off in the presence of a stranger for only the good and the friendly may know where he is to be found."

"Then your secret will be of little use to me."

"Why?"

"No one would tell me where to find him although it will be clear to everyone that I know his name."

"Then say that I have spoken to you of him; then the place where he can be found will be revealed to you. My name is known in the whole land of Tijari, and the righteous know that they can trust my friends."

"And what is your name?"

"I am called Marah Durimeh."

That was a mysterious bit of information, but it sounded so fantastic that I did not think it of much value. I said my goodbye and returned to my abode. Once there, I noted more than the usual noise coming from the kitchen. Something must have happened to the fine 'Myrte', to awaken her displeasure. In the current circumstances, even the tiniest event could have some value to me and so I entered the kitchen. Mersinah was scolding the brave Agha that much was obvious immediately. She stood before him and wagged her fists at him in a threatening gesture and he stood there with downcast eyes, like a boy receiving a rebuke from a parent. 'Myrte' saw me enter and immediately drew me into the argument.

"Will you look at this Selim Agha!"

She indicated the poor sinner in a manner equal to an emperor, then turned her head to the right and looked at him accusingly.

"Is this man an Agha of the Arnauts?" she asked disdainfully.

"Yes."

I provided this answer in a tone of certainty of course, but this tone appeared to cause a relapse of her rapture.

"What! So you too believe him to be the commander of valiant warriors? I will tell you what he is; he is an Agha of cowards!"

The Agha opened his eyes and tried to muster a gaze of contempt. It almost succeeded.

"Don't make me angry, Mersinah, for you know too well that I will be terrible then!"

"And what is the cause of your anger?" I dared to ask.

"These fifty piaster!" answered 'Myrte', while she pointed at the ground with disdain.

I looked down and saw two silver twenty- and another silver ten-piaster coin on the ground.

"What about this money?"

"It came from the *Mutesselim*."

Now I began to understand the rest and asked:

"What for?"

"For the capture of the *Makrej*. *Effendi*, you know roughly how much money that one carried on his person?"

"I guess that it was roughly twenty-four-thousand piaster."

"Then Selim has told me the truth. That hoard, that immense hoard of money the Commandant has taken from the *Makrej* and from that he gave this brave Agha of the Arnauts fifty piaster!"

With these words her facial expression changed into a display of contempt. She kicked the coins away and asked me:

"And do you know what this Agha of the Arnauts has done?"

"What?"

"He took the money and departed without saying a word! Ask him if I tell you a lie!"

"What else should I have done?" Selim excused himself.

"Thrown the money at his beard! I surely would have done that. Do you believe it, *Effendi*?"

"I believe it!"

I spoke the truth with that assurance. She honored me with a gaze of thankfulness and then asked:

"Shall he return it to him?"

"No."

"No?"

I turned to the Agha:

"Have you signed the statement that the Commandant is to send to Mosul?"

"Yes."

"How much has he reported?"

"Four-hundred piaster in gold and eighty-one piaster in silver."

"Nothing else?"

"No."

"The watch and the rings?"

"Not even these."

"He is your superior and you must not make an enemy of him; that is why it is good that you have taken the money without argument. Do you remember what I have promised you?"

"I do!"

"I will keep my word and I will speak with the Commandant. You shall at least receive a thousand piaster."

"Is that true, *Effendi*?" asked Mersinah.

"Yes. The money neither belongs to the *Mutesselim* or the Agha, certainly it comes into the hands of those who have no right to it and so it should remain where it is. But the Agha shall not be cheated in such a despicable manner!"

"But he should have received seven-thousand piaster?"

"Those he will never receive. That was just a ruse. Selim, has the *Bash Jaush* already departed?"

"No, *Effendi*."

"But he should have departed before noon today."

"The *Mutesselim* has to write a new report since he said that he would send the Arab in the original. Perhaps the *Bash Jaush* is to wait until we have caught the escapee."

"There would be little hope of that."

"Why?"

"Because he plunged to his death in the ravine."

"And if we are mistaken in that assumption?"

"How so?"

"The *Mutesselim* now believes that he still lives."

"Has he told you some more details regarding this?"

"No; but I did gather this from the way he spoke."

"Then I hope that he is not mistaken!"

I went to my room. Was a careless act of mine or of us responsible for arousing the Commandant's suspicion? It was possible. But then it would be advisable that we prepared ourselves for anything. But before I could inform my companions, I mentally reviewed all that had transpired. I could think of nothing obvious and I was still contemplating the past events when the Agha ascended the stairs and entered my room.

"*Effendi*, a messenger has come from the *Mutesselim*. He says that we are to join him in the prison."

"Is he already there?"

"Yes."

"Wait for me downstairs. I will come at once!"

Was this request made in friendship or with animosity? I decided to be prepared for the latter. Both my revolvers were loaded. I also armed myself with my pistols and then went to see Halef. He was alone in his room.

"Where is the *Buluk-Emini*?"

"The *Bash Jaush* came to fetch him."

That was not suspicious in itself but yet it was to me because of my own state of mind.

"How long ago?"

"Immediately after you went to buy the horse."

"Come with me to the Haddedihn's room!"

The Arab was lying on the floor, smoking his pipe.

"Emir," he greeted me, "Allah has not granted me patience to wait for the things I desire. What else do we need to do in this city?"

"Perhaps we will leave it shortly. It almost looks like we have been discovered."

Now he arose slowly in the manner of a man who may be surprised but who is yet strong enough to suppress this emotion and face its consequences.

"And from what do you determine this, *Effendi*?"

"I only suspect it for the moment. The Commandant has sent for me and asked that I should come to the prison where he waits for me. I will go, but I will be cautious. If I do not return within the hour, then something bad has happened to me."

"Then I shall come and find you!" cried Halef.

"You may not be able to get to me, for perhaps I might be inside the prison, and this time as a prisoner. You may then decide: - either you flee or you try to free me."

"We will not leave you!" assured the Haddedihn.

As he now stood, so proud and straight; with his long white beard cascading down to his belt, he was the very picture of a daring, yet prudent man.

"I thank you! If they should take me prisoner, it would only be after a fierce struggle, that much is certain. I would definitely resist being bound and if I am not bound, then it would be possible for me to indicate the cell in which I am held."

"How will you do that, *Sihdi*?" asked Halef.

"I will try to climb up the wall and give you a sign by pushing one of my garments as far as possible out of the hole so that you can see it. Perhaps it may be possible to send you a message via the Agha or even Mersinah. I would certainly not be a prisoner for long. But whatever the situation, always keep your horses saddled. Think about the situation further on your own; I do not have the time to discuss it further now for the *Mutesselim* is waiting and I still have to speak to the Englishman."

And he too sat on his carpet and smoked his pipe.

"Nice that you come, Sir!" he greeted me. "Want to go!"

"Why?"

"Its eerie here!"

"Make yourself clear!"

He arose, walked up to the open window and pointed to the roof of the house opposite.

"Look there!"

I scrutinized the roof and recognized the shape of an Arnaut who was lying on his belly and watched our rooms.

"Will also climb onto our roof," said Lindsay calmly, "and send that man a bullet!"

"I will now go to the prison where the *Mutesselim* awaits me. If I am not back within the hour then something happened to me and I am stuck. In that case I will push some piece of my clothing out of the hole in which I sit. You should be able to see it from the rear windows or from the roof."

"Very nice; will be great fun; shall get to know Master Lindsay!"

"Try to make yourself understood to Halef. He does speak a few words of English."

"Will make pantomime. Yes!"

I departed. Three men on whom I could depend were watching over me. Besides, Amadijah was almost deserted; half the garrison was under the influence of the fever and the *Mutesselim* I could handle by myself.

Selim Agha already waited by the door. My two conversations had taken longer than he liked and now he tried to make up the lost time with a rapid pace.

Just like earlier this morning, the Commandant again stood by the prison gate. He stepped back when he saw us coming. Since leaving my abode I had carefully scrutinized the surroundings but had not noted any man that might have had instructions to watch me. The two lanes through which we passed were deserted, and even near the prison no one could be seen. The Commandant greeted me very respectfully but with my heightened distrust, I soon discovered that there was some guile behind this formality.

"*Effendi*," he commenced as soon as he had locked the door behind me, "we did not find the body of the escaped prisoner."

"You have searched for it in the ravine?"

"Yes. People were lowered into it with ropes. The prisoner was not there."

"But his clothes were!"

"Perhaps he had just discarded them there!"

"Then he must have had other garments!"

"And perhaps he did. Yesterday a new suit of clothes was purchased."

He carefully studied my face for a reaction. He certainly thought that I would betray myself by a facial expression; but to the contrary, he had exposed himself to me by this very question, for I now knew what I could expect of him.

"For him?" I asked with an incredulous smile.

"I believe so. Yes, even a horse was purchased!"

"For him as well?"

"I believe so. And it is still in the city."

"He therefore intends to ride right through the city gate? Oh, *Mutesselim*, I believe that your system is suffering still. I will have to send you some more medicine!"

"I will never again drink such a medicine," he answered somewhat embarrassed. "I am convinced that he managed to escape from the prison but that he is still inside the city walls."

"And you know how he managed to escape?"

"No; but I am certain that neither the Agha nor the guards are to blame for his success."

"And where should he be hiding?"

"That I will yet discover and you shall help me, *Effendi*."

"I? Gladly, if I can."

I had quickly glanced at the top of the stairs when I first entered the prison and had seen many Arnauts gathered there. Obviously the intent was to make me a prisoner. I was further convinced of this by the careless talk of the

Commandant. A quick glance at the Agha's face revealed that he at least knew nothing of the *Mutesselim's* plan. So he too was under suspicion, and from that I deduced that the fugitive was believed to be on his rooms or mine.

"I have heard," continued the Commandant, "that you are a great and experienced tracker."

"Who has told you this?"

"Your *Bashi-Bozuk*, has heard this from your servant Halef."

So he had interrogated the *Bashi-Bozuk*. So that was why the *Bash Jaush* had fetched him! The Commandant continued:

"And that is why I beg you to look around the prison."

"But I have already done so!"

"But not carefully, as it needs to be done when one wants to discover any evidence. Then the tiniest thing might be of the greatest importance."

"That is true. So you desire that I search the whole building?"

"Yes. But you would probably want to first start with the pit in which he was, for there the escape began."

Oh, you clever Turk! Behind me, on the steps, I heard some soft crunching. The Arnauts were descending the stairs in a careful manner.

"That is quite right," I admitted quite nonchalantly. "Open the door to the cell!"

"Open up, Selim Agha!" he ordered.

The Agha pushed back the bolts and opened the door wide so that it was flush with the wall.

I stepped closer, but did so carefully so that a quick push could not topple me into the pit, then I scrutinized the pit.

"I see nothing noticeable here, *Mutesselim*!"

"From up here you can't see it very well. You will probably need to go right into it, *Effendi*!"

"If you think that it is important, I will do so," I replied without concern.

I stepped to the side and grabbed hold of the door, lifted it from its hinges and laid it lengthwise before the opening so that I could keep a close eye on it. That, the good Commandant had not expected; a big fat line had been drawn through his scheming.

"What are you doing?" he asked both disappointedly and angrily.

"I have taken the door off its hinges, as you can see," I answered.

"Why?"

"Oh, when one looks for evidence, one has to be very careful and keep an eye on everything!"

"But taking the door off is not necessary. You don't get any more light than you had before."

"That is right! But do you know what evidence is most clear?"

"Which?"

"That which one reads in the face of men. And those" I tapped his shoulder in confidently, "an *Effendi* from Germanistan knows to read very well."

"What do you mean by that?" he asked in dismay.

"I mean that I consider you to be a great diplomat. You know how to keep your secrets and intentions well. And that is why I will do as you ask and jump into the pit."

"What do you mean by 'intentions'?"

"Your wisdom has led you to the correct conclusion that only a prisoner could best discover how one could possibly escape from in there. Allah be praised that he created such clever men!"

I leapt down into the pit and bent down as though I intended to inspect the floor. But I kept an eye on the doorway and soon I noted that the *Mutesselim* made hand motions to the Agha. Both bent and intended to lift the heavy door and place it back onto its hinges. I turned around.

"*Mutesselim*, leave the door where it is!"

"It shall go where it belongs."

"Then I will go where I belong!"

I made a move as though I desired to leap from the pit, of course this was not an easy thing to do as the pit was quite deep.

"Stop, you stay!" he ordered me and waved his arm, at which a few armed Arnauts came running. "You are my prisoner!"

The good Selim was startled. He stared first at the *Mutesselim* and then at me.

"Your prisoner?" I asked. "You jest!"

"I am quite serious!"

"Then you have become mad overnight! How can you presume that you are the man that can take me prisoner!"

"You are already captured and will not be free again until the fugitive is caught."

"*Mutesselim*, I don't believe that you will catch him!"

"Why not?"

"Because for that a man with courage and wisdom is required, and with these two qualities Allah has seen fit not to burden you."

"Are you making fun of me? See how far you get with your own wisdom! Put the door back and bolt it!"

Now I pulled one of the pistols from my belt.

"I advise you, to leave the door where it is!"

The brave Arnauts, quite embarrassed, remained where they were.

"Put your hands to it, you dogs!" he ordered most threateningly.

"Don't let yourself be shot, you people!" I said whilst I cocked the pistol.

"Dare to shoot!" shouted the *Mutesselim*.

"Dare? Oh, *Mutesselim*, that is not a daring exploit. I will deal with these people quite well, and you will be the first that is struck by my bullet!"

The effect was characteristic of this daring hero of Amadijah, he immediately disappeared from the open doorway. Only his voice could now be heard:

"Lock him in, you scoundrels!"

"Don't do it, you men, for then I will shoot the first one who dares to close the door and surely send him to *Jehennah*!"

"Then you shoot back!" the voice sounded from the side.

"*Mutesselim*, don't forget who I am! Any harm to my person will cost you your head."

"Will you obey, you knaves! Or shall it be I who shoots you? Selim Agha, lend a hand!"

The nephew of the brother-in-law, of the sister of the grandson, of the mother of the stepsister of 'Myrte' had followed the example of his superior and had pressed himself against the wall some distance away. He certainly was now in some embarrassing difficulty from which I had to rescue him.

"Step aside you men for here I come!"

I pointed the maw of my weapon at them and the doorway thus became deserted. After a short and quick moment of exertion I was out of the pit and stood before the Commandant, holding my pistol under his nose.

"*Mutesselim*, I have not found any evidence down there!"

"*Allah illa Allah*! *Emir*, put that weapon away!"

The fact that he had a similar shooting iron in his belt with which he could defend himself apparently escaped him.

"It only gets put back in its place when the guards have returned upstairs. Selim Agha, lead them away!"

This order the Agha obeyed immediately:

"Get going and don't show your faces again!"

They quickly retreated up the stairs.

"There, now I will put my weapon away. Oh, *Mutesselim*, how you have disgraced yourself now! Your ruse failed, your might was useless and now you stand there like a *Fakara günakiar* [poor sinner], who has to beg for mercy. Why did you want to have me locked up?"

"Because I have to search your premises."

"And may I not be there when you do?"

"You would have prevented it."

"Ah, so you have respect for me? I like that very much! And you think that the others would not have objected?"

"You are the worst, but they would have been afraid."

"You are much mistaken, *Mutesselim*. I am the most congenial of them all. My Hajji Halef Omar is a hero; Hajji Lindsay-*Bei* is a brute, and the third, which you have not yet seen, exceeds them both. You would have departed from that company only as a corpse! How long did you think that I would have stayed in this hole?"

"As long as I desired!"

"You think so? You see these weapons and this bag of bullets! I would have shot out the bolts or the hinges and stood where I am standing now inside of two minutes. And then at my first shot, my people would have known that I was in danger. They would have hurried here to help me."

"They could not have entered."

"A bullet from a rifle would have easily opened your old lock. Come here, I will show you something!"

I turned him towards the cell and pointed at the hole that served as a window. Through it a little area of the sky could be seen; but now one could also see a figure clad in checkered red and black, holding a gun in its hand and intently watching the prison.

"Do you know that man?" I asked.

"Hajji Lindsay-*Bei*!"

"Yes, it is he. He stands on the roof of our abode and awaits a prearranged sign from me. *Mutesselim*, your life hangs by a hair. What do you have against me?"

"You have freed the prisoner!"

"Who says this?"

"I have witnesses."

"Must you hold me captive, me, an *Effendi* and a *Bei*, an Emir, who ranks far higher than you, who possesses the *Bu-djeruldi* of the Sultan and who has given you ample proof that he fears no man?"

"Yes, you are afraid of no man, and precisely because of that we had to keep you safe whilst we searched your rooms."

"You can search them in my presence!"

"Lord, now I will not do so. I will send my people."

Ah, he was now afraid of the hero and the brute and him who exceeded both.

"Even that I would permit, if it was done without causing a lot of fuss. They can rummage around in every corner; I have nothing against that. You see, *Mutesselim*, you don't have to lock me up!"

"I did not know that!"

"But your biggest mistake was to believe that I was so blind and that I would permit you to lock me up without objection. Don't try that again, for I tell you: your life hangs by a hair."

"But, Emir, if we discover the fugitive in your abode then we will have to take you into custody!"

"Then I would not resist."

"And I can not let you return to your rooms now."

"Why not?"

"I must be certain that you do not give the order to hide the fugitive."

"Good. But I tell you that my companions will not allow the searching of our rooms without my being there. Quite to the contrary, they would rather shoot anyone who dares to enter them."

"So write a note to them, tell them to permit my people to enter!"

"That I could do. Selim Agha can take the letter to them immediately."

"No. Not him!"

"And why not?"

"He could be involved and warn them."

"Oh, the Agha is loyal to you and knows not to speak or omit a single word regarding the fugitive! Is that not true, Selim Agha?"

"Lord," Selim said to his superior, "I swear that I know nothing and that the *Effendi* is innocent as well!"

"The latter you can not swear to, but the first I will believe for your sake. Emir, you will accompany me to my palace where we will discuss this matter further. I will present your accusers to you ."

"That I would demand as well!"

"One of them you can hear immediately."

"Who is it?"

"The Arnaut, who sits in that pit because of you."

"Ah! That one?"

"Yes. I investigated every cell today and asked every prisoner if they had noticed anything unusual. I asked him too and I heard something from him which is very bad for you."

"He seeks revenge! But would it not be better to send a guard to my rooms first? If I were to write a letter, a misunderstanding might arise, or my companions might think that it was written by someone else."

"They would believe the guard even less!"

"I don't mean that either. This man should fetch my servant so that he can assure himself that I permit the searching of my rooms."

"You will speak to him in my presence?"

"Yes."

"Then I will have him brought here."

He called one of the Arnauts over to him and gave the requisite order; then Selim Agha had to open the dungeon in which the erstwhile *Khawass* of the Englishman was incarcerated.

"Stand up," ordered the Mutesselim, "and answer my questions fully! Do you still maintain what you have told me earlier?"

"Yes."

"Repeat it!"

"The man, that you call Hajji Lindsay-*Bei* is an *Inglis*. On leaving Mosul, he took me and a translator along and to the latter he said that he was searching for a man that was on a journey to free a prisoner."

So, Master Fowling-bull has had a loose tongue!

"Did he name this man?" I asked the Arnaut.

"No."

"Did the translator speak the name of the prisoner that should be freed?"

"No."

"And not even the place where this prisoner is?"

"No."

"*Mutesselim*, does this Arnaut have anything else to say?"

"That is all."

"No; that is nothing! Selim Agha, lock up! Oh, *Mutesselim*, you are truly a great diplomat, of whose merit I will boast much in Stambul! They will hurry to provide you with an even higher rank than you have now. Perhaps the Padishah will elevate you to be the Viceroy of Baghdad. Hajji Lindsay-*Bei* seeks a man. Has he said that I am this man? This man wants to free a prisoner. Has he said that it is your prisoner? Would an *Inglis* leave his motherland, a land almost a thousand day's camel ride distant from here, to free an Arab from captivity? When he departed his country he had never even seen an Arab."

"But you, you are a friend of Amad el Ghandur?"

"I tell you that I have never seen him before I laid eyes on him here in this pit! Hajji Lindsay-*Bei* does not understand Turkish, or Arabic, and his translator could not speak good English. Who knows what this man heard or what he understood. Perhaps the Hajji merely told him a fairy tale."

"But he does not speak!"

"Back then he did. He made his vow much later."

"Then come, you shall also hear the other witness! Someone is rapping on the door. It must be your servant."

He opened the gate. The Arnaut had brought Halef to whom I said that I was in agreement with the search of our rooms and I added:

"I wish to prove to the *Mutesselim* that I am his friend. His people shall be allowed to search everywhere. Now go!"

"And where are you going now?"

"To the *Mutesselim*."

"When will you return?"

"I don't know yet."

"In an hour much can be discussed and much can happen. If you are not back within this time, then I will come and fetch you!"

He departed. The Commandant was clearly very doubtful now. The resolute bearing of my little Halef had impressed him.

In the anteroom of his *Selamlük* several officers and servants were gathered. He called one of the officers over to him with a gesture, that one also entered the *Selamlük* with us. We sat down, but I did not receive a pipe this time.

"This is the man!" said the Mutesselim, whilst he indicated the officer.

"What of this man?"

"Who has seen you."

"Where?"

"In the lane leading away from the prison. Ibrahim, you tell it!"

The officer saw that I was free and he looked at me with uncertainty whilst he recited his report:

"I came from the palace, Lord. It was very late when I opened my door. Just when I was about to close it again I heard hurried steps approaching. There were two men who were walking quite fast; one pulled the other along and the other was out of breath. When they had turned the corner I heard a raven croak."

"Have you recognized the two men?"

"Only this *Effendi*. It was dark but I recognized him from his build."

"And what was the build of the other?"

"Shorter."

"Did they see you?"

"No, for I stood behind the door."

"You can go!"

The man left.

"Now, Emir, what do you say?"

"I was with you the whole evening!"

"But you were gone for a few minutes when you went to fetch the lamp. I suspect that you spirited the prisoner away during that time and you did so in a hurry since I was waiting for you."

I laughed.

"Oh, *Mutesselim*, when will you become a good diplomat! I can see that your system truly does need some fortification. Permit me to ask a few questions."

"Speak."

"Who had the key to the prison gate?"

"I did."

"Could I leave, even if I wanted to?"

"No," he answered hesitantly.

"With whom did I go to my rooms?"

"With Selim Agha."

"Is this Agha of the Arnauts taller or shorter than I?"

"Shorter."

"And now, Agha, I ask you: Did we walk slowly like snails or did we walk quickly?"

"Quickly," he answered.

"Did we lead each other or not?"

"We led each other."

"*Mutesselim*, can a raven who croaks in his sleep or his dreams have anything at all to do with the fugitive?"

"Emir, that fits perfectly!" he answered.

"No, that does not fit perfectly, rather it is so simple and so natural that I am alarmed at the pettiness of your thoughts! I am quite worried about you! You had the key, and no one could leave the prison; that you had to know. I went home with the Agha, through the very lane in which that man lives; that too you knew. And based on a tale that only served to justify me, you wanted to condemn me? I was your friend. I gave you gifts; I led the *Makrej*, whose capture most likely brings you great honor and promotion, into your hands; I gave you medicine, to bring joy to your soul, and for all of this you thank me by trying to imprison me. Get away! You drive me insane! And what is equally bad is that you even put your own Agha of the Arnauts under suspicion, your own Agha of whose loyalty you know, and who would fight for you, even if he would loose his own life!"

Selim Agha straightened himself and grew a whole inch.

"Yes, that is true!" he affirmed, whilst he slapped his saber and rolled his eyes. "My life belongs to you, Lord. For you I give it gladly!"

That was too much proof. The Commandant proffered his hand to me and begged:

"Forgive me, Emir! You are vindicated, and I will not have your rooms searched!"

"You will have them searched. I demand it myself now!"

"But it is superfluous now!"

"I stand firm by my demand."

The *Mutesselim* arose and left the room.

"*Effendi*, I thank you, for clearing me from this suspicion!" the Agha said.

"You will soon hear that I will even do more for you."

When the Commandant returned, he wore a very morose expression and said:

"A *Bash Jaush* stands outside who is to go to Mosul ... "

"The one that fetched my *Bashi-Bozuk*," I interrupted him, "so that you could interrogate him! Have you heard a single word from him that puts me under suspicion?"

"No, he was full of praise for you. But tell me what I should write to Anadoli Kasi Askeri about the escaped prisoner!"

"Write the truth!"

"That would be most damaging to me, *Effendi*. Don't you think that I could write that he died?"

"That is your own business!"

"Would you betray me?"

"I don't have any reason to do so as long as you are my friend."

"I will do it!"

"But what if you are lucky enough to catch him? Or if he successfully reaches his home?"

"Then the deposed *Mutessarif* was mistaken and sent me a man he thought to be Amad el Ghandur, but who was not. And if I manage to catch him again ... *Effendi*, it would be best if I did not even search for him at all!"

That was the true Turkish manner, to finesse oneself out of trouble; but to me this was now most welcome.

"But the *Bash Jaush* knows that the Arab escaped?"

"That was another Arab, not a Haddedihn, but rather an Abu Salman, who denied me taxes."

"Then hurry, so that you dispose of your worry about the *Makrej*. If he too should be successful in escaping, then you are doomed."

"The convoy should leave within the hour."

"Have you already prepared the statement of all the *Makrej* had on his person?"

"It is complete and has already been signed by me and Selim Agha."

"You have forgotten one signature, *Mutesselim*."

"Which one?"

"Mine."

"Oh, *Effendi*, yours is not necessary."

"But desirable."

"For what reason?"

"I could be asked about this in Mosul or Stambul, if something were to be questionable. Then it would be better if I signed now; then everything will be in order. Even for you it must be a welcome opportunity to have one more witness; for I trust that the *Makrej* will no doubt slander you to get his revenge."

The Commandant was now in a most embarrassing situation.

"The statement is already closed and sealed," he said.

"Show me!"

He arose and went into an adjoining room.

"*Effendi*," the Agha whispered fearfully, "do not betray the fact that I told you everything."

"Don't worry!"

The *Mutesselim* returned carrying a sealed parchment. He handed it to me without a second thought.

I took it to assure myself that it was the correct one. I pressed the folded sides so that it formed a tube and I could see the inside, since it was not in an envelope. I discovered from some of the words that I could read that the Commandant had not deceived me, yet the numbers I was looking for were not visible. Despite that, I pretended that I could see them and slowly voiced them aloud:

"Four-hundred piaster in gold ... eighty-one piaster in silver ... ! *Mutesselim*, you will have to open this statement; you have made an error!"

"Lord, this matter does not concern you but only me!"

"Then it only concerned me that I stood by you and held the *Makrej* down whilst you took his money?"

"Yes," he answered naively.

"Good! But you promised me five thousand piaster, to which another two thousand were to be added as the paper money did not have the full value. Where is this sum?"

"Emir!"

"*Mutesselim*!"

"You said that you were my friend and yet you wish to torment me!"

"You said you were my friend and yet you tried to deceive me!"

"I must send the money to Mosul."

"Four-hundred-and-eighty-one piaster, yes. But your duty is to send all of the *Makrej's* money, including his watch and rings. If you do this I demand nothing; if you don't then I demand my rightful share."

"You are not entitled to anything," he declared.

"And neither are you, nor Selim Agha. Did he receive something?"

"Seven-thousand piaster in paper money," he answered quickly in order to cut off the Agha's answer. The latter made such a face that I almost burst out laughing.

"Well then," I said, "why do you withhold my share?"

"You are a foreigner and not one of my officers."

"You shall be proved right; but then I assign my share to the Padishah. Tell the *Bash Jaush* that he should come to my rooms before he departs. I wish to give him my report to Anadoli Kasi Askeri. Farewell, *Mutesselim*, and permit me to visit you this evening."

I went toward the door but had not yet reached it when he called to me:

"How much money will you report?"

"The complete sum of twenty-five-thousand piaster, a watch and four diamond rings."

"How much of it do you want?"

"My full share. Seven-thousand piaster in paper, or five-thousand in gold or silver."

"*Effendi*, truly there was not that much gold!"

"I can discern the sound of gold from that of silver quite well, and the bag had a substantial circumference."

"You are rich, Emir, and will be happy with five-hundred piaster!"

"Two-thousand in gold, that is my last offer!"

"*Allah kerihm*, I can not!"

"Farewell!"

Again I went toward the door. He waited until I had opened it before he called me back. Yet I walked on and I was already in the street when hurried steps sounded behind me. It was Selim Agha who came to get me.

When I again entered the *Selamlük*, the Commandant was not there, but soon he came from the small room next door. His gaze was sinister and full of animosity, his voice quivered hoarsely when he asked me:

"So you want two-thousand?"

"In gold!"

He sat down and counted out twenty one hundred piaster coins onto the carpet.

I bent, picked them up and pocketed them. He waited a moment and then asked in a sinister tone:

"And you don't show your gratitude?"

"I? I expect your gratitude instead since I gifted you three-thousand piaster!"

"You have been paid and have given me nothing. When do you leave?"

"I don't know yet."

"I would advise you to leave the city this day!"

"Why?"

"You have your gold, now go! And don't ever return!"

"*Mutesselim*, leave this farce, otherwise I return the piaster and write my report. If I desire to stay, I will stay, and when I come to visit you, you will receive me graciously. But to save your heart further worry, I will tell you that I will depart this day. But before I do, I will come to you once again to take my leave, and I hope that we will part in peace."

I now left him and returned to my companions. Before I reached the house, I encountered a troop of Arnauts, that timidly made way for me so that I could pass. Mersinah stood by the door and watched them. Her face seethed with anger.

"Emir, has something like this ever happened before?" she snorted in my direction.

"What?"

"That a *Mutesselim* searches the home of his Agha of the Arnauts?"

"I don't know, oh angel of this house, for I never was an Agha of the Arnauts."

"And do you know what they searched for?"

"Well?"

"For the escaped Arab! To search for the fugitive in the house of the guard! But when this Selim Agha comes home, I will tell him what I would have done in his place."

"Don't bicker with him. He suffered enough."

"With what?"

"That I and my companions depart."

"You?"

She pulled an indescribably shocked face.

"Yes. The *Mutesselim* and I quarreled and I don't like to remain any longer in the place where he rules."

"*Allah, Tallah, Wallah*! Lord, stay. I will force this man to treat you with respect!"

That was a promise that would have been most interesting to see carried out. But I unfortunately thought it impossible and left Mersinah standing downstairs where her voice continued to grumble like distant thunder. Above, the *Bashi-Bozuk* stood by the head of the stairs. He had heard my voice and now waited for me.

"*Effendi*, I will take my leave from you!"

"Come in; I will pay you!"

"Oh, Emir, I have already been paid."

"By whom?"

"By the man with the long face."

"How much has he given to you?"

"This!"

With a sparkle in his eyes he pulled a handful of silver coins from belt and showed them to me.

"Then come. As the man with the long face has paid you, I will pay for your donkey."

"*Allah kerihm*, I will not sell it!" he cried in surprise.

"I only mean that I will pay its due wage!"

"*Mash Allah*, then I come!"

He accompanied me to my room, which was empty. There I wrote a reference for him and gave him some more money, which overjoyed him.

"Emir, I have never met such a good *Effendi* as you. I wish you were my captain or my major or my colonel! Then I would protect you in battle like that time, when I lost my nose. That was a really great battle at ... "

"Let it be, my good Ifra. I am completely convinced of your heroism. You were with the *Mutesselim* today?"

"The *Bash Jaush* came to fetch me and asked me many questions."

"About what?"

"Whether a prisoner was with you; if you killed many Turks with the *Jesidi*; if you were perhaps a minister from Stambul, and still much more than I can remember."

"Your journey, Ifra, will take you through Spandareh. Tell the village elder there, that I start for Gumri today, and that I have already sent his gift to the *Bei* of Gumri. Also, in Baadri you go to Ali *Bei*, to attest to that which Selek will tell him."

"Does he go too?"

"Yes; where is he?"

"With his horse."

"Tell him that he can saddle up. I will give him a letter. Now farewell, Ifra. Allah protect you and your donkey. May you never forget that a rock should be tied to its tail!" ...

My three companions were gathered in the Englishman's room, ready for battle. Halef embraced me joyfully, and the Englishman proffered his hand with happiness written all over his face, so that I could not mistake his great concern for me.

"Were in danger, Sir?"

"I was stuck in the same hole from which I rescued Amad el Ghandur."

"Ah! Wonderful adventure! Was prisoner! How long?"

"Two minutes."

"Freed yourself?"

"Entirely! Shall I tell you the story?"

"Of course! Well! Yes! Nice land here, very nice! Better adventures every day!"

I told him everything in English and then added:

"We will depart within the hour."

The face of the Englishman took on the shape of an extraordinarily frightful question mark.

"To Gumri." I added.

"Oh, was nice here, very nice! Interesting!"

"Only yesterday you thought it was not so nice here, Master Lindsay!"

"Was frustrated! Had nothing to do! Still was nice though, very nice! Romantic! Yes! What's it like in Gumri?"

"Even more romantic."

"Well! Then we go there!"

He arose immediately to see to his horse, and now I had time to tell the other two about my experiences. None were as happy about our imminent departure as Mohammed Emin, whose heartfelt desire it was to join his son as soon as possible. Even he arose hurriedly to ready himself for the journey. I now returned to my room and wrote a letter to Ali *Bei*. I reported everything to him in a condensed manner and thanked him for the two letters, which were of great use to me. This letter, as well as the other two, I handed to Selek who immediately departed Amadijah. He did not join the convoy, but rather preferred to ride alone like a true *Jesidi*.

The steps of two people echoed outside. Selim Agha and Mersinah entered my room.

"*Effendi*, is it truly your intention to leave Amadijah?" Selim asked me.

"You have heard it when you were with the *Mutesselim*."

"They are already saddling up!" sobbed 'Myrte', who tried to wipe her eyes with her hand but unfortunately only got as far as the equally sad, dripping nose.

"Where do you go from here?"

"That, the *Mutesselim* need not know, Selim Agha. We ride towards Gumri."

"You will not reach it today."

"Then we stay somewhere on the road tonight."

"Lord," begged Mersinah, "stay at least this night with us. I will cook my best pillau for you."

"It is decided: we ride."

"Surely you don't fear the *Mutesselim*?"

"He knows best that I do not fear him!"

"And I do too, Lord," the Agha put in; "you have squeezed two-thousand piaster from him!"

'Myrte' was astounded, her eyes grew in size.

"*Mash Allah*, what a sum!"

"And even in gold!" added Selim.

"To whom does this money belong?"

"To the Emir of course! Emir, if you would have only spoken for me also!"

"Have you not done so, *Effendi*?" inquired Mersinah. "You had promised us that you would!"

"And I have kept my word."

"Really? Emir, when did you speak with the *Mutesselim*?"

"When Selim Agha was there."

"Lord, I heard nothing!" Selim protested.

"*Mash Allah*, have you suddenly become deaf! The *Mutesselim* offered me five-hundred piaster instead of the five-thousand I demanded!"

"That was for yourself, *Effendi*!"

"Selim Agha, you have said: you like me and are friend, and yet you believe that I do not keep my word? I had to pretend that it was for me!"

"Pretend ... ?"

He stared at me as though he had become stone.

"Pretend?" shouted Mersinah. But it dawned upon her faster than Selim. "But why did you need to pretend? Pray tell, Emir!"

"That I have already explained to the Agha ... "

"*Effendi*," she cried, "don't explain anything else to this Agha of the Arnauts, for he will never understand anything! Rather tell me!"

"If I had demanded the money for the Agha, then the *Mutesselim* would have become his enemy ... "

"That is right, *Effendi*," she interrupted quickly. "Yes, it would have even gone worse, for after your departure he would have had to return the money."

"I thought so too, and thus I pretended that I demanded the money for myself."

“And it really was not for you? Oh, say it quickly!”

Every bone in this noble 'Myrte' quivered with greed.

“It was for the Agha.”

“*Mash Allah*! Is this true?”

“Of course!”

“And he shall receive more money on top of the fifty piaster?”

“Much more.”

“How much?”

“Everything.”

“*Allah illa Allah*! When, when?”

“Right now.”

“*Hamdullillah*, Allah be praised! He makes us rich through you! But now you have to give it to us too!”

“Here it is. Come, Selim Agha!”

I counted the full sum into his hand. He tried to close his hand quickly, but he was too slow, for 'Myrte' managed to swipe all of the one hundred piaster coins from his hand with a single deft movement.

“Mersinah!” he thundered.

“Selim Agha!” she flashed back.

“It is mine!” he growled.

“And it shall remain yours!” she assured him.

“I can look after it myself!” he mumbled.

“It is safer with me!” she consoled him.

“Give me some of it!” he begged.

“Just leave it with me!” she said affectionately.

“Then at least give me the fifty piaster from yesterday!”

“And you shall have them, Selim Agha!”

“All of it?”

“All of it; except for the twenty-three that are already gone.”

“All of it! And twenty-three are already gone from it! Where are they?”

“Gone! On flour and water for the prisoners.”

“For water? That does not cost anything!”

“Nothing is free for the prisoners; remember that, Selim Agha! But, Emir, now you don't have anything!”

Now that she had the money in her hands, she was considerate of me.

“I don't want it. Yes, I may not even take of it.”

“You may not? Why?”

"My belief does not permit it."

"Your belief? *Allah illa Allah*! Faith does not forbid the taking of money!"

"Oh yes! This money does neither belong to the *Makrej*, who certainly did not obtain it through just means, or to the *Mutesselim* or to the Agha. But it would certainly disappear and would never have returned to the rightful owner. That is the only reason I forced the *Mutesselim* to part with a portion of it. If it should be in the wrong hands, then it is better that you have a part of it, instead of the *Mutesselim* keeping it all."

"*Effendi*, that is a nice belief!" Mersinah assured me. "You are a faithful adherent of the Prophet. May Allah bless you for that!"

"Listen, Mersinah! If I would have been an adherent of the Prophet then you would have received nothing, rather I would have filled my own pockets. I am no Moslem."

"Not a Moslem!" she cried in amazement. "What then?"

"A Christian."

"*Mash Allah*! Are you a *Nessorah* [Nestorian]?"

"No. My belief is different from the *Nessorah*."

"Then you believe in the holy *Omm Allah Marryam* [Mother of God, Mary]?"

"Yes."

"Oh, Emir, the Christians who believe in her are all good people!"

"How do you know this?"

"I see it from your example and I also know it from the old Marah Durimeh."

"Ah! Do you know her?"

"She is well known in Amadijah. She comes rarely, but when she does come, then she brings joy to all that meet her. She too believes in *Omm Allah Marryam* and she is a blessing to many. But I just remembered that I have to go to her!"

"She is already gone."

"Yes, she departed; but yet I must go non-the-less."

"Why?"

"I have to tell of your leaving."

"Who has asked for this?"

"The father of the girl whose life you saved."

"Stay here!"

"I must go!"

"Mersinah, stay! I order you!"

My command did not help; she had already bolted down the stairs and when I stepped up to the window, I saw her hurrying across the square.

"Leave her, *Effendi*!" said Selim Agha. "She made a promise. Oh, why did you give me so much money in her presence! Now I will not get one single Para of it!"

"Does she spend it on herself?"

"No; but she is a miser, *Effendi*. What she does not use for us or for the prisoners, she hides, so that I can not find it. She is very proud of the fact that I will have a great deal of money when she dies. But it is no good that I have to suffer for it now. I smoke the worst tobacco, and when I go to the Jew's place, then I may only drink the cheapest medicine. And that medicine is really bad!"

Chapter 36

The valiant Agha of the Arnauts departed in great sadness, and I followed him downstairs into the courtyard where the horses were being saddled. The Englishman and I took one last walk through the city to buy a few useful things. When we returned, everyone had gathered by the front door of the house. With them was a man whom I recognized to be the father of my patient.

"Lord, I hear that you are leaving," he began as he stepped several paces towards me. "That is why I came to bid you farewell. My daughter will soon be completely cured. She, my wife and I, we will pray to Allah that he might protect you. And so that you may think of us, I have brought a small *Jadikar* [memento], which I ask you to accept!"

"If it is just a *Ufak-Defek* [small thing], I will take it, but otherwise not."

"It is so small and inexpensive that I shrink at the thought to give it to you. Permit me to give it to your servant! Which one is he?"

"The one standing by my stallion."

He took a leather, pearl encrusted case from beneath his cloak and handed it to Halef. I also saw that he gave something else to Halef. I thanked him and we parted.

Now came the hardest part: to take leave from Selim Agha and especially from 'Myrte'. The Agha went from horse to horse and messed around with the reigns and buckles, which were quite alright. He rolled his eyes terribly all the while, like I had never seen him do before.

The tips of his mustache went up and down like a balance beam, and there and then he grabbed at his throat as though something were strangling him. Finally he proffered his hand to Halef in a farewell gesture. He commenced at the bottom.

"Live well, Hajji Halef Omar! Allah be with you, always!"

He did not listen to the little Hajji's answer, but rather leapt towards Mohammed's horse in order to swat a fly that sat on the horse's neck. He then turned to the Haddedihn with an energetic movement and proffered him his hand:

"Allah be with you in all things! Return to us again if your path leads you to Amadijah!"

He suddenly noticed that the girth of the Englishman's saddle was one-twentieth of an inch too far back. He hurried over and crawled beneath the horse to tuck and pull it into place with such fervor that one would think he pulled on a huge load. Finally he was finished and stuck out his right hand toward the rider:

"*Sihdi*, may your way be ... "

"Well!" the good master interrupted him. "Here!"

A coin dropped into the Agha's open hand, and it was, if I knew Lindsay well, quite substantial. This act of kindness confused the emotional leader of the Arnauts even more. He began again:

"*Sihdi*, may your way be the way ... "

"Well!" Lindsay nodded, and added a second coin to the *Baksheesh*. Lindsay thought that the offered hand demanded it.

"*Sihdi*," the Agha began again with a raised voice, "may your way be the way of the righteous, and ... "

"Well!" Lindsay said for the third time.

But the Agha suddenly pulled his hand back and took the opportunity, which my mounting of my horse presented, to grab hold of my stirrup. Now his face clouded over like a shadow moving across a sun-drenched field. He opened his mouth but instead of words coming forth, long held back tears streamed from his eyes. The words he wanted to speak became unintelligible. He stretched his hand towards me; I took it, squeezed it with emotion and then he suddenly disappeared into the passageway of his house.

Mersinah had waited for this. Now she came like the sun does through the dawn's redness. She wanted to start with Halef, I coaxed my horse closer and said:

"Halef, ride with the others down into the valley. I will have to go to the *Mutesselim* once more and will then quickly follow you." I then turned to Mersinah: "Here, take my hand! I thank you for everything. Farewell, never die and think of me as often as you taste the lovely foods you prepare for the prisoners!"

"Farewell, Emir! You are the most magnanimous ... "

I did not hear more. I rode off quickly towards the palace of the Commandant, followed closely by my dog. I left my horse before the gate and entered the palace. My dog followed me; I desired this. In the anteroom some of the same people were gathered that I had seen there before. They arose with fright when they saw the dog. No one had ever dared this.

"Where is the *Mutesselim*?" I asked.

"In his *Selamlük*," one of them answered.

"Is he alone?"

"The palace overseer is with him."

I did not bother to have myself announced, but simply stepped into the room. My dog was at my side. The palace overseer made a horrified gesture and the *Mutesselim* arose immediately.

"*Effendi*, what are you doing?" he cried.

"I come to take my leave of you."

"With a dog!"

"It is better than some people. You said that I should not return. I come with a dog. That is the answer of an Emir from Germanistan. *Salaam*!"

I departed as quickly as I had arrived. Once in the open again, I took my time; but no one came to demand an explanation off me. I mounted my horse and rode off. My companions had just ridden through the city gate when I caught up with them for Mersinah's words of farewell had taken quite some time.

"What you do with the *Mutesselim*?" asked Lindsay.

I told him.

"Brilliant! Hmm! Delightful idea! Would pay well if you were someone else! Yes!"

He murmured and laughed to himself for a long time.

Soon we had to dismount and slowly lead our horses down the steep incline. But it went much faster when we reached the valley floor and the place where we turned to the left earlier. Here Halef had to remain and hide himself in order to warn us if we were being watched. We reached the small clearing where we tied up the horses and then penetrated the thicket on foot.

"Here!" said the Englishman, when we reached the oak tree. "Magnificent villa up there! Well! Smokes tobacco!"

And really one could see small tobacco clouds swirl from the 'Villa Amad' one after another. The Arab lay inside the hole and did not notice our presence until we made ourselves known with a quick shout. Then he poked his head from the opening and recognized us. The fresh, invigorating forest air and the nutritious food had strengthened him considerably and he managed to descend from his 'villa' without our help. I got my lasso back, which he had kept with him yesterday.

We did not waste any time and returned to our horses immediately, we quickly mounted and started our ride for it was imperative that we put a good distance between Amadijah and us today. Halef reported that nothing suspicious had occurred and so we turned right onto the path that led to the summer homes of the inhabitants of Amadijah.

We rode up a valley that was watered by a wide mountain stream. A beautiful deciduous forest covered its sides. Further up, the stream divided into many arms; the valley became broader and provided plenty of space for the many tents and huts that appeared in picturesque order along the valley floor and on its slopes. These were the *Jilaks* or summer homes.

The place was very well chosen. Green forest and fruit trees shaded the huts and tents, and a thick carpet of climbing plants strove up the cliff faces. This healthy spot presented a glaring, yet desirable opposition to the poisonous air filled fort of Amadijah.

Whilst the others rode on at a fast pace to avoid the glances of spies, the Englishman and I dismounted before the house of a money changer, as Lindsay wanted to ensure a sufficient supply of the country's acceptable currency.

Although the distance was two English miles, we reached the top of the crest within a half an hour, and now we saw the Berwari valley open before us, where we would be safe from any Turkish pursuit attempts.

In the distance, the blue haze of the Tijari Mountains could be seen. In particular the peak of Ashiehtah stood out to the eye. The top of it sparkled with a bright white, for it was covered with snow. It seemed only a short time ago when we first rode through the pastures of the Haddedihn and stirred up the pollen with the legs of our horses.

To the right, up the mountains of Tkhoma, were the water rich valleys of the Zab, and further south were the heights of Tura Ghara, Jebel Haïr and Zibar-Landes. The old Marah Durimeh had spoken of Tijari and Tkhoma. I involuntarily thought of the secret she had spoken of, of the 'Spirit of the Cave', that inhabited those mountains.

We surely would reach a Kurdish village soon. My experiences with the Kurds and my meeting with the 'Spirit of the Cave' I will relate another time. But now I like to thank my dear readers who have accompanied me this far.

What will happen when Kara Ben Nemsi meets the *Ruh 'i kulyan*? What dangers await our hero and his faithful companions in the wild mountains of Kurdistan?

To find out, read the next part of this continuing Travel Narrative.

Oriental Odyssey III
Travel Adventures in Kurdistan

Authors Notes

The *Jesidi*, on whom this book is based, are the very same people who are also referred to as the Yezidi. These Kurdish people still exist today in very small numbers and are adherents of an indigenous secretive faith combining elements of Paganism, Islam, Christianity, Judaism and Zoroastrianism.

It should be noted that there is still a lot of confusion about their faith to this day and it is amazing that Karl May had a real insight into and understanding of their faith when he penned the original manuscript.

These people and their faith has been attacked by many western writers who no doubt heard sinister tales told by travelers into the remote regions of the Yesidi homeland. Tales of pagans performing dark satanic rites or paying homage to the Devil and ill-informed and fantastic rumors of heathens gathered around bonfires, adoring a copper *sanjak*, no doubt helped to put the Yezidi in a most terrible light.

This little Kurdish subgroup in northern Iraq that whilst showing strong similarities with the *Ahl-i Haqq* or *Yarsani* of Iran which include the true *Shaitan-parastiyyan* or Devil-worshippers are of course quite misunderstood.

Why Karl May chose these people as the subject of his travel narrative can no longer be determined accurately, but one can presume that given Karl May's interest in the fate of many oppressed people, the Yesidi must have touched his heart. Thus his description of their ritual and his enlightened understanding of their plight is more than just the result of extensive research. His touching description of the people and their faith holds a mirror to his own Christian belief and reveals an inner struggle within himself.

He asks the unspoken question as to how it is possible for a people so devout in their belief and so righteous and almost more Christian than those Christians born into the faith can get it so wrong.

But whether he asks that question of the Yesidi or of the Christian faith is of course left to the reader to ponder.

It is not my intention to do a dissertation of the Yesidi or to write a lengthy article about their faith and religion. I simply wish to provide a background to Karl May's original manuscript and confirm that the details he included in his narrative are indeed accurate as far as these people are concerned.

Translation Notes

The greatest possible care has been taken to render the original German text into a coherent English format. But some passages and concepts just do not lend themselves to fair English translation.

Wherever such passages occur, they have been translated practically verbatim. We then made changes in the sentence structure so that what finally emerged, might be considered intelligible English. The sentence was then further polished and a note was added to explain the foreign concept to the reader.

We (the translator and editor) both feel that in doing this we present a comprehensible (and hopefully enjoyable) English text that retains not only the spirit of Karl May's work but also his unique style.

Below are the concepts that could not be translated without making additions to the original text, as well as other references that elaborate on a concept that is only briefly touched upon within the narrative.

Reference	Notes
Ch 21. 1	**Yahu** This word refers to a creature called a Yahoo, or as it is known today, Yowie – possible corruption of the Aboriginal word *Yourie.* It refers to a large hominid reported to be foul smelling, covered in hair etc; possibly a relative of the yeti or sasquatch The native peoples of Australia viewed him as an evil spirit and we doubt if they ever prayed to it. There have been reported sightings of these creatures, even in recent times.
Ch 22. 1	**'I became a Christian because otherwise I would have received the bastinado from the Agha.' And that Agha was - a strict Mohammedan.** We feel that this is an expression of the duplicity so common in this region. It is certainly true that some people sought to escape from their suffering and persecution of their own people by taking on the mantle of another religion because to remain in their own religious group meant persecution by those in power. Historically, Christianity attracted those who were discontent –

Reference	Notes
	not only with their own religion but also with the government that ruled them.
Ch 23. 1	**Jenny Lind - The World's Sweetest Singer - 1821-1887** Jenny Lind was born in Stockholm, Sweden, in 1821, the daughter of a teacher of languages. She is said to have been able to repeat a song that she had heard but once at the age of three. At ten years of age she sang children parts on the Stockholm stage. After turning 12 years of age, her upper notes lost their sweetness, and for four years she did not do much singing. Her love for music continued and these years were devoted to the study of instrumental music and composition. At the end of this period her voice had recovered its power and purity and for a year and a half she was the star of the Stockholm opera. Next, she gave a series of concerts to obtain the means to go to Paris for further study, but the French teacher did not appreciate her powers and Jenny returned to her native city. When she was twenty-three years old, Jenny went to Dresden and when Queen Victoria visited that city the following year, she sang at the festivals held in the queen's honor. This opened the way to astonishing success in other German cities. In 1847 she went to London and was enthusiastically received. Here she sang for the first time in concert. Because of the influence of P.T. Barnum, Jenny Lind visited America in 1850. Because of his great influence and his power as an advertiser he roused the wildest enthusiasm. Tickets sold for fabulous prices in New York. But she did not disappoint the wildest expectation. She subsequently married Mr. Otto Goldschmidt of Boston, a musician and conductor. After her marriage, she appeared on the stage only at intervals and usually at concerts given for charitable causes. She was deeply interested in these charitable causes and we can easily add to her title of singer that of philanthropist. Her later years were spent in London where she died in 1887. Her life and songs are a sweet memory.

Reference **Notes**

Ch 24. 1 **Melek Ta-us** or **Melek Ta'us**

> Oh my Lord, you are the angel of men and jinns,
> Oh my Lord, you are the angel of the Throne and the Seat,
> Oh my Lord, you are the angel of the Bull and the Fish,
> Oh my Lord, you are the angel of the world and what is holy.
> from *Qewlê Tawûsî Melek*, "The Hymn of Melek Ta'us" [1]

This verse neatly demonstrates key aspects of Yezidi [*Jesidi*] thought. First, it places Melek Ta'us at the head of the *Haftan* (Heptad), or seven angels in charge of administering the world and the sacredness therein. Second, it makes Melek Ta'us protector of the Throne and Seat of God - the agent of the Almighty. Third, it positions Melek Ta'us within their creation myth, as the earth symbolically rests between the horns of a Bull which stood on the back of a Fish.

The seven angels (*Melek* may be assumed to mean this in English) represent various aspects and qualities of divinity and have different spheres of influence. There is a subgroup of four that are familiar to the western Hermetic tradition: *Mika'il*, *Jibra'il*, *Israfil* and *'Izra'il* (or *'Ezazil'*), the latter which is correlated to Melek Ta'us.

[1] Kreyenbroek, ibid, p. 244.

Ch 25. 1 **Not a drop of blood flowed. The Sheiks now came to open the veins in the necks of the fallen beasts and the Fakirs lingered close by with great vessels to catch the blood.**

Since the beasts were felled by a thrust of a blade between the neck bones, thus severing the spine, the beasts would have died instantaneously as described by Karl May. However, the beasts would now lie upon the ground, their hearts stilled and when the veins were opened, I doubt if the blood would have 'flowed', for without the heart pumping it, all it could do would be to ooze from the incision. No mention is made of hanging these beasts to encourage the blood to flow from the opened veins at their necks.

Reference	Notes

Ch 25. 2 **Notenpulte**

Karl May said the wooden frame resembled a '*Notenpulte*', I.E. a music stand, later in the paragraph however he describes the same as a '*Pulte*', I.E. a lectern. A music stand and a lectern are quite different and cannot be confused as either one or the other. The fact that two vessels are placed on this stand would make the object a lectern, as a music stand would be too flimsy to hold such vessels securely.

Ch 25. 3 **The religious sentiment of a Christian bristles against the use of this bird, but I did not observe anything immoral in this act.**

In Christian symbolism, the rooster is a familiar Passion symbol. Prior to being arrested by the soldiers, Jesus correctly predicted that Peter would deny Him three times before the rooster crowed on the following morning. At the rooster's crowing, Peter remembered Jesus' words and "went out and wept bitterly." [Mat 26:75; see also Mat 26:34-75; Mk 14:30-72; Lk 22:34-61; John 13:38-18:27] The rooster represents Peter's denial of Christ and also stands for his remorse and repentance upon hearing the rooster's crow. Because Peter later became the leader of the early Church, the rooster represents papal vigilance. In many cultures, the rooster's habit of crowing at the dawning of each new morning made it a symbol of the daily victory of light over darkness and the triumph of good over evil. This habit along with its fiery comb made the rooster the symbol of fire, the sun and Christ - the light of the world who announces an end to spiritual darkness and despair. In the Far East, the rooster was painted on the doors or houses to drive off evil spirits. During the Middle Ages, the rooster became a popular Christian image on weathervanes, also known as weathercocks. Its crowing made it an emblem of the Christian's attitude of watchfulness and

Reference	Notes

readiness for the sudden return of Christ, the resurrection of the dead, and the final judgment of humankind. [Mk 13:32 & 13:35-36] In many countries roosters were sacrificed to the gods. Early Germans sacrificed roosters during their funeral rites. The Greeks believed a rooster guided the dead to the other world where its crowing would awaken the souls to a new life. In the Orient, the Sun-god Attis had the rooster as a personal attribute to represent the myth that Attis had risen from the dead. In the West, the black rooster is the tool of Satan. Because of its aggressiveness, the rooster has been used to symbolize the soldierly qualities of vigilance, courage, supremacy, and pride. It is the national emblem of France and an image of war. This bird's aggressiveness and strutting have also caused it to be associated with base qualities such as arrogance, conceit, bossiness, lust, anger, bad temper, and frustrated desires. Karl May is probably referring to the use of a black rooster during satanic rituals. Otherwise his statement would not make sense.

Ch 26. 1 **Befördert**

It is important to note that Karl May used '*befördert*' here and later in the text plays with this word.
'*befördert*' can mean; to - carry, transport, convey, send, throw out, move up. But it can also mean; to promote;

Ch 30. 1 **Mastix** – originally comes from Greece and the mastix resin is still used to this day by them as an aromatic that lends flavor to wine and ouzo. For use as altar incense, mastix is mixed with aloe, thyme, spruce and incense and cured. In the European occult tradition, mastix is assigned to the sun and to the awakening of the second sight as well as exorcism. The smoke strengthens the spiritual power, improves and clears the charisma. Since mastix counts among the most expensive incense resins, it is difficult to obtain. In earlier times it was already an important part of the famous Egyptian Kyphi-mixture. In the Orient, mastix

Reference **Notes**

is used in the manufacture of confectioneries and as an elixir. Even today, the resin is used as a cure for diarrhea in children. It is chewed as a means to freshen the breath. In the west it is used in the manufacture of varnish and dentistry. Mastix is a good means of producing smoke that discourages insects. Mastix develops a fresh, herbal aroma and mixes well with lavender, orange and lemon grass.

Ch 31. 1 **Oak apples**

A common gall on black and Spanish oak Also called "spongy oak apple," "apple gall," "King Charles' apple". Oak apple galls are sometimes mistaken for an actual crop of the tree, such as apples on an apple tree, but are actually deformed leaves. The gall is about 1¼ to 2 inches or larger in diameter, globular, and smooth. The outside is green and darkens with age. The inside has a juicy, white, spongy substance with a small, hard center where the parasite is located. When the parasite leaves the gall, the gall dries and the insides become a mass of fibers.

Ch 31. 2 **osterländischer Zwölfspänner**

Osterland refers to a region that is bound by the Saale river and extends eastwards across the Mulde river up to the Elbe river and to the south is the city of Gera. The area is known for its farming and production of dairy products. The first use of the name Osterland can be traced back to the early 8th century but over the years, the name's meaning has been lost. Yet it has a long history that can be studied in the chronicles of the Weißenfels city. (*Wer zur Geschichte des Osterlandes weiterführende Informationen haben möchte, kann sich an die Stadt Weißenfels (Stadtchronik) wenden.)*

The word *Zwölfspänner* refers to a coupling of twelve horses, which presents a concept of something taking up quite a bit of room.

Reference	**Notes**
	So the image of a comfortable, possible quite rotund, farmer walking in a wide gaited manner comes to mind.
Ch 31. 3	**Alfenidegeschirr** **Alfenide** (*n.*) An alloy of nickel and silver electroplated with silver. **Geschirr** (*n.*) Dishes. Since the dishes used were certainly not of metal at all, the reference to *Alfenidegeschirr* refers to the fact that such dishes are pretentious. They are plated to look like something they are not. In the text we used 'delightful dishes' to reflect this very pretentiousness.

About the Author

Michael M. Michalak was born in Germany in 1953 and became interested in the works of Karl May after receiving his first *Winnetou* book from his father. Ever since then he has been captivated by Karl May's travel narratives. In 1965, Mr. Michalak emigrated to Australia with his parents and he was disappointed to discover that Karl May was virtually unknown in that country. Later, when Mr. Michalak moved to the United States of America, he re-discovered his favorite author. But since English translations of Karl May's writings are rare, often mangled, and usually abridged, Mr. Michalak and his wife Elaine were most disappointed by what they read and they decided to undertake a more accurate and complete translation of Karl May's greatest work. The *Orientzyklus* [Orient Cycle or Odyssey] has never before been translated from the original serialized version. This epic translation project was commenced in January 1999, but shortly after this project started, Elaine was diagnosed with cancer and the project might well have been abandoned had it not been for the dedication and courage of these two people. The initial book took a full year to translate and during the following year, an extensive editing effort was undertaken, to polish the translation and ready the manuscript for publication. The first book was published in March 2001 and work on the second book was well under way. But just two months later, Elaine succumbed to her illness and died. It was Elaine's final wish that the work continue and that the entire series would be available in the English language for the children of our modern world A wish that is being fulfilled.

Books by this Author

Oriental Odyssey I	In the Shadow of the Padishah Through the Desert
Oriental Odyssey II	In the Shadow of the Padishah The Devil Worshippers
My Life and My Mission	Karl May's Autobiography
A Voice from the Ashes	A Tribute to Elaine
Oriental Odyssey III	Travel Adventures in Kurdistan